# Endorsements for
## *We Are The Destroyers*

---

"This is one of the best works of science fiction I've read in a very long time. It made me think and had me quickly turning the pages—a rare combination!"

— DORAN H.

"I enjoyed the story of how the society of Syns evolved. I could visualize the story and characters even after I put the book down. I thought about the characters often . . . left me thinking will humans ever learn from their past mistakes."

— AMY C.

"Unexpected, different . . . it would make a great movie with good special effects."

— PHIL AND SAMMY W.

". . . good science fiction . . . a believable storyline, some great imagination!"

— RICK C.

# We Are The Destroyers

## D. K. Lindler

FIRST LIFE PUBLISHING

For information about this title or to order other books and/or electronic media, contact the publisher:
First Life Publishing
Phoenix, AZ 85014

ISBN:  978-0-9915090-2-7 (paperback)
       978-0-9915090-1-0 (eBook)

Printed in the United States of America
Cover and Interior Design: 1106 Design

Publisher's Cataloging-In-Publication Data
(Prepared by The Donohue Group, Inc.)

Lindler, D. K.
    We are the destroyers / D. K. Lindler.

        pages ; cm

    Issued also as an ebook.
    ISBN: 978-0-9915090-2-7 (paperback)

    1. Planets—Fiction. 2. Environmental degradation—Fiction. 3. Visions—Fiction. 4. Spirituality—Fiction. 5. Imaginary places—Fiction. 6. Fantasy fiction. 7. Science fiction.  I. Title.

PS3612.I545 W4 2014
813/.6

# Dedication

*There would be two distinct individuals in my life.*
*One from this life, K. G. Without him, this book would not exist.*
*He dedicated the past ten years to allow me to pursue my passion.*

*And the other, from the eighteenth century, a French*
*writer and philosopher, Denis Diderot, whose ability*
*with thought and words spirited me forward.*

# Table of Contents

# INTRODUCTION

Greetings. Sit back. Get comfortable. It is time we bring you up to date as to where you are in the scheme of things. We wish to tell you a story of a journey of discovery. It will be, and can be, everything you wish. So now let's see what your true wishes are.

# CHAPTER 1

# In Search of the Beginning

Ry Sing watched the dark-haired man from across the room. He sat in front of a wall-mounted display filled with star charts. He was in good physical shape nearing his 40th year. His tanned skin evidenced his Maureesh descent. He was born on the island of Mauree in the southern hemisphere, where the atmosphere had thinned over the centuries, creating the bronzed tones of the inhabitants.

His red military jacket was unbuttoned. He may have been in the act of removing it when his attention was diverted by the charts. She smiled at his singular focus. He was unaware that she was in the room with him, waiting for him to turn around. The information she was carrying had been weighing heavily on her heart for some time. It would be a relief to tell him, but that would only make it more real. That's why she had been content to remain unnoticed here in this room, delaying the moment. But it was time. She could wait no longer. He needed to know about the past.

"Bel'lar." She said his name softly.

He spun around. "Ry Sing. I didn't hear you come in." He grinned.

"Obviously." She smiled. "I have information about another voyage from a long time ago. It's time to tell you about it. Will you sit over here with me?" The long sleeve of her pastel-blue silk tunic fluttered as she motioned him to join her.

"Of course." He leaned back in his chair, stretched his arms overhead, and felt his shoulder muscles flex and then relax. With a sigh, he stood, shrugged out of his jacket, and left it on his chair. The insignia on the chest of his jacket was a cross within a circle with the letters ISOS stitched above it. Then, as an afterthought, he pitched his voice toward the display. "Finish." The charts vanished as the display darkened.

She watched him pull the shades and sit across from her.

He took her clasped hands into his own for a moment and then sat back. He sensed her reluctance and something else. What was it—sorrow? Something about this old voyage had upset her, and he kept silent so as not to distract her.

Breathing deeply, she closed her eyes and entered a relaxed state, peaceful and at ease. He couldn't detect any sign of the reluctance or sorrow now. *Her ability to focus must be overriding her emotions,* he thought.

Ten years ago, she had begun to focus within, accessing knowledge and speaking about things she didn't know she knew. At that time, she spoke of the existence of a planet similar to theirs, one capable of sustaining human life. This knowledge set them on this quest they were on today, in search of the blue-white planet.

She straightened in the chair and began to speak.

"Greetings, Exalted One."

Bel'lar's hand twitched at this greeting. He wondered what it meant but remained silent, unwilling to interrupt as she continued.

"We will tell you a story of long ago that will be of great interest to you as you embark upon this glorious journey to this new world. Let us begin. Relax, close your eyes, and you will see what we are about to tell you."

Breathing in deeply, he relaxed and, within moments, felt himself floating free of his body but unafraid—her voice the only thing penetrating his altered state.

"More than hundreds of thousands of years ago, in the solar system nearest to you, in what will come to be known by the inhabitants of the blue-white planet as the Belt of Orion, there was the Planet of Abundance. Those who lived there could be whatever it was they wished. We want to capitalize on the "be." Being there was all that was necessary to self-indulge oneself in *being* more than they had ever dreamed of and creating the wealth and prosperity expected. But even with the abilities to have all there was in this physical paradise, significant opportunities remained to alter this wonderful abundance. So as the inhabitants went about their existence on this Planet of Abundance, they began to feel that somehow they were the gods that created that place.

"As time passed they began to use up some of the abundance. A dire future was predicted by their holy men, one in which the planet would become overpopulated and unable to handle the abundance of human beings that would eventually lead to their own destruction. The holy men warned that what you sow you shall reap and so shall it be. Yet the warnings went unheeded. The inhabitants could not restrain the insatiable desire to alter their surroundings by making it better, they felt, than it was.

This continued for thousands of years until, as foretold, the planet reached the brink of self-destruction.

"Then a group of 'born again' ecologist holy men conceived a radical plan. They would give this planet a rebirth by setting off a chain of nuclear events around the circumference of the planet.

"Now let's go to this event. Come with us so you may see and realize what occurred."

Bel'lar felt a tug on his spirit. Then suddenly he was flying. Disconcerted at first, he let his fear fade away as he listened to Ry Sing's voice guiding him.

"As we're getting closer to this beautiful planet, realize you are a bird. A great soaring bird."

And indeed he was a bird. He flexed his wings in pleasure. He pushed away his incredulity of his altered state and flew.

Ry Sing continued. "See that gathering of many beings down below in front of a platform with a great stone backdrop."

Flying swiftly, his feathers ruffling in the wind, he saw the massive crowd. He shifted his weight and light glinted on his dark wings as he circled and then flew in closer. *What is that?* he thought.

And Ry Sing's voice answered, "A temple."

As he flew in closer, he could see men in blood-red robes arrayed along the edge of the platform. Holy men. He counted twelve. What was this place?

The holy men were attempting to comfort the crush of humanity around this platform. Children were crying. Bel'lar sensed the tension, the fear, the confusion. Some of the holy men were leaning over the platform's edge, placing their hands on the heads of people who surged up to them for blessing. What was happening? Did these people know what was going to happen?

Two holy men drew back from the crowd and moved to stand near a stone chair in the center of the platform. One turned to the other. Bel'lar could hear the speaker's voice clearly from his vantage point overhead.

"It has taken many difficult decisions to come to this moment. I hope it will be as the Great One sees it. For it has been written in very ancient scripture that rebirth through fire will heal and sanctify the spirit of this great place and allow the healing to begin."

The listener nodded but didn't speak.

The holy men at the edge of the platform backed away from the people and took up their places on either side of the stone chair. The people nearest the platform sank to their knees, and, as a wave, it spread throughout the congregation until all were kneeling, hands clasped in prayer. Now an air of great expectation and trepidation traveled through the people. They realized, as Bel'lar realized, that what was about to occur could never be rescinded.

Then from behind the stone chair, an exquisite man walked forward to greet the multitudes. He was tall, slender, godlike, with long, dark hair, wearing robes of distinction. These robes caught the light, reflecting many colors and then, at times, it seemed that this man was transparent. Bel'lar felt a stab of recognition but was confused. This man couldn't be familiar.

Ry Sing spoke. "He will be known in the future as the one that saved mankind."

This godlike man raised both arms, palms out, his robes of distinction fluttering in the breeze. His lips lifted in a loving smile; his eyes brightened with emotion. He gazed out over the congregation in silence for a long moment as if committing their faces to memory.

The multitudes stirred, getting to their feet. Calls of "our savior" and "save us, Great One," came from all over the mass of people. The holy men looked at each other and then dropped their eyes, their hands hidden in their robes.

The Great One continued to behold his people as the moments stretched on.

Then, lowering his arms, he walked back to the stone chair and sat, facing the audience. All waited as he remained in deep meditation.

The Great One stood. A long moment passed. The sounds of bodies shifting from one foot to the other, a child's whimper quickly shushed, a collective sigh as the people waited. Then his body emitted a glow, reflecting the sunlight. The glow intensified until he blazed with sunlight engulfing him in its iridescent halo. The energy of the stars focused through this man and streamed down upon the multitudes below. The Great One was now one with this powerful energy.

For one glorious moment, all present were at peace, basking in the benediction that blazed through the Great One. Even Bel'lar, observing from high above, was affected. A sigh of relief rippled through the crowd as they seemed to forget why they were gathered.

Then the Great One strode forward and raised his hands above his head in prayer to the god. The true god he knew. Down in front of him was a device of stone, waist high, cut in the shape of a pyramid. A metallic rod with a crossbar overlaid with a circle projected from the apex of this stone.

Bel'lar heard sharp intakes of breath as the people saw this device begin to glow. The holy men fidgeted, their eyes on their leader.

Then this great religious leader grabbed the crossbar and proclaimed, "As it was in the beginning, it shall be again. And I shall be the one to initiate the new beginning."

He drove the crossbar down into the stone.

Bel'lar hung in the sky, waiting, as all present waited. Then . . . there, off in the distance, flashes of light . . . and a thunderous roar erupted from underground. The ground shook. A huge cloud shot into the air. The sky turned dark. The great nuclear event that would circumnavigate and destroy the entire planet had begun.

"What have you done!" a voice cried out.

The Great One answered, "I have freed you from your sins."

"What about our children? They have done nothing. Save them."

The Great One turned away. He didn't answer. No one answered the people's cries.

The Great One and his holy men hurried into the darkened opening into the temple.

Bel'lar yelled, but it came out as a screech. He had forgotten he was a bird. The holy men were leaving the people to die. And he could do nothing but watch. He was gut-wrenchingly horrified, angry. Why did Ry Sing want him to see this? What could this have to do with the journey they would undertake? But most of all, he hated the feeling of recognition. He had nothing to do with this ungodly event. He couldn't do anything this terrible.

He continued to watch, afraid of what he would see. The terror emanating from the people was palpable, cramping his insides. The people were running in all directions. Some tried to climb on the platform, but it was too late. The holy men had gone inside the temple, and the huge stones of the opening were sliding closed, sealing completely forever. The people outside were left to endure the horror of what had begun.

Bel'lar drew back as a wave of light and wind blew through his existence. He could see other explosions off in the distance. More wind and light, intensifying as it reached him. His being must be disintegrating—how could it not?—but still he watched, holding onto his energy without substance. The platform collapsed, crushing the people nearby. Then another wave of wind and light blew through everything. The people disintegrated before his eyes. No sign of the platform remained. No sign of the people. It was as if nothing had ever been there—no holy men to have carried out this unthinkable act of religious purification.

His wings pumping, Bel'lar flew straight up into space. Then, leveling off, he looked down. From this great height, he could see the temple engulfed in fire and smoke. The planet exploded again and again. The force of one explosion cleared the clouds from around the temple for a second, and Bel'lar realized the temple was a pyramid. Then he spotted something. From underground, at the base of the temple, an object, a ship, sped out into space.

Suddenly Bel'lar was back in his body seated in front of Ry Sing, his hands clenched, his knuckles whitened, his body rigid. He couldn't stop seeing it. All those people, an entire planet, dead. My fault. But how could it be his fault?

"This chain reaction gave rebirth to the planet," Ry Sing said, "by cutting a rift that spread through the central part of the planet and spewed out its lifeblood. Ash and magma clouded the skies, and, when it finally settled, it buried the Planet of Abundance. Now it is a planet merely suspended in time.

"In the final days of the Planet of Abundance, before the religious purification, the holy men were people of vision and perception. They decided to take the seeds of their existence and transport them. At that time, they did not know of your planet, but they sensed an energy that could sustain life out there somewhere. The holy men left the Planet of Abundance on that final day and journeyed out and found the planet that you call home.

"Now, once again, as you embark on a new beginning, go out wishing that this time the human species will endeavor to understand why they were created. Do you have any questions?"

The horror of what he had just witnessed seemed burned into his eyes. They were so dry he couldn't shed any tears, but his throat was choked with emotion. He wasn't sure if he could recover from this terrible event. He squeezed his eyes tight, trying to awaken his tear ducts. He coughed. Coughed again. "Why, how . . . was this my fault? Why do I think this? And how could it be? Explain." He felt the pressure in his chest and struggled to breathe it out. He cleared his throat.

Ry Sing, still in trance, answered, "You were there, but that happened eons ago."

"How could that be?" he asked. He didn't want to accept this answer. He didn't understand. He was furious and sad and confused. He wanted to hit something but didn't. Not while Ry Sing was in trance. It would startle her.

He clenched his hands tighter. Pain radiated up his arms.

"Hold these thoughts in your heart, and they will be explained as you endeavor to seek the truth. With that, this session is ended." Ry Sing took a deep breath that ended in a sob and then released it. No longer the messenger, she leaned back in the chair. Her long, dark hair spilled over her shoulders. Tears slid silently down her cheeks, but she didn't open her eyes or attempt to brush them away.

He wanted to ask more questions, find out how it was possible that he was there, a participant in that event, but he let her rest. He'd noticed the tears on her face. He wasn't the only one reeling. She was hurting, too.

The aching in his arms caught his attention. He relaxed his hands, shaking them. The pain receded, and he felt relief.

He surveyed his surroundings, waiting for his heart to cease pounding, his equilibrium to return. White shades, gray furniture created sparse, functional space without decoration in this apartment. Most of his belongings were already aboard the Light Traveler.

Two traveling packs leaned against the wall by the exterior door. Tomorrow was the last day here for him and Ry Sing before they joined the rest of the crew on the ship. They had stayed, savoring this last chance to be alone together before the journey.

His mind cast back in time to how this all had started. Three years had passed since his appointment by the government to captain the starship, Light Traveler. His task had been to select a crew most capable of finding the blue-white planet, and if found, secure it for possible colonization. That's how he had met Ry Sing, this young woman of the Asian race. She had been brought to his attention by an old friend of his father's. He had selected her for this mission because of her considerable skill as a sensitive and healer. Though, he had to admit, he had been attracted to this young woman with long, dark hair and delicate features. Their working relationship had evolved into an intimate, increasingly committed personal relationship. But despite their closeness, she retained an aura of mystery because there was much about her that he didn't know or understand.

He glanced back at Ry Sing. Her chest rose and fell with each breath as she slept. She appeared at peace since she had been able to release this information. His eyes lingered on her face, enjoying her features softened in sleep. Her eyelashes fluttered. She would wake soon.

He got up quietly and crossed to the window. Lifting the shade, he stood there looking out. A haze filled the sky, partially obscuring the sun.

A young man from the apartment next door walked by. Then an older woman. Unlike he and Ry Sing, both of these people had thickened, stocky bodies, evidence of the genetic changes most of the people on this planet had undergone from decades of eating synthetic foods and breathing the contaminated air. They proudly called themselves Syns, shortened from "synthetics."

It saddened him to see this, but he knew it wouldn't change. That it couldn't change. The people were addicted to the synthetic foods, and their physical bodies had mutated accordingly. If only they could have continued eating real foods grown organically, things might be different. This journey might not be necessary. But he knew that was impossible. Even if they could eat it, the current population exceeded the supply of organic food and had for many years.

He wondered how many Organs like himself and Ry Sing and the few they knew remained on this planet. Or had they all shifted to consuming synthetics? He hoped not. In his own heart, he knew he could never do this. Seeing what his people, the Syns, had become, it was clear to him that they had once again created their worst fears, and it reaffirmed why this journey was imperative. His resolve to succeed strengthened.

A tone signaled an incoming call. He crossed to the display.

"Yes," he said.

The display filled with the visage of an older, gray-haired man.

"Captain Bel'lar." It was Ka'aya at the project headquarters. "We are sensing trouble in the Brotherhood of Syn. Your lives are in danger. We dare not wait for the correct rotation. Come at once."

"I've been expecting this. On our way."

He crossed the room to Ry Sing. He touched her shoulder, but she didn't respond. He grabbed her arm and tugged. She tried to shake him off. He just tugged more, pulling her to her feet. "No more sleeping. We have to hurry. The Brotherhood's coming."

Ry Sing heard the urgency in his voice and rubbed her face hard, pushing her hair back.

Bel'lar shoved his military jacket into his pack and then pulled on an old brown jacket with a hood. He tossed his pack over his shoulder and took one last look around the room. He knew he would never return here.

Ry Sing wore a similar drab jacket and was struggling to get her pack on. He jerked it onto her shoulders and then linked his arm in hers.

They passed through the door and hurried down the stairs. They were out of sight around the building when they heard the sound of running feet pounding up the stairs to their apartment.

A voice yelled, "Open up."

Something heavy crashed through the door.

They ran.

It was only a short distance to the public rail station, and Bel'lar and Ry Sing arrived without incident. They stood across the street in the shadow of an old tree growing at the corner of a small store. Bel'lar scanned their surroundings while Ry Sing leaned against the trunk of the tree, breathing hard. No sign of pursuit yet. They had easily avoided the guards at his apartment, but he didn't relax. This just made him more cautious. He turned his attention to the station. A white octagonal building with glass walls, it afforded him a clear view of the mass of people queued up inside to board the rail cars. Tall columns held up the portico which shaded the three entries through which many more people were entering. It was nearing midday, and this mob of people would continue for another two hours. Bel'lar noted the rail car filling with passengers and close to departure.

He anticipated problems inside the station but didn't see any unusual security. Yet. Could they slip through in this mass of people? Was the team sent to capture them working alone? More likely it would be just a matter of time before the guards in this station were alerted.

He knew Ry Sing was tired from her session and the run here. He wasn't sure how hard he could push her. He touched her arm, and she straightened and nodded. Pulling her along behind him, they blended in with a large group of Syns crossing the street and joined those waiting under the portico for entrance to the station. Bel'lar searched the crowd again.

When he turned back, Ry Sing was leaning against a column, her eyes closed. Her hood had slipped down over her face, and some of her hair had escaped. Her long hair was a rarity that drew the attention of several women. Thinning hair had become the norm among the population. One young woman touched Ry Sing's hair in wonder while two others watched. Ry Sing didn't seem aware of the attention, but this could get out of control fast. Organs were a rare sight for the Syns, and Ry Sing appeared in distress. The two women offered her pills. This wasn't unusual. The Syns carried various mood enhancers with them at all times because they required frequent doses to function. As Organs, Bel'lar and Ry Sing refused synthetic foodstuff or enhancements, eating only organic foods.

Bel'lar intercepted the women, accepting the pills, nodding thanks to the two women. He put his arm around Ry Sing and tucked her hair back inside the hood. She smiled up at him, unaware of the attention she had attracted. The pills spilled out of his hand unnoticed in this crush of people.

The line began to move, and the people forgot about the Asian woman with the beautiful hair.

Moving slowly, Bel'lar and Ry Sing entered the station building. Once inside, the clog at the entries loosened, and people scattered to board the waiting rail transports. They attached themselves to a family, moving when they moved. The closest guard on the platform was lazy, his mind on something else, and he wasn't paying any attention to the people streaming around him. Keeping the family between him and the guard, Bel'lar approached the platform, Ry Sing following at his elbow. The open door to the transport ahead would take them to their destination.

Then their path was blocked. A Brotherhood of Syn guard stood in front of Bel'lar. She looked him over, her eyes unfriendly. "Particulars," she demanded.

Bel'lar offered his right thumb and it was read by the guard's small device. Nothing. The guard shoved the device at Ry Sing. Ry Sing extended her hand, careful to keep her head down. This was it. They were going to pass. Bel'lar took hold of Ry Sing's arm.

Then the guard's device flashed *Detain for Inquiry.* Jerking his left arm up, Bel'lar slammed into the guard, knocking her to the floor. Tightening his grip on Ry Sing's arm, he dodged around the downed guard, carrying Ry Sing with him and sprinted toward the transport.

Sirens rent the air. All the Syns lay down on the floor as the doorways began sealing shut. The transport ahead was their only way out.

Erupting from everywhere, Brotherhood of Syn security guards were running toward them. The guard he had knocked down was up, blood streaming down her face from her broken nose, yelling orders to get them.

Ignoring the guards, Bel'lar and Ry Sing reached the edge of the platform and leaped into the air at the rail car. He knew the car doors were secured and the car was beginning to move. They had only seconds. They hit the car with a thud that reverberated throughout their bodies. He grabbed on to the railing at the back of the car and hung on. Ry Sing hung onto Bel'lar. He pulled her around in front of him, protecting her with his body. The car jetted away from the station with

Ry Sing and Bel'lar glued to it from the magnetic force field generated by the transport.

The strength of the magnetic field was so strong that Bel'lar was able to catch only a glimpse of the security guards clustered at the edge of the platform and saw the bleeding guard shouting something into her device. The next station would be swarming with guards, and escape would be impossible. What were they going to do?

The transport reached full speed as Bel'lar racked his brain for a solution. Somehow they had to make it to the teleport station.

The public rail sped around the bend, and the station receded into the distance. The wind whipped Ry Sing's hair and wrapped it around Bel'lar's face, blinding him.

Unable to determine their location, glimpses of trees told Bel'lar that they had entered the countryside. He knew when the trees ended, the next stop was moments away. The only chance would be to escape into the surrounding forest when the rail stopped and make their way from there to the project headquarters, which were just on the other side of the hill they were about to pass.

"Ready," Ry Sing yelled.

"What?"

She closed her eyes and concentrated. In her mind's eye, she expanded her energy field to encompass Bel'lar. Then, focusing on where they touched the transport, she created an opening in the magnetic field. Abruptly, they were hurled free into the hollow that paralleled the rail track. This section by the forest was thick with leaves that cushioned their fall as they hit the ground.

Rolling to his feet, Bel'lar resettled his pack. "Thanks for choosing a soft landing."

"I didn't," she said, laughing.

He pulled her to her feet, adjusting her pack.

"We weren't able to move. How did you do that?" he demanded.

"A little something I learned from Ka'aya."

She brushed at her hair, trying to get out some of the leaves. He tried to help but accidently pulled her hair.

"Ouch, stop it." She smacked at his hands. He dropped his hands, and she turned to face him. Still laughing, her face flushed, she kissed him, her lips soft and warm. He responded strongly, forgetting where they were for a moment. Then, remembering, he released her.

Together they started up the hill, away from the rail track. The hillside was blanketed with trees, and they were out of sight within a few steps. They had a chance now, Bel'lar thought, thanks to Ry Sing. If they reached the teleport station before the Brotherhood of Syn caught them, they would be safe. He looked over at her as they climbed. She was smiling, obviously enjoying this adventure. He was too, he realized. It felt good to be active, rather than waiting. And how did she breach that magnetic field? Impossible, he would have thought. Her abilities were unexpected and amazing. What else could she do?

Upon reaching the crown of the hill, they looked down. The remains of an ancient pyramid, nestled at the bottom, were discernible. With the passage of time and weather, this structure had become buried in this hill and, until its discovery ten years ago, unknown. However, from the rail path, none of this could be seen.

Ry Sing looked back, the rail cars no longer visible in the distance.

"Big surprise at the next stop for the Brotherhood," she said.

"We'd better hurry. It's only a matter of time before they stop looking and come here," he said.

They started down the hill.

The trees sported their fall colors of reds, oranges, and yellows. Ry Sing crunched through the fallen leaves and couldn't resist tucking some away in her pockets.

"It's so beautiful here," she said with a sigh.

The trek down was not a straight path; still, it was an easy walk but farther than it seemed from the crown. They kept up a fast pace, and both were hot and thirsty by the time they reached the station. They saw some familiar faces as they approached the restricted area, which was bustling with activity. Preparations were underway for the expected attack. Squads of guards were being sent to bolster the security along the perimeter. Supplies were being moved inside the building.

The guard at the entrance gate smiled at them. A walk-through scanner was situated to his right.

"Captain Bel'lar, we've been expecting you."

"Thanks, Zack," Bel'lar answered.

This guard was not a member of the Brotherhood of Syn but was part of the small contingency force that guarded the project that had been named "In Search of Shangri-La." His uniform bore the same ISOS insignia as Bel'lar's. However the guard's pants were gray rather than black like Bel'lar's, indicating his lower rank. He stepped aside and motioned for them to enter the scanner.

Bel'lar nodded to Zack and stepped into the scanner. Ry Sing followed him. Red lights flashed on the guard's monitor, but he waved them through.

Wasting no time, Bel'lar and Ry Sing reached a small building that appeared to be a guardhouse. They stepped inside, and the door closed behind them. Not a guardhouse, this was a personnel tube, running vertically, that would take them down inside the heart of the teleport station. The tube began its descent, stopping at level seven. The door slid open, and they entered the underground docking bay where the starship, the Light Traveler, was docked. Or should have been docked. The cavernous bay was empty.

Bel'lar's eyes widened with shock. "Where's my ship?" he demanded.

Ry Sing said nothing. She seemed unconcerned.

"Ro'ald!" Bel'lar shouted. "Get out here!" Bel'lar's voice was amplified in this vaulted bay.

The station manager came running, his arms full of files. Loose papers on the top were in imminent danger of escaping his precarious hold.

"Where's my ship?" Bel'lar shouted.

"Preflight test," the station manager gasped out. "Another frequency. Just found out. Back any time now." He sucked in a breath. Papers sifted to the ground.

Ry Sing picked up the papers and tucked them into one of the files Ro'ald was holding. He gave her a lopsided smile.

"Another frequency? What else can this ship do?" Bel'lar said. Of course it could move through dimensions. *I should have realized*, he thought.

"You'll have to find out on the journey," Ro'ald said. "You have to leave now. The Brotherhood has cancelled the project."

A disturbance in the air, a squiggle of light where the ship should have been drew their eyes. The air blurred, and then the outline of the ship materialized. Bel'lar let out an audible sigh of relief, and Ry Sing suppressed a giggle.

At first, the ship was transparent and seemed to have a modularity to it that created variable waves, pulsating back and forth. As it entered this frequency, its transparency solidified into a white, yellowish bright light so bright it hurt to look directly at it with the naked eye. The station manager buried his nose in his files while Bel'lar and Ry Sing covered their eyes until the light diminished to a bearable brightness. When they looked back, a hard, elliptical-shaped beryllium craft filled the bay. Covered in concave and convex crystals, the skin of the ship reflected light, distorting its outline and giving the appearance of breathing. A dome on the top contained the bridge.

"There you are, my beauty," Bel'lar greeted his ship. He walked up to her, reaching up to touch her skin. It warmed as if she were alive and responding to his touch. "Amazing. What other secrets do you hold?" He stepped back and turned around. "Somewhere in our past we created such a wonderful and magnificent ship. Yet," he glanced back at the ship, "we also created the Brotherhood of Syn—an irony I'll never understand."

Ry Sing, her demeanor serene, put her hand upon his cheek. She looked up at him, struck again by the almost elegant bone structure of his face. Something he had inherited from his mother. Dark hair, tousled by the wind, curled onto his bronzed skin. "Everything will be clear once we begin the journey. Come, let us enter the ship." She winked at the station manager and turned toward the craft.

Ro'ald nodded in relief. Then he hurried away, calling back over his shoulder. "I'll contact you from the control room." He disappeared into the tube.

Bel'lar strode up to the ship beside Ry Sing. An opening appeared in the convex, crystalline substance as if it were anticipating their need. They entered into a darkened corridor with many colored lights cascading down each side. This entry corridor was merely to keep the interior pure from outside contaminants on the home planet. With Bel'lar's initial step inside the corridor, air from beneath blew gently at first and then increased as they took a few steps inward. Microscopic pollutants that had attached to their clothes were being removed. Tones sounded, and the lights intensified. To Bel'lar, they always sounded like horns, blowing triumphantly as he entered his ship.

A final gust of air pushed at them as they exited the corridor. Ry Sing shivered. "I liked that." She stood on tiptoe to kiss him. "I'll meet you on the bridge." She turned down a side corridor and was gone.

Bel'lar continued walking to the bridge through a corridor of light. It was round and white, with ribs of shiny metal perforated by round holes that seemed to float through the space. The corridor ended, and he approached the lift, which took him up to the bridge.

At the entrance to the bridge, a feminine voice said, "Greetings, Captain Bel'lar. You may enter."

"Thank you, L.T." Bel'lar wasn't concerned any longer. He knew the Brotherhood couldn't stop this ship from launching, nor could they get inside her.

The lift door opened, and he entered the bridge. It was a vast oval-shaped room constructed of materials similar to the ship's exterior. The ceiling and walls flowed together with concave and convex facets that reflected light. The main deck floated above this bed of crystal, seemingly alive. As he stepped onto the deck, there was a negligible quiver as it adjusted to his weight. A walkway through the center of the bridge led to the six reclinable seats set in a half circle facing forward, with a view of space. The captain oversaw all the bridge's operations from his chair in the center of the room. In front of it was a control panel, one-meter in diameter with a half globe facing down, centered in the middle of the panel. Behind the control panel and seats, and to the left of the walkway, a smaller deck floated two steps above the main deck. It contained one station with a small crystal display for the First Officer's use. Opposite this small station was another deck with additional seating.

Ka'aya, already on the bridge, was seated in meditation, his hands steepled in front of him. His gray beard and long, curly gray hair lent him a wise countenance. His age was unknown. He never responded to Bel'lar's probing, but Bel'lar suspected that he must be more than 100 years old.

Ka'aya opened his eyes. His black eyebrows and mustache sharpened the intensity of his gaze, which was now focused on Bel'lar's face.

"You're here." He crossed the deck to the younger man, his relief apparent. His robe of gray and white shimmered when he moved, creating the illusion that he floated rather than walked.

"We were concerned for you. One can never predict what the Syns will do." Ka'aya always spoke in the plural because he had long ago understood that he was not alone and felt the singular inappropriate. An elder in the Sacred Ecology religion, he was a sensitive, with abilities that far exceeded others. Sensitives embraced more than the physical aspects of life. They understood that the life they were living was merely an aspect of their whole existence. As such, they were open to the possibilities of the future.

It was rumored that Ka'aya could warp the fabric of reality. What exactly that meant Bel'lar didn't know, but he had known him all his life. He had been part of Bel'lar's life, teaching and guiding him. He had served as a trusted advisor to Bel'lar's father, Aaron, who had been the head of the Sacred Ecology religion until his death five years ago. Ka'aya volunteered for this mission because he could sense the blue-white planet and knew he belonged there.

He embraced Bel'lar, sharing his energy with him. Bel'lar felt that tiny surge of warmth in the area of his heart that he knew somehow meant they were connected.

"Where is Ry Sing?"

"In her quarters; she'll be here soon," Bel'lar said.

"Good. It's almost time for rotation. Did you have any trouble?" Ka'aya returned to his seat next to the Captain's.

"Nothing I couldn't handle. Where's the rest of the crew?" Bel'lar glanced at the entrance to the bridge and walked over to stand in front of the globe.

"Mauleen has been conducting the preflight check in anticipation of your arrival. She should be contacting you any minute. Enis, of course, is in the galley checking his stock. Dobeman said something about a fudge icicle. He said he would return in time. Not to worry." The barest hint of a smile flitted across Ka'aya's face.

Bel'lar arched an eyebrow but refrained from commenting. They both knew this was an unusual crew.

The door to the bridge opened, and Dobeman entered. Alien to their home planet, he was a Sentinel and their guide on this mission. He could interpret many different languages. He had experienced many subcultures and was adaptable to environments which were hostile to human beings. As he approached, Bel'lar noticed again how unlike a human he looked with his dark, pupil-filled, almond-shaped eyes. His hairless head was larger than a human's. His skin's color, an iridescent gray. The rest of his body was thin and elongated, with large hands and feet.

Dobeman wore an orange cloth draped over one shoulder and tied at the waist, extending to above his large feet. He carried a staff of blackened tangle wood presented to him on one of his adventures. But it was what he held in his other hand that drew Bel'lar's attention. A fudge icicle in an advanced state of meltdown dripped down Dobeman's arm, splashing onto the floor. As it touched the floating deck, the drops were absorbed within seconds. Bel'lar wondered if the ship enjoyed the taste or was simply removing a contaminant.

Bel'lar grinned. "What's the purpose of this sticky trail all over my ship? Why don't you just eat it?"

There was a pause, and then Dobeman spoke without moving his mouth. His voice sounded as if he were talking from a far distance. This effect had been disconcerting to Bel'lar during his initial interactions with Dobeman, but now he didn't notice.

Dobeman said calmly and precisely, "It is the way the fudge icicle melts, as it runs down my arm and drips onto the floor. This is the enjoyment that I am looking for. If you remember, the last time I had a fudge icicle, I was holding it in the other hand so, of course, I would wish to experience the event from the other side." He turned and left the bridge, drips following each step, instantly absorbed by the ship.

Bel'lar thought this crew of six, all Organs, was going to be fractious. Especially Ry Sing. She was completely uncontrollable. When the Brotherhood approached him with this task, they urged him to choose his crew from among other Organs. He had, selecting a combination of technos and sensitives. The Brotherhood had insisted Dobeman be part of this crew simply because he was alien. Dobeman's ship had crashed on the home planet many years ago, and Dobeman had remained, unable to repair his ship. But Bel'lar knew Dobeman had extensive experience with other races, subcultures, and planets.

A chirping tone heralded an incoming communication. The wall in front of the control panel smoothed and flattened, coming to life as a display. The station manager, Ro'ald, looked harried as he greeted Bel'lar. Behind Ro'ald, the control room hummed with activity, making everything ready for this launch.

"Captain, it's time."

"First officer Mauleen needs a few more minutes. I'll contact you when we're ready."

The station manager nodded acceptance, and the crystalline display went blank.

"What's keeping Ry Sing?" Bel'lar tapped his fingers on the console.

"You know her. She's never where you expect her to be," Ka'aya said.

"L.T., locate Ry Sing."

"Locating, Captain," the Light Traveler answered.

What could be taking so long? Where was Ry Sing? Bel'lar had a bad feeling. Then the display focused in on Ry Sing. The Light Traveler had located her standing on a rise overlooking the city—not aboard the ship as Bel'lar had had every reason to assume.

He didn't wait for her to speak. "What are you doing out there?"

Ry Sing stared at him, eyes unblinking. "I had to see what was happening. Groups of angry, irrational Syns are collecting all over the city. They're angry about the money wasted on this project that's doing nothing immediate to better their lives. I'm sad and fascinated by them. The synthetic products have begun to slant their thought processes and short-circuit their brain waves. They're about to erupt. There's much to learn here."

Impatiently, Ka'aya said, "And no time. If you don't return now, you'll be left behind."

Her face lost its animation, her voice mournful. "But what about our people? They need our help." Here was the real reason behind her behavior.

Bel'lar started to speak, but Ka'aya silenced him with a hand on his arm.

Ka'aya, his voice gentle, turned back to Ry Sing, "You've done all you can here, my dear. Now allow them to live."

"Hurry, Ry Sing," Bel'lar interjected.

Ry Sing looked back once more at the city. Her shoulders drooped in resignation. The display went blank.

"Don't worry; she'll come," Ka'aya said.

Bel'lar turned to Ka'aya. "We can't wait." Bel'lar addressed the ship. "L.T., Bring her back."

"Yes, Captain," the ship responded.

A chirp signaled an internal ship's communication, and the crystal display focused in on First Officer Mauleen, her curly red hair hanging in her eyes, as usual. She brushed it back with an impatient motion. Her petite stature and feminine looks belied her seriousness and engineering capabilities. One of the first to join the mission, Bel'lar had chosen her for her impressive technical abilities. He had been rewarded by an unwavering loyalty to him and the project.

"Captain, preflight is complete. Ready to rotate on your command."

Ka'aya sat back in his seat in preparation for the imminent rotation.

Dobeman came in quietly and sat next to Ka'aya.

Mere seconds passed before Ry Sing appeared, preceded by a huge whoosh of energy. She was restored to her ebullient glory. She took center stage in front of the others, looking at Bel'lar. "What are we waiting for? The Syns will be here any moment."

Bel'lar glared at her. She didn't respond.

Without a further glance at anyone, she left the bridge.

Bel'lar's mouth tightened. What was wrong with her? Why did she leave the ship without telling him? He would have stopped her. Where was the playful woman he had just spent the past few days with? He'd thought earlier how amazing she was, but sometimes she was incomprehensible.

No time for these thoughts. He pushed them away and returned to the imminent departure.

"Is everyone aboard now, Ka'aya?"

Ka'aya nodded.

"L.T., contact the control room."

"Yes, Captain."

The control room was in crisis. The door was being barricaded with anything Ro'ald's people could drag in front of it.

"Captain. We're doing everything we can, but the Brotherhood's here. We can't wait any longer." Ro'ald raked his hair back with one hand. "You have to take off now."

There was a loud crash. Ro'ald glanced at the door behind him. He turned back to Bel'lar. "Good luck to you. And may the seeds of mankind prosper in your care."

"It will be what it is," Bel'lar responded, putting his hand upon the globe in the center of the panel. In the back of his mind was the memory of another ship leaving a planet with the seeds of mankind on board. An icy shiver ran down his back. Then he sat back and allowed the ship to begin her transformation. With a low muffled hum, the ship seemed to wake, creating an electrical field that generated momentum, lifting it off its stationary blocks. She rose up into the air, glowed white-yellow, achieved rotation, and was gone.

Back in the control room, the door burst open, and Brotherhood guards charged into the room. Only to find it empty.

✳ ✳ ✳

The ship broke free from the underground station and shot into space. Propelled by a light-frequency generator, it increased in velocity until it transcended light itself. This was at the exact time when the sunlight hit the generators and flooded in, increasing the velocity one hundred fold. Speed was dependent on the number of light rays. Light speed times ten for each light ray it let in propelled the ship by that speed. There was no limit to the speed, for there was no resistance. It would accelerate beyond light speed, for there was nothing known to inhibit this craft from achieving velocities into the area of infinity.

The crystalline display flexed and transformed into a window that encompassed the entire forward bay area of the bridge, enabling sweeping views into space on both sides and straight ahead.

"We have transcended light. The journey has begun," Bel'lar announced. "I hope Light Traveler is taking us to the blue-white planet, for I have no control over this craft."

"It is well that you understand that, Bel'lar," said Ka'aya. "Light Traveler is not mechanical or even physical. She is the emotions, the essence of all that is alive. She transports life from one beginning to the end and from the end to the beginning. We are merely passengers, visitors in time on this ship flying through the vastness of space to her destination. The journey will be fruitful, creating the experiences you wish. So enjoy. It is all in the hands of the ship." Ka'aya folded his hands and rested them in his lap, his demeanor one of allowance and peace.

Dobeman stared out into space. "It is as if time is moving, yet we are standing still. Time is the traveler; time the force that moves us."

Ka'aya nodded in agreement, "And we are merely observers."

Ry Sing entered the bridge dressed in a black, feminine gown that hugged her figure. Very unlike the tunic and pants she usually preferred. Bel'lar watched her approach, the dress swishing as she stepped onto the floating deck. Her waist-length black hair swayed with the movement. Her face was delicately shaped, her skin, fair and translucent. Her dark lashes and brows appeared as if drawn with a brush. But now her almond-shaped green eyes were full of mischief, and her melancholy, her irritation had all disappeared.

"Isn't this lovely?" She twirled in a circle to show off the dress.

"You are always lovely, my dear," Ka'aya said.

"Indeed, you are. But it looks like you're dressed for an ending," Bel'lar said.

She smiled as she looked up at him coyly. "This is an end and a beginning." She stepped closer and looked up into his eyes. Her breath lightly teased his skin as her green eyes drew him in. He leaned toward her, reaching for her when she laughed and danced away to sit next to Ka'aya.

Having forgotten himself in front of the others, he straightened, glanced around, and pulled back emotionally. The captain needed to maintain a certain decorum. She had managed to influence his behavior and get him to forget her dangerous trip to watch what was happening in the city. But she was beautiful.

Ry Sing was always at ease with whatever was happening and felt free to express her feelings in an often exuberant manner. He was perplexed by this as well as amused. He wanted to hold her close or punch something; to yell to release this excitement and anxiety he felt as they traveled to the unknown. But most of all, he felt out of control. And he hated it. Everything in him wanted to be more than just a passenger, but he couldn't, just as Ka'aya had said.

His need to be active drove him to find something he could control. He knew that wasn't Ry Sing. Her behavior over the past hours had shown him that if he hadn't known before. And he was angry with her for that crazy trip back to the city. She might have been killed or missed the launch. He heard her laugh and looked over. She smiled at him and turned back to Ka'aya. There was something strong and unbreakable between those two that hadn't diminished despite her romantic relationship with Bel'lar, and it bothered him. A lot. It seemed like the bond between child and parent, but, sometimes, he wasn't sure.

Yet, nothing in any of his actions supported the idea that Ka'aya's feelings for Ry Sing were anything other than parental. Besides, Ka'aya had been like Bel'lar's second father, supporting his choices, acting as surrogate parent after his sister died. It would feel like betrayal if Ka'aya changed his relationship with Ry Sing. Yet he didn't really think he would. It was Ry Sing's feelings that he wondered and worried about.

Ry Sing laughed again and put her hand over Ka'aya's.

It was obvious he wasn't going to get the chance to argue with her now. He took a deep breath and said, "I have some things to attend to."

Ka'aya shook his head but remained silent.

Dobeman followed Bel'lar off the bridge, leaving Ka'aya and Ry Sing alone.

Ry Sing watched Bel'lar stride away, her expression thoughtful. She knew he was confused and angry with her. She wanted to talk to him but wasn't sure if her reasons for leaving the station would be comprehensible to him. That's why she was avoiding him by staying with Ka'aya. She had needed to see the people once more and to be reminded why this voyage was the only way to help them. They had been irreparably damaged by the synthetic foods they had been consuming for hundreds of years. Mutations had transformed them into something far different than human beings. They no longer had free will and choice. The synthetic substances had corrupted them, and now they were unable to learn. Was the lesson at an end? She feared it was, but she was content to leave that question unanswered and go on this voyage to the blue-white planet. There would be time enough when they returned to determine the answer and its ramifications.

Sitting in companionable silence, Ry Sing and Ka'aya continued to look out upon the vastness of space. Ka'aya knew she was comfortable with him; they had known each other since her days at the Academy of Ecology. Her talents had manifested at an early age, and she was taken from the orphanage to attend the Academy, where she came to Ka'aya's notice. When she was six, her parents, both of whom were sensitives and healers, were killed in a transport crash on their way to a village where a virus was raging unchecked. Within moments of their deaths, they appeared to her in spirit, comforting and explaining what had happened. Even at that age, Ry Sing was able to grasp their message, see and feel their presence, and release her fear of death. From that moment, she had lived life in the present time, fully involved in each experience.

Once her educational studies were complete, she was apprenticed to Ka'aya for seven years. It was then that she learned to work with energy fields as she had done earlier with Bel'lar when she freed them from the rail. She attained the designation of Sower in the Sacred Ecology religion. She was the only one to achieve this designation in many, many years.

Ry Sing laid her hand over Ka'aya's, content to wait for him to break the silence.

After a moment, he squeezed her hand and said, "Here we are at the beginning of a glorious journey through time and space. The potential for learning is phenomenal, and we're proud of your willingness to embrace it with all of its uncertainties."

"I can do no less than my teacher has shown me." She clasped her hands together and bowed her head to him. "But the truth is I'm so excited. This journey—I know I've made it before. You feel this, too."

He smiled. Then, getting to his feet, he kissed her on the cheek and left.

She lingered, eyes focused far away. Then she, too, left the bridge.

* * *

Enis, the mission's botanist, was also the ship's cook. He had volunteered to cook because he enjoyed it. He was working in the onboard greenhouse, selecting ripe vegetables and fruit. The smell of the moist, potent soil filled his nostrils as he inhaled. This greenhouse would provide all the food necessary for the journey to the blue-white planet, and it astounded him each time he came here. It didn't require any attention from him other than harvesting the food. Everything else, the perfect climate, the water, even the propagation was in the hands of the ship.

It was peaceful and silent. The scent of the warm, fertile soil relaxed him. He enjoyed this work, preferring honest work to companionship. Bending over, he tenderly grasped a perfect specimen of squash; slicing its stem, he placed it in the basket. Then he moved on to the fruit trees, filling a smaller container with ripe, yellow fruit. Then another with tiny dark cherries. He stopped to pop one in his mouth. *Perfect,* he thought. He looked around this greenhouse and was filled with happiness.

* * *

Bel'lar sat in front of the crystal display in his quarters that allowed him access to the ship's data archives. It was the end of the first day on their voyage. He was tired from the high-anxiety escape from the BOS and the subsequent launch. He asked the ship to contact the station. He wanted to know what had happened to Ro'ald and the others. The BOS was breaking in the door as they launched, and he feared that they were dead or incarcerated.

Light Traveler was unable to connect to the station. It wasn't responding, and she didn't know why. Bel'lar thought that it was highly probable that those men and women had given their lives for this mission, In Search of Shangri-La. It was because of their heroic efforts that he and his crew were on this amazing starship embarking on this journey to save their people. He was determined not to waste their sacrifice.

Since there was nothing he could do about those people and their fate, he turned his thoughts to this journey, going back to the beginning.

The ship had been discovered 10 years ago but kept secret from the general populace. After he was contacted by the Brotherhood of Syn to undertake this mission, the Brotherhood announced to the people that they would solve the world's problems by building a craft that could fly to other planets. No mention that the Light Traveler already existed. But over the term of the project, the degrading living conditions reached an unacceptable level. Anger and frustration spread through the masses. Protests began against the project, citing the massive amount of money being spent and the lack of credible information about the development and construction of this craft. The Brotherhood thought they could control the people with bits and pieces of information while the money was diverted into other projects. But discontent over the shortages of basic needs and the specter of no real assistance in the near future erupted into riots that last day. He wondered about the outcome, what had happened to Ro'ald and the others, and if he would ever know.

Their destination, the blue-white planet, had been a mystery to all for a long time. Ka'aya said their ancestors, the thirteen holy men, had visited it, but no one knew what had happened to them, if they had actually gone there, or if they had taken this ship. They were embarking on this adventure blindly, trusting Light Traveler to take them there. He knew some of his crew were nervous, afraid that they might not return, afraid that family and friends would all be dead by the time they returned. Shangri-La might be waiting, but only time would tell.

As captain, he took seriously his responsibility for the lives of his crew. Yet all they knew was that it was written that this ship would take them to a new beginning, to a place of utter beauty where they might begin again in peace and joy and abundance. But there was no concrete information and no proof other than the Light Traveler's existence and some star charts provided by the ship. Bel'lar distrusted blind faith in scripture but remembered the Syns at the rail station. They deserved another chance to live in peace and harmony. His job was to provide it if it was possible.

This journey had become feasible 10 years ago, when some crystal stones of irregular shape, similar in size to a man's hand, were unearthed during the extension of the public rail track. Ry Sing had been the one to read the information stored on those stones and point the way to the location of the ship. Those stones were secured on this ship.

The ship was ancient. He and his crew hadn't any idea of its origin, nor did they understand all the technologies involved in the production of such a craft. The efforts of the team of Organ scientists to determine its capabilities had been in vain. All they could do was observe and record as the ship awoke from hibernation and its systems were activated.

The frustration of the scientists continued without change until the day Bel'lar was introduced to the ship. He had entered the bay when a voice greeted him, shocking everyone. It was the Light Traveler.

"Greetings, Exalted One. I am the Light Traveler. I have been waiting for you. I am preparing this ship for the journey to the blue-white planet. I am at your service."

The scientists shouted all at once, trying to get answers to their questions. She didn't respond to them. Instead she invited Bel'lar aboard. Bel'lar questioned her about her technologies, but she wouldn't elucidate further. She would only say that she had an automatic guidance system programmed in ancient times to find the blue-white planet. He asked if she would allow the scientists to observe her functions. She told him that it was unnecessary but that she would allow it. They were free to draw whatever conclusions they might.

Despite repeated attempts by the scientists to talk to her, Bel'lar was the only one she responded to, even though she didn't answer his questions, and the ship's operation continued independently, regardless of the scientists' attempts.

He remembered Ka'aya's comments earlier. The ship wasn't mechanical, he had said. She was the essence of life. That seemed to better explain her actions. She was much more than physical. And as Ka'aya had said, she had her own mind—or at least a guiding directive.

The Light Traveler seemed to be following a preset program as her decks formed themselves and then settled into their locations. Systems such as the greenhouse, and air and water purification commenced operation. When the bridge reformed one day to the preferences that he had been contemplating but hadn't mentioned, Bel'lar suspected that Light Traveler was more than a machine, actually responding to his feelings and thoughts. Before this day, the bridge had been vacant but for the one deck. The next morning he had entered to discover the six chairs with the small, circular console. Then the day he selected Mauleen as his first officer, a smaller deck appeared, floating above the existing one on the bridge. This one had a smaller station and crystalline display designed with Mauleen's needs in mind. These adjustments continued throughout the ship as crew members were selected.

※　※　※

Later that evening, the door to his quarters opened, and Bel'lar turned around. The lights dimmed. Straining to focus in the dark, he could just make out someone standing in the doorway. He recognized that silhouette. He smiled. It was Ry Sing. She moved forward, and he met her, holding out his arms. She stepped into his embrace, her robe slipping off her shoulders.

Several hours later, Bel'lar bolted upright in bed. Ry Sing slept peacefully beside him. He stared into the darkness of his quarters, tormented voices crying out in his mind. He rubbed his face hard, willing the nightmare to release him. When it had and all was silent, he lay back down, remembering.

※　※　※

The initial excitement and trepidation of the abrupt escape from their home planet subsided and his crew relaxed into routine. The ship was completely self-sufficient, allowing the crew time to spend on their individual pursuits. Some meditated, some contemplated and some tried to fix parts that didn't need to be fixed.

Bel'lar attempted to contact the ISOS installation again for news on the home planet, especially of that last day, but they had already traveled out of range. He didn't know if the installation had been destroyed or if anyone had escaped. There was nothing to be done but focus on the mission.

That would be easier to do if he weren't having these nightmares. Hardly a night passed that he didn't wake in a sweat from one of them. All were similar. He was on the platform, the multitudes of people spread out as far as the eye could see. The details from the vision with Ry Sing were the same. He heard babies crying and saw the Great One holding his hands out to the people. Heard cries of "Save us." Then it was he, Bel'lar, holding the cross, driving it into the stone Device. That's when he'd always awake.

* * *

Bel'lar walked into the lounge. He had requested everyone meet for dinner this evening. A week had passed, and he wanted to see how his crew was faring. Bel'lar wondered if anyone else was having nightmares. It could be something to do with the life force of the ship. Or just plain nerves about the unknown. He wasn't sure he wanted to bring it up.

At first glance, it seemed that everyone was here. Even Enis. Tall and lean, the ship's cook and botanist had not had much interaction with the others. He seemed content with interacting with himself. Ka'aya had vouched for Enis, and Bel'lar had readily agreed to add him to this crew. He had been chosen for his knowledge of plants but had offered to cook for them on the journey. Bel'lar had had reservations about this, but it turned out that Enis was an excellent cook.

Enis was busy setting up for dinner. He was leaning over the side table, arranging small plates in a semi-circle in front of a baked-fruit dessert. He stepped back and eyed the setup, adjusting one plate in the semi-circle.

"Enis, I haven't seen you since we left the home planet," Bel'lar said.

In slow motion, Enis looked up at him with his brown eyes, his head slightly tilted forward. His brown hair poked out of the edges of his brown-knitted cap. He acknowledged Bel'lar's greeting with a nod and then straightened.

"Captain, so far, the mission is a success. You have done what we couldn't do without you. You have accelerated the ship to pure energy, to become this pure light traveler, this explosion of opportunities. I thank you."

"Thank you for your gracious words and trust." He had thought Enis awkward and shy, but this speech surprised him. Instead, he was methodical, deliberate, and attentive to details as well as shy.

Enis gave a slight bow and moved away, disappearing into the food-preparation area.

Bel'lar joined the others, sitting in the vacant chair next to Ry Sing. Ka'aya was seated on her other side, with Dobeman across from them. Ry Sing squeezed his hand, and the others greeted him. The empty chair by Dobeman indicated one crewmember missing.

"Where's Mauleen?" Bel'lar asked.

As if she heard him, Mauleen's voice greeted him over the intercom.

"Captain, please excuse me. Permission to continue my analysis of the light generator. The best time is while she's underway. I'm spending as much time here as I can."

"Permission granted," Bel'lar said. It pleased him that at least one person on this voyage still needed guidance from him.

Ka'aya smiled.

Bel'lar leaned back and shook his head. "I should have expected that. Her focus borders on obsession."

"She's been sleeping down there," Ry Sing said.

Bel'lar grinned. "Dedication is an admirable trait." Then he was distracted by Enis bringing in the food.

They sat for a long time, enjoying the food and the companionship. When they had finished, they moved over to the lounge chairs.

Enis cleaned up the remains of the meal. He set up several pitchers of water and glasses on the bar. Then, sitting some distance from them, he began eating his own meal. Shy and withdrawn, he kept his eyes on his food.

Ry Sing poked Bel'lar in the arm with her finger and angled her head toward Enis, a mischievous smile on her face.

"Please don't tease him, Ry Sing. He's painfully shy. You know we intimidate him. He will grow accustomed to us soon," Ka'aya said.

"You're right. I'm sorry." But she didn't stop smiling.

Enis must have overheard them, because he looked at Ry Sing. Then he stood, bowed and excused himself without looking at anyone else. He tripped at the door to the food-preparation area but the deck drifted up to compensate, then lowered to allow him to catch hold of the opening as he left.

Ka'aya looked Bel'lar over, noting the dark smudges under his eyes. "You're not sleeping. We can see it in your eyes, your face. What's wrong?"

"It's nothing. Just some bad dreams."

"It's more than that. Talk to us," Ka'aya said.

"The dream is the same. It's the Planet of Abundance on its day of destruction. I just don't understand why I keep having it."

"Sit back and close your eyes. Let us help you understand," Ka'aya said.

"Forget it. No meditation is going to change anything. You know I'm not interested in religious rites. I just need to burn off this energy."

"Meditation isn't a religious rite," Ry Sing said. "It's a method of getting in touch with God and yourself."

"As I said. 'Religion.'"

Ka'aya and Ry Sing exchanged a glance. Dobeman watched all three of them.

Bel'lar disliked that look Ka'aya and Ry Sing shared. He stood, anxious to get away from any more of Ka'aya's insights. Ry Sing stopped him, her hand on his arm.

"Captain, please excuse me," Dobeman interrupted. "Light Traveler has a record of events from the original journey. It would be valuable for this crew to view it."

Dobeman maintained his gaze on Bel'lar, waiting.

Bel'lar nodded, relieved by the distraction. He sat and asked L.T. to contact Mauleen. She did so, and Mauleen appeared on the large wall-mounted display to the side of them.

"Captain, I'm here. What do you need?"

"We're about to view a record containing background on the Planet of Abundance. Watch it from your location."

"Certainly, Captain," she answered.

Mauleen's face disappeared from the display. Bel'lar turned to Dobeman.

Dobeman asked Light Traveler to play the record.

A voice began to speak, a soft-spoken female voice—it was the voice of the Light Traveler.

"Greetings. I am here to explain what has been and what will be. I will try to enlighten you. This ship is a constellation-class craft, and I am the energy of this ship. I am every facet and moving part. I am the intelligence, and I am here for the reason of continuing. I am here to continue the knowledge that has been gained in the past. I am here to send this knowledge into the future with you. I am here to assist beings like you to perpetuate the life force by expanding it and to continue it beyond the realms of immortality."

No one noticed Enis come in and stand by the doorway to the food-preparation area. Bel'lar had forgotten to call him, absorbed in his own fears.

The Light Traveler continued, "This ship was created for this very reason many thousands of years ago by beings similar to you. I was built with technologies that surpass those of today. These technologies will probably never be surpassed again in the future on any planet. I have been in hibernation for many thousands of years and have been activated at certain intervals to help civilizations move from one place and time to another, to continue the adventure. The first time this occurred was on the Planet of Abundance. That planet was bountiful, and it gave much to the inhabitants in the way of experiences, but as it grew and prospered and continued, it reached the point where it began to die."

Bel'lar was suddenly filled with foreboding.

The display filled with scene after scene of the Planet of Abundance. No green trees, no fields, just cities and people everywhere. Everything had been consumed. So much like the home planet they had just left.

"Then a religious movement started, the Sacred Ecology, which tried to turn the clocks back, tried to turn back the technologies, attempted to teach humanity to abstain from expanding, from consuming all. But this religion did not succeed, and, at the point where the Planet of Abundance was nearing extinction, the holy men, with their followers, decided to purify the planet and rid it of all living species that could do it harm."

Bel'lar wanted to close his eyes, to avoid seeing what he feared was coming. Then a thought: Maybe the vision Ry Sing had shown him was false. Maybe it had never happened.

The voice went on, "They ignited a nuclear-chain-reaction event that encompassed the planet and cleansed it, sending the planet into hibernation to come forth in a few million years. But before the chain reaction was complete, thirteen of the holy men were able to leave the planet on this ship that you journey on now."

The display filled with scenes of the violence of the destruction and then narrowed in on the multitudes of people spread out around the pyramid temple. Flames erupted from the ground. Where people had been clustered, now fires burned hot. Continuing explosions and fire decimated the people, everything. Huge plumes of smoke and debris shot into space from all over the planet.

This time, Bel'lar witnessed the destruction from space and not as part of the destruction. But this time also the effect on him was more powerful. He realized he had been harboring a hope that it wasn't true. Now he had to believe it had happened. It was recorded in the ship's memory. He couldn't refute it. The terrible truth created pressure in his chest, and it hurt to breathe. He felt as if his head would explode from the pressure.

✳ ✳ ✳

Watching this horror play out on her display, Mauleen whispered to herself, "Where is the compassion, the humanity in the human being? I don't understand emotions, the driving force of humans." This was why she focused on her responsibilities, performing to the best that she was capable of, if not more.

✳ ✳ ✳

Ka'aya put his hand on Bel'lar's shoulder, attempting to shift some of the pain from him. "I know this is difficult, but understand that this negative event that has horrified you has created opportunities for a great wealth of emotions, and through these emotions, knowledge is gained. So don't judge, but experience such events, and, from these events, become wise, and learn, so you may understand."

The pressure eased and, Bel'lar sucked in air. "I don't have patience for religion, Ka'aya," he gasped out. He had spent his life so far eluding religion's grasp, and it hadn't been easy. His father ignored his true wishes and continued to hope he would succeed him when the time came. Yet he refused, and one of his father's ministers was chosen, but many others still felt it should have been him. This mission was all that saved him from constant harassment by the followers of the Sacred Ecology religion to take up his, as they called it, "rightful place as chosen by God."

"This is not religion, Bel'lar, but a way to live your life in harmony with all-that-is by allowing what has begun to finish," Ka'aya explained. "Sacred Ecology is simply allowing the water to flow to the sea, the trees to grow, the air to move, the sun to shine, the animals to live."

The record resumed. "The holy men journeyed to your home planet on this ship. Your planet was perfect. Indeed, almost identical to their own Planet of Abundance, now extinct."

"Then these holy men went on to create a civilization with the local inhabitants that would become great in its own right." The crystal display blanked. The record was over.

"What will keep the blue-white planet from turning out like the Planet of Abundance and our home planet?" Bel'lar demanded.

"It is in the hearts of mankind to create what they need," Ka'aya answered him, his voice heavy with sadness.

Enis turned and escaped into the food-preparation area. His eyes filled with tears; he didn't want the others to see him crying.

*        *        *

In the light-generating room, Mauleen put her head down on the station in front of her. She was glad it was over. She couldn't stand any more.

*        *        *

That night, Bel'lar fell asleep and suffered through the dream again. This time the dream was even more intense, and, even while awake, Bel'lar remained frightened by what he had witnessed. His mind kept flashing back to when he was the one who drove the cross into the heart of the planet. He felt that he was the holy man. It didn't make any sense. He couldn't be that man. He was Bel'lar, and he lived right now. He knew what Ka'aya would say or Ry Sing or even his father. He knew we lived many lives—but not one as that holy man. Not he. Not Bel'lar. But he knew with absolute certainty, or perhaps it was clairvoyance, that some day he would have to account for what that man did. This was what terrified him the most—had him jumping at shadows. He opened his journal and started to write, "Oh God, forgive me for I know not what I have done."

It weighed heavily on him, this mission that was critical to save their people. If things continued as they had on their home planet, it seemed clear that the end would be the same. The home planet would be destroyed just as the Planet of Abundance had been. They had to find the blue-white planet. He hoped again that he could trust the Light Traveler to find it.

✳ ✳ ✳

Two days had passed since they had viewed the record and since he had endured that intense dream he couldn't seem to wake from. Bel'lar had begun walking the corridors each day in the afternoon to keep busy. At the end of his walk, he turned into the corridor leading to the crew's private quarters, intent on spending the rest of the day in his own quarters. Oblivious to his surroundings, he was walking, eyes cast down, shaking his head when someone touched his arm. Ry Sing was leaning against her doorway, smiling seductively. Normally, he wouldn't have thought twice about approaching her, but his thoughts about the holy man filled his mind, and he wasn't himself. Far from it. He looked at her more closely and thought she looked hungry, and this made him nervous. He wondered what she was hungry for.

"It's me. Bel'lar, what's wrong with you? Why don't you come inside?" She grabbed his arm and tugged. He looked ill, his cheeks were hollow, his eyes reflected pain.

He stuffed his hands in his pockets and tried to walk away. Her hold on his arm tightened. She wasn't going to let him walk away. He needed her help.

He mumbled something under his breath, then stopped, unwilling to jerk his arm away from her.

"Come in. I don't bite, at least not much."

He glanced up at her, considering. Then he followed her inside.

That glance unsettled her. He acted as if he didn't trust her.

"Sit here on the couch with me," she said, leading him by his hand.

"All right," he said. She sat first. He sat at the opposite end.

She couldn't believe he was sitting way over there. What had happened to him that would cause such a distance to open up between them? Where was the man she knew?

"I'll pour us some wine." She went behind the bar where she kept refreshments. She poured one for each of them. His hand shook some when he accepted his glass. A splash dropped onto his black pants, creating a tiny wet spot. He touched it with a finger and then put his hand over it. She sat next to him and began to stroke his arm. Her nails caused tremors to radiate up his arm, and he shivered.

She smiled at this and said, "You're a very troubled soul. You can't go through this life worrying about lives before. If you do, you won't accomplish your goals in this life."

He looked at her now, searching her face for the truth. Did she really know something that would help him? He sat up and looked directly into her green eyes.

She rested her hand on his shoulder and began to impart warm energy into his body.

He glanced away from her eyes.

"Drink your wine, Bel'lar."

He took a drink, more like a gulp. "But those holy men. How could they destroy that planet? All those people. How could they do it? I will never understand. Even if there was a compelling reason, I couldn't. I couldn't be that bold. I could not kill an entire planet."

"You can't look at it that way. The beings on the Planet of Abundance wanted that experience, and the holy men were just fulfilling the prophecy. Let me help you understand. Lean back. Hand me your glass."

He gave up his glass but sat upright, afraid to lay his head back—afraid to give into her help, afraid that it would release the emotion he was holding at bay with all of his being.

She walked around behind him and began massaging his shoulders, his neck, his forehead. Then, placing her hands on either side of his head, she said, "I'm going to allow the energy of my body to mix with the energy of yours to help you relax."

Bel'lar stiffened at her touch, but her hands were warm and getting warmer. The heat soaked into his body, into his mind, soothing and healing him. Soon his shoulders drooped and his head dropped back. His eyes closed. He stopped fighting her. He couldn't stay alert. He no longer cared. With each wave of heated, healing energy, he gave himself into her hands, trusting her.

Ry Sing's voice had dropped to a purr, sending her words into him with a vibration that further induced him to submit to her. "Understand the energy that flows from me to you also flowed through the beings of that planet. Through this, you will understand that the energy is not dead, that those people did not die—they only changed form."

Her words were arrows being shot into his body. At first, there was pain, but that soon dissipated, and warmth spread throughout his body. He moaned out loud with the comfort of it.

"Good. I'm going to count to three while you relax further. Visualize that this extinction wasn't a death but merely the end of a cycle. Everything changed. But it didn't go away."

The last bit of his tension drained away as Ry Sing counted and he melted into the couch. She left her hands on his head, maintaining the physical connection until she was sure he was asleep. Then, pressing a light kiss on the top of his head, she disengaged without disturbing him.

Picking up her glass, she took a sip.

"I did that too well, Light Traveler." She shrugged her shoulders, toasted the sleeping Bel'lar and took another sip. Then she walked to the door. Opening it, she leaned against the doorframe.

✳  ✳  ✳

Bel'lar's frustration grew as each day passed. Twenty-eight days they had been on this journey. He, along with the rest of the crew, had no idea when and if they would reach the blue-white planet. The Light Traveler would say only that the journey was proceeding as planned and that all systems were operational. Ka'aya and Ry Sing were committed to the journey, going about the days calmly and happily. Without their inspirational example, the others might find this journey more than they could handle. Enis and Mauleen managed to keep themselves busy, not stopping long enough to let any concerns surface. And Dobeman spent hours in silence and contemplation, writing in his log, without any sign of impatience or anxiety.

Bel'lar was glad that the others were coping well but couldn't help but be irritated that he wasn't. This command was unlike any that he had held before. He was used to being responsible for a much larger staff going about vital, necessary tasks, reporting to him each day, needing his leadership. But this ship required nothing from any of them. She functioned independently and reported to him only when he inquired. He knew his presence had activated her, but, as captain, he felt useless.

And he was still plagued by those nightly dreams.

To keep in shape and burn off his frustration, Bel'lar stressed his body physically each morning for two hours in the room he had named the warrior room. Light Traveler had responded to his unspoken desire, and, one week into the journey, a new corridor appeared on his route to the bridge. He stepped inside, and an opening appeared that led into this room. It had a full set of bars and hand weights, along with a running track. The track was incredible because it seemed short, but once he began to run, it continued until he stopped. It modified itself to accommodate whatever distance Bel'lar wanted each day.

✳ ✳ ✳

Bel'lar was running on the track in the warrior room when he sensed a change in the ship's speed. It was slowing. He stopped, listening. *Could this be it?* he wondered. Fifty-six days had passed since they'd left the home planet.

Light Traveler said, "Captain, we are changing from light speed to normal speed."

As the ship slowed down, Bel'lar felt heavy for a moment. Then the heaviness dropped away, and he felt his body lift as if he would float. Then, everything seemed different, yet the same. The ship continued to slow. He ran from the warrior room, increasing his speed. They had found the blue-white planet—a planet that had already been traveled to by their ancestors.

As the ship slowed, all of the crew except Enis converged on the bridge. Mauleen was seated at her station, eyes on space. The crystalline display was activated and they could see into the vastness of space.

A planet filled the view. It was blue and white, and its abundance could be seen and felt from the bridge. Ka'aya and Ry Sing had tears in their eyes, while Dobeman stared in fascination. Bel'lar was excited. This must be the blue-white planet.

# CHAPTER 2

# UNDERSTANDING THE PAST

As they hovered above the blue-white planet, everyone was infused with tremendous excitement. No one wanted to look away from the display, with its view of the beautiful glowing planet, fully lit with its atmosphere and sunshine. As they gazed upon it, many things went through the crewmembers' minds. Where would they live? What would happen to them? What would be different, and what would be the same? What would they tell the future generations about how it all began? They wondered what the intention of their ancestors, the holy men, had been.

Mauleen left to check on some equipment, and Enis had not appeared yet, but Dobeman, Ka'aya, and Ry Sing were present and waiting for Bel'lar to take the next step.

Ka'aya approached the crystalline display and gazed out upon the beautiful planet before them. *Yes*, he thought, *this is the next step in our evolution. It is where we will live, where we will teach and train all who come after us.* He breathed in the planet's energy, and he was pleased.

Enis hurried in, wiping his wet hands on his apron. He stopped near Ka'aya and was transfixed by the sight of the planet. Breathing out a deep breath, he put his hand on his heart and stood there, a peaceful smile on his face.

Bel'lar wanted to land immediately and experience this planet with all his senses, but he had cautioned the others against this very thing. Instead, he clamped down on his excitement and considered what the best course of action would be. Should they commence the studies that Dobeman would conduct, or was it possible that the holy men had left something here to aid them as they had on his home planet?

A tone sounded, and Mauleen appeared in a window superimposed in the upper left corner of the display; the blue-white planet filled the rest.

"Captain, what are your orders?" Behind her was the light-generating equipment.

"Run a scan for any signals or anomalies," he directed, as he moved to stand behind his chair.

"Yes, Captain," Mauleen answered.

"Anything?" Bel'lar kept his eyes on the viewing display.

"No. I'll run it again." She bent her head to the station in the light-generating room. "Captain, still nothing. But Light Traveler has widened the scan to encompass nearby planets. I don't understand."

"L.T., what are you doing?" Bel'lar asked.

"Searching for signs of the ancient ones' previous visit to this solar system," the ship answered.

"Wait a minute. Isn't this the right planet?"

"It's the right planet, Bel'lar," Ka'aya said. "There is no doubt."

The ship began to shift away from the blue-white planet.

"What are you doing, L.T.?"

Light Traveler responded, "Recalculating, Captain."

The ship increased her speed.

"Captain, she's changed course. She's leaving this planet," Mauleen interrupted.

"Light Traveler, I demand you stop immediately," Bel'lar said.

Light Traveler didn't respond to Bel'lar, and her speed remained constant. She was on a new course.

"Stop," Bel'lar demanded, his voice furious. "L.T., respond." His hands were white knuckled on the back of his chair.

Mauleen blurted out, "I've found something." She gulped a breath to get a grip on her excitement. "A faint signal. Light Traveler's set a course for it. We should investigate further."

"I don't think we have any choice, Mauleen. Light Traveler, where are you taking us?" Bel'lar asked.

"I have set course for a small red planet. A signal is broadcasting that bears the ancient ones' signature."

"I see. Do we need to make this detour?"

"Yes, Captain," the ship said.

"Trust her, Bel'lar, to provide an opportunity," Ka'aya said. "It will be valuable."

Bel'lar glared at Ka'aya and then faced the display, intent on where the ship was taking them.

Ry Sing smiled at Bel'lar's response to Ka'aya. She knew they had to go to the source of this signal before they could land on the blue-white planet. Critical information waited for them, but she didn't add any support to Ka'aya's comment. Light Traveler had everything under control.

Dobeman watched everything and everyone as they reacted to the unexpected detour. His recording device was active, and his thoughts were being entered. Much emotion was stirred up and released at every human event. It seemed a lot of fuss over a simple course change to receive important information, but he noted and enjoyed each occurrence.

Ry Sing had an idea and wanted to scan the blue-white planet before it was out of range, using her intuition as a guide. She took advantage of Mauleen's absence to sit at the small station. Blending her energy with that of the ship, she cast her senses wide and intercepted a signal almost immediately. She narrowed into this strange beam of energy that she couldn't quite make out, even though it seemed familiar. She focused the scanner on it, but no visual appeared as she listened. No one else heard it but her. It was a frequency, a wave, that was comforting to her as she sat there, floating in a twilight daze, taking it in but still unable to understand it. She remained in this state, oblivious to the others.

Ka'aya recognized her trance state and smiled. He knew she had contacted something which completely held her attention.

On the small display in front of her, an image appeared. Her harmonious state with the ship allowed this manifestation. It was a small pyramid, azure gold, shining in the sun. Ka'aya touched her shoulder, and she opened her eyes. She was about to call Bel'lar over when Ka'aya leaned in close to her and spoke softly into her ear. "This is for you alone. Don't be concerned. You'll have much time to explore it when we return to the blue-white planet."

"It's from Taurus. Why is that familiar?" Her voice was husky with emotion.

"It's where you're from," he answered.

She closed her eyes again, savoring and imprinting this beam of energy, this image in her memory, intent on reconnecting when they returned.

Bel'lar paced in frustration. Everything was out of his control. The Light Traveler was forcing them to this other planet for some unknown reason. He hated not knowing.

He looked down at Ry Sing. Her eyes were closed. How could she just sit there, unaware of what was happening?

"Ry Sing."

She opened her eyes abruptly at the sound of her name, his voice severing her connection. The azure gold pyramid disappeared from the small display. She slowly focused in on Bel'lar. He jabbed his thumb toward the main display. She recognized the source of his agitation. He was unable to allow. *What fun*, she thought as she grinned at him. He frowned back. Then she stepped down from the small deck and joined him. Together they walked closer to the display.

Everyone's eyes were glued to the activated display, waiting for the new location to appear. Then a small red planet was detectable in the distance. This was the source of the signal that Light Traveler had found.

Light Traveler adjusted her focus to zoom in on this tiny planet. She was capable of reaching and exposing details at great distances. Therefore, within a matter of minutes, the surface of this planet was viewable despite their distance from it. Her focus traveled around the planet and stopped. A pyramid rose up from the ground with something large and white gleaming next to it. This white shape became larger and clearer as the ship adjusted her focus.

Bel'lar drew his breath in sharply. The white shape was a face that resembled the great holy man himself. The one he had seen on the Planet of Abundance. The one he had been seeing in his dreams. He didn't look around at his crew. He knew they recognized the face. Everyone had been told the story of the Planet of Abundance and its demise. Now, more than ever, he didn't want to go to this strange planet. What was the significance of this large replica of the holy man's face? What would they find down there? And why wasn't any of this on the blue-white planet?

Enis sat quietly and didn't utter a word, hardly breathing. The image of the Great One had stimulated his interest in this planet. He wondered what the holy men may have brought with them. And if any of it was still here. Somehow he had to find out.

"L.T., why are you taking us to this planet?" the captain said.

"This is where the holy men landed," the ship said.

"But this is not the blue-white planet."

"No, Bel'lar," Ry Sing interrupted. "It's the red planet, where the holy men lived for some time. We must find out why they came here. This is the next step in your mission."

"What do you know?" Bel'lar looked at her and then at Ka'aya. The older man merely gave a small bow and raised his hand toward the crystalline display's image of the red planet. Ry Sing looked at the red planet, too. Bel'lar shook his head as he walked away from her, considering his next move.

Mauleen had quietly entered the bridge while the others were fixated on the red planet and had seated herself at her station. She sat straight, her uniform crisp as she tucked her hair behind her ears.

Bel'lar turned around and noted his first officer's appearance. "Mauleen, you're here. Good. Can we access anything from here?"

"No, Captain. It's simply a distress signal. We'll have to investigate to discover the reason."

"That seems to be Light Traveler's plan. Nothing to do but wait." Bel'lar looked around at the others. "L.T., estimated time of arrival?"

"At this speed, arrival will be in thirty-two hours," Light Traveler answered.

"Thank you." Bel'lar looked at his crew again. "Since we have little choice, we're going to this red planet. But only as long as necessary to find out why the holy men were there. Then we return to the blue-white planet."

✳ ✳ ✳

The ship entered the atmosphere around the red planet, as estimated, in just more than thirty-two hours. Bel'lar announced the arrival from his position on the bridge.

Ry Sing and Ka'aya walked together to the bridge. They had been in meditation for the past two hours and were refreshed and ready to explore this red planet.

Dobeman closed the record he was reviewing in preparation for the studies he would conduct on the blue-white planet. He was very interested in this outpost and wanted to explore it. He met up with Enis at the entry to the bridge, and the two entered together.

On the bridge, Bel'lar and Mauleen had completed preliminary scans, and, by the time the others arrived, Bel'lar had made the decision to land.

Bel'lar nodded to his crew as they entered.

"L.T., land at a safe distance from the pyramid over by the face. We need to be sure there's no danger," he said. "The sensors say the atmosphere is too thin for us without life suits, and no life forms are detected anywhere on the planet."

The ship traveled through the atmosphere and landed next to the pyramid. She set down so easily no one felt the landing. The pyramid loomed over them, shining like red glass in the red light that colored everything.

"Captain, suits will not be necessary. I have connected to the passageway leading into the Red Planet Complex. You may exit through the bottom level of the ship and take the lift down into the complex," announced the ship.

"Good, L.T. Obviously, you've been here before. Mauleen, you're with me. Dobeman, I'll need your abilities. Ry Sing, Ka'aya, one or both of you as well."

Enis was the only one who remained on board. He was glad to be excluded because he was trying to work out how to make a trip to the surface alone.

The five quickly dispersed to pick up their gear. Bel'lar stopped at his quarters for his weapon.

They met at the lift and traveled down one level to the bottom. Ry Sing giggled and did a little dance step, as she stood next to Bel'lar. He smiled down at her. Mauleen checked everyone's gear, her face that of the perfect officer, and then grinned, letting her guard down for a second. Each of them except for Ka'aya carried a small pack clipped to a waist belt that contained a small torch, a multipurpose tool, and a scanning/recording device.

Bel'lar was smiling, too. The excitement was infectious. Ka'aya smiled at Bel'lar, enjoying the high spirits of the others. It had been a long trip, and the chance to leave the ship was not to be missed. Dobeman, as usual, observed dispassionately but enjoyed this experience.

At the bottom level, the lift door slid back, revealing the ship's open hatch and secure connection to the Red Planet Complex. Bel'lar took the lead as they stepped into the dimly lit lift of the Red Planet Complex. Silently, it took them down two levels. The lift opened on to a long, dark corridor built of stone, similar to the pyramid on the surface.

Bel'lar peered into the darkness cautiously, the silence eerie. Ry Sing stepped up right behind him. Impatient, she tapped his back with her finger. When he didn't move, she pushed him and tried to step around him. He frowned at her and then held her back and entered first. The lights came on in this section of the corridor, but darkness still waited up ahead.

Unable to see where this corridor was taking them or what might be ahead, Bel'lar led the way slowly, the others following in single file, with Mauleen the last one out of the lift. The corridor was constructed of perfectly cut and fitted stones similar to the stonework on the pyramid they had found on the home planet. Bel'lar couldn't resist running his hand along the stones, marveling at how smooth and cool they were beneath his fingers.

Dobeman stood next to him, his hands touching the stones, his fingers following the crevices. "Exceptional craftsmanship."

"I agree," Bel'lar said.

No dust or debris of any kind littered this corridor. It was pristine and clean inside here as if someone maintained it; the air was fresh and comfortably cool. It made Bel'lar uneasy. "Hasn't it been eons since any human beings were here?" he said.

"It's a little creepy, isn't it?" Ry Sing added and then giggled again.

Bel'lar couldn't see her face since she was right behind him, but Ka'aya could. Ry Sing was teasing Bel'lar, but he hadn't noticed yet, completely absorbed as he was in seeing to their safety.

The hair on the back of Bel'lar's neck prickled, not knowing what to anticipate. He led his group toward the darkness ahead. The corridor curved to the left, and they followed him into the darkness, Ry Sing still close behind him. Dobeman and Ka'aya followed her, with Mauleen behind them.

Expecting the light to come on in this stretch of corridor as it had in the first segment, Bel'lar didn't hesitate to enter, but the darkness continued. They walked forward until all of them were in the dark. Bel'lar stopped.

A whooshing sound had them spinning around to witness a door sliding shut, cutting off their access to the ship and the light. Now in total darkness, no one moved, no one breathed. Bel'lar pulled his torch out and switched it on.

Then Mauleen cried out. She took a deep ragged breath. "I felt something. Behind me."

They heard a dull thud. Something had fallen.

"Mauleen, are you all right?" Ry Sing called out.

Bel'lar shone his torch in Mauleen's direction, and he could see she wasn't all right. She was lying on the floor, unmoving. Hurrying back to her, he bent down to check on her when she moved, pushing up to a seated position. He jerked back out of the way as she began getting to her feet, her body moving mechanically.

She began to speak, a deep, distant-sounding voice that was not hers; yet her mouth was moving. "I have been waiting for you." Her head turned to face the others. She stared at them with closed eyes.

Bel'lar took a step back, the others behind him.

The voice issued from Mauleen again, "Don't you recognize me? I know you. You are holy men, my brothers and sisters." The voice sighed. "It has been so long. Why do you back away from me?"

Ry Sing stood next to Bel'lar now, unafraid and unconcerned, Bel'lar noticed. She took a step toward Mauleen, and he pulled her back.

Ka'aya stepped forward. "Greetings, brother." He cupped his hands together in front of him. Staring intently into his hands, he drew energy into them. His hands began to glow. Then the glow brightened, and he lifted his hands, releasing an orb of yellow-orange fire that floated up, bathing the corridor in light.

"Indeed, you are the holy men," the voice exclaimed.

"Release Mauleen," Bel'lar demanded. "The one you're possessing."

Mauleen's head turned to Bel'lar, but her eyes remained unnaturally closed. The voice addressed him. "Do not be afraid.

I am merely transferring my energy through this one's body. No harm will come to her."

Dobeman had taken his recorder out. He was making a visual as well as audio recording of this event and was embedding his observations through mental telepathy into this record. In his experience, such entities weren't bad, and, thus, there was nothing to be concerned about. It was how this group of humans would react to this situation that he was more interested in discovering.

Bel'lar had had enough. He drew his weapon, a device that discharged a beam of energy that could disrupt the magnetic field of a body temporarily, causing it to collapse.

"Release her," he ordered.

Ka'aya put his hand on Bel'lar's forearm. "Bel'lar, you can't use that. You will hurt Mauleen."

The voice said, "Yes. That is true."

"Ry Sing, what do you sense?" Bel'lar asked. He didn't lower his weapon.

"There's a life force here," she answered as she closed her eyes and focused in on Mauleen. "I believe he's one of the ancient holy men. She's not being harmed." She opened her eyes. "He won't harm us."

Mauleen's head turned from side to side as if looking at each of them, all the while with the eyes eerily closed.

Bel'lar still didn't lower his weapon, his senses disturbed by the unnatural thing in front of him.

The ancient holy man in possession of Mauleen's body remained motionless, waiting.

Dobeman made a note in his journal. *This is turning out to be quite fascinating*, he thought.

Bel'lar lowered his weapon but didn't holster it. He didn't trust this entity that had Mauleen in its grip.

"We are ready, ancient one," Ry Sing said.

Mauleen's hand rose and then dropped to her side.

"Thank you. Now, if you will follow, I will take you into the station."

Bel'lar and his companions stood to one side while Mauleen's body, under the holy man's direction, proceeded past them, her arms and legs moving out of sync in a stilted fashion. Ry Sing was the first to step out behind the ancient one. Bel'lar followed her, the others behind him. Ka'aya's fire orb moved with them, illuminating their path in golden light.

The corridor seemed to end up ahead, but, on closer examination, they discovered it was a closed doorway. The ancient holy man stopped before this door.

A different voice hailed them. "This station is closed."

The ancient holy man inhabiting Mauleen's body was clearly surprised as he said, "Why is it closed?"

The station answered, "A very long time ago, the last three inhabitants expired. Their final request was to put the station into stasis, waiting for the return of the nine who had gone on before. You do not match the visual records of the nine. You are intruders."

"I gave those orders. Don't you recognize my voice?" The ancient one sounded distressed.

"Access denied," the station replied.

"If you deny us access," the ancient one said, "you deny us the knowledge and information that lies within this station. It is your obligation to allow this knowledge from the past to be exposed."

The station didn't respond, and they waited in silence.

Ka'aya raised his hand, and the orb of fire floated near him, positioning itself directly above his left hand.

Bel'lar looked around at the others. "Enough of this. Everyone stand back. I'll burn through the door with my light pistol."

He raised his weapon to fire, but Ka'aya was swifter. He hurled the orb against the door. Bel'lar jumped back, with a yell, raising his hands up to cover his face. The orb exploded into thousands of tiny winking sparks that fell away and burned out, leaving the door undamaged.

Ka'aya was perplexed at this and paused in contemplation. Then he smiled and approached the door. He touched it gently, and it opened. He turned to the others still smiling. "Force will accomplish whatever you desire. But knowing the right amount is the key."

Bel'lar looked at Ka'aya in amazement. Ry Sing hugged her mentor, and he smiled down at her.

The ancient holy man stepped through, and they followed.

Dobeman paused to inspect the door, curious about the bits of light that sparkled and winked out. He used his device to scan the door as he contemplated how Ka'aya had accomplished this feat.

They walked cautiously into the Red Planet Complex, and the lights came on. They were in a great round room, which appeared to have been the station's headquarters. A large pyramid-shaped sky window crowned this room in the center. The pyramid window was about ten meters in height and ten meters in width. Outside, sand had drifted up on one side, partially obscuring the view, but the crimson glow was discernible.

Beneath this window in the room was some kind of control panel where the holy men must have worked. Off to one side was a grouping of chairs and small tables. A workstation ran the length of the wall on the other side. Several lighted corridors led off from this room.

Bel'lar circumnavigated the room quickly, making sure it was safe. He stepped into the corridors, looking for anything that might be a threat. The others followed Mauleen to the center of the room and waited. When Bel'lar felt secure, he returned to them.

Dobeman had turned his attention to the instruments. Some sort of automatic program was running, and he exerted his energy toward determining what it was and how it worked.

Mauleen's eyes opened. Blinking several times, she looked around the room. But when she spoke, it was still in the ancient one's voice. "I had forgotten how the station looked through the eyes of a human being. This is something that I shall cherish." She smiled.

Ry Sing closed her eyes. "I sense another life force in here. It's very strong." She turned to Ka'aya.

He waved his hand through the air, dispelling any impediments to communication. "Greetings to all who are present but not in physical."

"Thank you for seeing us and knowing we are here." This voice appeared to issue from the air around them. "We apologize for our brother who has taken possession of your beautiful lady companion. He did not do this out of malice. He just wished to be physical once again."

This strange new voice made Bel'lar edgy. He looked around for the source, all his senses on alert. He didn't like this station and wasn't certain he wanted to know what secrets it held.

Mauleen's head turned, as if searching for the location of the voice, as she answered, "You won't believe how wonderful it is to be physical again. But I shall, as you wish, relinquish my hold over the lady."

With that, Mauleen's body shuddered, and her knees buckled. Bel'lar caught her before she fell. He put an arm around her, holding her upright, but her legs were like rubber.

She opened her eyes, blinking rapidly. "Where are we? What happened?"

The voice from the air around them spoke, "We are sorry we intruded into your consciousness, but realize you have experienced something not many human beings could handle—multi-consciousness. We hope this won't prejudice you against us."

Mauleen rubbed her eyes and tried to shake off the dazed feeling. She didn't understand these words or who was speaking. She felt disconnected, unfocused, out of control, and this disturbed her. She struggled to stand on her own, but she was too unsteady. Bel'lar tightened his supportive hold on her.

"Bring her over to this couch, Bel'lar, she needs rest," Ry Sing said.

He helped Mauleen to the couch, and she collapsed back. She still had not regained her strength or control.

Ry Sing placed her hands on Mauleen's forehead and chest. She closed her eyes and scanned Mauleen's energy field, searching for deficiencies or disruptions. Nothing concerned her. She squeezed Mauleen's hand.

"You'll be fine. Just rest."

"We once again apologize," the voice said. "We will not intrude upon your physical space any more. We hope this incident in no way will alter the future. And, once again, we welcome you back."

"What does that mean—we've been here before?" Bel'lar said under his breath.

"Just listen. You may learn something," Ka'aya whispered.

Ry Sing went to stand by Ka'aya.

"We chose to stay here when you left to find a home to build a new civilization. Now you return but act as if you don't know us."

"We do have some knowledge," Ka'aya replied. "But it has been eons since we made that journey."

The voice continued. "It has not been eons for us. Time is irrelevant in our state. How can you not know us? We know you."

"That is why we seek you out, to reconnect to the past," Ka'aya said. "So we can understand ourselves and progress through this difficult time."

The voice laughed. "You beings of physical are always suffering in your present condition. This is why you have chosen this path."

"Who are you then? Tell us," Bel'lar said. This was taking entirely too long in his opinion.

Mauleen sat up at Bel'lar's question, listening. She felt almost normal again.

"We are the three holy men who remained. Our bodies ceased to function many years ago, but we stayed to tell the story of why we are here and what we have done."

"You sent the distress call," Ry Sing said.

"We wanted you to come here so we could explain what happened."

"You deceived us," Bel'lar said. "Why should we trust you?"

"We must tell you what we have done."

"Does this have anything to do with the blue-white planet?" Bel'lar didn't want to waste any more time than they had to here.

Ka'aya and Ry Sing exchanged a look that Bel'lar couldn't read. Were they smiling? Probably at him.

"Please continue, ancient ones," Ka'aya said.

The voice said, "We are the three who remained. We have joined with the station so that you might hear us. You may think of us as apparitions, for your folklore mentions many of them. Apparitions exist for many reasons. But one reason is they have not fulfilled their mission in the physical world, so, when the body has disintegrated, the essence of that body remains until it is completed."

All eyes were suddenly drawn to an area just beyond Mauleen's couch, where the apparitions appeared, flickering in and out of view and then becoming distinct; three beings, one female and two male, standing together. Their individual forms blended into each other, the edges indistinct, their eyes clear and sad. They were dressed in long, blood-red robes.

As one entity, the apparitions drifted closer to the five. Bel'lar took a step back in reaction and nervousness. He reached for his weapon but didn't pull it. He knew his weapon wouldn't banish the apparitions. Unsure what would, he stepped in front of the others determined to somehow protect them.

"Stop, Bel'lar," Ry Sing cried out. "These beings are our ancestors, our friends. Allow them to feel our energies as we feel theirs. Then we will understand what has happened here."

She stepped in front of Bel'lar and greeted the three. They glided to a stop in front of her and stretched out their hands to touch hers, which she extended to theirs. She closed her eyes and sighed.

Bel'lar reached for her, intent on pulling her out of the apparitions' grasp, but she moved too fast. Reluctant to let her be that close to the apparitions, he moved closer. Then, sensing how profound the connection was for her, he waited, not touching her. The travelers watched her communion with the three holy men, Bel'lar and Mauleen nervously, Ka'aya and Dobeman interested but unconcerned.

At the moment that Ry Sing's energy touched the ancient ones, she felt a surge of love tinged with happiness and recognition. And relief. They were relieved to finally complete their task. The surge of energy caused her to sway, and then it supported her; the story flowed into her at an amazing speed, faster than she could process. She didn't try to slow it down but just allowed it to encompass her, knowing that she could recall it afterward.

Ka'aya began to explain to the others in a low voice so as not to disturb Ry Sing. "These beings are our ancestors, not new life forms. They are just like us, but they have not allowed their life resonance to decay. When one has a belief to complete something, it will remain steadfast until its assignment is complete. Most people don't understand this, but this is the way it has always been and will always be. So if you stumble through your physical life and never accomplish your intentions, you might hang around after your body passes."

The flow of information slowed and then stopped. Ry Sing was surrounded once more in that flood of emotion, love, and, now, thanksgiving. The beauty of it brought tears to her eyes. She opened her eyes and stepped back from the three holy men. She bowed to them.

Then she turned around. Bel'lar moved over to her, catching her hand. She smiled at him, and he knew she was unharmed. He led her over to where Mauleen was resting. Several chairs were clustered, and they looked soft and, strangely, dust free.

The three holy men floated over to be near Ry Sing, hovering at her side. They were close enough to experience her energy again. One reached out a hand to touch her shoulder, and she smiled.

Ka'aya and Dobeman moved their chairs in closer to her.

Mauleen scooted to the edge of her seat on the couch. She could feel some tingling that seemed to be coming from the apparitions, but, unlike Ry Sing, this only made her jittery and wanting to escape it.

Bel'lar remained standing. He was feeling edgy again, and, now that Ry Sing was safe, he was impatient to look over the control panel and access the station's archives. He wanted to discover the reason they were here and get back to the ship.

The holy men bowed their heads to Bel'lar. "Greetings, Exalted One. We understand why you are disturbed about being near us again. We won't give up your secret." They bowed again.

Bel'lar just stared at them. Then, dismissing them, he said, "Mauleen and I should be investigating this station. Are you feeling well enough, Mauleen?"

Mauleen got to her feet quickly. "Yes, of course." She couldn't wait to get away from the holy men.

"Wait, Bel'lar," Ry Sing said. "As we are intending to create a new civilization on the blue-white planet, it's imperative that you hear the ancient ones' story."

Bel'lar looked at her, shaking his head.

"The reason we came here is to hear their story. Come here and listen." She sounded angry with him, and he was surprised. If she felt it was important, he would give her a few moments. He turned to Mauleen and waved her on to the control area. He sat and turned his attention to Ry Sing.

Ry Sing smiled up at the three holy men. The man on the left bowed. "I am called Ne'lan," he said. His hair was fair and wispy. His aged face reflected abject sadness and shame.

He began his story. "When we left the Planet of Abundance on that fateful day, there were thirteen of us. We were all that was left of a once-great civilization. As our journey progressed, our leader, the Great One, suffered more than the rest of us from the weight of what we had done. He decided that he could no longer go on. He refused nourishment and passed from physical shortly after we arrived here."

Bel'lar fidgeted. This information about the Great One was disturbing him. Ry Sing put her hand on his arm, hoping to calm him.

Ne'lan looked at Bel'lar and continued. "But before he passed on, we found the blue-white planet and were confronted with an unforeseen problem. The planet was extensively populated with dinosaurs, animals of gigantic proportions, making our dream of a new home only a dream. Determined to secure this planet for mankind's new beginning, we began to discuss ways to rid the planet of these animals. We argued that they were only animals and should give up this planet to us. After all, we were humans, we said at the time. The Great One was unalterably opposed to this thinking. He said that *all* living beings, including animals, were creatures of God and should be respected. We were in a quandary. How could we travel all this way and not achieve success? Then the Great One passed on, and we were free to follow our desires."

He looked down, even more ashamed. The woman nudged him. He looked up and said, "We discovered this red planet. It was going dormant, but we found some inhabitable areas. A pyramid library had been erected here in the far distant past. Unable to settle on the blue-white planet, we began life here, building this station, and the face. The face we dedicated to the Great One, because he had suffered and completed his penance for the destruction of the Planet of Abundance."

Ne'lan ceased speaking and turned to the woman. She had short black hair and a pale face. With a bow, she introduced herself. "I am called Sha'ra. I will continue our story."

"Gazing on the blue-white planet, we were consumed with the desire to take it for mankind. We discovered an asteroid that seemed to be on a possible trajectory with the blue-white planet. It became the answer to our problem. We decided to take matters into our own hands and nudge it, creating the collision that encompassed the planet and choked out all life. The dinosaurs were gone, and the planet was in the throes of healing but not yet habitable. As we watched, the horror of what we had done came home to us. We were morally corrupt in thinking that we could take this planet for us at all costs. We were heartsick at what we had done. Unable to land on the healing planet, we didn't know what to do. Then another planet was discovered in the ship's records. Nine of our brothers traveled on to find this new planet, choosing to make amends in that way. The three of us decided to live out our lives here in penance." She paused and looked down. This was a difficult story to tell, despite no longer being in a physical state.

Bel'lar half rose in his chair, impatient for this to be over. But Ry Sing put her hand on his arm. He glared at her and then sank down. Ry Sing looked at the three again. "Please continue," she said.

Sha'ra turned to the man next to her, who hadn't spoken yet. He nodded and bowed. Gray hair and a stern, aquiline face, he said, "I am RaTa. We wanted you to come here, as indeed all who seek the blue-white planet must come here, to hear of the terrible thing we have done. So that you will understand and not commit our evils. No matter how important the planet, it is reprehensible to kill animals or any living beings. It is morally corrupt to steal a planet as we tried to do. We know now that we thought we were gods, and the result justified our actions. For that we continue to do penance, gazing on the blue-white planet so that we will never forget." He stopped speaking.

Dobeman was recording this story and adding his own comments. The soul was an amazing thing, to remain focused and determined to expiate its transgressions, to assist those in the physical plane. The beauty of the God energy brought tears to his eyes, which was a rarity for him.

Ry Sing looked at Ka'aya. He stood and bowed to the three ancient ones. "You are not in physical anymore. You cannot cause the animals on the planet any more distress, for you have paid your debt to the ancient ones. Come with us. Your time here is at an end. You have a new mission."

The three shook their heads. "We do not deserve this. We cannot," Ne'lan said.

"Let me declare your penance at an end," Ry Sing said. "Go with us to the blue-white planet. See what you have created."

"Wait a minute," Bel'lar said. "We're not taking anyone anywhere. Certainly not them." He stood.

"They're not physical beings any longer," Ry Sing said. "We can't stop them from going anywhere."

"We're done here. It's time to be about our business." He turned away and joined Mauleen at the control panel.

Ry Sing was irritated by him, but she realized it was his fear of hearing about the Great One that had him on edge. She turned back to the three ancient ones. "I'm sorry about Bel'lar. He's confused by these events and his reaction to them."

Ne'lan nodded. "We are not surprised at his anger with us. We understand and do not judge him."

Sha'ra smiled. "He was the only one who didn't want to sacrifice the animals. In tribute, we sent the Great One's remains to the blue-white planet."

"Indeed," Ka'aya said. "Thank you for your strength in abiding all these years to complete your mission. We accept your trust and will do all within our power to learn from your experience."

✳ ✳ ✳

Several hours passed while the five travelers explored the complex. Down one of the passageways, they discovered the original crew's quarters, recreation areas, and a dining space. They also found one area devoted to the holy men's religion. It was simply arranged and had as its focal point an unrestricted view of the pyramid marking this planet as a one-time home of mankind. Visible through a huge window almost the size of the end wall was the carved face outside. The rest of the room contained twelve chairs facing this window. White candles were spaced evenly apart on the windowsill, one meter up from the floor. Everything in the room was mantled in the planet's crimson glow. The sky was beginning to darken as the planet rotated away from the sun and the red gleam smoldered, imparting a feeling of gloom and sadness. It made them shiver, and they quickly moved on.

* * *

Enis simply had to see what was inside that pyramid. He studied it on the main display on the bridge and discovered a shadow. He asked Light Traveler to adjust focus to afford him a better view. It was an arch, and underneath it was a doorway. That decided it. Taking the lift down, he entered the locker where the life suits were stored. He struggled into one, and, hooking a bag to his waist belt, he stepped out onto the planet. Not knowing how much time he had before the others returned, he hurried. He took the path that led around the stone face because it kept him out of view through the windows in the station. He reached the doorway and searched it for a way to open it.

* * *

Inside the station, Bel'lar and his crew reached the entrance to the pyramid, but the door was secured. After a cursory examination of the doorway, he decided it was unnecessary to spend any more time here. This had been a waste of time. The blue-white planet was their destination. He led everyone back to the control room.

Mauleen was satisfied now that all controls were at their original settings and the complex would shut down as they left. The doors closed behind them, and the lights began blinking out as they walked down the corridor to the ship.

At the ship's entrance, the Red Planet Complex door was open. The access to Light Traveler slid open, and the lift waited. Bel'lar stepped forward to go in when a huge gust of energy passed right through him and into the ship. He stopped abruptly, caught off guard by wind in a windless tunnel. Ka'aya and Ry Sing stepped forward with smiles, each taking one of his arms, and got into the lift with him.

"What was that?" He shivered as the energy left his body.

"Just old friends coming on board," Ka'aya said.

"What old friends?" Bel'lar asked. But he knew. The only beings it could be were the three holy men spirits. He wanted to bar them from the ship but didn't know how.

"Don't worry," Ry Sing said. "They won't cause any problems."

"You'd better be right, or I'll be looking to you to handle it," Bel'lar said. He glanced around seeking any sign of them. *And keep away from me, holy men,* he thought. Then he banished them from his mind. "Let's meet on the bridge and discuss our transit to the blue-white planet."

Enis was waiting for them with great anticipation as they exited the lift. He had barely made it back on board before the others. Slightly out of breath, he fell in step with Bel'lar. "Welcome back, Captain. Are we going back to the blue-white planet now?" He looked over at Bel'lar shyly. He was still afraid to stand up straight and look the captain in the eyes.

"We are," the captain said. "That was a complete waste of time."

Enis looked confused.

"It was necessary, and we learned much, Bel'lar," Ka'aya said.

"Then you be sure and explain it to Enis." Bel'lar entered the bridge with the others following him. "Sit down. Now, where is

Ry Sing?" Everyone was accounted for except Ry Sing. She had been here just a moment before. He looked at his crew.

Ka'aya shrugged. No one else had noticed her leave.

The chirp of the intercom sounded. "Bel'lar?" It was Ry Sing's voice.

"Where are you? You're supposed to be here."

"I'm supposed to be where I want. That's the fun of being me," she answered, her voice full of excitement.

"And exactly where is that?" he asked. He wasn't sure he wanted to know.

She giggled. "Activate the display, Light Traveler."

The display focused on her face, then pulled the focus back. She was on the red planet's surface, dressed in a long cloak. And she wasn't wearing a life suit.

"Ry Sing, you'll die without the proper oxygen!" Mauleen bit out her words. She wanted to order Ry Sing back on board, but that was for the captain to do.

The display adjusted focus again. Ry Sing was standing on a narrow band on the stark planet, the ice cap beyond her in the distance. On closer inspection, the band was green vegetation of some kind.

"I've found the only place on this planet where life exists," she said. "Isn't it lovely? Oxygen is created here, enough for my use. Other than being quite cold, it's a lovely experience." Ry Sing wrapped her long cloak about her to hold in the heat and inhaled deeply. Her breath frosted in the thin, icy atmosphere. Her face was suffused with happiness.

"Get back here, right now," Bel'lar ordered. His voice hardened as he tried to control his anger.

"I'm not ready to come in. And Bel'lar, I'm not in any danger. Truly." Ry Sing turned away to face the ice cap. Her breath created a nimbus of frosted air around her head. Her long, dark hair silvered and sparkled from the bits of ice forming in it. "I'll enjoy myself a little while longer and be aboard in plenty of time before you leave the planet."

He knew she was a capable and remarkable being, but she was also the most exasperating, infuriating person he had ever known. She continually pushed him past his limits. He turned from the display to see Ka'aya smiling. "What are you smiling at?" Bel'lar demanded. Would these sensitives never recognize his authority as captain?

"We were reflecting on how proud we are of Ry Sing and her initiative. She has exceeded all our hopes and expectations."

Bel'lar glared at Ka'aya and then turned back to the display. He knew the only thing that would get her aboard is if he threw her over his shoulder and carried her. Well, that would just have to do. "Mauleen, I need assistance." He turned and left the bridge. Mauleen hurried after him.

They entered the locker where the life suits were stored. One suit hung crookedly, one glove on the deck under it. Mauleen wondered about it but then forgot in her hurry to help Bel'lar into a life suit. Once he was suited up, she released the hatch and assisted him to leave the ship safely. She stood by for his return.

On the bridge, Dobeman, Enis, and Ka'aya watched Ry Sing enjoying her respite on the red planet.

Bel'lar walked toward her, the cold noticeable even through his suit. He was surprised that Ry Sing could endure it. Since it was only a short distance to where Ry Sing was standing, he reached her in a few minutes. She turned at his approach, smiling. He said nothing and merely hoisted her over his shoulder. Completely caught off guard, she shrieked at him, hitting him, kicking her feet. The suit tempered her blows so that he felt little, if anything. He ignored her, tightening his grip, and kept walking.

On the bridge, Ka'aya, Dobeman, and Enis watched all this with amusement. Dobeman made comments in his record. Sometimes humanoids were entertaining.

By the time Bel'lar reached the ship, Ry Sing had run out of oxygen and was silent. Mauleen met them inside the hatch and quickly hooked her up to oxygen. Ry Sing was still furious but too oxygen deprived to yell anymore. Her eyes promised retribution. He grinned at her. "Excellent. Everyone's on board."

He removed his suit and left. Mauleen helped Ry Sing to her quarters and returned to the bridge.

Bel'lar was waiting for Mauleen's arrival. He took a deep breath and squared his shoulders. He turned to Dobeman. "Now, where were we?"

"It seems to me," Dobeman began, "that we can proceed to the blue-white planet, where we will conduct the examinations and gather the samples to make our final decisions. I'm in favor of setting course directly for the blue-white planet. During this transit, we will begin an analysis of the planet and its characteristics and decide where to conduct the examinations. I will work with Mauleen to gather this information." He looked over at Mauleen, who nodded agreement.

Everyone agreed with this plan. Bel'lar instructed Light Traveler to set a course for the blue-white planet. Hunger became the main issue now that the next step had been agreed upon. Especially for Bel'lar, who had worked up a big appetite after his rescue of Ry Sing. Enis left the bridge to make something for them. They all went in search of food with the idea of eating and sleeping and then to work. There was much to be done in a short period of time before the ship entered the blue-white planet's atmosphere, and they were anxious to begin.

The following morning, the travelers were well on their way to the blue-white planet.

Mauleen and Dobeman were working in Dobeman's quarters, which were set up as a laboratory. He had access to the ship's archives and systems and could retrieve and initiate surveys from here. He and Mauleen spent the transit time working there. Bel'lar came in and out for short periods to discuss their findings. The ship again needed no monitoring during this journey. Mauleen and Bel'lar knew that, when they arrived, Light Traveler would alert them.

Enis appeared only at meals, and then briefly. He seemed anxious and on edge, constantly looking around him. He felt sure the holy men must know what he had taken from the pyramid.

Ka'aya noticed his behavior and realized that Enis must be sensing the three holy men's spirits. The young man's sensitive abilities were making themselves known, but it was causing difficulty. He resolved to get a few moments with Enis and explain, but Enis was adept at disappearing and gave him no chance.

Ry Sing hadn't discussed her foray onto the red planet with anyone, preferring to keep her information to herself. She was irritated with Bel'lar's highhanded behavior and ignored him. She had been spending her time in reflection and meditation, analyzing the many sensations and information she had received over the last few days. The surprise of the azure gold pyramid, her ability to read it, and finding the three holy men had triggered a flood of emotions and memories, which were moving too fast for her comfort. That was why she had gone out on the red planet. She needed the clarity that the thin, cold atmosphere would afford her. It hadn't been enough. Bel'lar had ruined it for her. Finally, she decided to take her concerns to Ka'aya.

She had raised her hand to knock on Ka'aya's door when he opened it. "You were waiting for me, weren't you?" She hugged him. "I badly need your help. I can't sleep. I know it's because of that pyramid from Taurus."

"This is so." Ka'aya stepped back from the embrace, his hands sliding down her arms to hold her hands as he looked her over. He easily detected the signs of sleeplessness and anxiety. She had shadows under her eyes, and her hair was messy. She must have been raking her fingers through it. Her characteristic serenity was missing.

"Please help me," she repeated, holding his hands tightly.

"Of course, dear one." He smoothed her hair, then led her into his quarters. "We have some information for you about your home planet, Taurus."

He guided her over to the couch.

His quarters reflected his approach to life. They were plainly appointed, with a few comfortable chairs beside the couch and a large soft carpet with a few pillows piled in one corner. He sometimes meditated sitting on this carpet. She heard the sound of water running and turned toward it. Water flowed down one wall, disappearing into a channel filled with crystals at the base of the wall. Light glinted off the crystals as the water splashed on them. The light and sound eased the emotions in her as she watched. It was healing and nourishing to come here, and she was already feeling better.

"Let us fetch some water, and we will get started." He walked into the bar area and poured a couple of glasses and brought them over. "Ry Sing, life is about the enjoyment of what is about to happen. Take a deep breath. Let it out."

"Usually I do this, but the information just won't come," she said. "I'm too close to this, this planet, and my connection to it so long ago." She ran her hand through her hair and sat back.

"It is of understanding." He sat in a chair across from her.

Then, mentally pulling herself together, she let her wayward thoughts go and concentrated on her mentor.

Silence settled down around them as he closed his eyes and leaned back. She knew he was taking control of the energy in the room. His breathing slowed and then deepened. She felt the energy flowing through her as well, for it was all the same energy. She felt very connected to him at this moment.

After a short time, he sat forward on the edge of his seat, crossed his ankles, put his hands together, and said, "Now is the time of knowing. Now is the time of seeing. Now is the time of understanding. We are all there is. You have come before us at this time because you are concerned about your connection to this planet that you know as Taurus." He paused.

She could almost see images as she watched him. She was not sure of what, but it was as if he were phasing in and out of this physical dimension. His body became light and bright like the sun, focusing back and forth as he sat there.

"You're glowing." She smiled, filled with the joy of this experience.

He smiled. "Of course, we are. We are the energy that is. We are all there is. All the energy that exists within this body is complete because in this body we can control it and we understand it. Be with us now as we explain why you are concerned."

She murmured "Thank you", and, tucking her legs up beside her, she leaned onto the arm of the couch.

"Relax and breathe with us, and we will tell you the story. It has been many thousands of years since you were on this planet of highly evolved beings. They were not concerned with merely existing on Taurus, eking out a living, trying to survive in the elements. They had progressed way beyond this. This is the reason that some of them left and came to the blue-white planet. They came here to create the challenge of existing in the physical again. Many beings do not wish to be part of the technological age but wish to try to survive with nature itself, living harmoniously in what God has created. Only this and nothing more."

She watched Ka'aya as he spoke the words that gave clarity to her confusion. His gray hair curled around his shoulders, his eyes closed, his face turned in her direction. She didn't want to imagine what it would be like if she couldn't come to him for answers.

He smiled as he continued, "Your planet of Taurus is advanced beyond what you would consider recognizable. They can create themselves in their own images and reproduce their own food substances. They can create alternating electrical impulses, which can be turned into pure energy. They can shift this energy in and out in different frequencies to create multi-dimensional lives. In these multi-dimensional lives, one can live in two or three dimensions simultaneously, experiencing all the different solutions to one situation. For example: choose to do one thing in one dimension and experience what occurs. Then choose something different in another dimension, experiencing both events simultaneously. So this planet of Taurus creates the possibility of multiple living frequencies. If you don't understand this, you will. It is prophesied that you will return to claim your place in this society."

He took a breath and then said, "You may not quite understand what we have said, but allow the knowledge to infiltrate your being. As we speak you are experiencing the words and the truths of these words. So breathe, and enjoy the experience because it will be all you have hoped for."

He stopped speaking, and the glow surrounding him dimmed as he began to return to the physical.

"Ry Sing, do you have questions for us? Otherwise we will drift back into the physical."

"I'm perplexed and confused, but I've been this way many times before, so I'll let it sit with me for a day or two. Bear with me, and I'll attempt to become what I need to. Thank you so much, Ka'aya."

He inclined his head in her direction. "It is not thanks that we need. It is merely the knowing that we have been of some help. With that, allow us to come back to the physical completely."

The room was quiet once again. Ry Sing rested while Ka'aya refocused his thoughts. After a few moments, he jerked a little bit, opened his eyes, and looked at her. She was slumped back; her eyes were closed. The energy created here was beyond her abilities to hold. She had allowed herself to collapse into a deep, restful state.

Ka'aya took a long, restorative breath. He sipped water and then got up and walked around the room to get the blood circulating in his body. He lit a candle and allowed it to burn. While Ry Sing slept, the candle burned, absorbing the energy from within the room and changing it.

* * *

Ka'aya had been waiting for Bel'lar to come to him for help, but Bel'lar was avoiding it. Later that day, he decided to go to Bel'lar's quarters and confront him. He knocked on the door, but there was no answer. He knocked again.

"Bel'lar, we know you're in there. You can't continue to ignore us because we will never go away."

Bel'lar opened the door. "I wasn't avoiding you. I have many responsibilities. It's never ending. But come in. I have a few moments." He knew the purpose of this visit, and he had been avoiding it. Ka'aya wanted him to face the emotions brought up by those dreams he had been having. But he didn't want to be forced to look at things that made him uncomfortable.

Ka'aya smiled. "Thank you for allowing us these few moments." He knew Bel'lar's feelings. He was just hoping that, this time, Bel'lar would allow himself to be helped before something more serious happened.

"Sit over here," Bel'lar invited. "Do you wish refreshments?"

Bel'lar's quarters were very austere—nothing but necessity and functionality. His jacket was lying over the back of the couch. Ka'aya sat next to it. He saw the active display. Bel'lar seemed to be working on information the sensors were receiving about the blue-white planet.

"No, we would just like to sit and talk for a moment."

"All right." Bel'lar sat on the chair in front of the display. His eyes glanced away from Ka'aya, distracted by the display's contents.

Ka'aya watched him for a moment and then leaned forward. "It is our understanding that you are disturbed about lives you have lived before."

Bel'lar looked back at him. "Well, not exactly. I . . . it's just that, once in a while, disconcerting situations arise," he answered with reluctance. "But I've trained myself to disregard them and focus on what's important." He fidgeted with a small stone that he pulled out of his pocket.

Ka'aya noticed the fidgeting. "That is commendable, but it doesn't address the core of your being. At some point in this life, you will be required to account for and focus on these issues that you are now setting aside. If you don't, they could manifest themselves as a disease or ailment that will inflict your body with serious consequences."

"I disagree. I'm very healthy." Bel'lar stood. "I appreciate your concern."

Ka'aya looked up at the young man, ignoring the cue to leave. Then he shook his head and got to his feet. He knew there was nothing more to be done. Bel'lar wouldn't accept his help. "We understand, and, of course, we accept your position. Know that we are here if needed."

"Thanks, Ka'aya," Bel'lar said as he walked him to the door.

Ka'aya entered the corridor and had gone only a few steps when he looked back. Bel'lar stood in the doorway, watching him. Their eyes met and, for an instant, Bel'lar's were unguarded, the pain and anguish evident. Then Bel'lar stepped back inside his quarters.

✳   ✳   ✳

Ka'aya and Ry Sing were enjoying tea in his quarters. She was watching the light play on the falling water that ran down his wall as she sipped her tea. "I wish I could tell Bel'lar about Taurus, but he's absorbed in his own issues."

Ka'aya smiled gently at her. "The message was for you."

"I know, but I wish he could understand the way you do."

He nodded. "He's caught up in the physical, and this information would only confuse him right now. We have tried to get him to talk about his nightmares, but he's refused. Some people don't want to be bothered with knowledge that's beyond the physical realms. You'll learn who is ready to hear your information."

She was turning this over in her mind when the intercom chirped.

"We're nearing the blue-white planet. The best view is from the bridge," Bel'lar announced.

Ry Sing jumped to her feet. "Let's go, Ka'aya. I'm so excited about this planet. And I want to visit the pyramid from Taurus. There may be more information there."

She grabbed Ka'aya's hands, pulling him toward the door. He gave in, laughing.

Ka'aya and Ry Sing were last to arrive on the bridge. Bel'lar waved them in. He was smiling broadly because it was time to begin preparations to land on the planet. Mauleen was at her station and Dobeman was standing beside her.

Bel'lar looked at his crew and said, "Everyone's here and accounted for, even Enis. Thank you for taking time from your daily activities to view the planet."

Enis was very excited and appeared to have shaken off his fear. "I'm ready and willing to do whatever it takes to start a new life."

Bel'lar laughed at Enis's exuberance.

Dobeman lifted a hand, drawing their attention.

"It is my turn to provide my expertise. In our surveys of this planet, evidence of another race was found. This race is the Asian race, Ry Sing's race."

Bel'lar looked at Ry Sing. She was nodding, anticipating his question. "Yes, I know about it."

"But you didn't say anything. Why not?" he asked.

"I knew that Dobeman would discover it and include it in his report," she answered.

Dobeman was looking from Ry Sing to Bel'lar, waiting. Bel'lar turned to him. "Go on," he said.

The Sentinel gave a slight bow to the captain and continued. "They built a pyramid to mark their arrival and settlement. We found it on a visual scan. I have decoded the message transmitted by its capstone. The Asian race, from a planet known as Taurus, landed here centuries ago and intermixed with the indigenous population. I don't anticipate any problems with this race settling here, because the Asian race is well known to me from my previous travels."

He pointed to the display, and the azure gold pyramid gleamed in the sunlight.

Dobeman went on, "However, a physical analysis of the indigenous peoples will remove any questions or concerns. We will run tests to insure that the humanoids have sufficient genetic material to allow the intermingling of your species. The First Officer and I have been studying the landmasses on this planet. In the southern hemisphere in the high desert on the western side, there are primitives that appear to be uncontaminated. The surveys of the other landmasses indicate the Asian race has infiltrated significantly enough that our testing may be obscured. However, we will test everywhere to make sure we have complete data on the life of this planet. The only landmass where no humanoids exist is that of the one where the Asian pyramid was placed.

"I recommend we go first to the landmass in the southern hemisphere to take samples and do testing. Then move around the planet continuing the testing and finish where the Asian race have placed their pyramid." He looked around at the others.

Suddenly the lights dimmed on the bridge, and, over the intercom, they heard a male voice speaking, "We wish to address all on this ship."

Enis jerked his head around, seeking the source of this disembodied voice. He thought this voice came from the spirits he had been sensing since they left the red planet. His earlier excitement had left him, and now he cringed, seeking escape. But there was no escape from a voice that was everywhere. He glanced at the door and then saw Ka'aya watching him. He gave up the idea of running and moved over to stand by the older man. Whatever happened, he felt that near Ka'aya would be the safest place to be. Ka'aya rested his hand on Enis's shoulder to give him support.

Bel'lar turned around seeking the source of the voice. "Who's speaking?" he asked.

"We are the ancient ones. Forgive our interruption. We wished to give a farewell as you are at the point of disembarking. We know that this adventure you are about to partake of will satisfy the beginning of the third planet. Take your first steps on the blue-white planet on the plateau near the Asian pyramid. That is where the great holy man's remains reside. With that, we say with affection we will be yours forever." The transmission ended. A surreal wind rushed through the bridge, and then the lights resumed their original brightness.

"Thank you and farewell," Ka'aya said quietly, knowing the holy men heard him. Now he knew the general area of the Great One's final resting place. He was positive he would find it once they landed.

Enis looked around and then appeared reassured now that the energy had stopped speaking. Mauleen also felt this relief but kept it to herself.

Ry Sing said, "Somehow, somewhere we shall reconnect with them."

Bel'lar shook off the disquiet he felt and remembered Dobeman had presented an idea before the ancients interrupted.

He stood, drawing everyone's eyes. "Now that that's over, we can return to business. Take us to the first location, Mauleen." He motioned toward the planet showing on the display. "Let's see what these primitives are like," he said.

Mauleen moved to the center console. She put her hand over the globe and pinpointed the exact location of the first group of primitives. The ship slowly descended, and, in a matter of moments, it reached its destination. The crystal display activated and initiated scanning for humanoids. The settlement that Dobeman had selected was nearby in a mountainous area. The ship moved closer, and they could see the settlement. There was green vegetation surrounding clay huts with some fires burning. There were about fifty in the population.

Dobeman reviewed the data. "This is excellent for our purposes, Mauleen. Take the ship to fifty meters from this settlement."

The ship dropped to tree height and hovered. It was daylight, but, as of yet, no one from the settlement had seen the craft.

"Hold it there, Mauleen. What's next?" Bel'lar turned to Dobeman expectantly.

"I will be the one to bring the primitives aboard. They should see only me because they will believe I am an alien being. They will be more confused if they see any of you since you look similar to them. We have a device that will call them to the ship."

Dobeman instructed Mauleen to sound the device. This sound created a hypnotic state to the primitives, keeping their fear in abeyance but compelling them to come to the ship. She sounded the device, and Dobeman walked to the corridor. "I will go to the surgery where I can control this experience and bring aboard the primitives. I will need a male first, a female second. This is all I will need."

Ry Sing turned toward Dobeman and took a couple of steps. "What exactly are you going to do? You're not going to hurt them, are you?" Ry Sing was torn between concern and curiosity. Dobeman stopped and looked at her; his face showed no expression.

It was Ka'aya who answered her. "Have no concern, Ry Sing, for it is just to take some tissue samples so that we may understand their genetic code and determine if we could harm them or they could harm us by walking with them."

Dobeman left for the surgery room.

Below them on the planet, the primitives were drawn from their huts and came in answer to the sound. They stopped near the ship, gazing in awe at this structure floating over their heads. They dropped to the ground in some kind of tribute. A man with a colorful headdress, a staff in his right hand, walked through the kneeling people. He halted directly under the craft and looked up at the Light Traveler.

Ka'aya contacted Dobeman. "Take the chief first. It will give him great status to be taken inside this structure that floats."

Ry Sing was pacing. "How can I be part of this without them seeing me?" She stopped and looked at Ka'aya. "What can I do?"

Mauleen glanced at Ry Sing. "Go down to the third level and pick up a life suit. The helmet will cover your head so they won't see you." Mauleen turned her attention back to the controls.

"Perfect." Ry Sing looked at Bel'lar. "You don't mind, do you?"

"Would it matter if I did?" He could see the excitement on her face. "Go."

She rushed from the bridge and entered the surgery fully suited up just as Dobeman levitated the chief from the surface of the planet into the surgery. The chief stood upright, trembling, unable to speak. The sound device would keep him slightly sedated for only a short time.

Dobeman noticed her suit and said, "We must work quickly."

The chief looked at the two, one this distinguished-looking Sentinel with large dark eyes, long fingers, and wearing an orange sarong. Next to him the chief saw a creature in a silver suit with a round spherical helmet and darkened facemask. They knew if he could think clearly he would be attacking them. They approached him. He didn't move. They took his staff and laid it down carefully. They guided him over to a table and helped him lie on it.

Dobeman began examining the man. He looked into his ears and eyes, his mouth, and using a handheld device, scanned his brain. After about ten minutes of examination, he took a blood sample.

Then he looked at Ry Sing, "That's it. Did you think I was going to dissect him?" She looked surprised as he continued, "Maybe in the future people will have horrifying stories about being abducted into alien crafts and having unthinkable medical procedures performed upon them. But that is not what we are going to do."

She laughed. "Things do have a way of getting distorted over time."

They both helped the chief up and led him over to the spot where he would be levitated back down to the planet. They stood him up straight, returned his staff to him and waved goodbye as he descended to the planet. Once he reached the surface he collapsed into a deep sleep. Then they brought a female of the species aboard and performed the same examination and took a blood sample.

When the woman was safely on the ground by the chief, Ry Sing called Bel'lar on the intercom, letting him know they were finished here and could move on to the next location.

As the ship began to move, and move quickly, the primitive people, now free of the influence of the sound device, looked at the ship in astonishment, wondering if this was God in all his glory. Reaching the chief and the woman who were taken aboard, they tried to wake them. As everyone crowded around them, they opened their eyes.

The tribe members spoke at once. "Was that God? It had to be. We know of nothing that can float in the sky like a bird. What was it like inside?"

The chief slowly sat up. He and the woman looked themselves over and saw that all was as it had been before. They were not harmed. He looked around at the spellbound faces of his people and knew this was the opportunity he had been waiting for.

"Yes, it was God, and he bestowed upon me and this woman special powers. He told us we must go out and spread the word of God. I was commanded to let others know that I speak on God's behalf, and if anyone questions or denies this truth, he does so at his own peril."

All the people dropped to their knees and worshiped the chief and the woman.

Over the next eight hours, Dobeman and Ry Sing completed the same examination on eight more pairs of humanoids at various sites on the blue-white planet. Both were tired but wanted to deliver the information to the crew today. They completed the processing of the information, and then Ry Sing contacted Bel'lar on the intercom. "The examinations are completed, and Dobeman has processed the results. We're on our way to the bridge."

The ship had reached orbiting altitude. Ry Sing and Dobeman were back on the bridge with all the rest of the crew. Ka'aya went over to sit by Ry Sing.

Dobeman moved to stand before the others. "It is as I suspected."

The crew waited for him to continue. Enis tensed up, and Ry Sing patted his hand.

"Everything is perfect," Dobeman said. "We may land the ship. The test results show that you may share your genetic code with them without danger. The Asian race seems to have improved their genetic material so it is beneficial to you, rather than contaminating it."

Enis sighed loudly.

Bel'lar stood. "Light Traveler. Take us back to the plateau to the azure gold pyramid. We will touch the blue-white planet there for the first time."

"Where the great holy man was laid to rest," Ka'aya added softly. No one heard him.

The ship began to descend. Everyone talked excitedly as they stared at the display. At first, from this great height, only a vast expanse of green was visible. Then, as they watched, slowly a small, barren patch of land grew larger and larger—it was the plateau, and, shining in the sun, the Asian pyramid beckoned to them.

# CHAPTER 3

# IMPRINTING ON THE BLUE-WHITE PLANET

The Light Traveler hovered over the plateau as Bel'lar began the meeting on the bridge. He looked around at his crew, their excitement plain upon their faces. Finally, they had arrived on the blue-white planet. And the sooner they completed their work, the sooner they could return home with their findings.

"I know everyone is excited and impatient to be about our tasks. But now the serious, in-depth studies begin. Dobeman, you're continuing your studies of the indigenous peoples."

Dobeman nodded. He had his pouch with his devices belted about his waist.

Bel'lar looked at his first officer, noting that she was formally dressed in her uniform. "Mauleen, you will commence your analysis of the planet's natural resources and its viability and suitability for our people."

She saluted him, suppressing a grin. She had already begun her work on the transit from the red planet and was anxious to continue.

"Enis, as our botanist, you will be studying the plants to determine the planet's ability to provide food and medicine."

Enis patted his bag slung over his shoulder; then with a grin, he imitated Mauleen and saluted.

Bel'lar smiled and turned his attention to the sensitives in his crew. "Ka'aya, what are you going to do?"

"We will begin with a study of the energy vortices to identify them and determine if they will cause any harm to humans."

Bel'lar nodded and turned to Ry Sing. "And your plans?"

She looked thoughtful as she considered. "I must resolve the questions about the Asian pyramid and its past influence on this planet."

Bel'lar looked at each of them in turn and said, "Excellent. I will expect preliminary reports within seven days. Let's get to it. Our home planet awaits our results."

The Light Traveler descended the last few meters and came to a resting position on a flat surface near the azure gold pyramid from Taurus. Ka'aya knew that this was where in ancient times they had ejected the capsule with the great holy man's remains in it. The capsule bore itself into the ground, where it remained.

The crew hurried to exit the ship with Bel'lar and Mauleen in the lead. Light Traveler had already completed a scan of this plateau and found nothing of concern.

Enis pushed his way by the others, mumbling apologies, and out the hatch.

"I'm so happy to be here," he called out as he darted off.

Ry Sing stepped out into the soft soil that covered this plateau. The sun was high in the sky, the air enticingly fresh after all this time spent on the ship. She turned in the direction of the Asian pyramid and walked toward it. Ka'aya and Dobeman followed more slowly.

Bel'lar joined them, keeping his eye on Enis. The ship's botanist/cook had already greatly outdistanced them. "Should we stop him?"

As they watched, Enis stopped his headlong rush and began walking around, looking at everything.

"He's just letting off energy, and he's still within sight." Ka'aya watched Enis with a smile. His unabashed enjoyment of this new planet was a joy to behold.

Mauleen reached Bel'lar. "Captain, I will remain on watch."

He acknowledged her, and she returned quickly to her post on the bridge at her small station. She had test results to review and other tests to initiate. There would be plenty of time for her to explore the planet after she had completed her work, she thought.

Ry Sing reached the azure gold pyramid. She stood looking up at the ancient Asian symbols inscribed on it. She cocked her head first to one side then the other, considering her first course of action. Then, simply going on instinct, she touched it and received a jolt of energy at the moment her fingers made contact. A flood of powerful emotions surged through her, knocking her to her knees. She knelt in the dirt beside the pyramid and wept, unable to hold these feelings back. She accepted and understood that she was from this planet, this culture that built this pyramid. Yet, she was unprepared for the strength of the sadness, the yearning, she felt at her separation from this culture and couldn't stop crying. It was unbearable not to go immediately to what her soul told her was home.

Ka'aya sensed Ry Sing's distress and increased his steps. He reached her side before Bel'lar and put his hand on her shoulder. He motioned to Bel'lar to wait while he leaned down to her. Softly, he spoke in her ear, "It's good for you to realize who your ancestors are and to make this connection now, because, in the future, it will not be of benefit to you. Allow the tears to flow, enjoy the emotions, and spend some time alone. We will leave you until you are ready." He patted her shoulder again and then moved away.

Bel'lar ignored Ka'aya's motion to not approach Ry Sing and continued walking. He stopped in front of her, crouching down, intent on seeing for himself if she was all right.

She was crying, but she gave him a tremulous smile. "I'm fine, really I am. Go on."

He looked her over and, satisfied that she was all right, kissed her on the forehead. Then he left her there, going in the same direction as Ka'aya.

As he walked, he saw that this plateau was a flat, desolate area, many hundreds of meters wide where nothing grew. A light breeze shifted the sand beneath his feet. This plateau was very unusual looking, almost as if man, not nature, had formed it. But yet, there was nothing on top of it other than the Asian pyramid.

Pondering the puzzle of this plateau, he watched Ka'aya walk slowly, his eyes partially closed, nodding his head as if he was responding to instruction. Bel'lar continued to follow him, realizing that Ka'aya was reading the energy on this plateau.

The holy man stopped, turning around to Bel'lar.

"This is a place of great power, and," he waved a hand toward the azure gold pyramid, "the Taurans recognized it, too. That's why they built that pyramid here. This planet has great promise."

The two walked on, Ka'aya's senses expanded, seeking information from the energy. Bel'lar, however, was simply intent on joining Enis and Dobeman, who were talking up ahead.

The four met and decided to leave the plateau and walk down through the vegetation.

Away from the barren plateau, the countryside changed into a lush tropical forest. Following the sound of a river, they pushed through the thick growth for a short distance and emerged on the bank. They found a place to rest with a clear view. The river was wide, but the opposite bank was visible. Many kinds of fish swam in the river. And birds. Birds everywhere. Tall white birds with long legs and black bills. Gorgeous scarlet-colored birds foraged through the foliage near the water's edge. Little birds abounded in the trees, chattering and calling. They heard scurrying in the underbrush and caught sight of some small furry, rodent-like animals.

The sun dropped lower, the sky turned oranges and yellows, burnishing the river with copper light. The beauty of this sight mesmerized everyone. Unwilling to leave, they stayed until the purple twilight settled down over the land. Then they returned to the ship for the night.

Expecting the decontamination corridor, Bel'lar was surprised to discover that the blue-white planet was exceedingly pure and that no decontamination was required. The one used on the home planet had been absorbed by the ship to be resurrected if and when needed. This was an exciting indication of the purity of this new world they had found.

That evening, they gathered for dinner, full of excitement to talk about the day's events. Enis had brought in some fruit from his foray into the surrounding area and served it simply sliced as the scrumptious end to the meal. Everyone had finished eating. Enis got up to clear the remains of the meal, tired and satisfied with his first day on this planet.

An idea occurred to Bel'lar. "Light Traveler, is there any information regarding this planet that would help us expedite our work here?"

"An archived message is available," Light Traveler answered. "It dates to the first voyage to the blue-white planet."

His stomach reacted, twisting. The Great One's face was never far from his mind since Ry Sing had shared that vision with him. He stood to one side of the others as they gathered around the display, not wanting to be too close.

The crystal display glowed with light, and then the light coalesced into a person. Everyone recognized him. It was the Great One from the Planet of Abundance. He appeared much thinner than in the vision Bel'lar had witnessed. He was seated, his eyes looking down as the display focused on him. He raised his eyes but didn't look directly into the display. He appeared on the verge of death. And the pain in his eyes was bottomless. It seemed a tremendous effort for him as he began to speak. His voice was quiet, and they strained to hear his first words.

"If you are viewing this message, you must have reached the blue-white planet. And once again, you wish, as I did, to begin a new civilization on this pristine world. I offer this advice. I, too, was impatient to begin a new civilization, and I take full responsibility for what I have done. But I didn't realize how difficult it would be to free the souls from the Planet of Abundance in order that they might receive a new opportunity. I shall carry this burden throughout eternity. And I know this: In my future lives, I will re-invent the planet which I have destroyed. I shall leave a record so that all those who come after me shall know what I have done."

Bel'lar's stomach sickened further.

"Yet I shall be unwilling to choose a planet that will have to be destroyed. However, once again, I will start the cycle—but hear these words: I shall not finish it ever again."

He paused and steadied himself with a shallow breath. Someone extended a hand to him from the side, but he waved whoever it was away.

"I must go on," he said. He looked forward again.

"As I'm dying, I'm looking into the future, and I can see myself." He looked up. He seemed to be looking directly at Bel'lar. There was a great silence. The others looked at Bel'lar, too.

Bel'lar backed away from them, his hands up, blocking them from coming closer. "No," he said. "I'm merely a military man. No more. I don't believe—."

He felt a pain shoot through his chest above his heart. He grabbed the spot, but the pain knocked him down. What was happening to him? Was he dying?

Ry Sing ran to him. He pushed himself to a seated position against the bulkhead with her help. She placed her hand over his heart and quickly determined that it was unharmed. But heat radiated through the fabric above his heart. Then, as she watched, a reddish swelling began to show through his white shirt. She unbuttoned a few buttons of his shirt, and found that the swelled area was his birthmark above his heart, red and angry looking.

The Great One continued, his voice stronger. "The one who carries the mark shall continue me. Do not deny this sacred trust. Do as you are intended upon." The dying man pulled his robe open from his neck and showed a birthmark in the shape of a cross enclosed in a circle on his chest above his heart. It was the symbol for ISOS. The display blacked out. The message was finished.

Ry Sing looked at Bel'lar's birthmark again. The swelling had marred its shape somewhat but it was similar in form to the Great One's mark. Bel'lar's wasn't a complete circle, however. The right outer edge of the mark was blurred, almost as if rubbed off. And the cross was distended from the irritation but still recognizable inside the open-ended circle. She had seen it before but never paid much attention to it. Then, as she watched, the circle closed and the cross thinned. Now it was an exact match to the Great One's mark. She put her hand over it again, intending to cool the irritation, but Bel'lar grabbed her wrist and held her away.

"No," he gasped out, his voice guttural with emotion. "I don't believe. Leave me." He couldn't bear to be here with them anymore. What had that holy man done to him? He got up and staggered out of the room.

Ry Sing started after Bel'lar, but Ka'aya touched her arm, stopping her.

"He has much to understand," he said.

She looked up at Ka'aya. "He is the Great One," she whispered.

"You always knew, didn't you?" he answered softly.

Ry Sing continued to look into Ka'aya's eyes, her expression changed to ominous, almost fear. She turned her gaze to the door where Bel'lar had exited. Softly, under her breath, she said, "You must fulfill your destiny, my love." She didn't see Ka'aya's nod.

Bel'lar's abrupt exit put an end to the gathering. Ry Sing and Ka'aya left within minutes of Bel'lar's withdrawal. Enis began cleaning up, and Mauleen hurried out.

Dobeman sat for a while, contemplating what he had just witnessed. *Humanoids,* he thought, *they're a very unusual species. They believe they have choice. But I have never seen one choose their destiny. They merely stumble through their life, banging into it time and time again. And never see it. I'm going to put this in my journal. Someday it will be one of the great books of the universe. The Practical Guide to being Humanoid.*

*　*　*

Ry Sing stopped by Bel'lar's quarters before coming to eat the next morning. She wanted to make sure he was recovered, but he didn't answer her knock. He didn't appear for the meal, either. She mentioned his disappearance to Mauleen, who searched the ship but didn't find him. Ry Sing and Ka'aya weren't disturbed about his absence, but Mauleen didn't like it. He was the Captain and shouldn't disappear. But she had surveys and samples to take and got busy with her responsibilities.

* * *

Ka'aya went to see Ry Sing that night. She had been in her room all evening, not venturing out for dinner. She'd spent the day at the azure gold pyramid and, when she came in, she'd gone directly to her room without seeing anyone. When he knocked at her door, she answered it after a pause. He noticed immediately that she looked distraught and teary eyed.

"Oh, come in," she said. "Don't look at me." She turned away as he followed her in.

"It doesn't matter, Ry Sing. What matters are your emotions and what you really wish to do." He followed her and sat next to her on the couch.

Everyone's quarters on the ship were different since they had been created according to each one's wishes. Ry Sing's quarters had changed since Ka'aya's last visit, reflecting her new vision. Before, they had been simple and plain. Now green plants grew out of the walls and trailed to the floor. The sounds of birds seemed to come from the plants. It felt almost as if they were in a forest enclave. The couch was covered with brightly colored pillows. The bar had several crystals arranged to catch the light and some candles.

She sniffed and brushed her hair off her face. She was wearing a robe of silken fabric in a soft blue shade. "I don't know what I want to do. I want to be with you to learn. But my people are calling me back to Taurus, to my beginning, to see for myself. I need to know what happened there—what I accomplished. It's very important for me to go there." She leaned her head back onto his shoulder.

He stroked her hair. "You don't have to make any decisions today. Just relax. Get the feeling of this planet. It will take some time for us to complete the necessary studies."

"I'm worried about Bel'lar. That message from the Great One interrupted his dedication to this mission. He's hiding out, ignoring Mauleen."

"He will recover his sense of duty. For now, he is in shock. He doesn't understand his connection to his life as the Great One. He is refusing to acknowledge it. But when he recovers, he will return to the home planet. The duty he lives for forces him to return to face the Brotherhood of Syn and tell them of this wonderful place."

"Do you want the Brotherhood of Syn on this beautiful planet?" She played with the hem of her robe.

"That is not for us to decide. That is for the Brotherhood of Syn. If they need to come to this planet for this experience, then we will not stand in their way. And if they wish to remain where they are, since they are in the end stages of their civilization, this also is acceptable.

"Don't try to manipulate the life force because it will end up manipulating you. Let the force flow where it needs to. Let it gather knowledge and move forward. What you must do is be the observer. If you become too attached, it will guide you in the wrong direction."

She smiled up at him and cuddled close. "Tell me more, Ka'aya. I'm so relaxed and at peace with you. Your voice, indeed your very presence, makes everything clearer."

"We must seek out the truth of our existence," he said. "Understanding your existence is your task in the lives you live.

So live these lives with the knowledge that the search is about this understanding."

"This is what draws me to the planet of my ancestors. Yes, I'll go. Thank you." She stretched up and kissed him lightly on the lips. "But while we're here, I'll learn all that I can."

"Then sleep now. I will stay a while."

She curled up against him like a child, trusting and happy. Her eyes closed, and soon he could hear her breathing slowly, rhythmically. He settled himself to enter an inner focus while she slept. Later he would slip out and return to his quarters for the night.

✳ ✳ ✳

Several days passed, and Bel'lar didn't appear for any meals, nor did he respond to the knocks on his door by Ry Sing and Ka'aya, both of whom checked on him each day. Ry Sing wondered if he was actually inside his quarters. She suspected that he might be outside somewhere, trying to make sense of this—as he would see it—terrible turn of events.

Mauleen was impatient with Bel'lar's absence. She wanted to discuss her results with him. What was Captain Bel'lar doing? She needed his direction. He was the captain, after all. But wasn't she in charge now? She wished he would just take charge again so that she could devote all her time to her work.

At the early meal, Mauleen asked Ka'aya and Ry Sing if they had any news of Bel'lar. And Enis was missing, too.

"Don't worry. He will rejoin us soon," Ka'aya answered.

Ry Sing faced the activated crystal display in the lounge with its view of the plateau. She wasn't really listening to the others' conversation. The azure gold pyramid gleaming in the sun was enticing her. She was eager to visit it, but frustrated.

Thus far she hadn't found any way inside it. And this distraction was keeping her from her responsibilities to discover this planet's past experiences. She had begun to wonder if there was a way in and whether it mattered if she found it. Perhaps the answers she sought about her past didn't lie within that gleaming structure. Maybe the Asian settlers on this planet had the answers. Perhaps she should seek them out.

Then a thought occurred to her, and she turned to the others. "We should have a ceremony to consecrate this planet and to appreciate the ones who have come before."

"Of course," Ka'aya said. "This plateau will be renowned throughout history. Once Bel'lar returns to us, I will conduct this ceremony."

"What about Enis?" Mauleen asked. She wasn't interested in a ceremony. "Have any of you seen him today?"

"New plants and fruits have been offered at each meal." He indicated the carefully arranged plates with sliced fruit and greens. "He must have been here, then. Don't worry about him, Mauleen," Ka'aya answered. "He has been in a euphoric state since we arrived. We are positive he is busy collecting plants and conducting analyses."

Mauleen shook her head with frustration. "I hope so. Two missing crew members is a serious cause for concern." *And it's driving me crazy*, she thought.

Ka'aya patted her on the shoulder. She smiled in response. "We're going to the river. Anyone want to accompany us?"

"And I'm going to the Tauran pyramid," Ry Sing said. She headed out of the lounge.

"I can't, Ka'aya," Mauleen answered. "With Captain Bel'lar absent, I must stay on watch."

"Bel'lar has made the correct choice in you, my dear," he said. This time, her smile was a bit embarrassed, and she looked away.

* * *

Hot and tired, his body forced into submission, Bel'lar finished up his workout in the warrior room and stepped in the corridor.

"There you are!" Ry Sing hurried up to him. She hugged him tight and then gave him a quick kiss.

He struggled a bit, and she released him. She touched his chest where the birthmark was and looked up into his eyes. They were haunted, underlined with shadow. "Have you been in your quarters these past days?"

"There and working out. I can't get the Great One's eyes out of my mind." He rubbed his eyes hard. "I'm not going to destroy anyone. My mission is to save our people." He looked around nervously.

This consuming anxiety was out of character for him. He was usually confident, in control, but this shock had shaken him badly. She reached up to touch his cheek tenderly.

"But Bel'lar, you must fulfill your destiny."

He pulled away. "Stop right there. My destiny is to save our people. I don't care what that crazy holy man said. I want him out of my mind."

She sighed. "I understand. Are you ready to rejoin us? Mauleen's very uncomfortable with your absence. At least speak to her."

"I don't want to talk to anyone. Ka'aya will want to discuss this with me, but I don't want to."

"He'll do whatever you want. But what about your first officer? You're the Captain. You should see her. Will you?"

He nodded, reluctantly. She took that for a yes.

"I'm so glad." She stood on tiptoe to kiss him on the mouth. He pulled her close, kissing her hard, then released her.

She left him standing in the corridor as she walked away, a pleased smile on her face that he didn't see. She knew he would eventually get through this and accept his responsibilities. He was simply fighting the inevitable.

*　*　*

Mauleen answered her door that night and discovered Bel'lar standing there.

"May I come in?"

"Of course, Captain."

She led the way to her table, where they sat across from each other. Her quarters were similar to Bel'lar's in their simplicity. Yet she had an oversize chair with pillows and a small blanket. She had pushed it in front of the wall-mounted display. The display had a diagram of locations with callouts that he couldn't read from here. It looked as if she had just hopped up to answer the door; the blanket was thrown back over the arm. He wondered if she slept there sometimes. Probably, knowing her compulsion for working. Again, one of the reasons he had chosen her for this mission.

He met her eyes. "I must apologize for the last few days. I had some things to work out. But I know that you've been handling yourself admirably, taking responsibility for this ship and its crew."

"I understand, Captain. I'm glad to see you. I just wish you had stayed in contact."

He looked sheepish for a second, and then his military bearing took over. He straightened and looked her in the eye.

She gave a sigh of relief. He looked like the Captain again.

*　*　*

Bel'lar rejoined the crew the next morning at the early meal, but his mood was serious and touchy. He was short with

Mauleen when she asked if he wanted to discuss her findings so far, saying, "Not yet." She walked away, disappointed.

Ka'aya, having heard Bel'lar's response to Mauleen, waited until later to discuss the consecration ceremony. He came upon Bel'lar sitting in the shade of the ship, staring out over the plateau toward the Asian pyramid. The sun was high in the sky, and the shade was welcome. Ry Sing wasn't visible, but he knew she was out there.

"Greetings, my son. It's wonderful to see you outside."

Bel'lar didn't look at Ka'aya. "I have nothing to talk about."

"That's not why we're here. We should hold a consecration ceremony for this planet."

Bel'lar stood abruptly. "No ceremonies."

Then Bel'lar walked away, leaving Ka'aya staring after him. This was much worse than Ka'aya had thought. Bel'lar was in complete denial. Ry Sing had tried to help him and succeeded in getting him to return to being Captain. But now she was absorbed in her past and her search for who she was. Ka'aya would have to continue keeping watch on Bel'lar and be ready to assist when needed. And he knew he would be needed. It was only a matter of time before Bel'lar's emotions would crack him wide open.

Something intruded at the edge of his consciousness. All thoughts of Bel'lar fled from his mind. He realized he was feeling Ry Sing's distress. Immediately, he began walking toward the Tauran pyramid, his gray and white robe billowing out behind him in the breeze. He followed his instinct, knowing that she must need him. When he arrived at the pyramid, she was nowhere in sight. Pausing to consider, he expanded his awareness and again followed his feeling. He turned left and began the walk to the corner of the pyramid. He had gone only twenty steps when she appeared at the corner. She broke into a run when she saw him.

"Ka'aya, you knew I needed you." She hugged him tight. Her hair was blown about by her run, her eyes distraught.

"Yes, my dear. We felt your distress. Now what's this all about?" He smoothed her hair back and then took her hand and tucked it into his elbow. Together they walked slowly, arm in arm, in the direction of the ship.

"I haven't been able to get inside. I've been coming out here for days, but there doesn't seem to be any way in. I have to know about my planet, my people. About who I was. Please help me. Do you have any more information for me?"

"This is something so important that you must find out on your own. We won't tell you."

She sagged on his arm, and he squeezed her hand. "This is hard, my dear, but don't let this stop you. You have attained the ancient level of Sower. As such, you are the beginning and the end. All knowledge is available to you."

"You're right. I'm discouraged, but I can't stop. I have to know. I'll think of something." She shook her head and stood straighter.

✳ ✳ ✳

In the middle of the night in his quarters, Ka'aya grew restless and felt a desire to open himself up to the universe. He knew this meant knowledge was attempting to reveal itself to him. He got up and seated himself in a cross-legged position on the floor by the wall. Prepared, he opened himself up to it and thereby accepted the invitation. He waited for the knowledge to overwhelm him. And it did, flowing into his body and his mind. Breathing heavily, he leaned back against the wall as he began to make sense of what he had just learned. He knew now that Ry Sing would make a great discovery. One that would alter everyone's futures on this planet. He got up, putting on his robe, and went to Ry Sing's quarters. Several hours remained until dawn.

Her door opened of its own accord, and Ry Sing stood there fully dressed in an azure tunic and pants. She had been waiting for him.

"Come, my dear." He turned, and she followed him through the ship and outside. They knew each other so well that she didn't ask, and he didn't explain.

Ka'aya led her out onto the plateau. The night sky was clear and bright with stars. The horizon was not yet lit with the promise of the new day. A soft breeze was gently blowing, and the smell of moisture came with it. Rain must have fallen earlier in the night, washing everything in anticipation.

They reached the spot that Ka'aya had identified earlier where the energy vortex was intensely powerful.

They stood facing each other ten paces apart. Ry Sing felt something brush her hair as it passed her. She smiled.

Softly, she said, "They're here. The three holy men. Can you feel them?" She shivered in anticipation.

"We have been waiting for them. They wish to participate. They wish to always be in spirit on this planet," said Ka'aya. "Let the ceremony begin. Let's bow our heads and imagine a shaft of light coming down out of the sky creating a circle around us."

He raised his hands to the heavens, the night sky seemed to open, and a beam of light shot through the darkness, creating a huge circle on the plateau that included both of them. Just before this beam of light blinded them, forcing them to keep their eyes closed, it illuminated an enormous structure that had been invisible to their eyes without this holy light. It was a pyramid residing invisibly on this plateau, waiting for activation.

Ka'aya and Ry Sing smiled at each other. They had both sensed its existence. And both knew, as well, that between this invisible pyramid and the azure gold pyramid, deep inside this energy vortex, were the Great One's remains.

He continued. "The vast knowledge contained in this shaft of light will intensify and become smaller and more focused." As he said this, the circle of light narrowed, smaller and smaller, until it encompassed only the space between them. He and Ry Sing were able to open their eyes, and, within this circle, the three holy men from the red planet appeared.

They spoke with one voice. "We wish to become one with this new place, this new beginning. Our intention is to grow in knowledge as the planet grows, assisting where we can. We will remain in spirit as guardians of every physical being in this place."

"Thank you, ancient ones. Your sacrifice is valued," Ry Sing said.

The holy men smiled at her. "No thanks are necessary. It is what we wish. We know you are questing for who you have been. We wish to help with this quest. Merely walk in the direction of the setting sun, and the next step in your destiny will appear before you."

"Thank you for your assistance." She bowed her head to the three as her mind wanted to explore their words.

The holy men expanded until they towered over them and began to speak. "Our Great One intended to create a new beginning on this planet. It is now that time, the new beginning. In his honor we consecrate this planet."

Then the holy men seemed to recede, melting into the powerful light. "Remember. It is you that will create the reality you live in."

The circle of light narrowed until it was one meter in diameter. Then, as the light reached the ground, it shot out in five directions, diminishing in size but increasing in strength. Like a blade of light, it burned the outline of a star pattern into the plateau. As the star was burned in, a whirlwind built around them, encompassing everything. They covered their faces instinctively. There was a loud crack of thunder, and the wind blew through them, taking with it the light.

* * *

Inside his quarters, Bel'lar jerked awake from the resounding crash of thunder. Activating his display, he looked outside and saw the light flash on the plateau, illuminating two figures, their clothes and hair blowing wildly in the storm. He knew who they were. How dare they go against his orders? Quickly dressing, he ran through the ship.

* * *

Now it was very quiet and still on the plateau but no longer dark. The horizon glowed with pink light, casting faint illumination on the plateau. Between Ka'aya and Ry Sing, etched in black in the stone of the plateau, was a five-pointed star with a circle in its center.

Ka'aya stepped into the circle. He felt rejuvenated, and a focusing calm settled down over him. He closed his eyes again, raised his arms to the rising sun, and spoke, "This plateau is now etched with the god energy. This will be the point of beginning. Below this circle burned into this plateau, lies the capsule where the holy man's remains have been entombed. These five points represent God and the four directions, and the circle in the middle is the connection between all. As above, so below." Ka'aya opened his eyes and looked at Ry Sing. He clapped his hands together once. "It is done. Go in peace."

Ry Sing and Ka'aya hugged and then started back to the ship.

At that moment Bel'lar erupted from the ship and ran toward them. His anger had been building until he was furious. He ran faster.

Ry Sing raised her arms to hug him, and he blocked her. He stared down at her, and she realized he was furious. She took a step back.

"You two never follow orders. I'm the captain of this ship," he yelled. "You and your secret meetings! I can't stand this anymore. You have to stop." Bel'lar's eyes were wild, his chest heaving.

Ka'aya put his hand on Bel'lar's shoulder and was pushed back. "Relax, son. Let's talk about this."

"I don't want to talk. I've told you that. And you had to do it." He gestured toward the site of the ceremony. "What have you put in motion? Can't you leave things alone? I won't be forced into anything. Do you hear me?"

Ry Sing's momentary confusion cleared. She didn't like being yelled at, and now she was angry. She poked Bel'lar in the chest, staring up at him. "No one's going to force you to do anything. How can you say that? We've been waiting for you to figure it out. But how can you stand there and ignore your destiny? I don't understand you. I'm tired of all this. Stay away from me."

She stalked away, sending her anger into the ground. With the rising sun at her back, she went in the direction of where the sun would set later on that day. She didn't look back.

Bel'lar watched her walk away, a blue figure fading into the distance, too irate to try to stop her. Then he spun around and began the walk back to the ship, with Ka'aya following at a discreet distance.

This was what Ka'aya had been expecting. Bel'lar had finally let his emotions out. Maybe now he would be open to discussing this later. As for Ry Sing, he had an idea where she was going and knew it would all work out. He relaxed and shook off the energy from the emotional confrontation.

The birds were singing as the sun began its ascent into the sky. There was every indication that it would be a perfectly beautiful day. Ka'aya decided against returning to the ship and meandered around on the plateau, enjoying the temperate weather. All around this great plateau a riot of vegetation grew. Over toward the east, the tops of the trees clustered where the plateau sloped down into the forest. He could hear birds calling and saw them flying about in the sunlight.

Following the line of the forest southeast, Ka'aya saw the undergrowth moving. Something was in there. Then he recognized Enis as he crawled out and stood upright on the plateau.

The botanist shaded his eyes with one hand and scanned the plateau. He caught sight of Ka'aya. He waved his arms. Ka'aya waved back. Then Enis hoisted a large bag onto his shoulder, and, walking half bent over, he went in the direction of the ship.

✳ ✳ ✳

Ry Sing didn't come to dinner that night or the next, and by the following morning Bel'lar went to her quarters. He had achieved a measure of calm, and this had gone on long enough. He had been overwhelmed by the visions of the Great One and then the pain. His birthmark still hurt, he realized, as he rubbed it. Well, he felt he was being forced into being something he wasn't. He had been forging a life for himself since he was old enough to choose that didn't involve religion or prophecy, and he refused to give in now. He was simply a military man with a duty to perform, and he would fulfill that duty. Ry Sing was purely doing what she always did, which was whatever she wanted or thought she should do. He had assumed she was still mad or just absorbed in her exploration of the Asian pyramid and that was why he hadn't seen her over the last few days. But he was truly worried when she didn't answer her door. He asked Light Traveler to open the door, and she complied. Ry Sing was not inside. Her bed had not been slept in.

"Light Traveler, is Ry Sing on board?"

"No, Captain."

"How long has she been gone?"

"Today is the third day," Light Traveler answered.

He was speechless. Where could she be? He went in search of Ka'aya and found him sitting alone on the bridge, the view, the plateau with the azure gold pyramid sparkling in the sun.

"Where's Ry Sing?"

Ka'aya didn't turn around. "In search of her destiny."

"You knew she was gone. Where is she? Why didn't you tell me? Is she all right?" Bel'lar was terrified that she might be hurt or lost and there was nothing he could do about it.

Ka'aya looked at Bel'lar. "We don't know the answer to any of those questions. Just allow what has begun to finish. She will return when and if she can."

"You're so infuriating, old man. She may be in danger, and you let her go, didn't you? I can't trust you." Bel'lar couldn't believe that Ka'aya would have let her go. Ry Sing was impulsive and might get into a dangerous situation.

"That's good. Explore your emotions. It was not for us to stop her. And you know this, Bel'lar. She is in search of her identity, and nothing will stop her. You would do well to observe and learn from her." Ka'aya turned away and, steepling his fingers in front, turned his attention to something else, dismissing Bel'lar.

Bel'lar stood there fuming, unable to do anything but wait and worry. Then he turned and stalked away, his destination, the warrior room, where he could bash something to his heart's content.

✳ ✳ ✳

The next morning Bel'lar wasn't angry anymore. Just worried. He couldn't imagine where she had gone and why she wasn't back yet. Four days. This was taking her argument with him too far. He didn't think she could still be angry. More likely, she had found something that compelled her interest and attention. What worried him was that she might be in danger and there was nothing he could do about it. But what danger? He had read the surveys, and no humanoids lived on this continent. And the mythical dinosaurs were just myth now. Dobeman had found nothing to alarm him. Perhaps he should be patient and allow her to do what she needed to, as Ka'aya suggested. She would return. Would she forgive him? Her last words to him had been to stay away from her. And he had been pushing her away. He didn't want to lose her. But where the hell was she?

He left the ship and walked to the site of the star burned into the plateau. That was the last place she had been. Maybe there was some kind of clue. He reached the star and stood in the center, looking around. Nothing in any direction. The sand sifted on the plateau in the mild breeze. Lines developed as the breeze caught handfuls of sand and lifted them and then scattered them on the ground.

Then he was angry again. How could she just walk off like that? He began walking fast, stomping, scattering the sand. His foot hit something. He stumbled, he fell forward, and smashed his forehead on an invisible object. The contact was forceful enough that he bounced off and fell back, crumpling to the ground. Unaware his forehead was bleeding, he lay there in an altered state. His mind drifted, and once again he found himself on the platform on the Planet of Abundance, watching events unfold . . .

. . . The Great One stood on the platform in front of the pyramid. Ranging out from this platform, multitudes of people were focused on him. He raised his hands to heaven. *God give me strength to do what I must and to endure the aftermath,* he prayed. All was silent. Everyone waited.

One of the priests approached and whispered in his ear. "This shall not be the last time you save humanity from themselves." Then the priest's features seemed to blur and reform. Now, as this priest looked out over the crowd, he was someone Bel'lar recognized. It was Ka'aya.

As Bel'lar watched, the Great One turned to the priest who now wore Ka'aya's face. And the Great One's face transformed into Bel'lar's countenance. He drove the crossbar into the stone . . .

Ka'aya was walking on the plateau when he saw Bel'lar lying on the ground. He quickly made his way to Bel'lar's side and knelt down. The wound on Bel'lar's forehead was streaming blood, but Ka'aya covered it with his hand and healed the wound. Minutes later, Bel'lar woke.

"Ow. What hit me?" Bel'lar touched his forehead carefully, finding only a small bump. But the pain was minor when confronted with the vision. What did it mean? Was Ka'aya really there all those years ago? And the Great One . . . no, he didn't want to remember. He covered his eyes, trying to block what he had seen.

"Your destiny hit a little harder than you expected." Ka'aya laughed.

Bel'lar pushed up on his elbows, then struggled to his feet. "You don't know anything, old man. Just leave me the hell alone." He stomped away.

"It's your pyramid!" Ka'aya yelled.

Bel'lar waved dismissively but didn't turn around.

Ka'aya turned and patted the invisible object. "We've got to make you visible. It's time the world sees you for all eternity."

✳ ✳ ✳

Ry Sing had been gone for four days. She had walked out in search of her destiny as the three holy men directed her, traveling in the direction of the setting sun. She had not eaten for these several days, but she had been able to have a few sips of water after a rain. It might have been yesterday. She wasn't concerned. This search was more important than food, because it was the spirit that she sought to nourish, not her physical body. Her frustration with Bel'lar had been merely the catalyst to leave when she did. She left the ship to seek the reason for her existence. This search was what drove her to keep walking.

Earlier in the day, she had begun to feel seriously weak but pushed on, her feet dragging with each step. She had almost reached the limit of her endurance without food or water when she saw a clearing ahead. Determined to reach this clearing, she forced herself to the edge of her endurance, propelling one foot in front of the other, her mouth parched and dry. Only when she reached it would she allow herself to rest.

The nearer she came to the clearing, something began to intrude on her senses. She looked around for the source but could see nothing. Sagging to the ground, she dragged herself into the clearing and stopped. Something was here that she couldn't see. But, it was here. She was sure of it. It must be in another dimension, another frequency. She felt its vibrational waves as it sat there, invisible.

Unable to stand, she crawled to the source of the vibration and pulled her body into a seated position on the sand. She slipped immediately into a trance, her body close to complete surrender, her spirit free to soar. With her spirit unfettered, she turned her attention to breaking through the frequency of this invisible object so that it would be revealed to her.

Time passed in this state, and yet there was no change. She shifted back and forth into different frequencies, but nothing. She pulled energy into her body at different rates. She held some energy and expelled others, until the frequency level of the vibrations of her body soared even higher.

Through sheer effort of will, she increased her vibrational waves to the maximum she could sustain and opened her eyes to witness this object coming into view. She spoke these words aloud, her voice cracking with the strain, "I've been sitting in this place to welcome you into my reality. I know you're of intelligence, and I know that I should be here. It now falls to you to welcome me and help me visualize who and what you are."

With the last word, she collapsed, falling over onto the sand. No one answered her, and she slipped into unconsciousness, her body vibrating rapidly. At the rate she was expelling her energy, she would be totally exhausted in a matter of minutes. Somehow she realized this and regained some thread of consciousness, enough to shut down the energy encapsulating her. She lay on the sand barely alive, only a tiny spark of life sustaining her. The sand collected about her from the breeze.

Her eyes closed, her body partially buried in the sand, she concentrated on rejuvenating her body. Something interrupted her concentration. She felt the tingle of a presence. This presence touched her shoulder. Exquisitely comforting, it sent an infusion of energy into her body, recharging her. Then water, cool, refreshing, was dribbled on her lips until she was able to drink. Still too weak to open her eyes, she attempted to move her head without success. Her voice barely above a whisper, she said, "Thank you. I've tried so hard to reach you, and yet you avoided my advances."

The hand moved off her shoulder, and then two beings lifted her gently off the sand. She struggled to open her eyes, but her eyes were blurry and unable to focus. She was carried a short distance and then taken up into the invisible object. Once inside, they carried her for some time and laid her on a bed. She could tell it was dimly lit because of the comforting glow of light through her eyelids.

A hand touched her shoulder again. A voice spoke quietly and reassuringly, "Rest now. You need to restore your body. I will return when the time is right."

The unknown beings crossed her arms on her chest, tucking in a covering around her. Finally, without the strength to move or even open her eyes, she let go of her fear and let it be whatever it would be. She was critically tired. She drifted off into sleep.

Four hours later, she opened her eyes and moved her head carefully. Where was she? What had happened to her? She couldn't remember. Then it came back to her, this life force she felt she must connect with. It had been her life's purpose to challenge reality, exploring what others believed to be non-existence. It was satisfying that she had once again proven this to herself. Now she truly knew there were things beyond the physical realms of existence.

She slid back into sleep. Time passed. Drifting back to awareness, she sensed the presence again. She opened her eyes and focused on this life force. Was this being one of the primitives from this planet? But as her eyes focused, she saw that this being was not of this planet, or at least hadn't been detected by the surveys that Dobeman had taken. Who were these beings? Why didn't she know of them? They were black skinned, a deep, rich black, shimmering in the light. She found them so lovely. She felt she was where she belonged. She felt she was home. How could this be?

This being with the gleaming black skin was male and very tall. He placed his hand on her shoulder. He was a slim, very handsome and distinguished-looking man, with clothing similar to Dobeman's. He was wearing a robe, draped over one shoulder, gathered at the waist and extending to his feet. The fabric was imprinted with the black-and-white-striped pattern of an animal.

He appeared both formal and relaxed at the same time, as he said, "Are you recovered now? Are you able to speak? At the rate of expiration of energy, you would have diminished to merely a lump of physical matter. Your willingness to give up your life was enough for us to aid you. We want to appreciate what kind of being is willing to surrender her life for something she can't see, for something she merely believes in. This is a mystery to us, and we must understand it."

He sat down next to her while she looked up at him and smiled at his beautiful, serious face. She felt a soft nose sniff her hand and then noticed the dog that was a silent shadow of this being. It had a long face with long, slender, pointed ears. Its body was tall and very slim, with a black smooth coat. The dog sat beside the man when he was finished sniffing, and they both watched her.

She smiled at the dog before answering this man's question, unconsciously responding in the same formal speech pattern that he used. "This is my life, and if you're not willing to give it up, then you will and must live many lives to my one." She struggled to sit up but was too weak, so he helped her. "It was your life-giving force that enabled me to live. I'm in your debt. For this, I will allow you to be my friend and I will be yours."

The tall man smiled.

She noticed the smile but continued, "I do not allow many to be my friends. It's not of interest to me because I'm absorbed in my life. Friendships merely distract me from my goals. So hold this dear because I'm your friend and will remain so as long as my body breathes, my heart beats, and beyond." She began to cough, caught up in the emotions of the moment. She lay back down. Not knowing the being's name or his race, she knew there was more here to pursue. She looked deeply into his eyes, and, when she had finished coughing, she asked, "What is your race?"

He returned her look and said, "Can you not see? Look at my hands, my face? I am of the black race. I am the race of all races. This is the race I am, and this is the race that will be." His voice was rich and deep, and she resonated with it, feeling inexplicable recognition and affection. Yet she knew she hadn't met him before in this life.

Impulsively, she reached out to him and then dropped her hand. She was confused by this recognition and her strong emotions. She asked, "What are you known by?"

He answered, "What are you known by?"

"I am Ry Sing."

"Lovely," he said in that rich voice and stood. The dog stood as well. "I must go now, Ry Sing. I have to tend to my ship. Food is being prepared for you and will be brought soon. You may stay with us as long as you wish." He smiled and left, the dog following close at his heels.

Outside in the corridor, he stopped. Who was this woman whose life he had saved? She called herself "Ry Sing," an ancient name. One he had heard only when his holy man read from the holy book. He felt a strong connection to her and didn't know why. He wanted to stay with her, be near her, a powerful emotion that disturbed him and excited him at the same time. He wondered what his holy man would say about her and walked on. Later, he would ask him.

Ry Sing pondered why he didn't tell her his name as she looked around this room for the first time. It was some kind of healing facility. There were cabinets and surgery tables and different apparatuses to sustain physical life. The room was quite large and contained two other beds besides the one she was lying on.

Exhaustion enveloped her, and she lay back down. Moments later, she turned as the door opened and a pretty woman of the black race entered. This young woman was smiling as she approached. Her black hair was wrapped in a colorful scarf, with big needles sticking through it.

"Hello," she said. "I've brought you a special drink to rejuvenate you. What is your name?"

Ry Sing smiled up at her and answered, "I'm Ry Sing." She had been fascinated by this young woman's headdress and now looked into her eyes for the first time. Almond-shaped, beautiful green eyes looked back. This young woman's eyes were just like Ry Sing's.

The woman's eyes widened. She stared at Ry Sing. She stammered, "What-t-t . . . what did you say?" all the while staring at Ry Sing.

"My friends call me Ry Sing."

"Oh, no." The young woman covered her mouth and broke into tears. Then Ry Sing was stunned as she faded from view. She just dissipated as if she hadn't been physical at all but some kind of energy. The container of liquid fell from a hand no longer there. Ry Sing watched it hit the floor, spilling.

Ry Sing stared intently at the place where the young woman had been standing, seeking any minute variation in the air or an unseen but felt signature. The spilled liquid and its container were all that remained. The ship absorbed this liquid within minutes, leaving only the container on the floor.

"Who and what was that?" Ry Sing said. *And why did this being react that way to me? And where did she get those green eyes that were like mine? What is going on?* She pushed up cautiously into a sitting position. The room spun, darkening at the edges. She closed her eyes and waited for the lightheadedness to pass. She opened her eyes. The room was still. She slid to the edge of the bed and then waited for her legs to hold her. Finally, she walked slowly to the door. She wanted to find out where the young woman had gone.

Leaning on a chair for support, she studied the door but couldn't decipher how to open it. She saw an indentation for a hand. That must be the opening mechanism. She tried it, but nothing happened. She pushed and tapped and rubbed the indentation. It wouldn't open. Was she being held captive? She wouldn't know what to do about that since she was too weak to attempt to escape. There was nothing for it but acceptance. She returned to the bed and sat down to wait. Bringing her legs up into a cross-legged position, she leaned back against the wall. Perhaps she could sense what was going on. She took some deep breaths, and, just as she was slipping away, the door opened. This time, the young woman returned with the man and the dog from before. Could they all disappear and rematerialize at will?

This young woman urged the man, "Look at her eyes."

He approached Ry Sing and looked down at her.

She opened her green eyes slowly and focused them on them both, unblinking. The young woman still seemed nervous; Ry Sing could tell by the way she phased in and out of focus, but the man wasn't. Neither was the dog. It watched her with interest. She tried to remember if she had touched the man and the dog before. She had. They had seemed physical to her.

The man turned around and looked at the young woman. He seemed not to notice or care that she was indistinct around the edges. "They are most striking and unusual. Like yours, Char."

"They are like mine. But don't you recognize her? I just feel I know her. Almost as if I'm being drawn into her. It was such a strong feeling, it startled me."

He turned back to face Ry Sing. He looked bewildered now, and he and this energy, this woman, exchanged a look. "What are you searching for, Ry Sing?"

She considered this seriously for a moment. "I'm searching for my life and for the lives I have yet to discover. I'm searching for the lives I've spent. I'm searching for the people that need the knowledge I carry within. That's why I came to find you."

He moved back a step and swallowed. "This I understand. It was written by our holy men that one day we would come upon one such as you. I hear your words, and they seem to me to be the voice of prophecy speaking from the holy book. We are honored. But, it's for our holy man to confirm, so you must speak with him. Kowangii carries the knowledge of the prophecy."

The young woman looked up at him and pulled at his arm impatiently. "But can't you see? Look at her eyes. Isn't she the one we all search for? I feel she is." Her eyes shone with her belief, and she knelt in front of Ry Sing. She stretched out her hand.

Ry Sing felt a compulsive need to touch this young woman but resisted. Her energy was very strong. Something was going on here, and she wasn't going to allow this until she knew what was happening. Ry Sing felt the young woman's sadness as a small wave of energy when she didn't respond. Ry Sing looked up at the man. He was still contemplating her identity and knew he was undecided.

"You could be right, Char," he said. He looked at Ry Sing again, searching her face for some answer. Then his indecision cleared, and he knelt before her. "I am but your servant. I'm Zander, of the animals, here to help you discover your path and future. If it's with us, I am truly blessed. With me is Chapatata, my dog friend and companion. He goes everywhere with me. And you must excuse Char Charengo. She never thought she'd find you in her lifetime."

"Please call me Char. Everyone does. And please forgive my behavior. It's as Zander says. I was shocked and excited to find you."

Ry Sing regarded this young woman kneeling before her with some trepidation. She felt herself drawing toward her. She pulled back. She didn't understand these feelings.

"Char will assist you with whatever you need. She's our ship's physician. We had some concern as to your motives in the beginning. When we discovered you were giving your life to see us, we had to discover who you were. So we brought you aboard and allowed you to rejuvenate your life force. Now, what are your wishes, Ry Sing?"

"Zander, Char, please get up. I have many questions about you, your race." She offered her hand to the dog. She felt no trepidation here. Chapatata licked it once and then looked up at her. He cocked his head to the side, and she nodded. He seemed to be smiling, too.

Zander got to his feet with a smile at her kindness to the dog. He didn't miss that little exchange they had, either. "We have the same questions of you and about the curious little craft that you arrived here in, and your band of misfits."

"These misfits, as you call them, were highly chosen from our home planet. We are top scientists, sensitives, and technos. We're here on a special mission."

"Yes, I know your mission," he said. "It was written by our holy men that we would come to this blue-white planet and meet the two other races. We would be the third race to settle here. But this planet isn't suited to us, so we've decided to bypass it this time. What we do have is a very precious cargo that we brought to help stabilize the planet energetically. It's a collection of animals you must see. Come with us now, and we'll show them to you."

He held out his hand to help Ry Sing stand, but she stumbled. Char rushed forward with another drink in her hand. She had placed it on the counter by the door when she returned this time. "Oh, I'm sorry. I forgot I brought this. It will give you energy so that you can move around. Later, we will take you to eat."

Ry Sing accepted it from her and drank. Unusual, but delicious, it tasted like a combination of cream and fruit with some herbs she couldn't identify. She felt the concoction fortifying her as she sipped. "Thank you, Char. I do feel better now. I'm ready to see the animals, Zander."

"You will be surprised at the different and unique animals we have gathered from throughout the universe. Some are from places where they were becoming endangered. We brought them to this planet where they can flourish and enjoy life. We chose this location because there are no humanoids on this continent to interfere with them. Come, let us show them to you. You will love them as we do."

Zander offered Ry Sing his arm, and they walked out of the room, with Char following. His love for the animals permeated his being, and it was almost palpable to those around him. Ry Sing understood as she listened to him speak that this was his mission and focus in life. She was surprised that she felt so much affection for this man that she had just met. What could this mean?

They walked down the corridor to a lift. The dog walked calmly at Zander's side, glancing up at Ry Sing every few feet. They rode the lift down two levels and entered a vast space divided by corridors with different rooms sectioned off. The rooms had clear partitions that opened on to the corridors. The animals were contained in these enclosures. They could see out but couldn't see what was next to them. They walked up to a horse-like animal with stripes. "I named this animal after my brother, Zebra. All of my family has names beginning with "z." Let's move down. Here are the cats of Orion. Aren't they beautiful and majestic?"

Ry Sing approached the partition and put her hands up to the glass. One of the white cats padded over to the partition and sat looking at her with expectation. He tilted his head from side to side as if he were trying to figure out what she was, this being that stood on two legs, not four. Apparently satisfied, he put his paws up to the partition where her hands were. She closed her eyes, and the big cat closed his eyes. She conveyed to the cat through telepathy that Zander was taking him to a wonderful place and would release him so that he might breed and create more of his own species and live in harmony on a new planet. She sensed his immediate relaxation when he knew this, because he hadn't known where they were going or what was going to happen to them. The cat dropped his paws to the floor. He almost seemed to smile at her, giving her thanks that she felt inside like a warm wave flowing through her. She smiled back at him. Then he lay down and rolled over with his feet in the air, a look of complete contentment on his face.

Zander watched this exchange with amazement. "Were you communicating with him? I sense how calm he is now. What did you share with him?"

"Of course, I can communicate with him. We are all one. I can communicate with all the animals here just as you can. I'll teach you this, for you have a great heart." She put her hand on his chest over his heart and felt the warmth of his body. "You took it upon yourself to rescue these animals from planets where they were not of value to the inhabitants. They were treated as less than their equals. Merely trophies. I commend you, Zander." She grabbed hold of the scarf around his neck and pulled him down to her level and kissed him on the mouth, putting her hand on the back of his neck. "This is from the animals to show their appreciation." Ry Sing didn't know why she had kissed him. It had been simply instinct. She noticed Char watching her with confusion.

Zander was overwhelmed with emotion, and a tear slid down his cheek. As he reached up to brush it away, one of the other members of his crew approached him, "Excuse me, Captain. When will we release the rest of the animals into the environment?"

"In a short time. Don't be impatient, Isaac. Ry Sing will communicate with them first."

Isaac looked at her in disbelief. "You're the ancient holy one? You don't look at all like I thought." Then he sucked in air and shut his mouth. He bent his head to her. "I'm sorry. I don't wish to be impertinent. I must be about my business of taking care of the animals." He turned back to Zander. "I apologize for my remarks."

Zander looked this man over with disapproval. Isaac straightened in response. Then Zander nodded. "You may return to your duties." Isaac hurried away.

Zander and Char introduced Ry Sing to all the animals and allowed her to spend time with each of them. There were thirty-six animals on board the ship, the Light Wanderer. All were in excellent health and spirits, especially after they met Ry Sing. Zander and his crew had brought lions, tigers, zebras, and the white cats from Orion, impalas, wildebeest, and others. Ry Sing learned that the Light Wanderer had a full crew of forty-nine even though the ship seemed to be sparsely populated, with only one or two crewmembers seen from time to time. This was because they spent most of their time down in the animal quarters, getting to know the animals and taking care of them.

"Ry Sing, it's time for you to eat. Let's go to the lounge and get you some food. While you eat, we can talk. Maybe we can find our minister, Kowangii." Zander led her back to the lift where they rode up one level and got off on the floor containing the lounges and the galley.

"I would like to meet your holy man. Why do you call him a minister?" Ry Sing asked as she walked beside him.

"In our culture he's a holy man, but he's also a holy man that ministers to the crew of my ship," Zander explained as he took her elbow and led her toward the second doorway in the corridor from the lift. They entered a lounge much larger than the one on the Light Traveler, although similar. There were many tables with chairs and a serving area along one side. Many crewmembers were eating and talking, and most of the tables had people sitting at them.

When Ry Sing walked in with Zander and Char, everyone stopped what they were doing and looked expectantly at Zander. Ry Sing wondered if they stopped because he was the captain of this ship or because she was an alien being with her light skin and long dark hair.

Then Zander said, "As you were."

The crew relaxed and returned to their business of eating and talking, but their conversations turned to talk of the alien woman standing with Zander and Char.

Zander and Char glanced around the room and found Kowangii sitting by a wall reading a book. The book looked worn and very old. He was holding it reverently as he read. This ancient man, with close-cropped curly gray hair and beard, was weathered and bent by time. Round spectacles had slid down his nose. His robe was similar to Zander's but was of fabric marked like a leopard. Ry Sing learned later from Char that this race of beings preferred to wear fabric that looked like the animals they loved and cared for, but they would never have worn the actual skin.

Kowangii looked up and smiled when he recognized Zander and Char. Then he stared at Ry Sing as she smiled back at him. Who was this? No, could it be? Could she possibly be who he thought she was? He noticed the profound reaction she had engendered in Zander and Char. They both seemed to be hanging on her every word. He got to his feet, one hand resting on the table for support. The book was forgotten on the table.

"Kowangii, I want you to meet Ry Sing." Zander watched the old man's reaction as he introduced her.

Kowangii looked deeply into her eyes, searching her soul. She responded by opening herself to him, inviting him to find the answers to his questions.

She smiled. He shook himself as if waking up.

He bowed his head to her. "You're the holy princess Ry Sing Su Tong." He took her right hand and held it to his cheek. "This band of misfits, as Captain Zander named you, is of such exalted stature. To have met you, it's beyond our wildest expectations." He squeezed her hand and released it. "This has been foretold on our home planet by the Sacred Ecology religion."

She noticed he referred to himself as we, speaking in the plural as Ka'aya did.

Kowangii continued to look at her as if unable to believe what he was seeing, his hand on his heart. Then he recovered and said, "We were just reading some passages about something you told us in the early time." He gathered up the book and tucked it inside his robe. Then he put away his glasses.

Ry Sing fixed Kowangii with a steady gaze, this time looking inside him and spoke flippantly, "I have written much. It does my heart well to know that some of you still follow in my footsteps." She smiled an arrogant, self-assured smile. They continued to look into each other's eyes, and the connection solidified and bonded. Then both gave a little laugh, breaking the moment. *Why did I say that? What's going on here? I've really gotten myself into something this time,* she thought.

"Come, please sit down. Do you need to eat?" Kowangii patted the seat next to him. She sat down. Char took the seat opposite Kowangii. Zander sat across from Ry Sing and Chapatata curled up on the floor by his feet.

"She does, Kowangii," Zander answered. "She hasn't eaten in some days, and she was close to death but a few hours ago."

Kowangii put his hand on her forehead. "Yes, we sense this. You must eat now."

Zander signaled to a crewmember, and she brought some refreshments for Ry Sing. For the next two hours while she ate, they told her the story of why they were here now. They were directed in scripture to come to this planet, at this time, because there was going to be a convergence of the three races: black, Asian and white. They decided to bring some of the endangered species here to release onto this wonderful planet and see if the convergence happened. They didn't feel they were going to stay at this time, but when they saw the misfit group on the Light Traveler arrive, they decided to watch and see what they were going to do. They had completed their own surveys and knew the Asian race had mixed well with the primitives, creating many tribes throughout most of the continents of this planet. Because of this, they didn't feel it would be of value to settle here.

Then Ry Sing told them that the white race came eons before, when the planet was inhabited by the dinosaurs, but didn't stay. She and her group were here, now, as the advance party to determine if it was safe to inhabit. The original travelers were thirteen holy men looking for a new home for their race. She went on to tell them that the leader of the holy men died on the trip and his fellow holy men had buried him on the plateau near the azure gold pyramid.

"Why won't you bring your race here?" she asked.

Zander got up and stretched as he thought this over. The four were the only ones in the lounge at this time. "I don't think we want this experience. Let these humanoids try to move past their inability to perceive anything more than they are."

"I understand your reluctance." Ry Sing sipped the tea that Kowangii poured for her. She was feeling stronger all the time. "How much longer will you remain on this planet?"

Zander sat again. The dog laid his head on Zander's leg. He rubbed the dog's ears with a gentle touch. "We release the animals slowly and take care of them as they become acclimated to their new environment. Sometimes we've had to move them from the initial place because we discover a better place for them. We've been here for several of this planet's moon cycles."

Ry Sing decided to change to another topic. "Why is your ship in an alternate frequency?"

"We didn't enter this frequency until we sensed your ship. We knew you had the technology to sense us but felt you wouldn't think to look in other frequencies because the humanoids on this planet were primitive. We thought you wouldn't find us unless we wished it," Zander explained.

"Will you at least come to our ship and meet the others? You know," she paused and smiled, "the misfits, before you leave?"

"Let's do that," Char said. She sounded excited. They had not left the ship since the smaller Light Traveler had landed, and she was looking forward to exploring the planet.

"We would love to go. We're very interested in the one known as Ka'aya," Kowangii said.

Chills ran down Ry Sing's back. "How do you know about him?"

"We have always known of Ka'aya," the old man said cryptically.

"We've been monitoring your ship," Zander added.

"Then you know we mean no harm to the planet and the beings on it. Our mission is simply one of discovery," she said.

Kowangii covered her hand with his. "We know this, and we want to meet your companions. But first you need a chance to rest and eat a few meals to replenish your energy. Finish your tea, and Char will take you to where you can rest for the night."

"Thank you. I'm feeling much restored by your friendship and that of the animals. I feel very much at home with all of you." Ry Sing drank more tea as Kowangii watched her paternally.

Char stood. "I'm glad you'll be staying. I'll arrange some quarters for you and be back soon. Is that all right, Zander?" Char smiled endearingly at him, feeling he could be coaxed with a smile.

"Yes, of course, my dear. We'll stay with her until you return." Zander smiled indulgently at her as he thought how delightful she was to have on board this trip. She was very excited about everything. He knew she thought her smile coaxed him to say yes, but he gave in to her enthusiasm. He found her fascinating and didn't need to be coaxed, but he wouldn't tell her. It was more enjoyable this way.

Kowangii and Ry Sing exchanged a look. It was apparent to them what was going on between the two.

Char hurried off. Zander watched her go and then turned his attention back to the others. "Now, Kowangii, you greeted her as the holy princess Ry Sing Su Tong. What exactly does that mean?"

Kowangii looked at both of them, considering his words.

"The holy princess is mentioned in the early writings of *The Book of Knowledge of the Sacred Ecology Religion*. But that is all we will say. The rest is for Ry Sing to discover. This cannot be told—only experienced."

Ry Sing looked at him. "I wish you would explain, but I understand, holy one. Ka'aya gave me the same advice just days ago. It's my lot in life to discover everything for myself."

The old man smiled at her with approval.

They continued talking until Char returned and took Ry Sing to her guest quarters. Kowangii and Zander talked for some time until Kowangii retired for the evening. Zander went to check on the progress of the animal-shelter construction.

* * *

Since Ry Sing's disappearance, Bel'lar had replayed their argument over and over again. It wasn't like her to stay mad and leave. He couldn't shake the fear that something had happened to her that prevented her from returning to him. He searched the areas near the ship and around the Tauran pyramid; he had explored both sides of the river up to the distance that he thought she might reasonably have traveled. She had left without food or water, and he kept expecting to come upon her unconscious and near death. Dobeman hadn't found any trace of her on his travels, either.

One place he didn't explore was that part of the plateau where he had been knocked unconscious. He was careful to stay clear of that invisible thing that Ka'aya had called a pyramid. Bel'lar preferred calling it a thing. The other name made him sick to his stomach, and his birthmark itched. He had told no one about that day, and Ka'aya hadn't tried to discuss it with him. He just watched him with a smile that irritated Bel'lar.

* * *

Ry Sing woke refreshed. It was hard to imagine that she had been near death a few days ago. She was looking forward to seeing Zander and Kowangii, but Char was another matter. The young woman or energy, she didn't know what she was yet, had been unfailingly kind last night. Ry Sing didn't understand her own reluctance to be around her. It wasn't that Char was able to materialize at will. Physical and non-physical were all the same to her. It was the feeling Ry Sing had when she was near Char that she would be absorbed by her that disturbed her. She felt the other's feelings as if they were her own. Or was it that somehow this being could influence her emotions this way, that she could invade her essence—that once she gave in she would be lost? She instinctively held back.

There was a knock on her door. She answered it. A meal was being delivered to her by one of Zander's crew. She was relieved it wasn't Char as she stepped aside to let this woman enter.

But Char did arrive at midday to take her to meet Zander and Kowangii. Now that Ry Sing was recovered, Char chattered on about how excited she was to go on this walk to see Ry Sing's ship and her fellow travelers. Ry Sing listened but didn't add anything. She could tell Char was also affected and confused by the strength of this attraction, but Ry Sing felt she needed to stay emotionally distant from her to avoid any intensification of the connection they felt to each other.

Kowangii was waiting inside the lounge. He embraced Ry Sing and touched her cheek. "You are looking well today, my dear."

"Thank you, Kowangii; I feel entirely recovered. Your healers are most expert at their jobs. But I'm not sure I'm ready for a four-day walk."

The old man laughed. "It may have taken you four days to reach us but that was because you took a circuitous route. It is actually about two and a half hours of comfortable walking."

Zander was giving instruction over the intercom to bring the ship back into the frequency of the planet's dimension. At the moment this occurred, the Light Wanderer was visible and detectable by the Light Traveler. Ry Sing realized that Bel'lar would be alerted to the presence of this ship long before they arrived. This should be fun. She hoped he wasn't too angry at her. She missed him. She could hardly remember what they had argued about, with all that had happened to her since then.

With Chapatata in front, the four set out on the trip to the Light Traveler. Despite the distance, they decided to walk and enjoy the beauty of this planet. Zander had kept the crew sequestered aboard once the smaller ship was detected. It was a treat to watch the dog enjoy himself running here and there, sniffing everything.

※ ※ ※

Back onboard the Light Traveler, an alarm sounded. *Alien object in distance* began flashing on the crystal display.

The Light Traveler found Bel'lar in his quarters reviewing a study completed by Dobeman and Mauleen. "An object has appeared to the southwest of our location."

Bel'lar hurried to the bridge. Mauleen was right behind him. The ship's sensors informed them it was a ship about three times the size of their ship. Sweat trickled down his neck at this news.

"We need everyone back inside now." He put out a call to the others. Was this where Ry Sing was? Was she a prisoner or worse? Maybe it had nothing to do with her.

The crystal display filled with the black ship. It was immense.

Ka'aya arrived immediately. He had been resting in his quarters. He saw the black ship revealed on the large crystal display. He saw the consternation on Mauleen's and Bel'lar's faces. He hastened to explain. "It looks like our ship, but merely a different color. There is no fear here, for they are us."

The ship displayed was a beautiful black craft. And Ka'aya was correct; it did look like theirs but was much larger. The size alone made Bel'lar concerned for the people in his care.

"You always say that," Bel'lar said, "but not now. I'm trying to protect you. Get everyone in here. And where is Ry Sing?" He paced back and forth, tension evident with each stride, as he tried to decide what he would do if Ry Sing was on this ship or—he didn't know if this was better or worse—not on it.

Enis was just coming in from exploring when he heard the alarm going off in the ship. He dropped his bag in the galley and rushed to the bridge. Bursting through the entry to the bridge, he came to an abrupt halt, his mouth open. The sight of the immense black ship filling the crystal display had his complete attention.

Moments later, Dobeman arrived and examined the black ship. *What a stimulating day it was turning out to be*, he thought. He looked forward to meeting these new travelers and the information to be gained by interaction.

"Mauleen, scan for life signs around that ship," Bel'lar directed.

Seated at her station, she initiated the scan. Five life signs were detected not far from that black ship, moving in this direction. "Captain, five life forms coming this way."

"Put it up on the main display," Bel'lar said.

Everyone turned to the main display, where the life forms were shown by their flickering heat signatures.

"Are they armed, Mauleen?" Bel'lar asked.

"Wait, Bel'lar," Ka'aya interjected. "Let's not get carried away. Can we see these aliens more clearly?" Ka'aya wanted to calm them down. He knew there was no cause for alarm.

Adjustments were made, and the aliens' features became clear. What was instantly apparent was that one of the aliens was Ry Sing. She was walking freely with three other beings. Then she linked arms with the older man. She seemed to be laughing. No weapons were discernible on any of the strangers.

"That's where she is," Ka'aya said. His attention strayed to the old man with Ry Sing. He seemed familiar. His pulse quickened. *It begins*, he thought.

"Who is that with her?" Bel'lar demanded. What kind of trouble had she gotten herself into this time? He hoped the friendly appearance of this group was the reality.

"I don't know. They have dark skin, but they look like us. I haven't seen anyone like them before," Mauleen said. "And what's that with them? Look. It's a dog. I haven't seen a dog in years."

The dog was so excited by being outside that it was running around the aliens, with a stick in his mouth, trying to get them to play. Enis laughed at the dog's behavior and relaxed.

Dobeman moved closer to the main console, his tangle-wood staff tapping with his steps. "I have seen visuals of this race before. I am related to them ancestrally. They won't harm us. Their mission is to work in harmony with the animals and create balance in ecological environments. I don't believe they are dangerous."

"Ry Sing obviously doesn't believe they are dangerous, either," Ka'aya said. "She is walking arm-in-arm with them. Like long-lost souls that have been reunited. There is no need for alarm. They don't pose any threat." In fact, Ka'aya knew that these aliens were indeed just that—long-lost souls with whom they were about to be reunited.

Bel'lar frowned, reluctant to let down their guard just yet. "That may be, but I will meet them alone when they arrive. The rest of you will stay here. Mauleen will protect you."

The four with the dog weren't in any hurry. They seemed to be strolling along, looking at everything and discussing it. They appeared in total harmony with their surroundings.

"Captain, it looks like it's going to take them some time to get here," Mauleen said as she watched the display.

"Monitor their progress, and let me know when they're close," Bel'lar said. He left the bridge.

When he returned several hours later, he had donned his dress uniform. Mauleen, also wearing hers, was announcing that everyone should return to the bridge as he entered.

✳ ✳ ✳

Ry Sing and the three of the black race climbed up out of the foliage and crossed the plateau. They came within a stone's throw of the invisible pyramid as they approached the ship. Kowangii looked at the star burned into the ground and smiled. He sensed the presence of the hidden library waiting for recognition. Then all their attention turned to the small ship, the Light Traveler, situated on the plateau before them. They stopped. Zander called Chapatata over, patting his leg, and the dog stood next to him.

Ry Sing stepped out in front of her companions. "Bel'lar," she called out. "I know you see us. Come out and meet my friends." She looked at Zander and the others in apology. She had hoped they would be outside to greet them.

Inside the ship, Bel'lar was about to give the order for Mauleen to remain there while he greeted the visitors when he saw Ka'aya leaving the bridge.

"You're in charge, Mauleen. Find Dobeman and get him back here." Bel'lar sped after Ka'aya.

He caught up to him at the ship's exit.

"As Captain, you should go out first," Ka'aya said as he stepped aside to allow Bel'lar a clear path through the hatch.

Frustrated with Ry Sing and now Ka'aya, he straightened his shoulders and walked out toward Ry Sing. Ka'aya followed more slowly.

Ry Sing noticed immediately that Bel'lar was wearing his formal dress uniform. He presented a distinguished impression as he stopped in front of her. "We were concerned about you, Ry Sing." He leaned closer and embraced her. "Where the hell have you been?" he whispered. He straightened, and she grinned.

"Look what I've found," she said. He wasn't mad anymore. That was good. But he was upset with her. He would probably try to get her to promise not to do anything like this ever again. It would take some coaxing on her part to smooth this over between them. That would be fun, too.

"What have you found?" Bel'lar turned his gaze to the three strangers.

"Let me introduce Captain Zander of the ship, the Light Wanderer. Zander meet Bel'lar, Captain of the Light Traveler."

Bel'lar looked the captain over, sizing him up. Zander was confident, powerful and very tall, forcing Bel'lar to look up to meet his eyes, despite Bel'lar's height. Not friendly or unfriendly, he merely inclined his head to Bel'lar in greeting. Bel'lar responded similarly.

Ry Sing introduced Char next. "This is Char Charengo, the ship's physician."

"And this is Kowangii, the Minister, and holy man of the ship."

Bel'lar bowed to each one as Ry Sing introduced them.

Kowangii spoke up, "We are very pleased to meet you." Then he turned to Ka'aya. "You must be Ka'aya."

Ka'aya smiled and stepped closer to greet Kowangii. He extended his arm, his hand palm up to the holy man. Kowangii responded by extending his arm with his palm down. They grasped each other's extended arm at the elbow and spoke simultaneously, "There is no difference between us. We are all of the One." Then they stepped back smiling, surprising everyone with their apparent connection.

"To have met Ry Sing, and now you, Ka'aya . . . we are almost speechless." Kowangii grinned. "We are making history today.

This has been foretold in ancient scripture." He pulled out the tattered book he was reading yesterday and held it out to Ka'aya.

Ka'aya accepted it, turning it over with astonishment. "We didn't think any of these were in existence anymore." He handed it back carefully to Kowangii who tucked it in his pocket.

"Is that *The Book of Knowledge of the Sacred Ecology Religion*?" Ry Sing stood at Kowangii's elbow to get a better look.

Kowangii said, "Indeed it is, my dear. It's all in there and is now coming to fruition." He looked at Ka'aya and Ry Sing and smiled in excitement.

Bel'lar regarded all of them. There seemed to be nothing overtly hostile about these alien visitors, but he wasn't ready to relax yet. "Apparently everyone knows everyone else. Let us offer you some refreshments. Your walk must have made you hot and dry. Come in. Be welcome."

Bel'lar offered his arm to Char and led the others inside to the lounge. Enis and Mauleen were waiting there. Enis had rushed to make things ready when he realized they were all coming inside. They sat down, and Enis brought out a tray of glasses with juice made from fruit that he had picked early this morning.

After everyone was introduced, had something to drink, and was seated comfortably, Bel'lar turned to Zander. The two Captains had taken seats across from each other at the table. Bel'lar held up his glass in greeting to his guests. "Welcome." Everyone drank. Then he looked at the other Captain. "Why are you here, Zander?"

"We're here," Zander answered, "because it was written in the scriptures that on this planet, at this time, there would be a meeting of three races, the black, the Asian, and the white. We decided to come because we have animals on board that we rescued from planets that are only marginally supporting life now. We are the caretakers of the animals. We bring animals where they're needed energetically to balance and provide the harmony the planet and others need. This planet supports life very well." Zander looked around at the others.

"However, we haven't decided to inhabit this planet. We wanted to see what was happening here first. We found the Asian race already here, and discovered that they settled here wishing to live in total harmony with the planet. We didn't know about the white race's motives, so we've been waiting for you to arrive. We expected you earlier."

"Well, we would have been, but we took a detour to the fourth planet in this system to discover what our ancestors, the holy men, had left for us. They inhabited that planet for a time."

Zander took a drink, nodding to Enis his approval of the juice. "Why didn't they come here?" He was leaning back, relaxed. The dog lay at his feet, asleep.

Bel'lar took a long drink of his juice before he answered. He was stalling. He had a hunch that this race, devoted to animals, would be disturbed at his ancestors' actions. He decided to be vague. "This planet was inhabited by dinosaurs."

Zander stiffened and stared at Bel'lar. "Are you the race that destroyed those animals?"

Bel'lar inhaled a deep breath, noting the controlled anger in Zander's body. Deliberately casual, he said, "It looks like our ancestors had a hand in something like that."

Zander slammed his hand down on the table. The others jumped. "How could you do this? How could your people do such a thing to innocent animals?" Zander's voice rose in anger. Chapatata jumped up, growling, his head swiveling around, seeking the source of Zander's anger.

Bel'lar sat forward aggressively. "How can you blame us for something our ancestors did?"

"You really are misfits," Zander said.

"Misfits? What do you mean by that?" Bel'lar demanded.

Kowangii stood. "Enough of this."

The two Captains glared at each other.

Ka'aya came over to help get Bel'lar out of this fix. He stood by Zander to draw his attention. "Sometimes holy men of all races do things they think are right but wind up being wrong. In your eyes, we can see that this was the wrong thing for our ancestors to do. But we can't change that. All we can offer is our solemn promise, as we now inhabit this planet, that we will cherish and keep safe all the animals you bring."

Zander's eyes bored deeply into Ka'aya's. "I will return to see what you have done. I will be looking after this place and the animals that we bring, so beware." Chapatata stared at Ka'aya, telling him with a growl that he would be back, too.

Ry Sing, sitting next to Zander, put her hand on his arm. "Zander, maybe that's the reason for your race to settle here. You need not travel around this planet. Stay on this continent where you release the animals, and be their guardians. That way you can trust in your future generations to be the custodians of the animals and keep the land inhabitable for them."

Zander shook his head at her words, still angry. He wasn't yet prepared to let this go.

Bel'lar didn't like the way her hand rested on Zander's arm. What was going on here? He didn't like this Captain.

This subject had to be dropped; it was too combustible. Ka'aya thought it time to bring it to an end before bad feelings hardened into permanent grudges. He looked at Zander. "It has been written that you will be part of this planet. Whether you choose to do this now or in the future is up to you, but you will be here for the end."

Zander expelled a breath and considered him more calmly. He turned to Kowangii with a question in his eyes.

"Yes, Zander, it is true. We didn't tell you because we knew you didn't want to come here and participate in this planet. But it is written in the scriptures that there will be participation of the black race on this planet and that it will begin here on this continent." Kowangii met Zander's eyes, showing him the truth of his words.

"All right, old man," he said reluctantly. "I understand your words and yours, also, Ka'aya. I will consider them." Zander sat back and patted Chapatata, reassuring him, and the dog lay back down. Ka'aya returned to his seat.

The two holy men had been able to dissipate the anger, and everyone settled down. Enis sensed this was the perfect moment and served the food. Char opened the pack she'd brought and set out food and water for Chapatata. Zander smiled at Char, and she fluttered her eyelashes at him; then she returned to her seat next to Bel'lar.

While they were eating, Zander began again to talk to Bel'lar. "Ry Sing told us that a Sentinel is a member of your crew. We would like to meet him."

"Dobeman is our anthropologist. He's studying the inhabitants to help us determine if we can coexist comfortably with them. Where is he, Mauleen?"

"He's off the ship completing some surveys. He should be here shortly."

"Good," Bel'lar said. "I'm sure he wants to meet you. How long are you going to be here?"

"Six more moon cycles. We build shelters for the animals. Then we release them, and continue monitoring to make sure they acclimate to this place and are comfortable. We have a very high success rate when we release them this way." Zander's face softened as he talked about his life's work.

Ka'aya bowed to Zander. "Your ship is an ark carrying the animals that will re-inhabit this planet. It is just as it was written in the scriptures. The Ark of Knowing has great responsibility for caring for these animals and taking them to the places where they have an opportunity to multiply their species, to live, to grow, to understand. It is a very worthy path."

Zander bowed in response to Ka'aya and said, "It's the knowing that makes it so worthwhile. When you speak of it, my heart lightens. Thank you."

Bel'lar saw a different side of this tall, stern man and recognized another like himself, devoted to completing his mission. However, he still didn't like the way Ry Sing was reacting to this man. Time for them to leave. He stood, bringing this evening to a close. Ry Sing frowned at him, but the others got to their feet.

On the way out, they met Dobeman coming in. He had taken the small transport early in the morning and spent some time away from the ship working on his surveys. Dobeman regarded the three from the black race with interest and waited for them to speak.

Kowangii walked up to Dobeman and addressed him. "Greetings. Don't you recognize us?"

Dobeman paused, considering Kowangii, and then responded, "I know I have ancestors from the black race, but I had given up hope of encountering you since I haven't met any of you on any of the planets I have visited."

"We would like to spend some time with you, Dobeman. We have to return to our ship now, but we will see you in a few days. Would that be all right?" Kowangii walked alongside Dobeman as they went outside.

"That would be very satisfactory. I shall look forward to it," Dobeman replied.

They all stood outside talking in front of the entrance to the ship.

"It's getting dark," Bel'lar said. "Are you concerned about making the journey back to your ship in the dark?"

"No. I'll just call for transport to pick us up." Zander pulled out some kind of transmitter. He stepped away from the others and made the request. Then he walked back to Ry Sing. Taking her hand in his, he raised it to his lips. She smiled up at him. "We would be honored if you would accompany us back to our ship. We want to spend some time with you."

"I don't think that's a good idea," Bel'lar protested. He didn't like the way Zander was looking at her or the way she was responding to him.

Ry Sing looked at Bel'lar. "But I do." She turned back to Zander. "Thank you. But I'd like to wait on that invitation. Kowangii has given me the key to something I've been pondering." Zander nodded and stepped back.

Kowangii kissed Ry Sing's cheek in farewell. "Of course, my dear." He turned to the others and gave a little bow.

The transport, piloted by a member of Zander's crew, appeared out of the dark sky and came to a halt in front of Zander and the others. They said their farewells. Zander, Kowangii, and Char climbed aboard, and the transport disappeared into the night.

❋ ❋ ❋

As soon as the three from the Light Wanderer left, Ry Sing excused herself, intent on retiring. Bel'lar followed her. He had waited all afternoon to talk to her and now, finally, they were alone. She attempted to close the door in his face, but he blocked it, stepping inside. She turned around, irritated at his high-handed manner.

He didn't give her a chance to speak. "How well do you know that man? I thought we were together. Why didn't you contact me? I thought you were hurt or even dead. How could you do this to me?"

Ry Sing just stared at him, letting him get it all out. When he paused, she said, "What are you talking about? We are together. Why would you think that?" He opened his mouth to interrupt, and she pointed at him. He closed his mouth. "I didn't contact you because I almost died. They rescued me, helped me get well. And I'm here, aren't I? I refused Zander's invitation."

"Invitation!" he yelled. "Why is he inviting you anywhere?" She infuriated him. He just wanted to strangle her. Instead he looked about the room and, grabbing a candle, he threw it against the wall, he was so angry. It smashed to bits.

She looked at the broken candle and then fixed him with a cold glare. "Are you done?" she demanded, her hands on her hips.

He looked at her. He was really in for it now, he thought. She was mad. *Good. That makes two of us.*

She looked down, breathing deeply. He watched, saying nothing. He didn't know if she was getting ready to smack him. Then she looked up, and the tension in her drained away. She stepped forward into his arms, completely surprising him.

"I missed you," she whispered into his shirt. He held her tight.

"You have no idea how much I missed you. Why do you do these things? Going off, getting lost, almost dying. I know you want to be free to follow your own path, but, honestly, Ry Sing, you're killing me." He rested his chin on her head.

"I know," she answered. "Let me make it up to you." She put her arms about his neck and pulled him into a stimulating kiss. In answer, he picked her up and carried her to her bed. They didn't argue about anything else for the rest of the night.

* * *

On the Light Wanderer, Zander was eating a meal at the Captain's table. It was the following morning after meeting the crew of the Light Traveler. He was eating alone with his dog because only those invited would sit with him. They did this out of respect to their Captain.

Kowangii entered, the old book clutched in his hand. He saw Zander eating and approached him. "Captain Zander, may we join you?" Kowangii didn't have to wait for an invitation to sit, but, out of courtesy, he always asked.

"Please sit, old man." Zander gestured to the seat across from him.

Kowangii sat, and a crewmember brought tea for him. Kowangii placed the book on the table. He got settled, stirring some sweetness into the tea. He took a sip. Then he looked at Zander. "What do you think of the people who have come to claim this planet as their own?"

Zander grimaced. "If they hadn't destroyed those animals, I might come to like them a little bit. But the arrogance of their race to think they were better than the animals. It's very difficult for me to get past that." Zander looked regretful as he continued to eat.

"Ah, well, give us a moment here to find it." Kowangii moved his teacup out of the way and put his book in front of him. He bent over the ancient tome, opened it, and began looking for something.

Zander watched this dear old man with amusement. "You're not going to quote scripture at me again, are you? I'm scriptured up to here. You know it doesn't matter to me, and I don't think you can influence me to change."

Kowangii smiled as he thumbed through the book, finally settling on a page. He put his finger on the passage that he wanted. "Just a moment. Here it is. Let us read from this passage."

"It is written that there will be three great events in the experience of mankind that will be so catastrophic, they will bring tears to the multitudes, for they will weep for many thousands of years beyond the events. These events will render the planets completely useless for thousands of millions of years.

"It is written that beyond that time they will start anew, but they will carry with them the remembrance of these events. The cleansing of the planets will be necessary, because the lessons learned will be at an end. The inhabitants of these three planets will not benefit by the continuation because determinate time is placed upon all lessons, and these times were at an end.

"It has been written that the holy man who cleansed the first planet so that it may be reborn will sacrifice his own life. This man will be reborn as the man who unites the population upon the third planet once again."

"Now, it is foretold that the second and third cleansing of a planet will be done by a man not considered holy, by a man not scripture read, but by a man of law and order bound . . . ," Kowangii began to weep, overcome by this passage, but then through an effort of will continued, ". . . by a man bound by his duty. This binding of his duty will force him to take actions to create events that will destroy his home planet, which he feels . . . ," Kowangii was once again overcome by weeping, and Zander waited patiently with tears in his own eyes for him to continue.

In a moment, Kowangii resumed, ". . . which he feels will be better cleansed than continuing. But this will not sit well with him, for it is written that he will end his life within the year after this event."

Zander had stopped eating and was unconsciously pushing his food around his plate. This passage had erased all interest in eating. He waited for the old man to compose himself.

Kowangii closed the book and wiped his eyes and sniffed. Then he fixed Zander with a serious gaze. "It's very important that you understand what I have read and that you learn that, every once in a while, great beings come along and do unthinkable things that they feel are completely out of their realm of existence. That is what will happen because the white race will do much penance for what these holy men and this one military man will do. They will go through their history on this planet, continuing to fight ever increasingly amongst themselves, in punishment."

"Are you telling me that this military man is Bel'lar?" Zander seemed shocked.

Kowangii answered, "We can't say for sure, but in our heart we feel he may be the one."

"Yes, the one who destroys. That's what he can be," Zander said angrily.

The old man put his hand on Zander's arm. "Don't be short-sighted. Realize your anger toward them is nothing compared to the anger they carry within their own being. Free yourself of this anger. Grant this old man his wish. Help them to achieve what they need, and let them do what they feel they should."

Zander was sad and somewhat ashamed at his emotions now. "Are you telling me we should help them inhabit this planet? That's not in my orders. My orders are to observe, to release the animals. What you're telling me is that this white race will come to this planet and inflict much pain and suffering." Zander shook his head. This was too hard for him to bear—to think that his animals would be hurt. "How can I be part of that?"

"Yes, Zander, but through pain and suffering, much knowledge is gained. You cannot deny yourself the opportunity to assist the white race to continue. So, yes, if we can help them, wherever possible, we should. We are going tomorrow to see what we can do to help him accept his destiny."

"Old man," he said, affectionately; he had known Kowangii since he was a boy. "The wisdom you carry within is greater than anything I have ever known. If you leave me, I will be lost in my one dimension to protect the animals. However, I will do this for Ry Sing. Not Bel'lar." Zander got to his feet.

"Certainly, my son." Kowangii took a last sip of his tea, and then Zander helped him to rise. "Why not give Bel'lar and his crew a tour of your ship? Show him the magnificence of this vessel. Try to be his friend. We will be sharing much over the next few cycles while we place the remaining animals."

"Let me sleep on it. Again you attempt to command this ship." Zander laughed. He looked down at Chapatata and silently summoned him to come. Together they walked out.

* * *

The next day, Kowangii returned to the Light Traveler. He came to help Bel'lar fulfill his destiny. He knew Bel'lar wouldn't be receptive from the discussions he'd had with Ry Sing, but he was determined to try. She had told him about Bel'lar's birthmark changing and his extreme reaction to the message from the Great One.

Bel'lar was sitting on the bridge when Light Traveler notified him that a transport was arriving. He left the bridge and exited the ship just as the old holy man climbed out and walked over to him. The transport zipped away.

"Greetings, Kowangii," Bel'lar said, nodding his head in respect.

"Greetings, likewise, Captain Bel'lar." Kowangii nodded in response.

"To what do I owe the honor of your visit?" Bel'lar led the old man toward some chairs that had been set up in the shade of the ship.

Kowangii took a seat opposite the younger man and looked directly at him, taking stock of this man who was avoiding his destiny.

Bel'lar felt the intensity of Kowangii's gaze and squirmed. Then he stiffened his resolve. "I hope you haven't come to talk to me about scriptures and destiny. I have my duty to fulfill, and that's what I intend to do."

"Indeed, Bel'lar. You must complete your mission. What you don't realize is that your mission *is* your destiny. There is no difference. But we wanted to offer you the opportunity to discuss this because your future is poised to transpire, and we wanted to help you prepare for those events." Kowangii took the ancient book from his pocket and held it on his knees.

Bel'lar glanced at the book with some trepidation; then he looked at Kowangii. The old man was regarding him with a pensive look. Was there a trick in here somewhere? Was Kowangii another holy man trying to get him to become a holy man? He considered his words carefully before answering.

"I'm simply a military man bound to fulfill my duty to find a future home for my people. Nothing more." He continued to look at Kowangii, unconsciously sitting up straighter.

"That is exactly what you are, and exactly what you are supposed to be. Be at peace with this, and you will meet your destiny prepared to accept it."

Bel'lar smiled. "That's certainly a twist. No coercion disguised as flattery to get me to acquiesce to the scriptures? No offers to discuss my feelings? You're a strange holy man, Kowangii," he said, searching the old man's face for explanation or at least a clue as to where this was going.

"That is the nicest thing ever said about us. We're pleased. We don't want you to share your feelings. We won't read from the book. We won't bother you with ancient rhetoric. We will only offer our assistance."

Bel'lar laughed. This old man had a way about him that was hard to resist. He found himself liking him despite his suspicions. "It seems, then, that I would be graceless to turn away your help. I will seek it if I find myself in need."

"Excellent." The old man leaned forward, his eyes boring into Bel'lar's.

Bel'lar looked back and felt a surge of energy in the area of his heart. It spread warmth into his chest.

The old man extended his hand to grasp Bel'lar's in the way he had with Ka'aya when they first met. Bel'lar responded in kind.

Kowangii looked into Bel'lar's eyes while maintaining his physical connection.

Bel'lar felt great emotion sweep through him.

Kowangii smiled broadly.

✳ ✳ ✳

Since Ry Sing had returned with the people from the Light Wanderer, Bel'lar had been keeping an eye on her. He didn't want her to disappear on him again. He had no wish to repeat that experience. But after the early meal, she had mentioned she had something to check out. He had been busy with Dobeman and Mauleen reviewing reports all day and hadn't thought any more about it. But now the sun was setting, and she hadn't returned. He was getting worried. He made his way to her quarters, but she wasn't inside.

"L.T., find Ry Sing."

"Yes, Captain," the Light Traveler answered.

Moments passed as he waited.

"Captain, she is not within the ship. And I do not sense her in the vicinity," Light Traveler said.

Bel'lar strode off to Ka'aya's quarters. Ka'aya answered his door immediately. "What is it?"

"Ry Sing's missing again. Do you know where she is? No dissembling this time," Bel'lar demanded.

Ka'aya didn't take exception to Bel'lar's accusation. Instead he closed his eyes, seeking her energy. "We cannot sense her anywhere. The pyramid is the only place we cannot sense, but we don't think she can get in there."

"I didn't, either." Bel'lar sounded concerned. He walked quickly away from Ka'aya.

Ka'aya followed.

They exited the ship and started across the plateau in the direction of the azure gold pyramid. They arrived at it quickly. After a look around, they couldn't find any access. They walked to the corners, but found nothing. In frustration, Bel'lar picked up a stone and started beating on the pyramid, yelling, "Ry Sing! Ry Sing! Are you in there?" He pulled his pistol and fired into the pyramid. A shower of stones flew out of the impact site, spraying them both with dust.

"What about your crack gun? We could blow the top off," Ka'aya said, smiling.

Bel'lar stepped back, incredulous. The crack gun was an antimatter weapon that fired a burst of energy, exploding apart its target. A meter and a half long, it could be fired from the shoulder, but not at all what he would choose for this purpose.

Ka'aya continued, "Are you ready for us to try now? If we can penetrate into this pyramid at this proximity, we might be able to reach her, if she's actually in there." Ka'aya sat on the ground with his legs crossed and closed his eyes.

Too distracted to listen to Ka'aya's suggestion, his mind busy with what to do next, Bel'lar paced away and then came back. He eyed Ka'aya and said, "What are you doing? Am I the only one worried about her?" He was at a loss as to how to find her. If she wasn't inside, where was she? Why did she do this? She drove him crazy.

A grinding sound split the air. Bel'lar jumped back, seeking the source of the sound, as a crack opened in the azure gold surface of the pyramid in front of the seated holy man. Ka'aya got to his feet, and, as they watched, one side of the crack opened further, sliding up inside the exterior surface creating a triangle-shaped opening. In the center of this opening, a glorious-looking Asian woman appeared, her waist-length black hair blowing gently in the breeze. For a moment, they didn't recognize Ry Sing, she seemed so different. She was wearing a short black dress of some soft fabric, embroidered all over and fringed in gold, leaving some sheer areas which exposed some of her white skin. On her head she wore what looked like a crown higher on one side and swooped up at an angle. She looked radiant.

Bel'lar was struck speechless at this vision in black and gold.

Ka'aya smiled. Then Bel'lar dropped to his knee. Ka'aya heard him say, "You look like a goddess."

She looked down at Bel'lar. "You know I am."

Ka'aya continued to smile at Ry Sing's transformation and Bel'lar's confusion. She stepped forward out of the doorway into the setting sun. When the sun touched her finery, rays shone out from her like a star.

"I sensed an urgency," she said. "Do you need me for something?"

Ry Sing had lost track of time. She had found a way inside the Asian pyramid, where she was shielded from the ship's sensors. Kowangii had given her a hint, and she had figured it out. She examined the symbols on the stone and realized which ones made up the opening sequence. When she traced them on the wall, the wall had opened.

"Well, yes, I, I, I don't remember," Bel'lar stuttered, still visibly moved by her appearance.

Ka'aya decided to help him out since he was stricken almost dumb by Ry Sing's beauty. "We do, my dear. Bel'lar was concerned when you didn't appear."

She regarded him, her eyes slightly out of focus. She appeared to be in a daze. Whatever she had experienced inside the pyramid had had a profound effect on her.

"Well, that's nice. But don't worry. If I'm not concerned, there's no reason for anyone else to be. As I walk, I'm in determination of my future. This is my destiny. Allow me to do this. I will do more that you will find disturbing if you continue to place restrictions on me."

Ka'aya walked up to her and put his hands on her arms. She shook a little at his touch as if she were coming out of a trance. Then she saw him for the first time. She smiled a silly smile. "Hi."

He smiled at her, searching her face, her eyes. She did seem restored. "Hi, yourself. Are you all right?" He continued to hold on to her, making sure she didn't fall. She was wavering, still unsteady.

"I have never been better. I've discovered the true meaning of my existence, and it's wonderful. I'm going to fulfill it without any concern for the rest of my life. I know what it is now. I must journey back to Taurus and bring them to this planet. Then we can be together again to fulfill our destiny. I know now it's with you. The pyramid guides me back to the future."

Bel'lar sat back on his heels, watching them. He didn't know what to do. What did she mean it was with Ka'aya? Was he going to lose her?

Ry Sing finally noticed him when he moved and turned that silly smile on him. "I didn't see you. How long have you been there?"

"I was the one beating on the pyramid, trying to get you to come out." He observed her closely to see if she was really coherent.

"Oh, you can't hear anything inside there once the door is shut. It's soundproof."

Bel'lar got to his feet, brushing off his pants. "You'd better come now. Where did you get these clothes?"

"In a big golden box. It was very strange. When I touched it, the lid opened. Inside, I found these clothes, and I just had to put them on. I felt I was in a dream." She looked down at the dress, touching it, and then stepped clear of the pyramid. The stone door slid closed behind her.

Bel'lar ran forward, jumping up to stop the door. But that was an impossibility. It closed. "Wait. Wait. We won't be able to get back in." He pushed on the stone slab but nothing happened.

"Don't worry, I know how." She was unconcerned as she stood there staring at him.

Bel'lar stared back, breathing hard. He was afraid he had lost her inside this pyramid. He didn't like this feeling of fear and impotence. She was distant, totally unfazed by his heightened anxiety. She was more frustrating than he could even begin to verbalize. He grabbed her arm. He was torn between being gentle and just dragging her back to the ship.

Ka'aya sensed the debate going on inside the younger man and smoothly interrupted. "Ry Sing, before you rule the world, you must put your crown on straight." He turned the large part of the crown to the front, revealing a huge ruby set into the middle of the crown. "That's better. Come, you two." He could see Bel'lar was still upset with her.

"Wonderful—I'm ready," she said. "Thank you for coming to get me." She gave them both a big smile.

Bel'lar supported her on one side, Ka'aya, the other. She was still a bit unsteady, but this wore off as they walked.

The sun was low in the west. They watched the clouds change from a dazzling orange to a brilliant multitude of colors as they walked. It was breathtaking. Then the sunlight illuminated a black dot coming in their direction. It grew until it seemed to block the light, becoming recognizable as the massive black ship, the Light Wanderer, flying swiftly toward them. Three times the size of the Light Traveler, it appeared to be constructed of the same material as their craft but black, elliptical in shape, along with a similarly designed raised-bubble-shaped bridge.

Bel'lar stopped in mid-stride. "That ship, it's huge. Look at how tiny our ship appears next to it." His eyes traveled up and down the craft. Then he realized he was holding his breath and let it out.

The ship hovered overhead, casting an ominous shadow.

"What are they doing here?" He began running, Ka'aya and Ry Sing following him.

Then the ship lowered and set down quietly on the plateau near the smaller ship.

As the three neared it, the hatch opened, and a ramp extended from the hatch to the ground. Then three people exited.

Dobeman and Enis were standing by the Light Traveler, waiting for the Light Wanderer to discharge her passengers.

Enis stared at Ry Sing and her finery. Ka'aya grinned at him. Enis's smile was uncertain, a question in his eyes.

Zander, Char, and Kowangii waited at the bottom of the ramp.

Bel'lar, breathing hard, reached the black ship first. "Captain, some notice would have been appreciated."

Zander smiled. "Did we startle you?"

"Why are you here?" Bel'lar asked, ignoring Zander's question.

"Greetings, Bel'lar," Kowangii said. "We're here to get better acquainted. We have a few days before we have to release the rest of the animals."

Kowangii grinned at Zander and then turned his attention to the crew of the Light Traveler. He was clutching his battered old book. It looked even older than the last time, Bel'lar thought.

"Greetings to—." Kowangii stopped in mid-sentence. He stepped forward, took Ry Sing's hand and bowed to her. "Greetings, Holy Princess Ry Sing Su Tong. You are a vision of loveliness."

Ry Sing giggled. "Greetings, dear Kowangii." She kissed his cheek and whispered, "I got inside."

The holy man smiled, his pride in her showing on his face. "We knew you would."

Zander greeted Ry Sing with a kiss on the cheek. Then he bowed to her. She smiled happily at all of them.

Bel'lar's eyes narrowed at this display of affection. He didn't mind Kowangii, but Zander kissing Ry Sing, he didn't like. He glanced up and noticed that Char was staring at Ry Sing, too. She didn't like Zander's kiss, either.

Bel'lar and Zander stared at each other.

Kowangii recovered from his surprise at seeing Ry Sing dressed as she was and greeted the other members of the crew.

Zander approached the Sentinel. "Greetings, Dobeman. It's a pleasure to see you again. It's always an honor to speak with one of your race."

Dobeman was taken aback by Zander's comments. "You have met others like me? I haven't seen another like me in many years. I thought I had become a race of one."

"On our planet there are many like you," Char said. "They are devoted to the study of mankind. And what you learn will make you the race of the future."

Dobeman smiled at Char's comments and looked pleased. This voyage was turning out to be much more stimulating than he thought it would be. His chances of meeting others like himself had just increased.

Kowangii nudged Zander.

Zander shot him an irritated glance, and then he looked at Bel'lar. "Would anyone care to see my ship? I felt it would be of interest to you and to. . ." Zander looked around as he said this, "Where is, what was her name?"

"You mean Mauleen, my first officer."

"Yes, the one with the red curly hair. I thought she would be interested also."

"She would be, but she's working and taking the watch."

"Isn't your ship self-maintaining? Isn't it a life force like mine?" Zander was intrigued. Could it be that they didn't understand their ship? Yes, the name "misfits" definitely applied to this group.

"It is, but some of us technos still need the feeling of being in charge. And she's compiling data about this planet to be used in our analysis."

"I see," Zander said. "Now come aboard. It's my pleasure to show you the craft that is your craft's big sister. She's similar in operation to yours, as the same race of beings created both ships. Before the separation between the black and the white race, there was one race that created ships like these."

"Indeed, Zander. It was from the time before. Most people don't even realize the greatness that came out of that era," Ka'aya said.

Kowangii smiled and looked at Ka'aya. "We come from that era." He laughed.

Ka'aya took Ry Sing's arm and said, "We're not the only two that came out of that era."

Ry Sing laughed and shrugged him off. "I don't know what you're talking about. Let's see this beautiful ship." She turned her attention and her smile to Zander. He offered her his arm, and together they walked up the ramp and stepped through into the ship, motioning for Bel'lar and the others to follow him. Bel'lar moved in front of the others to catch up with Ry Sing. Char and Kowangii stood to one side to let the crew of the Light Traveler pass and then followed.

Bel'lar walked up to stand next to Zander and Ry Sing. He wanted to separate these two, so he began questioning Zander. "Do you have many of these ships on your planet?"

"We do. We've mastered the technologies and can reproduce the ships at will. But it was difficult and took us many years. What about you?"

Bel'lar shook his head regretfully. "The Light Traveler is our only ship. Our scientists spent much time with her, but we haven't conquered the technologies yet."

Zander looked around to see if everyone was inside. Char came up to him and pulled him aside. She whispered that she would make arrangements for some refreshments and left.

Kowangii came up behind Bel'lar. "Realize, Bel'lar, it is only technology. It is the advancement of the door opening without touching. Remember when you had to touch the door to open it. Before this, you had to turn a handle to open the door, before that you had to push it, and before that when you had to roll the door and so on."

Ka'aya added, "And before that, the humanoids were still living and dying the way they are today. So what has technology given them but a different way—"

"—to do the same thing," Kowangii finished. The two old ones linked arms and walked off together down the corridor laughing. The others were stunned at their antics and amused. They seemed to be old friends.

Ry Sing linked her arm with Bel'lar's. "I'm going with you. Those two scare me." Then she laughed, and everyone laughed.

Enis felt shy in this group and was standing off to the side, not saying anything. Bel'lar noticed him hanging back and encouraged him to join them.

Zander smiled at Enis as he approached. "Greetings, Enis. Please join us."

"Th-thank you," Enis stammered. His shyness had intensified with Zander looking at him. He looked down at the dog instead, standing silently by Zander's side.

Bel'lar interjected smoothly, "Zander will show us his ship and you will learn things you've never thought of before. You too, Dobeman, come with us."

"Yes, Dobeman. You might find this ship interesting. It's a hybrid, like you," Zander said.

Dobeman looked mildly surprised. "I might find it interesting if you have any fudge icicles."

"Fudge icicles. What's a fudge icicle?" Zander asked.

"It's a frozen concoction of sweet, dark liquid on a stick," Bel'lar explained. "And you should see the way it melts. Dobeman is very interested in how they melt."

Zander considered this and said, "We don't have fudge icicles, but we have something similar we call a dream icicle. It actually matches the color of your robe. It tastes wonderful."

"Very well. I will be happy to tour your ship with the anticipation of trying one of these icicles." Dobeman smiled in anticipation.

"Then, let's start in the lounge and galley. We'll get an icicle for you to enjoy as we tour the ship." Zander led them into the lounge and asked a crew member to get the treat for Dobeman. The others looked around the lounge until a dream icicle was brought out and given to Dobeman. Chapatata seemed to know what this frozen treat was because he became very attentive to the Sentinel.

They began their tour of the rest of the ship with Bel'lar and Zander discussing everything without any repeat of their earlier hostility. Ry Sing walked between the two men enjoying this tour even though she was familiar with the ship. Enis and Dobeman followed along behind, with the dog hanging back by Dobeman. Dobeman had unwrapped his icicle and was holding it out in front, allowing it to drip directly onto the deck of the ship. Chapatata tried to lick up the drips, but the ship absorbed them too quickly, leaving no trace. Then the dog caught on and began to hover just under Dobeman's arm. He caught a drip every so often, but more dropped on his head. This amused Enis. In no time, Enis and Dobeman were talking and asking questions, having been put at ease by Zander's easy manner and the dripping frozen treat.

The evening ended with refreshments in the lounge.

✳ ✳ ✳

Ry Sing and Bel'lar crossed the plateau, their destination, the black ship.

"I'm going to be sorry I agreed to this, aren't I?" he said. "You three are up to something."

"Bel'lar, don't worry. This will be fun. They're both very interesting holy men." Ry Sing linked her arm with his and gave him a little squeeze.

They arrived at the black ship and were greeted by the Light Wanderer. "Welcome, Captain Bel'lar and Ry Sing. You may board."

An opening appeared in the side of the ship, and they entered. A female crewmember met them just inside this opening, and they followed her to a smaller lounge, where Kowangii and Ka'aya were waiting for them. A small table had been set up for the four to enjoy a private meal while they talked.

Kowangii and Ka'aya greeted Ry Sing with hugs and Bel'lar with clasped hands.

"Please sit, you two," Kowangii said. "Here on each side of us. Ka'aya, take the seat at the end."

The four sat, and a crewmember brought in a tray with the meal. The meal was a thick, hearty soup, a mixture of squashes with peppers in a variety of colors, green, yellow, red with pink beans and spicy greens. It was accompanied by a round loaf of brown bread. Kowangii tore off a hunk and proceeded to dunk it in his soup. The others followed his example. It was accompanied by a refreshingly cool fruit juice that had been diluted with water, creating the right amount of sweetness.

"Well now, what's this all about?" Bel'lar asked. He looked at each of the others in turn, waiting for someone to explain.

Ry Sing smiled and looked at Kowangii.

Ka'aya looked at Kowangii as well. "Kowangii, why don't you explain?"

"By all means," Kowangii responded. "Bel'lar, we wanted to talk to you about the sleeping pyramid on the plateau."

Bel'lar visibly stiffened. Kowangii put up his hand as he quickly continued, "Please, hear us out, Bel'lar."

Bel'lar stared at him, then gave an almost imperceptible nod. He relaxed a bit.

"We feel it's important to your destiny, and that of mankind, to light the pyramid and thereby bring it into this dimension, where it will be visible. It currently can't be seen because it's in a dormant state. The holy book tells us that this can be remedied by the installation of a capstone."

"Bel'lar," Ry Sing interjected. "The capstone is here on this planet. Kowangii can find it with the help of the holy book. The Light Wanderer is ready to retrieve it for you."

Bel'lar shook his head. "But I don't understand how it got here. Who built it?"

Ka'aya turned to Ry Sing. She nodded.

She pushed her chair back and settled more comfortably into it. "For the truth, I need to go within." She closed her eyes and began to breathe deeply. She turned her focus inward and easily entered a trance state, facilitated by the close proximity of the two holy men. Then she began to speak.

"In the beginning, there was one race of humanoid beings that began the whole great adventure. This one great race of beings known as the God Race was so close to God that they carried the God Energy with them. They created ships of wonder, among them, the Light Wanderer and the Light Traveler. These ships enabled them to embark on a journey to find and identify those planets that could sustain a life force that would captivate and support the humanoids. And once they found these planets, on each one of them they erected a library of the God knowledge of everything. They were built so that the humanoids could, as they advanced on the planet, begin to understand and utilize this knowledge to advance their civilization. These pyramid libraries were set in an alternate dimension to avoid influencing the potential of the humanoids' existence. But yet, when they were civilized enough, the activation would be essential to further their society."

As quickly as she had slipped into trance, she was back, looking at Bel'lar.

"But what about our home planet? The pyramid was disassembled and buried. Why didn't we get that knowledge?" Bel'lar asked.

Ka'aya responded. "The pyramid library was activated, but over the centuries, people were distracted by the home planet's energy, and, for some reason beyond our knowledge, they disassembled it, not realizing what it was for, and lost the God knowledge."

"Look where it got them," Ry Sing said.

"No planet has succeeded, Ry Sing. Not the Planet of Abundance, not our home planet," Bel'lar said, flatly. He looked at all three of these holy people.

"We don't know if they would have succeeded if the library had been available. They need this chance," she argued.

Bel'lar had had enough of this conversation. He stood.

"Why do you persist in this? I've made my wishes plain. I don't want any of you to do this. Nothing good happens to a planet that has a pyramid on it. Maybe the only chance this planet has is if this pyramid remains undiscovered. No . . . No. I won't be a part of this. I won't take responsibility. I have one mission. This isn't it. Now, if you will excuse me." He left the lounge.

Kowangii looked sadly at Ry Sing and Ka'aya. "We had hoped he would listen."

"Indeed," Ka'aya said.

"But scripture says that it's Bel'lar. He must be the one to activate the library," Ry Sing said, looking at the other two for agreement.

Ka'aya looked thoughtful. "Maybe we can work around that. If we get enough holy men, we three and the three from the red planet, we can perform the activation. The pyramid must be brought into this dimension."

"I agree," Ry Sing said. "We must be the ones to do this if he won't. Mankind needs this information." She looked at Kowangii. "How do we proceed?"

Kowangii looked from one to the other and noted their resolve with satisfaction. "We will do this. The holy book will direct us to the location of the crystal from which we will cut the capstone. We have everything we need on board. We are about to make a final trip to distribute the remaining animals. It will be a simple matter to make a detour and collect the crystal. Once we return, the ships will place it, and, if Bel'lar still refuses, we will initiate the infusion of the God knowledge of all-that-is."

"Will Zander be in accordance with this plan?" Ka'aya asked.

Kowangii nodded. "Indeed, he will, as we have already discussed it."

"That's wonderful, then. We're in agreement," said Ry Sing. "Is there anything for dessert?"

"Yes, there is, my dear, and Bel'lar will be sorry he missed it."

* * *

Enis was on his way to the azure gold pyramid. He knew that both Bel'lar and Ry Sing were on the black ship, and this was a perfect opportunity. He had watched Ry Sing from a distance the other day and saw her trace something on the outside of this pyramid. Then the pyramid had opened up to her, and she entered. He felt sure that he could duplicate her actions and gain entrance. He carried his usual bag, large enough for his botany or his ship's cook duties. But today he had other plans than finding fruits and plants.

He reached the pyramid and approached the spot where she had been standing just before she entered. In front of him on the stone were a series of symbols placed two across with six rows and a bar at the bottom. Now, how was it that she had chosen? He looked closely at these symbols and noticed that three were smooth, probably from her hand where she had touched them, brushing off the dust. He considered them for a time and noticed a glow coming from those three. He tilted his head to the side, and it was clearer. Each of the symbols flashed in a sequence. This was clearly an access control, and Ry Sing had left the sequence active. He grinned. He touched the bar, and a grinding noise reached his ears. He stepped back and watched the door slide open. He looked around and then stepped inside.

❋ ❋ ❋

Ry Sing was sitting on the couch in Bel'lar's quarters. He was pacing back and forth in front of her. He was hurt and angry after the meeting on the black ship today.

"Please stop, and sit by me," she said. "I didn't betray you. I would never do that. It's just, you know how I feel about destiny. I was willing to give my life to discover the black race, and, still, it's not completely clear why I needed to find them. But I'm willing to trust that it will become clear in time."

He stopped and looked at her. She could see that he was hurt. "Please, Bel'lar. I'm sorry. Come here."

He sat next to her, and she put her arms around him and hugged. Then she just held him, her cheek against his neck. Slowly, he relaxed and leaned his head back. They sat this way for some time. Then he put his arms around her and kissed her.

"No talking," he whispered as he kissed her again. She responded by tugging him to his feet and leading him to his bed.

❋ ❋ ❋

A few days had turned into five, and the Light Wanderer was still on the plateau. Zander went to meet with Bel'lar. The two walked slowly away from the Light Traveler, gazing out over the plateau as they talked. Neither was comfortable with each other.

"Bel'lar, it's time for us to go about our mission to distribute the animals. This will be only a short trip. Then we return home to re-provision, and we're off to bring another group of animals to new homes. You're welcome to join us on this last trip."

"I appreciate that, but I'll remain here. Dobeman has completed his studies, and I need to review the information and check out locations. Dobeman has identified an ideal location at the crossing of two rivers in a fertile valley some distance from here."

"I understand. Some of your crew wishes to go with us, and I thought I would ask for them."

"Take them all if you want. They're spending all their time with you and your crew anyway," Bel'lar responded, his voice tinged with irritation.

Zander smiled. "Then you won't mind."

"I didn't say that, but I expected it," Bel'lar said. "Who are they?"

"Ka'aya and Dobeman have expressed interest."

Bel'lar sensed that those two weren't all who wanted to make this trip, but he waited. "And . . . ?"

Zander glanced at him. "Ry Sing expressed interest, but she was going to talk to you personally about this."

"All right, I'll talk to her. But as for Ka'aya and Dobeman," he said, "their work is done. Mauleen and I have the next stage, preparing the final report."

Ry Sing came into view, waving at them. She was coming from the Asian pyramid. "There she is now," Bel'lar said, waving at her.

"Our ships can communicate with each other. I can return within a few hours if you need me," Zander replied.

"I'll see you when you get back."

The two men nodded to each other, and then Zander walked away. He stopped to greet Ry Sing. Bel'lar watched as he hugged her, giving her a kiss on the cheek. Zander turned once and watched her reach Bel'lar. Then he continued on to his ship.

When Ry Sing reached Bel'lar, he burst out, "Why must he kiss you every time he sees you?"

She stood, staring up at him. "Are you through complaining?"

He looked down at her. "You don't want to go on this trip with them, do you?"

"I do."

"I don't like you being on the same ship with him."

"Stop being silly. This is a great chance for me to work with the animals before we return to the home planet. And there's something about Char that I must discover. This trip will give me the time to do that."

They held hands, walking back to the ship.

"I wish that my work here was done and we could depart for home now, but it's not. So how can I not support you in the adventure you're about to have? I'll miss you for the time you're apart from me." He pulled her to him, kissing her.

"I'm so glad. I'll miss you, too. I believe you're starting to understand me. It's my mission to keep you in the dark, wondering who I really am." She smiled up at him.

He squeezed her tighter. "Truer words . . ."

She put her finger to his lips. He kissed her again.

* * *

The Light Wanderer left the following morning with Ka'aya, Ry Sing, and Dobeman on board. Dobeman had already stopped in the lounge and picked up a dream icicle for observation. He joined the rest in the large meeting room where a map filled the crystal display on one wall, the locations for releasing the animals marked on it. Zander had called a meeting to discuss the journey. The guests were attending along with Char, Kowangii, and several of Zander's officers. Dobeman found a seat, and Chapatata came up behind him. The dog watched Dobeman with intensity, silently waiting while the Sentinel unwrapped the icicle. Dobeman held it out to drip onto the floor when suddenly he felt a jerk and heard a snap. He turned in time to see Chapatata run off with the dream icicle in his mouth.

"You can only tease the dog so long, and then he gets even, Dobeman. He won't just watch it drip." Zander laughed. He was the only one to see the dog steal the icicle, and he couldn't blame him. "Now that we have had that nice little break, let's get back to the map."

After several hours of discussion, it was decided they would go to the east and release the big cats first. The white ones would be released in a mountainous area where the climate was colder. Then they would release the tigers in a rainforest area. Once the cats were released, they would move on to the west to the next continent and release the buffalo. Finally, they would return to this continent.

Zander gave his officers their orders and adjourned the meeting. He turned back to the three from the Light Traveler. "We should arrive at the mountainous area in a few hours. Our crew will begin building a shelter for the cats over the next few days, after we have determined where to build it. You're free to amuse yourselves, and, of course, Ry Sing, you know this already. Char, will you see that they're comfortable? The midday meal will be served in one hour, and you're welcome at my table if you choose. You must excuse me now. I need to consult with my building staff and make sure the cats are ready. Ry Sing, if you would like to work with the cats today, that would be wonderful. They sense something is happening. I'd like it if you would be available when we release the cats into the environment." Zander smiled at everyone and left.

In the middle of the afternoon, the ship arrived at the area where the white cats would start their new lives. A small expeditionary force, along with the habitat specialist, Gorn, a shorter, wiry man with close-cropped curly hair, went out to determine where the shelter should be built.

Over the next two days, a shelter was built. Located in a copse of trees with a rocky backdrop, the cats would be protected from the wind and snow. This family of white cats, a male and female with three kits, were in full winter coat and should have no trouble with the cold. The enclosures on the ship had provided the temperature that would cause the cats to grow winter coats.

Ry Sing and Zander visited the cats. They were going to be released today. The white female came up to the clear divider and put up her paw to thank them. First Ry Sing placed her hand there, and then she asked Zander to come close. "She wants to thank you, Zander. She knows you're responsible. Put your hand here, on the other side of her paw."

He knelt and put up his hand to the female's paw. A flood of emotions flowed from her through his hand into his body. He felt her excitement and her gratitude for saving them and bringing them here. He shared his happiness with her, and then she removed her paw. He stood up and turned to Ry Sing, a big smile on his face. "They're ready to see their new home. Let's take them out."

The big cats lay down with the kits between their paws. The clear enclosure rose up and floated above the floor, held in place by two remote control devices. The cats looked around calmly, and the kits stood up as they floated down out of the ship; they were guided towards the shelter built by the crew. Everyone walked alongside, with Gorn leading the way. They were suited up in warm, thermal clothing.

Snow lay on the ground, and the trees were bare. No wind disturbed the calm. Yet winter was beginning to lose its grip here, and soon green would start to shoot up through the snow. Already patches of ground were visible.

Ry Sing was exhilarated by the cold, and wished Bel'lar was here to experience it with her. It was beautiful and forbidding at the same time. The mountain range rose into the air, blanketed in snow. Clouds flitted across the sky. Underneath it all, new life was sprouting. She was looking forward to seeing the cats explore their new home.

When they arrived at the shelter, four crewmembers and Gorn moved forward with the cats, while the others stayed back, out of the way. The enclosure was lowered slowly to the ground. Once they were happy with the location, they retired to a safe distance to observe. The adult cats watched motionless as the panel started to rise, waiting until it was all the way up. Then they walked sedately out into the beautiful day. Their heads were up, their noses tasted the air, and their ears were twitching as they listened to the sounds of their new home. The kits followed, wanting to run, but the parents gave them the eye to stay behind until it was safe. The cats sniffed the shelter, and then the female crawled in. The male directed the kits in after her, and then he crawled in. After a short time, they crawled out. The kits began to explore, dancing and playing as they went.

Gorn walked up to Zander. "I'm satisfied. The cats have approved the shelter. I will stay for the rest of the afternoon. Others will join me throughout the night, taking shifts to watch and make sure they are adjusting. I'll report to you daily with their progress."

"Thank you, Gorn. Well done. I'll see you tomorrow morning for the first report."

* * *

They had been monitoring the cats for two weeks now, and during this time the crew had time to spend in their own pursuits. One day, Kowangii went in search of Dobeman.

He found him in the late afternoon. The Sentinel was out in the surrounding countryside, sitting on a rock, watching the clouds form these great shapes in the late afternoon skies. He was dressed in his usual cape and seemed unaffected by the cold. He was fascinated by the hues of color that could be seen only when the sun reached certain angles in relationship to the land. Dobeman heard footsteps and turned. He saw Kowangii walking toward him.

Kowangii was bundled up in a thermal robe and was stepping in the same spots where Dobeman had walked to get there. Using his walking stick for balance, he had one hand on his robe holding it up out of the snow. As he got closer to Dobeman, he called out. "There you are. We have been searching for you for some time. Then we decided to find you through simple deduction. We closed our eyes and picked the spot that we thought you would not be at, and here you are."

Dobeman could see the big grin on Kowangii's face.

"I always try to do what I think I should not," Dobeman explained. "Then I realize it was what I was supposed to do. So I'm literally back-stepping through my life."

"Yes, trying to discover your past, your beginnings," Kowangii said, "For who are you Dobeman, this magnificent being? Who created you?"

Dobeman responded, "That is a very good question. For the longest time I've wondered if I was the only one of my kind left. All my life I have been searching for the answer. And wondering what will happen to the knowledge I have gathered. Please sit down, Kowangii. I believe you have something to tell me."

Kowangii sat next to Dobeman on the cold rock and said, "We would like to read you something from this book." He pulled out the tattered old book covered in leopard-skin cloth and opened it. He scanned down the page with his finger. "Here it is."

He cleared his throat. "As I am, and as I could be, and as I will be, I can see the future. The future is for me to create the perfect humanoid. This race will all be similar in color and not restricted by the emotions carried in my species. It will have the intelligence quotient of ten to the power of mine. The body will be sustained on minimum resources and will live three times my species' longevity. These beings that I create will move out through the universe and gather knowledge and wisdom and will indeed be the gods of the future." Kowangii looked up from the book and said, "That's all there is in the book that refers to your race."

"I already know most of what you have told me," Dobeman said. "But you have not told me what I seek."

Kowangii put his hand upon Dobeman's knee. "Yes, my son, and now we will tell you what we feel. We feel that, eons ago, in a distant part of the universe, beings such as you were created to be the caretakers of the human beings. You contain all the wisdom and knowledge and none of the animal instincts that we carry and many of this species carries to the detriment of us. It is through these emotions much violence is manifested. Through these emotions much inequality and hurt is accomplished. So, as you go through your life, realize that the mission is to be the non-involved being, the one with focus, direction and purpose—the one that can see through the clouds in the sky and realize the sun always shines upon those that know it is there."

Dobeman put his hand on top of Kowangii's where it rested on his knee. "I do feel emotions because now I feel the emotion of truth coming from you. It does not cloud my thoughts but clarifies them, and I know who you are."

Kowangii said, "And that is the key to your existence. To see clearly what species like mine cannot. To help the humanoids understand themselves. It is as if your mission was to be the god creature that inhabits this universe without the burden of the rest of humanity. So if you come back with us to our planet, you will meet others like yourself who hold great positions in our society. Positions of knowledge and wisdom. But right now, it's freezing out here. We're going back to the ship. Will you walk with us?"

"Thank you, but no. You have opened up much expansion in my knowledge. I will now contemplate your words."

"Very well, Dobeman. We're going to have something warm to drink. We will see you inside." He walked away, leaving Dobeman silhouetted against the sky in its deepest, most colorful hues yet.

✳ ✳ ✳

At the morning meeting, Gorn reported that the white cats of Orion were adapting very well, beginning to eat mostly what they brought in on their own. They seemed to be having no trouble with the weather, and the snowstorm of three days ago appeared to have invigorated them. "I recommend we move on to place the tigers. We will make return trips to monitor the cats every few days." Gorn completed his report and looked at Zander.

"I agree, Gorn. We will move the ship later this morning to the next location." Zander pressed the intercom and requested the crew make ready to move to the next location.

✳ ✳ ✳

Back on the plateau, Bel'lar left the ship as the sun was coming up. The small transport was waiting outside. He had just finished talking with Ry Sing. She had been gone with the Light Wanderer for one moon cycle. He was looking forward to her return. He had talked to her many times, but it was not the same as spending time with her. Soon she would be back. Then they could all go home.

* * *

The Light Wanderer was on the continent to the west where the buffalo were released some weeks ago. The buffalo were doing well, and it was the appropriate moment to find and collect the capstone for the dormant pyramid and then return to the plateau. The ship journeyed to the southernmost tip of this blue-white planet, into the ice and snow to cut the capstone. They arrived on this cold, frigid continent in the early evening. It was decided to locate and cut the capstone the next day.

They were here because Kowangii had read from *The Book of Knowledge of the Sacred Ecology Religion*. There was a symbolic axis point of the planet in the northern and southern hemispheres. This was where all the energies of the planet collected into a stream and projected themselves up through the central core of the planet. At this confluence, between the light energy of the atmosphere and the dense energy of the planet, a clear blue crystal shaft grew up out of the earth. It was of sufficient size that a piece large enough to form a capstone for the pyramid could be fashioned. Once cut and placed on the pyramid, it would become the greatest focal point on the planet.

Zander was already on the bridge when their guests arrived. Ka'aya, Dobeman, and Ry Sing had been invited to observe the cutting of the capstone. Zander waved at them as they took seats out of the way of his crew. The main crystal display was on. They could see the ice extended as far as the eye could see. The ship's sensors registered a hit. They had found what they were looking for, the axis of the planet. Submerged in ice and snow, they would have to clear space around it to see where to cut. Zander directed the ship to move closer to the axis to shorten the distance his crew would have to travel outside.

"The axis is ten meters ahead, Captain Zander. You may proceed," the ship informed him.

"Thank you," Zander responded. Then he activated the intercom. "We are ten meters from the axis. You may proceed to collect it."

"Very well, Captain Zander," answered the leader of the team waiting to disembark. Suited up in frigid-weather clothing, they exited through the large hatch one level down from the animal deck.

From the bridge, they watched the five-man team move through the snow carrying two small, remote-controlled tugs. The man in the lead was using a hand scanner to locate the axis. When he found it, he motioned the two men behind him to come forward. Using headsets that channeled their thoughts, they directed the tugs to blow the snow off the axis and then began to cut the ice away from it. After a short time, the blue crystal of the axis appeared, protruding from the ground like a huge, gleaming spear. Using the dimensions that Kowangii supplied, they made the cut. Carefully, they righted it, and, there, shining through the ice, was a blue crystal pyramid. They used the tugs to levitate it and carefully returned to the ship. It was placed in storage, on the deck below the animal deck.

Zander turned to Ka'aya, Dobeman, and Ry Sing. "My first officer will escort you to where the capstone is being stored now, if you wish to see it."

"Oh yes, we want to see it. It's beautiful," Ry Sing answered as she stood up.

Ka'aya agreed. "Thank you, Zander." He got up, followed by Dobeman. The first officer led them off the bridge as Zander directed the ship to take them to the next location to release the last group of animals.

✳ ✳ ✳

Ry Sing had been avoiding Char, and Char had been avoiding her for the last two moon cycles. They had managed to be polite but distant when they met, nothing more. Char had remained in the background when Ry Sing visited the animals with Zander each day.

The compulsion to touch Char hadn't decreased. If anything, it had increased. Ry Sing was drawn and repelled at the same time to Char, who now seemed more afraid of her than before. She knew the other woman was feeling what she felt. It only remained to decide what to do because something must be decided. Ry Sing had been meditating on this over the last few days. It was time to resolve this mutual love/hate attraction they had. This ship would soon return to the plateau, and the opportunity would be lost. It had to be now.

Ry Sing wandered around the ship, seeking Char without success. Finally, she met Char in the corridor leading from the main lounge. "Char, could we talk? I really think we need to."

Char just looked at her for a long moment. Then, she glanced down and sniffed. When she looked back at Ry Sing, her green eyes, so mysteriously identical to Ry Sing's, were full of tears. Ry Sing took Char's hand. There was a shock; both women jerked, but they didn't release their hold. Then it seemed as if Char's hand melted into Ry Sing's and Ry Sing's into Char's. They both watched their hands phasing in and out. Then looked at each other and smiled slowly.

"Come, Ry Sing. I know where we can talk."

The two women walked hand in hand down the corridor, Char leading the way. The corridor was deserted, and no one noticed them enter a meditation garden, one specifically provided for the holy man, Kowangii. It seemed empty when they stepped inside. Immediately a sense of peace pervaded the atmosphere, and both women were at ease. Char led Ry Sing down a pathway to a bench that was placed in front of a pool surrounded by plants with water trickling into it. This was just one of several meditation benches arranged throughout this garden, none visible from the others because of the vegetation.

Light sparkled on the water, drawing their eyes. They sat in silence, hands still touching, for some time. They were very much alike, these two young women, with their identical green eyes, their bodies the same height and size. Yet, the colors of their clothing were complete opposites. Ry Sing was dressed in her usual tunic and pants, today a soft blue-and-green design. Char wore a dress patterned in bright reds and yellows.

* * *

Unknown to the two women, Zander was a short distance away. He had entered the garden earlier and was deep in thought. A noise brought him out of his reverie, and he walked softly, since, at first, he didn't realize who they were; his intention was to leave quietly without disrupting them. But when he recognized them, he remained hidden, unable to stop from watching.

* * *

Char broke the silence, her voice soft, but Ry Sing didn't have any trouble hearing her. "I have been afraid that if I touched you, you would absorb me, and I would cease to exist. Never before in my life have I dematerialized as I did that first time I met you. I didn't understand how this could be. But watching our hands I see that we're part of each other—that we are each other. And I understand that I won't be absorbed if I don't wish it. But I see your mission, your destiny; in fact, I can see all of you, and I want to be part of it—something I can't do if I remain separate from you."

Ry Sing listened with awe and amazement to the young woman's words. Her physical connection only intensified her spiritual connection as she felt the answer to this situation and knew it to be right. She wasn't sure that she could release Char's hand now that she had touched her. The bond was strong and increasing. No longer was the dark color of Char's hand visible. Only Ry Sing's hand could be seen.

Ry Sing turned to face Char and put out her other hand. Char met her eyes, and they gazed into each other's soul and discovered—it was the same soul. They had been separate for the space of this life thus far. And the desire to be reunited, to come home, permeated their beings. With tremulous smiles, tears again brightening both their eyes, Char extended her hand to Ry Sing. Then she said one word. "Yes."

※ ※ ※

Zander listened, not comprehending what was happening. He saw their hands blending into each other's, heard Char agreeing to something, and he wanted to shout, *No! Stop!* but he kept silent.

※ ※ ※

The two women's hands met, clasped with a great shock. The circle of energy was complete. Their energy swirled and surged through each other, sparks shooting off what became a whirlwind of energy that completely encompassed them as they sat on this bench. Everything around them continued: the water trickled into the little pool, sparkling with bits of light, seemingly unaware of the momentous creation that was happening in this beautiful place; unaware of two halves of the same soul coming together.

The whirlwind of energy slowed and then ceased. And sitting on the bench was only one woman. Ry Sing. Char was no longer a separate being. She had been completely absorbed. She had come home and was now reunited and one with Ry Sing.

Ry Sing sat in silence enveloped in a sense of unconditional love, the presence of Char very real and substantial inside of her. This love seemed to pour out of everywhere, and Ry Sing felt complete. For the first time in this life, she was complete. She smiled, and tears of joy flowed down her cheeks.

Kowangii entered the meditation garden and discovered Ry Sing sitting on the bench, still caught up in the wonder of reunion. The energy was palpable, and he sensed it, knowing something sacred and holy had just occurred here. He stood before her, waiting for her to speak.

"Dear old man, you're so like Ka'aya to arrive at just the perfect moment. I'm not sure that I can explain what just happened, but I'll try. Char and I have discovered that we are two halves of the same soul. And we have reunited in one being." She brushed at her face, wiping away tears.

Then her happiness changed to confusion and fear. She looked up at the old man, who gazed at her with tenderness. "What have we done? Did I kill Char? It felt so right but . . . help me." Suddenly, she was exhausted.

Kowangii put his hands on her head in benediction. "You didn't kill Char. You have found the part of yourself that waited for you in her. You are now whole. You are now the holy princess Ry Sing Su Tong. You will remember this day because you are the beginning. You will go to this planet where the beginning occurred and bring forth the knowledge, wisdom, and understanding that, without the spirit, the wisdom is lost.

You will attempt to combine these wisdoms here, back on this blue-white planet." He leaned down and kissed her on the top of her head. As he did so, there was a flash of reds and yellows; it was Char accepting the kiss. Then, a shift, and it was Ry Sing who looked up at Kowangii.

* * *

Zander watched all of this with horror and grief. What had happened to his dear Char? He recognized the flash of color, and, for one second, she was there, then gone.

* * *

"Rise, my dear, and go forth. Your life awaits you." Kowangii smiled and she smiled in return.

Her arms hung limply at her sides. She wanted to lie down on the bench and sleep. "I don't know if I can, just yet."

"You must tell Zander."

"Oh, no." Ry Sing felt the love Char had for Zander wash over her and saw memories of their time together. Bel'lar and Zander. This was going to be complicated.

"He loves Char and will miss her when you return to the Light Traveler."

Zander interrupted them. "What have you done to her? Where is she?" He demanded.

"She's here, inside me," she tried to explain.

He grabbed her arm, shook her. "Answer me."

Kowangii lifted his walking stick and rapped Zander on the shoulder. "What are you doing? Let her be."

Zander stepped back, letting her go. He understood only one thing. He had watched Char disappear. His eyes were wild as he looked from one to the other. Then he turned and stormed out of the garden.

Tears burned in Ry Sing's eyes.

"Come, my dear." Kowangii helped her to her feet and left the garden, with her leaning heavily on his arm. As they walked, every few steps, she phased back and forth from Char to herself. It would be a while before she would be in complete balance and in control of this phasing back and forth.

* * *

Zander didn't eat dinner in the lounge with the others that evening. Ry Sing ate with Kowangii and Ka'aya. Then Dobeman joined them and mentioned that he had passed Zander on his way in. The Captain had been on his way off the ship. The Light Wanderer had landed on the same continent as the Light Traveler but in the southern portion. He was somewhere outside.

Ry Sing excused herself and went in search of him. She knew this meeting wouldn't be easy. She felt the strength of Char's love for Zander. She already knew how he felt. But she had to talk to him. Char had hopes that he would accept her choice and not grieve too much.

She left the ship and walked for a bit. The sun was setting and soon it would be dark. She didn't think he would have gone far since tomorrow they were returning to the plateau. She decided to wait by the ship. She sat on the ground near the entrance to the ship and waited. She closed her eyes and relaxed. The sun set, and twilight suffused the land. Then she heard soft steps and opened her eyes. Zander stood before her.

She held out her hand, and he helped her to her feet. They stood facing each other in the half-light.

"I saw it all," he said. "What has happened to Char? Does she still live?"

"Char's not dead, Zander. She still lives inside me. She was able to accomplish her dream today of becoming me, and I will carry her essence with me for my remaining days in this body. She and I are one now. She will truly be me as we continue with our life. It's an amazing accomplishment, and you should honor her for it. It's comforting to have her essence inside me because it awakens me to my memories of all of you and the black race." Ry Sing put her hand on Zander's cheek, and her essence shifted; it was Char looking up at him. His breath caught in his throat as she continued speaking in Char's voice, "I still love you, Zander."

Relief showed on his face as he embraced her. "Stay with me, and return home to our world," he said.

Char returned his embrace and then stepped back. "I can't."

"But if you're truly Char, then you will." He wouldn't let go of her hands.

Once again it was Ry Sing who answered, now in her own voice. "I'm much more than Char. I am the Ry Sing Su Tong. I have been seeking my past, and Char is a part of that. Most human beings will seek out other human beings to try to attach to them. I've moved beyond that. I'm physically two parts in one human being." Her essence wavered, phasing in and out between her physical appearance and Char's.

"I don't care about any of that. I want Char back. I don't want to spend my life without you. Change back. Be Char again." He tightened his hold on her hands.

"I'm so sorry, Zander," she said with infinite compassion in her eyes. "I can no longer be with you in this life—not in that way. My destiny calls me to other paths. But there will always be future lives to be with you again."

He shook his head in disbelief. "How could you do this without talking to me first? How could Char leave me? I don't understand any of this. Isn't there some way to reverse what you've done?"

"There is only forward, no going back. I have much to accomplish in this life, and now Char and I will do it together."

He stared at her, anguish in his eyes. She embraced him, holding him close, her cheek on his heart. Then she released him and went inside the ship. He remained standing there for a long time, filled with deep, wrenching sadness. He had just lost his love, and it was too late to do anything about it. *Damn those holy men and their scriptures. Why couldn't they leave well enough alone?*

* * *

The final release of the animals had been completed. Zander and his crew were satisfied that the animals were adapting well, and the chances of survival were excellent. It was time to return to the plateau and deliver the capstone. Captain Zander announced over the intercom, "We have onboard the blue capstone for the white race's pyramid. All the animals have been placed in their habitats, and I believe most will flourish. Our mission, now, is complete. We will return to the plateau. Prepare to leave this area in one hour."

The Light Wanderer reached the plateau while the sun was peeking over the horizon and took up a position above the invisible pyramid. The plateau was still as the ship hovered. A beam of light shot out of the black ship and connected to its little sister ship below on the ground. The two ships were in conversation while the beings inside waited. Then the beam of energy connecting the two ships intensified, expanding, and in that beam, the capstone materialized near to the black ship. Supported within that beam by the two ships, the capstone began its descent to the top of the invisible pyramid, where it settled quietly into place. Glowing in the rising sun, it remained visible, perched atop an invisible pyramid. The ships had completed their task. The pyramid was ready and waiting to be infused with light—ready and waiting for its awakening.

On board, the Light Traveler announced the arrival of the black ship. Unaware of the placing of the capstone, Bel'lar made his way quickly to the exit.

The black ship landed near the smaller ship, and people spilled out of both of them. Ry Sing ran up to Bel'lar just as he exited the ship. Every part of her being exuded excitement.

Throwing her arms around him, she said "We set the capstone."

"What?" Bel'lar said. He felt as if he had been kicked in the stomach.

"We set the capstone," she said again. She felt him stiffen. He disengaged from her embrace and stepped back.

He looked up at the capstone that appeared to be floating in the air. He sucked in a breath. He couldn't believe what he was seeing. Now clearly discernible was a platform jutting from the still unseen pyramid about six meters above the plateau. But what took his breath away was the appearance of the Device at the forefront of the platform. In size and shape it was the same as the one the Great One used to destroy the Planet of Abundance. Yet he could see that no rod protruded from this one. Instead it was pushed into the Device.

"What have you done?" he said. His birthmark began to burn and itch. He was scratching it before he realized.

"Now mankind can begin to live again on this planet," she said.

Ka'aya and Kowangii joined Ry Sing and Bel'lar. Bel'lar glared at them. This was a conspiracy to force him to do what he didn't want to do. He was having none of it.

Both holy men simply looked at him without speaking.

Then Ka'aya said, "You have to do this. It is your destiny."

Bel'lar shook his head. "No."

Kowangii echoed Ka'aya. "It is your destiny."

Bel'lar looked at the two old ones standing in front of him. "I'm not a holy man. I don't have the authority. I renounced that way of life long ago." He was rubbing his chest hard; the mark was driving him crazy. Now he was well and truly incensed. And afraid.

Ry Sing stepped between the two holy men and faced Bel'lar. "You can't do that," she said. "You have and possess certain inalienable rights that you cannot deny. Make up for the transgressions of your past lives and infuse this pyramid so that life can begin anew here."

Bel'lar was distraught. "How many times do I have to do this?" he demanded.

Ka'aya smiled. "Enough times until humanity can get it right, my son."

"Will this free me of my obligations?"

Ka'aya looked at Kowangii; then both looked to Ry Sing, waiting for her to speak.

"For a time, this will free you from your obligation, but it's really not your destiny to control the events of the future but merely to be a player in them," she answered. She felt compassion for Bel'lar, but he needed to accept and face his past lives. They couldn't wait any longer for him.

Bel'lar looked at all of them in turn, searching their faces. He saw compassion and love but also strength and determination. He looked up at the platform again. Energy was coalescing above it, swirling, shifting.

Ka'aya noticed it and said, "Those are the ancient holy men, your brothers. They await you."

"Not in this lifetime," Bel'lar said. "If I awaken this pyramid, I will just have to come back in a future life and destroy what I've started. I will not. I cannot do this. I'm still living with the memory of the Planet of Abundance."

Ry Sing said, "Then we shall be your surrogate. We will invoke all the powers that are needed. And we will take complete responsibility for the awakening of this new civilization with the hope that this time they will get it right."

Bel'lar stared at her. "Do what you have to. I don't care. I'm not involved. I'm merely the Captain of this ship, and that's all I want to be," he said. He strode inside his ship.

All eyes turned to the energy movement on the platform above. And as they watched, the energy thickened like fog and then began to drift into shapes—three forms in silhouette that revealed themselves as the spirits of the three holy men from the red planet. Gathering the energy about them, they extended their arms toward the ones on the ground, sending this energy down, where it surrounded Ry Sing, Ka'aya, and Kowangii. The three ancients raised their arms to heaven and drew this energy up, raising the three to the platform.

Down below, the two crews were in awe of this astounding delivery of the three holy ones to the platform.

The spirits of the three ancient holy men waited with their arms lifted to the heavens as Ry Sing went immediately to the Device. Ka'aya and Kowangii stood on either side of her, the three ancients towering over them.

The holy men's spirits released their energy questing into the sky, and clouds began to form and swirl. The swirling clouds dropped lower and circulated around the sleeping pyramid. Then the clouds ignited with millions of sparkling singularities pouring from the sky.

✳ ✳ ✳

Bel'lar watched from inside the ship; his birthmark seemed to burn through his uniform, and his stomach clenched tightly. The main display on the bridge was activated, and he had a clear view of everything. He was amazed at the sight of Ry Sing and the two holy men lifted to the platform. But he knew that they were setting into motion something that, no matter how hard he tried to avoid it, he would have to face at some point in the future of his existence. He didn't know if he could survive that event. He wished he could hate them for what they were doing, but it wasn't possible, so great was the affection he had for those three on the platform.

* * *

Ry Sing watched the singularities surging faster and faster. "Are these the souls that will inhabit this planet?"

"Yes, my dear," Ka'aya answered. "These are the souls from all the planets that ever existed, the souls that never die. These are the souls that will create the opportunities forever and ever."

"Amen," Kowangii said.

Singularities swirled around her, sparkling on her hands, her hair. She felt their encouragement. They wanted her to initiate this new beginning.

"They want the opportunity to be here, so how can we deprive them of such an auspicious and fertile event?" she said.

She wrapped her hands around the bar and pulled. It resisted her. She braced her feet and continued to pull. It felt as if it had been in that position a very long time. She looked at the two holy men on either side of her. They stepped up to assist. Placing their hands on the bar also, they added their strength to hers and pulled. Still it resisted them. Then the ancient ones floated forward and placed their transparent hands over the three in physical form. Ry Sing felt the unlimited surge of strength as it focused into a massive wrench of the bar. It broke free, and they pulled it into the upright position, all three staggering back with the force of the upward thrust; the ancient ones merely floated back.

In response to the Device, the energy stream of singularities narrowed into a lightning bolt that shot up into the sky and then dived for the capstone. In that instant, everyone's eyes followed the lightning bolt as it struck the blue crystal capstone with great force, suffusing the sky with a brilliance of white light energy. The capstone glowed white hot.

The ones down below shaded their eyes.

It seemed the top would blow off, but it lasted only fifteen seconds. Then a single tone sounded, clear and sharp. And the capstone shed its energy down the sides. As the energy of singularities descended, the pyramid entered this reality, one section at a time, as if it were being built from the capstone down, right there in front of their eyes, until finally the entire pyramid was revealed. A river of white-hot light cascaded down the sides. The pyramid glowed in many different colors of the rainbow. It shimmered, and then another tone was emitted, loud, clear, and unmistakable.

The two crews held their breath as they watched in fascination and awe.

The surface of the pyramid liquefied, a river of knowledge flowing down from the point of light of God. It flowed down and out from the pyramid, encompassing the surrounding area with a breeze that touched everyone, bathing them in the God energy. It created a state of utter bliss in all those who experienced it. Then the singularities melted into the pyramid until none remained outside.

The three ancient ones bowed to Ry Sing and the two holy men. Then they turned and walked into the pyramid, where they would take up their post to be available to this new planet and its inhabitants.

Then, as it began, it ended.

Ry Sing, Ka'aya, and Kowangii found themselves standing on the plateau among the members of both crews.

Those who witnessed this event would always remember this day; it was one of the greatest events that mankind had ever beheld.

The two old men were laughing now, gazing upon this wondrous structure, fully realized in this reality. Ka'aya turned to Kowangii. "This must be the greatest planet ever, for the sheer size and brilliance of this pyramid shall guide and direct mankind into infinite possibilities."

Kowangii gazed upon the pyramid as he said, "Behold, this is the beginning of mankind upon the beautiful blue-white planet. It shall be as it has been written, and will extend as long as it is needed, to provide mankind with opportunities. This pyramid shall ever hold this infusion of knowledge and as long as it's intact, this wisdom will be available to the future generations that wish to understand."

"It is of understanding," Ry Sing said. The three holy men bowed to each other.

Zander approached Ry Sing as the two crews split up and returned to their respective ships.

Pulling her aside, he held both of her hands. "I want to talk with you. Would you eat with me and we can talk?"

She looked up into his eyes and saw the longing, the earnest need to talk to her. She couldn't be cruel to this man who was suffering. She felt she owed it to Char to listen to him. She nodded, and they went into the black ship.

He led her to the private room where she had taken Bel'lar to meet with Kowangii and Ka'aya. The table was set up for a meal, but no food had been brought in yet. They sat down at one end of the table. He leaned forward and held her hand again. His eyes were sad when he looked at her. She waited.

＊　＊　＊

On the Light Traveler, the crew was coming in when Bel'lar noticed that Ry Sing wasn't there. He asked where she was.

Enis spoke up. "I saw her go aboard the Light Wanderer with Zander."

Bel'lar was furious. He stormed out. First he had worried about Ka'aya and Ry Sing. Now he had to worry about Zander and her. It was too much. He was going to bring her back, by force, if necessary. He ran the short distance and entered the black ship, and no one stopped him. They knew who he was and merely nodded to him as he passed by. Not sure where to go, he asked the ship. Light Wanderer told him he would find Zander in the small room he had visited before when he met with Ka'aya and Kowangii. He hurried toward that room.

＊　＊　＊

"I can't accept that Char is gone," Zander said. Ry Sing was about to speak; he held up his hand. "I know what you've said. I don't care. My Char is inside you. Come back with me to my home planet. We can be together. Our lives will be devoted to the animals. I can see how you love them. It will be a wonderful life."

Now Ry Sing was sad. She couldn't give this man what he yearned for, desired. She squeezed his hand in preparation for her answer. He misread her feelings and pulled her into his arms and kissed her. Unprepared for the surge of emotions from Char, Ry Sing responded, kissing him back.

The door opened and Bel'lar burst in. Seeing the two together, "What the hell are you doing?" he shouted.

The two sprang apart and faced Bel'lar. Ry Sing looked shocked. Zander was furious. He stepped in front of her as Bel'lar advanced.

"Ry Sing, get over here. It's time to leave," Bel'lar said.

Zander blocked him from reaching her. Still shocked she just stood there, watching these two.

All reason fled from Bel'lar's mind as he rushed Zander. He had to get her away from him.

They grappled with each other, Bel'lar trying to get past him to Ry Sing.

Ry Sing's shock drained away to be replaced by fury. What was wrong with them? How dare Bel'lar order her around? She grabbed up two plates from the table and bashed them over the two men's heads. Dazed, they broke apart and turned to look at her.

"You're both idiots. Bel'lar, you can't order me around. And Zander. I'm sorry, but I have to return to the home planet."

Bel'lar made a move toward her. "Keep away, Bel'lar." She left the room.

The two men glared at each other. Then Bel'lar left the ship.

✳ ✳ ✳

Bel'lar joined the others for the evening meal on the Light Traveler. Ry Sing didn't attend. Bel'lar was quiet, and no one was pressing him to talk.

When they were finished eating, Ka'aya cleared his throat, and everyone turned to him. "Bel'lar, we have had some time to plan our futures since we arrived on this blue-white planet, and some of us have decided not to return to the home planet. Zander has invited us to join them on their journey back to their world, and Dobeman and I wish to go with them. We feel our destinies lie in another direction." He paused to allow this to sink in. "How do you feel about this change in plans?"

Bel'lar looked into his surrogate father's eyes as he considered. "Well, Ka'aya. I always thought you would be returning with us. It saddens me that this is the last I will see you." They gazed at each other, Ka'aya freely showing his grief at leaving this man he considered a son. Bel'lar was more guarded, but Ka'aya could see the unhappiness he felt. Then Bel'lar turned to the Sentinel. "You will find your people, if you go to the home world of the black race. I understand your desire to go. And, of course, I'm pleased that Ry Sing is going home with me, as well as Mauleen and Enis. Together we can find a way to deliver the information to the Brotherhood of Syn and assemble those who will make the journey back here."

He nodded to them. "I'll miss you both, and I wish you success in your search. And Dobeman, don't forget to take the rest of the fudge icicles so you can have variety."

✳  ✳  ✳

Bel'lar left the lounge, surprised at how melancholy he felt after hearing that Ka'aya wasn't coming home with them. Here he'd been wishing that Ka'aya wouldn't be around to distract Ry Sing, but now he was sorry he wouldn't be. He realized how much he counted on the old man to provide the balance that Bel'lar had difficulty achieving. But he had to be honest with himself. Ka'aya was more his father than his birth father had been, and it hurt to say goodbye to him.

Outside Ry Sing's door, he shook off the feelings and focused on what he would say to her. Then he decided that he was just going to say what he felt. Put it all out there.

He took a deep breath and tapped on her door. She didn't answer. He knew she was ignoring him. He tapped again, louder. Then he called out, "Ry Sing, open the door. We need to talk. I won't leave until you talk to me." He continued to wait. He had no intention of leaving. Then the door slid open. He looked inside but didn't see her. The light level in her quarters was very low. He stepped in and, looking around, finally located her. She was sitting on the floor near the wall that was covered with vines. He reached her and sat on the floor facing her. Now he could see that her eyes were red and swollen. She had been crying. He tried to hold her hand, but she pulled away.

He sat in silence, thinking. He wanted to yell at her, but he knew that wouldn't get him anywhere. He took a deep breath and said, "You make me crazy. Why were you kissing him? Don't you want to be with me anymore?"

She looked at him, seeing his hands clench as he tried to be calm. "He was kissing me. This is all so confusing, Bel'lar. I'm not sure I can explain. But Zander feels very connected to me because I can speak to the animals. Kowangii recognized me as part of a prophecy in their holy books, and this has confused him. If you hadn't interrupted, I would have told him I was going back with you. I've never wavered in my love for you. Why can't you trust me?"

Bel'lar hung his head in embarrassment.

"Were you really going to drag me out of there? I can't believe you," she added.

"I didn't know what else to do. I thought I was losing you. See it from my viewpoint." He grinned as he continued. "He has a bigger ship, and all those animals. What have I got? A little ship and, maybe . . . what about bringing a tiny animal back with us. I could talk to Kowangii."

She leaned forward and embraced him, smiling. "You're so silly."

✴ ✴ ✴

The last day on the blue-white planet had arrived. Both crews had gone through the site, making sure nothing was left in the few hours since breakfast. All that remained now was to say goodbyes. They decided to meet at the southwest foot of the Great Pyramid, as everyone was calling it. The sun was shining off the Great Pyramid, which glowed white and blue in the light. A gentle breeze was blowing.

The crew members from the Light Traveler gathered near Zander and Kowangii. The remainder of the Light Wanderer's crew stood near them. After last night, Zander and Bel'lar were uneasy around each other. They stared at each other but said nothing.

Captain Bel'lar stepped forward and looked around the group. "Now that you have activated the pyramid library, I hope this planet will be different from the others. I truly hope that the humans who come to inhabit this planet will believe in something more than their own greed and selfishness and use this library to learn what happened on the planets that have gone before. Learn from those mistakes so that this planet will be a showcase of its humanity and won't have to be destroyed again."

Ka'aya put his hand on Bel'lar's shoulder. "Well said, my son. This is the beginning of a new civilization, and the potential for success runs very high if the inhabitants set aside their animal instincts."

Zander joined the two facing the group. "I, too, wish to speak. I hope that the people who inhabit here will learn from living with the animals that we have brought. This is an opportunity to live an austere life and take from this planet only what is necessary to exist. If they act as the caretakers of the animals and allow them dignity in their lives, the animals will allow dignity in theirs." He looked at Ry Sing and then looked away.

Kowangii stood by Ka'aya. "Societies that abuse their animals will fall and fail as a species, and will be again destroyed by their own hands."

Ry Sing put her hand up. "I want to speak. My new friends, you're now taken into my heart. This friendship will transcend all time, and I will hold this experience dear to me. I wish to hug everyone once more. I will start with you, Kowangii." As she walked over to him, his eyes beamed with anticipation, and they hugged. She whispered in his ear. "You knew what I was searching for and allowed it to happen. I will always honor Char, every thought her mind creates. She gives me the perspective of duality. I owe you a debt of gratitude for this life and beyond." She kissed him on the cheek.

He hugged her tight. "And you are the youth, full of anticipation we will remember."

Then she approached Zander. His eyes were sad as he waited for her to reach him. She embraced him, her cheek on his heart. His arms encompassed her, and he leaned his head to rest on hers. In a whisper, she said, "We will love you all the days of this life and look forward to a future life when we will be with you. Don't grieve, for this is what we want, what we need to do." Then she kissed him on the lips.

He tightened his embrace, and whispered, "Goodbye, my love." Then he released her and stepped back. He looked away so that the others wouldn't see the tears clouding his vision.

Bel'lar watched this with concern and jealousy. He wondered what had gone on between these two all that time on the black ship. He hated feeling this way. He was glad they were leaving. No one would be there to receive her attention but him. He wanted her all to himself.

Ry Sing proceeded to hug everyone else. Then she embraced Ka'aya, and they stood in silence while all the rest started to hug and say their goodbyes. When it was all finished, Bel'lar, Ry Sing, Enis, and Mauleen stood on one side. On the opposite side were Zander, Kowangii, Ka'aya, and Dobeman. They were almost in a line facing each other.

Ka'aya borrowed Kowangii's walking stick. He drew a circle around the two groups in the sand. He then took the walking stick and drew a straight line between the two groups from one edge of the circle to the other edge. He stood at one end of the line between the two groups. He returned the stick to Kowangii and put his hands out to encompass both groups.

"The circle represents this life and all that is about it. It represents the knowing and understanding. It represents the whole, the All, the One. And as God's energy is one, we are one with all of you standing together in our life. As this circle splits in two, even though we are on one side, part of our life that is leaving will never be whole until we reunite. We will always remember this point in time to be that of the point of light of God. For knowing all of you, and participating with each and every one of you, has brought us closer to the God energy. May we all live and grow in understanding, as we have, from this experience. We will always be there for each and every individual." Ka'aya dropped his hands to his side and started to walk back toward the middle of the group.

Ry Sing rushed up to him, crying. "I can't let you go. I thought I could, but I can't. You must come with us. I can't bear being without you."

He gently held her arms and kept her back a little bit so that he could look into her eyes. "Remember the times we taught you to be strong. This is one of those times. We will not be gone forever, and you will be in our heart, so you will not be far. But it is your time to go and discover what you will create on this planet."

She looked up at him. "I hear your words, but my heart breaks." He looked into her eyes and then hugged her. Crying, she held him tight.

Emotion had welled up inside almost everyone now. Zander felt he could take no more of this sadness. It was time for these two crews to depart.

Zander said, "This has been a bittersweet experience, and I shall leave it that way." He looked at Ry Sing with longing; then he turned and walked toward the ship. His crew began to enter the black ship.

Bel'lar gently pulled Ry Sing away from Ka'aya, and then he hugged Ka'aya. "You've been like a father to me." He felt the comforting gush of energy that entered his heart. His sadness intensified at this parting.

"And you've been like a belligerent son to us," Ka'aya said tenderly. "Take care of Ry Sing."

"Of course," Bel'lar responded.

"Bel'lar, there will be a time in your lives when you will not be wondering, 'Should I do this, should I do that? Was that the right decision or maybe not?' We will be there when you will know again who you are. We will be there for your great triumphs. Don't worry. Be happy." Ka'aya hugged Bel'lar again.

"Good bye, Ka'aya." Bel'lar walked away with his arm supporting Ry Sing. Her head was down. Ka'aya could still hear her sobbing.

Everyone was aboard both ships except for Dobeman and, of course, the dog, Chapatata. Dobeman turned around and saw Chapatata was sitting, staring up at him. He had been silent throughout this whole emotional outburst. Dobeman looked down at him now. They stared at each other. "It's left to me and you, Chapatata, the two that don't quite understand what has happened, the two that realize it would be a sad place, indeed, if we didn't have the species with emotions. If it were up to me, I would have been gone long before now. And if it had been up to you, you would have been lying in the sand, enjoying the warmth of the sun above. So, it is fitting that the two of us are the last to leave this beautiful, serene blue-white planet. Come walk with me to the ship. I think there is an extra dream icicle aboard."

They boarded the Light Wanderer, and the opening closed behind them. The ship began to emit a sound. It pulsated and vibrated harmoniously with its surroundings. It rose up and slowly turned, increasing in altitude. In a moment, it was gone.

The Light Traveler then hovered, and, in an instant, it was gone in the other direction.

Now upon this planet, and on this special plateau where people had come to mark the planet as their own, there was but the sound of the planet itself, as it moved, breathed, and lived.

# Chapter 4
## Traveling Home

Aboard Captain Zander's ship, several days had passed since their departure from the blue-white planet. The ship was journeying home. Six days out, the Light Wanderer requested Captain Zander to report to the surgery. As he turned onto the corridor, he saw Ka'aya walking into the surgery before him.

"I didn't hear your name called, Ka'aya."

Ka'aya waited at the doorway for the Captain. "We know, but we're needed here."

They entered and discovered Kowangii, in a seriously ill state, lying on the bed.

Zander hurried over to Kowangii, his face tightened with concern. "What's wrong? Are you all right?"

A healer, Lorelle, stood next to Kowangii. She looked up at Zander, tears in her eyes. "It's time for him to leave us."

Zander was shocked, unprepared for this news. "No. It can't be. I can't bear to . . ." He lapsed into silence. He didn't know what else to say.

Ka'aya put his hand on Zander's shoulder as he said, "Can't bear to what? To release him? It is his decision to be released, not yours."

Zander sighed. "Yes, it's our custom that one who lives in this physical life may leave at any time, no questions asked. When they reach maturity, they have the right to stop their life. And, yes, they may do so . . . in the manner they wish."

Kowangii opened his eyes and looked at them. "What's all the commotion? This is a poor old man trying to die." His voice quavered as he spoke. "You're disturbing us, and we wish it stopped. Ah, Zander, old friend and companion. We're glad you're here. And Ka'aya, our new brother, the one we have known before." He stretched out his hand to Ka'aya.

Ka'aya came closer and leaned down. "What is wrong, Kowangii?"

Lorelle looked at Ka'aya somberly. "It's his heart. It's failing. The life force is leaking out at a rapid rate now."

Ka'aya took Kowangii's hand. "Did something drain your life force?"

Kowangii looked up at him, "Nothing has done us any harm. Our connection is allowing this, freeing our spirit, freeing our soul from this stricken body. We shall float off into the heavens beyond, with no regrets and with positive reinforcements from you." He struggled to breathe, his face contorted from his difficulty in expanding his chest.

At that moment, the crystal display activated in the surgery, and they turned toward it. Ry Sing and Bel'lar, far away on the Light Traveler, joined this sad group and were witness to this event.

"What's happening? Light Traveler connected us without explanation," Bel'lar said.

"Kowangii is dying. He has only moments left," Ka'aya answered.

Ry Sing was distraught. "I wish I were there. I could heal you, Kowangii. Lorelle, I'll direct you how to do this. I know I hold the power now. I can do this. I will it to be." She stretched her hand to the group clustered near Kowangii, pressing it on the display.

Lorelle looked at Zander with hope. He shook his head. Tears were running down his face. "No, Ry Sing. It's not our way."

The others were completely absorbed with these traumatic events and didn't notice Dobeman enter and stay by the door. *This is going to be interesting*, he thought. *What way is theirs?* he asked himself.

"Ry Sing." Kowangii's voice was very weak.

Ry Sing and Bel'lar learned forward with the others, straining to hear the old man's words.

Kowangii coughed and then swallowed with great effort. The healer patted his forehead with a cloth.

"It's not our way, not our civilization's belief to extend the life where it's not necessary. You come into this existence, this life, to appreciate, to understand, to experience all of the emotions you can. Then, on the other hand, you're here to experience the transformation—the transformation from this physical life to where you were before you were born. Because of this knowledge you carry in the physical, you think this end is somehow worse than the birth. But we tell you, and we believe this throughout our soul. There is no difference between being born and . . . "— he gasped for breath—". . . being all, becoming one with your brothers and sisters, your ancestors and enemies. To be all with the ones who helped you through this life to understand who you are, what you have created, and what will be left over after you have . . . " He gasped again, and the healer arranged his pillow, tucking a tiny one in to elevate his head to help him speak.

Ka'aya grabbed his hand and held it while he began to cry. "Kowangii, we foresaw that we would unite, that somehow we would become one. But we never thought it would come to this, that you would transfer before these eyes into the God energy and drift off, leaving us here."

Ry Sing was crying now. Bel'lar's face was stoic as he held back his grief, but he put his arm around her and held her close.

Kowangii grabbed Ka'aya's hands and pulled him toward himself. His difficulty in speaking hurt those listening. "We're not leaving you. We're merely changing forms. If you will allow, we shall become one consciousness. We shall become one in the body of the Ka'aya. As the two become one, this is the way of all things. When the God created all, he began to separate. He separated man from woman, mankind from animals, animals from plants, plants from water, water from earth, earth from planets and so on, and on. Now we have that rare privilege of coming back together so we may build upon this knowledge and be one. Moving backwards to the All. Coming closer to the All as we unite."

Ka'aya and Kowangii stared into each other's eyes, searching for the measure of each other's heart. Then Ka'aya released the old man's hands and straightened.

"We are honored. We will accept the consciousness of the greatest man who has touched us in this life. We will carry the Kowangii consciousness and the Ka'aya consciousness to become this multi-conscious being. This multi-consciousness will defer to each other and become the one, as you wish." He bowed his head to Kowangii.

"Can you do this?" Ry Sing cried out. "Will this hurt you?"

Zander was completely grief stricken and blurted out, "I forbid this. I forbid the joining of the two races. I forbid you to take over the body, the spirit, the energy, the essence of my favorite holy man." His voice broke on the last word.

Kowangii grabbed the cloth of Zander's robe and, with surprising strength, pulled him down to him. "We are no longer a holy man. We don't need the book. We've already given the book away, the book that held all the answers for this life. This is the next step, and you will deny us this? We think not. For you cannot go through your existence denying us anything. We are willing this upon you, and you must allow what has begun, to finish." Kowangii let go of Zander's robe and his arm fell weakly at his side.

Zander hung his head as his tears fell. He kissed Kowangii on the forehead and then stepped back. It hurt too much to say goodbye to this dear old man.

Ka'aya lay down on the couch and closed his eyes. Lorelle put a pillow under his head and leaned down to him. "Is there anything I can do to help you?"

He smiled up at her. "Dim the lights, and allow the transference of the energy. Kowangii will give us the knowledge to do this."

"Very well." She did as he asked and returned to Kowangii's side.

Dobeman watched intently, trying to understand what they were feeling. He was in awe of the great experience that these humans were having. They were suffering much, but they were also gaining in knowledge. He remembered that Ka'aya had said much was learned through great adversity. If there was any adversity going on right now, it was in the transformation of one old man going limp in his body.

The healer sat down next to Kowangii. Zander was seated on the other side, and they were touching him. Ry Sing's hand was up to the display as if she were there touching Kowangii, too.

Kowangii sighed, deep and long. And, with his last breath, he uttered, "Shall we be more than a man. We think so." The last words escaped in a long sigh. Kowangii's body went limp. Silence engulfed the room for a long moment. The healer choked back a sob. Tears fell from Zander's eyes, but he didn't move, letting them fall on the arm of the old man he loved.

Ry Sing gripped Bel'lar's hand tightly, the two helpless to do anything but watch.

Kowangii's body seemed to shrink in front of them.

Time stood still as they came to the understanding that this man they all loved had died.

Then a cloud of energy, the light essence that was Kowangii appeared above his empty body. Multicolored, but transparent, it had all the colors, the soft hues of the rainbow. It sparkled as it moved effortlessly through the air toward Ka'aya; the colors constantly changed and mixed with one another. Ka'aya was completely calm and relaxed as the energy floated over him, taking the shape of a human body with a head, arms, legs and a torso. Within this energy, the colors pulsated and sparkled.

Ry Sing held her breath as this energy stopped above Ka'aya. Bel'lar jerked in his chair.

Ka'aya opened his eyes and turned his hands up. "All that we are is a man. All that we ever wanted to be was a man. All we shall ever be is a man."

As he completed those words, the energy drifted down, seeping into his body. The pulsating energy was absorbed into Ka'aya's body with some jerking, as the body rejected some of the energy. But this joining grew in strength. Ka'aya twitched and jerked, and then, with a great sigh, as a last bit of energy entered his body, he surrendered to numbness.

The healer held his wrist, checking if the heart was beating. It wasn't. The joining had stopped his heart. She put her head on his chest, listening for the heartbeat, but she couldn't feel or hear anything.

Ry Sing called to the healer. "You must start his heart."

Zander stood. "That's not our way. If the heart has stopped, there is a reason. We allow this to be a sign." He watched her sadly.

Ry Sing became frantic. "How can you do this? Don't let him die. Do something." She was standing, desperate to help in any way but frustrated that she wasn't there at Ka'aya's side.

Lorelle's hands were on Ka'aya's chest, but her eyes focused on Zander. Then a hand clasped hers. It was Ka'aya's, almost scaring her. He spoke softly, "It is not necessary to revive us. This heart beats upon itself. It beats and beats. We are united with the one once known as Kowangii. We now possess the two. Once we receive the third, then we shall be as we once were. We shall be all there is. We shall be all there was, and we shall truly be born again. Born again to help, born again to understand. Born again to know."

He started to shake uncontrollably. Lorelle took his hands and crossed them on his chest, holding her hands there, giving of her energy to comfort him.

Everyone had moved away from Kowangii. The one that was, was no more. Or was he? Was he now better than he was? Only he knew. Looking at Ka'aya, they saw the smile on his face, they somehow knew that the two were better than when they were apart. They were better because they were together, creating what was sacred in life. Something no one else could ever create.

Ka'aya slowly pushed up to a seated position with the healer's assistance. "You should not be rising yet," she protested.

"We are all right."

Zander was the farthest away and the closest to Kowangii. He backed up even further when Ka'aya's body became fluid, vibrating with waves of energy. With one wave of energy, he was the Kowangii, and then, with the next wave, he was Ka'aya. He lifted his head. He held out his arms, his hands palms up. He sat fully erect now and spoke with the voice of Kowangii. "Zander, come forth and touch the hands of Kowangii."

Zander hesitated, listening. But he strode forward because that was indeed the voice of his dear friend, Kowangii. He clasped the left hand of Ka'aya and bowed his head.

"A secret has been revealed to us, and we are filled with joy," Ka'aya said. "Together, we have enough energy and the free will and choice to abandon this body. We choose to do so."

Ry Sing was stunned. Then fear loosened her tongue. "No, please, no. You can't do this. You can't leave me. It's hard enough that I can't be with you—but to lose you now? No. No." She burst into tears.

Bel'lar sat next to her, frozen in his chair. He couldn't believe this was happening.

Ka'aya looked into the display, into Ry Sing's face. "Don't cry, dear one. We're not dying. We're merely taking advantage of this energy to seek out the third, the third that will make us complete. We're going in search of the third. There will be a triad of souls in the body we wish to be."

Ka'aya crumpled sideways.

Zander caught him and helped him lie back down. The healer held Ka'aya's wrist and then leaned to his chest. She looked up at Ry Sing and shook her head sadly. No life remained in this body that only a moment ago had held two magnificent beings, two holy men now off in pursuit of the third.

Ry Sing was beside herself with grief and despair. She turned to Bel'lar and pressed her face into his chest, sobbing uncontrollably. He held her, smoothing her hair, attempting to comfort her, without success. He couldn't believe that Ka'aya was dead. It was the last thing he had expected. He was devastated with grief at this unexpected loss of both men. He hated this feeling.

"Zander, we leave you to your grief. L.T., please terminate this connection," Bel'lar said formally, struggling to hold his grief at bay.

The two from the Light Traveler were gone, the display dark. Lorelle sank to the floor with tears running down her cheeks. She covered her face with her hands and sobbed.

Dobeman observed her distress and Zander's. "Why do you weep? This should be a celebration. Did you not hear Kowangii and Ka'aya say they were free?"

Zander looked at Dobeman wonderingly. "Dobeman, don't you understand? As much as human beings speak of being free, it's our worst fear. Just look at all the humans you know. Don't they say they wish to be free and then make themselves dependent on physical things they don't need? Then they write books that they deem to be holy. Someone will pick up one and bind themselves to its words, which may or may not have meaning to them. What's worse may be the fear of being free from these words. I grieve because I know the book will win out and bind so many individuals to its words—these words that were written to set them free. But no. They will interpret these words to be laws that bind them to this physical book. They will never be free. This makes me sad. I have seen two men freed from the physical. It was so easy, because they were willing."

Dobeman gazed at these two humans, attempting to see their faces in a different perspective. "I am starting to understand about the human beings. I have seen the wildebeest begin to run in one direction and to increase in speed. When the first started to run, he knew why he was running, but do the rest? No, they merely run as the others, wishing to be part of something."

Zander nodded. "To be bound to one another no matter the reason or the cause."

"And to run right off the edge of a cliff following each other because they know not why the first one began to run. They merely follow because they are afraid not to be part of the herd. Why?" Dobeman waited for Zander to answer.

"Their fear won out. It's exactly what we all fear. That's why human beings are always running from something. If they would only look behind them, they would see it isn't really back there, but up ahead, where they are running to."

Dobeman smiled at that statement. "Of course. They always get what they wish."

Zander looked down, his eyes reddened with tears. "With Kowangii's passing, much knowledge has been gained. I know the old man would have loved that. I'm going to my quarters now." He left quickly, wanting to be alone with his grief.

Dobeman left a moment later. The healer remained. In a moment, she would go about the business of making arrangements for the remains of these two amazing men.

* * *

While everyone grieved their passing, the two holy men who had joined together left Ka'aya's body without a backward glance. They passed through the hull of the Light Wanderer, an energy burst infused with excitement that appeared as a comet with a twin tail that accelerated until it coalesced into a driven pursuit of the heavens and disappeared.

*  *  *

Ry Sing was no longer crying. Bel'lar had left a while ago. She knew he was grieving, too, and had asked him to go with her to her room. He had carried her to it and put her to bed. She threw back her blanket and got up. Then, kneeling on the floor, she settled comfortably into the familiar cross-legged position. Many times before she had done this, but now she needed it to help her deal with this grief. Closing her eyes, she turned her focus inward, breathing deeply. She felt the stress, the grief, fade away with each breath, to be replaced by a sense of connection and peace. She floated for a time in this boundless space, absorbing the healing energy. Then light and at ease, she opened herself up to the universe, seeking the beloved soul of her mentor. In her mind she called out, "Ka'aya."

And was rewarded with a response. "Yes, my dear, we are here," Ka'aya answered.

"Are you no more? Have I lost you in this life?"

"No one ever is. You know this," he answered.

"I need you in this life."

There was a pause, and then he answered, "It shall be done."

Ry Sing remained where she was, filled with the knowledge that all would be resolved. Time passed, and she drifted in a meditative state.

A twin-tailed comet swooped down from the heavens and sped toward the Light Traveler. Reaching the ship, it collided with her hull, infusing her with its energy. The Light Traveler's skin sparkled with stars as the energy was absorbed. No one inside felt this collision, but Ry Sing knew the moment that it occurred. She cried tears of relief as her quarters filled with the combined essence of two highly memorable holy men.

* * *

In Bel'lar's quarters, he sat alone in the dark. He couldn't believe that Ka'aya was dead. He couldn't remember a time in his life when the old man wasn't there, poking and prodding him to do something. He wished for just a moment that he had been more considerate, at least pretended to listen to the old man. But only for a moment.

Then he realized something else. Something that disturbed him. Lurking underneath his grief was a tiny bit of relief. Now he had Ry Sing all to himself. It sounded petty when he considered this, but, still, he feared that her feelings for Ka'aya transcended her feelings for everyone else, and he hadn't been sure if she would leave him for Ka'aya at some point. Now that would never happen. And he felt bad that he could be this mean-spirited.

* * *

Zander sat quietly in his quarters on the Light Wanderer. It had been several weeks since Kowangii and Ka'aya had passed over. A tone sounded. Zander roused himself.

"Yes."

"Captain Zander, Kowangii's last request is available for you to view," the ship said.

"Thank you, Light Wanderer. I thought the old man would have some kind of last request because he always seemed organized."

The display on his wall brightened and came into focus. It was Kowangii. He gazed gently at him. "Greetings, my son. We know you're missing us, but we have achieved the greatest prize of all: Understanding that the physical life that dwells within this body that we cherished and coveted is to be released and given back to God. Being aware during this release returns a better physical life than when God gave it to us. This is our gift to you. Don't fear when it's your time. Step up and choose to be as God wanted you to be. Know your own direction."

Kowangii's face crumpled with emotion, tears welling in his eyes. Then he brushed them away and continued, "We have graduated from this life and worn the hat of graduation. Now, our last request will be somewhat difficult, we know. Zander; we wish our physical remains to be encapsulated upon the spot where you will build . . ."

Zander shook his head as he listened to Kowangii. *Here it comes,* he thought.

". . . our own pyramid library . . ."

And Zander completed the sentence with Kowangii, ". . . on the blue-white planet."

"Oh, yes, dear friend. When you build our great pyramid, our government will not be a problem; they will do as you wish. It has always been in the writings that the blue-white planet would be inhabited by our race. It is only you who, as of yet, has not chosen this path." Kowangii smiled and nodded. The record terminated.

Zander sat in silence, lost in contemplation after viewing this message. Finally he addressed the air, "I feel in my heart, old man, that the habitation of the blue-white planet will cause our race much anguish and loss of perspective. Yet, as we stand now, no one can even mirror our abilities and stature. We are the race that always has been. The race that will endeavor."

But it was the ship, not Kowangii, that answered him. "You are the race that will create situations to tax the multitudes that inhabit the blue-white planet. Through this it will enable your race to move from this place with great knowledge and understanding. It is through adversity that they shall conquer their greatest fears. So, let your fears be subdued to the wishes of this old man, who will walk on that planet that creates so much controversy in your soul."

"Thank you, Light Wanderer. I'll carry this with me. When we reach home I will address the governing agencies and allow them to decide."

✳ ✳ ✳

Light Traveler sped through space, changing form and light and color, intent on her destination, the home planet. Bel'lar was seated on the bridge looking out over the vastness of space as it flashed by. Light Traveler had accelerated well beyond light speed. He was attempting, with the ship's assistance, to get home as soon as possible.

Ry Sing entered the bridge. He smiled, watching her cross the deck to reach him. She looked happy, her step energetic. He was glad to see that she had recovered from her grief over Ka'aya's passing. Or at least she wasn't talking about it.

"Bel'lar, I wish to talk to you about my desire to journey to the planet of Taurus."

He stood up to greet her. "I thought—I hoped—that you had forgotten about that wild idea. There's nothing there for you."

She pushed him down in his seat and then perched on the edge of the chair next to him. "I never really felt you understood my desires about this planet. Deep in my heart, there's a void, and this void grows every day. Eventually it will take over my being unless I fill the void by going to Taurus. I thought, maybe in your infinite wisdom, you could plan a side trip and drop me off and then shoot home and do what you need to do there. Pick up supplies and the people wishing to immigrate, and, on the

way back to the blue-white planet, swing by and pick me up."
She gave him a big smile as she straightened his collar.

Bel'lar didn't try to laugh this off. He knew this was very
important to her. He took hold of her hand. "I've always wanted
to fulfill all your desires. I fully intended to take you to your
planet. But, when I consulted with the ship, she explained it
this way. Traveling faster than light causes a time-warp factor,
which I hadn't taken into consideration."

Ry Sing looked bewildered. "What does this mean?"

"I'll explain it the best I can. When you travel faster than
the speed of light, time slows down relative to the time on
the planet. I have some trepidation about how much time has
passed. We've been traveling for less than a year, but the time
that may have elapsed on our home planet may be hundreds of
years. L.T. can't calculate this because of the many unknowns
in space—any of which could alter or slow our transit time."

"I didn't consider that."

"That's why I can't drop you off at your planet and come
back for you later. You would have grown old and perhaps died.
Of course, I'd still be this young, virile man, and you wouldn't
like that."

"But I might be dead and happy," she teased, smiling again.

He smiled and then grew serious. "If you weren't there, I
don't think I could bear it. So, I have a new plan. I haven't final-
ized it yet, but what about this? We go back together to the home
planet. We hide the ship, and only I go down to the planet to find
out if it's safe. If it is, then the rest of you can visit the planet.
Afterwards, we'll get the people who want to immigrate to the
blue-white planet, and on the way, we'll go to Taurus, and you
can do whatever you need to."

"You mean what I feel is necessary."

"Yes, that's what I mean. When we're finished, we can journey together to the blue-white planet."

She considered this idea. "All right. Can this ship go any faster?"

He pulled her into his lap and hugged her as they gazed out at the stars.

*       *       *

Bel'lar had just come from the warrior room. He caught a glimpse of blue from the connecting corridor as someone passed by. Walking quickly, he turned into the corridor and recognized Ry Sing. She was about ten steps ahead when he called out to her. She stopped and turned, but it wasn't Ry Sing any longer. Char was looking back at him, dressed all in reds and yellows. A long moment passed while Bel'lar stared, nonplussed. Then he recovered and said, "I thought you were Ry Sing. But how . . ."

Char smiled. As she began to speak, Char's appearance grew indistinct. "I am Ry Sing." She smiled again as she walked to him. With each step she seemed to change, her image fading and strengthening alternately, until her appearance solidified, and now it was Ry Sing who stood before him, looking up. She held out her hand to him.

"What happened? What was that?" He cupped her face with his hands, examining her closely, but it was indeed Ry Sing, not Char. How could he have seen that?

"I'm in the process of gathering all of my personalities. Char was one of them." She watched Bel'lar's face and knew his mind was frantically trying to figure this out. It made her smile. She loved challenging his reality.

"What do you mean—personalities?" he asked.

"In existence, there is more than one of you, and, if you can seek them out and together be one, you will have the understanding of who you really are, which, of course, is more than one, more than two. But in your case, you have all that you need in this life."

"Me. What about me?"

"Simply put, Bel'lar, you are it. No one else will get inside you."

"That's a relief. I'm having enough trouble with one of me. But Char. Why did I see her?"

"Char and I reunited on the black ship. She is a part of my soul that I was seeking. From time to time my appearance phases in and out. This will stop once I become acclimated to this reunion."

"What about Char? Is she gone?"

"Of course, she's not gone. She and I are one now. We will spend the rest of this life together. Don't worry, Bel'lar. She made the choice, and I'm glad she did. It did upset Zander, though. He was very much in love with her."

"That explains it. When I saw you kissing him, I—"

"You were jealous." She touched his face tenderly. "There was no need to be. He was grieving, but I had made it clear that my path wasn't with him in this life. Char's emotions are mine now, and Zander remains dear to me. But we talked about all this, silly!"

She watched his face, realizing that he was still disturbed about this but knew he would have to learn how to accept her feelings for Zander and let it go. She was finding it confusing as well trying to tell the difference between her feelings and Char's.

They parted ways, and he went to his quarters to wash up.

He didn't like that she had feelings for another person. He had worried about Ka'aya, and now he had Zander to worry about. Except he probably wouldn't see Zander again in this life. And she had chosen to return with him to the home planet.

* * *

Several weeks had passed, and, as Bel'lar was walking down the corridor, he kept hearing in his head, *I must complete my life's mission.* This refrain continued as he walked.

Ry Sing spent most of her time in her quarters thinking about Taurus. The days were long now, the nights longer, but she would endure. Shortly they would be home, and it would be exciting to see what had happened while they were away and to bring them the news of the beautiful planet they had found. She hoped they still wanted this news.

Ka'aya's passing had hurt terribly. It had been so unexpected and had almost torn her apart. That is, until Ka'aya had answered her need and his soul had become part of the ship, sustained by the Light Traveler. She had begun going to his quarters each day to talk to him. She didn't need to be inside his quarters to do this, but she felt comforted being in there. It was as if she had a daily meeting with him, one she truly enjoyed. She didn't tell Bel'lar about this. It was something she knew he would rather not know.

The days wandered on. There wasn't much to do. The ship was self-sufficient. Bel'lar felt lost. He tried to write in his journal about his experiences on the blue-white planet. He detailed his experiences with his newfound friends, the black race. This race was unknown on the home planet.

He had much time for thought, and this brought him round to the home planet. He remembered their escape and didn't know what type of welcome, if any, they might receive upon arrival. He wondered again how much time had passed and if his mission even mattered anymore. Was it too late? Had the Syns degenerated to the point of mental incapacity?

And again his thoughts turned to Ka'aya. He couldn't believe that he was gone. He had seemed eternal.

✳ ✳ ✳

Bel'lar, hands clasped behind him, stood in front of the main console on the bridge. They had passed the midway point to the home planet. He was staring out into space when he started to wonder what Ry Sing was doing. He asked the ship her whereabouts.

"She is in Ka'aya's quarters."

"Thank you, L.T." He continued to stare out into space. *What is she doing in there?* he wondered.

He had nothing else to do. He'd go find out. He left the bridge and made his way to Ka'aya's quarters. He hadn't been in here since the last time he and Ka'aya had spoken on the trip to the blue-white planet. Despite Ka'aya's death, this felt like trespassing. He hesitated before the door. Then, feeling silly, he touched the panel, and it opened. He stepped inside. Ry Sing was seated in meditation, her legs crossed, in the center of the room. She opened her eyes and looked at him.

"What are you doing in here," he said.

"I come here frequently to feel his energy. It comforts me. Were you looking for me?"

"I was restless and wondered where you were."

"Well, it's perfect that you're here now. I have a message for you from Ka'aya. Come sit near me."

He hesitated, and she smiled. "You're not afraid of him, are you?"

"Not afraid, just cautious. Your last message for me was about the Planet of Abundance, and that didn't work out too well for me." He scratched the birthmark on his chest. "So I'm understandably hesitant to receive another one."

"Just sit down and listen." She pointed to the spot.

Bel'lar sat on the floor across from her, his legs loosely crossed. He wasn't as comfortable as she was in this position. He hoped this message wouldn't take too long.

She closed her eyes once he was seated and began to breathe rhythmically in and out. She turned her focus inward and felt the boundless energy enter, opening her to unlimited possibilities.

She straightened and began to speak, "Greetings, Bel'lar. It's Ka'aya."

Bel'lar stared at this Asian woman, who was speaking the words of his surrogate father.

"You must be halfway to your destination by now, the home planet. We understand your duty comes first, and you shall fulfill all that is required of you. Kowangii has explained to us that, on the home planet, there will be times when you will need guidance. Since we won't be there to help you to understand the situations that will be thrust upon you, he graciously left you a present. With this present, we hope that you will understand what you will do, why you will do it, and how you will continue afterwards."

Bel'lar scratched his head. What did the old man say? Ka'aya has always spoken in riddles to me. "Why don't you just give me the facts?"

Ka'aya smiled. "The facts are this present is given to you to hold and to use for only a determinate period of time. When you see that the time has expired, you must pass this on to another. Another you will know to be like you. Ry Sing can show you where it is. Be surprised, amused, and perplexed."

Bel'lar shook his head. "You haven't changed at all. I thought death would have some effect on you. Can't you tell me anything more?"

Ka'aya, speaking through Ry Sing, smiled again. "My son, now you have grown up and must decide. Now is the time. Remember our love and the love of all that know you go with you."

She sagged, his message clearly over. He watched her, knowing she would come out of this trance without help from him.

The message for Bel'lar was complete, but Ka'aya had a message for her. In her mind, he told her that the combined essence that he had become had reached a decision. It was time for them to continue on their journey. They were departing for the home planet, where the next step in their evolution would occur. They were in search of the third and would find it there. They were leaving now so that Ka'aya would have time to be reincarnated and grown when she arrived. "Search for us," Ka'aya said in her mind. "We may have need of your help. Remember to give Bel'lar his present."

Ry Sing shivered as Ka'aya's energy left her. Knowing that it would be some time before she would see him again, she was sad, already missing him. She felt his energy leave the ship and speed away toward its new destination. Then her eyes fluttered open, and she glanced around the room, coming back to reality. Finally, she focused on Bel'lar.

"I know where it is," she said. "It's inside this room."

She rolled her legs to the side and began to rise. Bel'lar helped her stand. She looked up at him. "Do you want to know?"

He stared at her; moments passed. "Sure, why not? Nothing else to do until we get home."

She walked over to the cabinet in the corner of the room. She opened it, pressed the catch inside, and a panel slid up inside the wall, leaving a small opening. Inside lay something wrapped in a cloth printed like a leopard skin. She stepped aside for Bel'lar. He took it out carefully and smoothed the cloth. "It's beautiful." He unwrapped what was a very old book. On the cover of this weather-beaten old book was written, *The Book of Knowledge of the Sacred Ecology Religion*. Bel'lar couldn't believe this. "Kowangii was willing to part with this. How can this be?"

A tattered piece of paper was sticking out of the book. He opened the book to that page, and on the paper was written a little note. "We have achieved our lifelong mission. Our goals were accomplished. Now we must pass this book on to our successor. That is you, Bel'lar. We will be yours in spirit as long as you need us. Kowangii."

Ry Sing stood next to him, reading the note, too. "Isn't that wonderful."

He was overcome and dropped into a chair. He couldn't believe Kowangii would leave this for him. He looked up at her with a confused look on his face. Then his confusion became consternation. "What did I do to deserve this? Gifts from holy men. This can't be good."

"Don't be so suspicious. They're only trying to help you. What are you going to do with it?"

"I don't want to do anything. Here, you take it." He held it out to her, but she refused to accept it.

"Oh, no. They left it for you. You're the chosen successor."

"I'm not their successor. If anyone is, it would be you. You're the holy person. What did Kowangii call you, 'the holy princess Ry Sing Su Tong'?"

She put her arm around him, pressing her cheek to his. She could tell he was very overwhelmed by this gift even though he'd tried to hide it. "There is no doubt that this gift is for you. You must decide if you will use it. I'll leave you to contemplate this gift." She kissed him on the forehead and left him sitting there in a daze.

Bel'lar sat for a while with the book on his lap open to where the marker was placed. Finally, he got up and took the book to his quarters. He tucked the note between the glass and the frame of the mirror where he washed up each morning. Then, he could read these words each day, remembering what a lovely thought, and what a lovely man. As he returned to the main room, he glanced at the book lying open on the table and wondered why Kowangii had put the marker in that location. It marked a place about two thirds of the way through the book.

He had to admit that he was curious. What could possibly be written in a book like this one? What ancient information did it contain? Ka'aya and Kowangii had revered it. Might there be something that would help him? He held it closer to read the passage and stopped, wondering if the scripture would be difficult to understand. *Without Ka'aya or Kowangii, I might have some difficulty. Maybe Ry Sing can help me if I need it.*

He began to read. Unaware that Kowangii had read this very passage to Zander some months past when he was enlisting his aid in helping the Captain of the small ship to reach his destiny, he didn't notice at first that it was Kowangii's voice that he heard in his mind as he read.

"It is written that there will be three great events in the experience of mankind that will be so catastrophic they will bring tears to the multitudes for they will weep for many thousands of years beyond the events. These events will render the planets completely useless for thousands of millions of years. It will be written that beyond that time they will start anew, but they will carry with them the remembrance of these events."

Kowangii's voice continued, and Bel'lar listened, full of wonderment as to how this could be happening. It was as if the old man were right here, speaking to him. ". . . It has been written that the holy man that cleansed the first planet so that it may be reborn will sacrifice his own life." He considered this passage. This must refer to the Great One. Disturbed but intrigued, he read on.

"Now, it is foretold that the second and third cleansing of a planet will be done by a man who is not considered to be holy, but by a man of law and order. A man who is bound by his duty. This binding of his duty will force him to take actions to create events that will destroy his home planet, which he feels will be better cleansed than continuing. This will not sit well with him, for it is written that he will end his life within the year after this event."

The voice in his mind said, "This man is you, Bel'lar."

He felt the shiver move throughout his whole body. This voice from beyond had raised the hair on his neck, terrifying him to his very core. He looked up from the book and stared at the far corner of his room. He didn't want to believe this, but it had the solid ring of truth, and that frightened him even more. Holy men, alive or dead, were an awful lot of trouble. They seemed to make it their mission to ruin his life with their dire predictions. But nothing was written in stone. He would treat this as a warning and do all that he could to make sure this didn't come to pass. His mission was to transport his people to the blue-white planet, and he wasn't going to let anything turn him from this path.

He wrapped the cloth over the book and put it on the table. *That's more than enough for now,* he groaned.

✳ ✳ ✳

The time seemed to accelerate as they got closer to the planet. A couple of weeks passed. Intermittently, his curiosity got the better of him, and he took out the book and read some passages. On one such occasion, he just opened the book randomly and began to read.

"What is left after a man frees the souls that trusted him to do his duty, not understanding what his duty really was? How does this man go on living?" *How did this man continue to live when he destroyed everything that he knew and loved?* Bel'lar wondered. He took a deep breath, not knowing the answers, and read on.

"As I walk alone on this desolate path, I know that what I have done was of value, was and will be appreciated, because

I have focused the God energy. I have taken that point of light and created a multitudinous and faceted experience that the children of God will need, will appreciate, and will carry on through their existence to their next lives. They will be better equipped to handle their next experiences.

"I will beseech them to take me with them, so that I may experience the happiness, the forever gratitude that they will indeed bestow upon me in the ever after."

"My spirit will grow beyond what my expectations could ever be. I will become the one who will move back to the center, where all light was created. To the center point, where God sits. I will then be equal to all that have come before me and to all that will follow in my footsteps."

Bel'lar dropped the book, in a hurry to get away from it, and made his way to the warrior room. Changing into running gear, he stepped onto the track and began to run. Today the path led through a forest, and the trees whispered to him as he passed. The scenery responded to his thoughts, his need. Even a cool breeze blew on him, easing his torment somewhat. But his mind returned to the words in the old book. He ran faster, but his thoughts would not be held back. Did this mean that he would do the unthinkable and then allow himself to die, as the Great One had? This book was not helping him despite what the two old holy men had hoped. Instead he was plagued again with those dreams of the Great One on the Planet of Abundance. *No. I'm not a holy man. That's not for me.*

He increased his speed, running on and on, letting the trees' whispering soothe him, letting the physical exertion burn away the dreams, the words, his fears. When he had finally exhausted himself, he collapsed on the track.

He realized one thing, however. The home planet was not going to be as he remembered and probably not as he wished.

With those thoughts, he knew that there would be a great challenge for him on the home planet. Well, he had been forewarned. Now he would prepare, anticipating as much as possible.

The ship alerted them that the star of the home planet was in view. With that notice, the ship began to slow. The four gathered on the bridge to view the star. They all, in their own ways, realized that this first part of this great adventure was now coming to an end. Each one approached this next step with some trepidation, because they knew that what they left on their home planet would be different. With that thought, the unknown dampened the excitement and enthusiasm.

CHAPTER 5

# CAN WE EVER GO HOME?

A hush came over the crew grouped on the bridge of the Light Traveler. Fears seeped into their thoughts now that they could see the planet. Would it be like they remembered? What had changed? Was it better? Was it worse? Each one was lost in their own thoughts as the ship brought them closer to their home planet.

Bel'lar broke the silence. "Light Traveler, can we cloak this ship? I don't want to be identified until we're ready."

"Yes, Captain, I will move into a higher frequency than that of the planet. This frequency will not be detectable, and we will be invisible."

"Very good. Do it." Bel'lar was intent on the planet visible on the display.

"Do you really think harm will come to us?" Enis said, his face reflecting his surprise. "We're here to take them to their new home, the beautiful blue-white planet."

"Enis, you don't know what's in the hearts of the humans on this planet," Ry Sing said. "You don't know what direction they've taken."

"You've forgotten they were shooting at us when we left," Bel'lar said.

Light Traveler caused the ship to vibrate at a higher frequency. For a moment the ship was visible. The next it vanished from sight.

Mauleen sat at her station, watching the Light Traveler's actions.

"Everything is now as you wish," Light Traveler announced. "You can bring the craft in close to whatever you wish to view."

"Excellent." Bel'lar began issuing orders. "Take us in low over the capital city, and begin surveying the planet."

The ship took them in, traveling at an altitude that allowed them to see the ground through the main crystal display. A great city, the one they had escaped from, spread out ahead of them, shrouded in a yellowish haze that at first looked like fog. But then they realized the fog was pollution.

"Oh, no," whispered Ry Sing.

Enis sighed, and Mauleen exchanged a sad look with him.

The pollution blocked their view of the details of the city. Bel'lar gave the order to fly below this pollution. The ship pierced the haze, and the home planet was unaware they were there.

On the outskirts of the city, they saw a large sign at the entrance to a huge manufacturing plant set in the middle of a stark and desolate area. The sign read, *Syn Foods Corporation. We feed the World.* The plant hummed with activity, but they were still too high up to see details.

Bel'lar scanned the city as they flew over but couldn't find any trees or grass around this plant. Nor, in fact, anywhere in the city or outside of it. Nothing seemed to be growing anywhere at all. Not one bit of green existed.

"What's happened to our planet?" Enis asked. "It looks dead. Where are the fields? Where's the food grown? The blue-white planet was truly paradise, wasn't it?"

He looked at Ry Sing, who smiled sadly. "We're too late," she said. Then she covered her mouth, sorry that she had said that out loud.

"Let's monitor the communication transmissions and the visual reporting to see what's going on here," Mauleen suggested.

"Do it. It's changed so much. This doesn't look like the same planet we left." Bel'lar continued to watch as they traveled over the city, a sense of dread settling over him. He feared it was as Ry Sing had said—it was too late.

Mauleen tuned into a video broadcast on the planet, and she put it up on the display. A news program. The date was shown on the screen. Mauleen's mouth dropped open, as she continued to stare at the broadcast. Then, recovering, she said, "Look at the date, Captain."

"That has to be wrong," he said. "That means it's been what—about 350 years since we left this planet. I expected a time change, but . . ." He shook himself. "L.T., compute the date."

He held his breath as he waited. No one else spoke.

"The date is correct, Captain. To be precise, 349.2 years have passed since we embarked on the journey to the blue-white planet."

The realization came over them that their home was not their home anymore, but merely a place they used to live. They sat quietly while their anticipation seeped away. Numbness set in. They knew now that all their friends and loved ones, and probably even places they remembered, no longer existed. His crew sat dazed, without direction or purpose.

Bel'lar recovered first, his duty asserting dominance over his emotions, pulling him back to the present. Clearly, knowing the possibilities was completely different than living them. He looked at each of his fellow travelers and wanted him and his crew to live through this event. To do that, he realized he would need to refocus them.

"L.T., take us out a safe distance and orbit the planet," he said. "We have decisions to make."

* * *

Bel'lar had given his crew one day to recover from this shock. Now it was time to refocus them on the task at hand. The four had already eaten and assembled on the bridge in anticipation of Bel'lar's orders. He stood in front of them. When all eyes were on him, he began to speak.

"We'll take the ship in as close to where it was originally launched as possible and land. I knew that area well. I'll go alone and find out what has transpired here over the past 350 years. I'll determine if it's safe for the rest of you to leave the ship and venture into the city. You'll be able to monitor me. And, of course, the ship can always find me. When I'm finished, I'll return to the ship."

Ry Sing shook her head. "I'm going with you."

Bel'lar smiled gently at her. "Not this time. The second journey out, it may be possible, but right now I want to know you're safe. If there are any problems, Mauleen will take the ship out of range, and all of you will be safe." He looked at the other two, including them in this statement.

Ry Sing frowned at him, not liking this at all, but didn't say anything more. She glanced at the other two, but no support came from them. Enis was nodding, agreeing with Bel'lar. Mauleen, as first officer, was following Bel'lar's orders.

The ship reached the site of the teleport. Another shock awaited them. Three hundred and fifty years ago, the pyramid had only been partially excavated. Now it sat exposed, alone and silent inside a fenced enclosure. Its facing had been removed and the underlying stones exposed. The hill and the forest were gone, along with everything else that had once been there. The secured yard, the buildings, all dust.

The ship set down next to it in a vacant area, still cloaked in its dimension that rendered it invisible to this planet both energetically and visibly.

Bel'lar had used his day to analyze the city, its inhabitants, gather what information he could with the help of the Light Traveler; he wanted to give himself the best chance of passing unnoticed among the inhabitants. His people still looked much the same as when he left. Same thickened bodies, now devoid of hair. He wondered if their mental processing had deteriorated more. They seemed functional, and calm.

He planned to alter his clothes so as not to look conspicuous. He would have to cover his hair, of course. He was able to find something similar to what he observed that the inhabitants wore. It wasn't identical, but he hoped it would let him blend in. Donning a white jacket with a hood, he prepared to leave the ship. Ry Sing walked him to the hatch, neither saying anything. They both knew how serious this could be, perhaps even dangerous, but he must do it. They held each other close. Then stepping back, Ry Sing pulled a syringe from her pocket, held it to his temple and inserted a microscopic transmitter under his skin. Now he could be tracked by the ship.

He carried another device as well that would let him speak to his crew. He hid it in an inside pocket.

The Light Traveler opened a hatch, and he walked out on the home planet. Aware of the pollution level, still he was surprised at how his breath choked in his throat. The air was fetid, sickening, trapped under the stagnant layer of pollution. *How do these people stand it?* he wondered. Pulling a cloth from his pocket, he tied it around his neck, pulling it up to cover his mouth as he looked around. It wasn't much better, but it kept him from gagging.

An enormous sign mounted on the fence attracted his attention. He walked over to read it. The lettering was faded, but he could just make it out. He assumed it must be very old.

The sign read, "Here was the last stronghold of the race of Organics. This race lived with and among us for many years. Then they stole our technology in the form of a light ship and left us with nothing." Underneath, written in small print, "There may still be Organs living on our planet. If you see one, report this to the authorities. There is a great reward for the discovery of any Organs."

He paused, considering the import of this message.

He realized that there was danger here for him, but it didn't matter. He must go on with his plan. He had to find out what had happened since he left and if his return would be heralded as the return of a savior or if he would be incarcerated or killed. He hiked away from this area and into the center of the city. His plan was to reach the area near where he used to live, if it was still there.

It was a good distance from the old teleport's location. Not too many people, Syns, were around, allowing him to travel unnoticed for the most part, making good time. The last time he traveled this route, he and Ry Sing were hanging off the back of the rail transport. It was hard to believe it was 350 years ago. He couldn't forget, however, that one thing hadn't changed. If that sign at the pyramid was any indication, they still didn't like Organs on this planet.

It was almost midday as he approached the center of the city; more people were on the street, going about their business. They completely ignored him and he felt encouraged. The city was in varying states of disrepair. This didn't improve as he reached the city center. Most of the buildings had broken and marked walls. Refuse cluttered the walkways and lay in the gutters. The people appeared to take no notice of this, simply stepping over and around this debris.

A network of public transport was running through the streets. The transport cars floated above the streets as they moved, sinking to the ground when stopping. People poured out at each stop here in the city center, and, in no time, he blended into a moving sea of people. He wondered why he didn't see any personal transports. A Brotherhood of Syn Security transport passed him. He stepped further into the crush of people to avoid being seen. The government had vehicles, it seemed.

Bel'lar stopped and stood looking up at an old building. The glass windows were all cracked on the top floor, but it didn't matter because they were sealed up with panels. All the buildings around here were in a similar state. This building seemed familiar, and he racked his memory to place it. He backed up to read the name over the entry when he bumped into someone. He turned and faced an old man. This old man, with his heavy, thickened and hairless body, was obviously a Syn. Even his eyebrows were gone, giving this man an odd, blank look.

He peered at Bel'lar, trying to see his face. He poked him with his finger. "Are you real?"

Bel'lar backed up and, keeping his head down, countered with a question, "What do you mean 'real'?" He had a good view of the old man's clothes. Basic garments, pants and a baggy tunic, dingy and worn.

"We defeated you in a great battle and drove you off this planet," the old Syn said. He poked him again. "I never thought I'd see one like you. It's only in our video history that we see ones like you. You're so thin you look close to death. Disgusting."

Bel'lar moved closer, lowering his voice. He didn't want to attract more attention. "I'm a Syn like you, but I'm ill. I have a rare disease."

The Syn hopped back, wiping his finger off on his tunic. "What kind of disease? Will I catch it?" He backed up more, wiping his finger harder on his tunic.

"They don't know yet."

The Syn backed away and hurried off, glancing back once.

*That worked*, Bel'lar thought. *I have a disease. Perfect. That explains everything. This hood hides my hair.* Then he remembered his eyebrows. He pulled the hood down over the top half of his face. *Maybe I'll get by with this thin disease.* He walked on.

He saw people lined up at the pharmacies, everyone dressed in similar fashion to the old Syn he had met. This area of the city had many pharmacies, and all of them had lines of people emerging from them, stretching out into the street. This seemed to be what they did at midday. The ones coming out of the pharmacies held small packets of something and bottles of liquid. Many of them just stopped on the street and ripped open the packets. They emptied them into their mouths and then gulped the liquid down. What could they be doing? Why were they in such a hurry?

As he walked on, he came across a Syn lying on the sidewalk, mumbling to himself, his eyes rolled back into his head. Bel'lar started to approach him, and then decided it was too risky. Other Syns bent to touch this man and walked on. They were repeating something, too, but he couldn't hear what it was. No one made any attempt to help him.

*What has happened here?* he thought as he hurried on.

He turned a corner, keeping his head down. When he glanced up, a short distance away, within easy sight, two Brotherhood of Syn Security guards were questioning a couple with a child. It was the first child Bel'lar had seen today. He stopped, watching. Maybe he should allow himself to be captured. That might be the easiest way to disclose who he was and why he was here. Then the child wandered away in Bel'lar's direction. The couple started after the child. The security guards turned and discovered Bel'lar as he turned away. They called out for him to stop.

Bel'lar ran. He'd changed his mind about being captured.

The two BOS guards ran after him, following him across the street and into a group of people.

Bel'lar bumped into a woman. She fell down, and Bel'lar tripped and fell over her. The guards reached him, dragging him to his feet. The Syns backed away, giving the guards room.

Stocky and bald, both guards wore what looked similar to the uniform from Bel'lar's time. Red jackets with gray pants, BOS insignia on the breast of the jacket. The larger man stood in front of him, turning his head this way and that as he tried to get a good look at Bel'lar's face. He jerked the cloth away from Bel'lar's mouth.

"Let me look at you," the guard demanded, forcing Bel'lar's head up. "You don't look like us. What's wrong with you?"

Bel'lar pulled back and attempted to drop his head down again. Unnoticed by the guards, he slipped his hand inside his jacket pocket and turned on his audio transmitter, allowing the crew on the ship to hear him. At least they would know what happened to him. "I have a disease," he answered. "I'm going to my surgery."

The big security guard grabbed Bel'lar by the shoulder and held him. "You're coming with us."

✳ ✳ ✳

Meanwhile, aboard ship, Ry Sing, Mauleen, and Enis sat together on the bridge listening to the events unfold for Bel'lar. Light Traveler had alerted them when the signal from his device contacted her. When the security guards took him into custody, Ry Sing stood.

"We can't let this happen. What can we do, Mauleen?"

"He instructed me to let him finish what he's started," Mauleen answered. "But don't worry. We can blast him out of any place they put him. We'll be able to swoop down, and no one will know we're there."

The two women exchanged a look. Then Ry Sing left the bridge.

Ry Sing hoped Mauleen was right, but she wasn't willing to wait. She went to her quarters and gathered some things in a small pack. Water, food, a recording device. She also donned a hooded jacket but made no attempt to cover her hair.

Stepping outside her quarters, she greeted Light Traveler.

"Yes, Ry Sing."

"I'm going to find Bel'lar. While I'm out there, I have a few things to accomplish. Then I'll be back. There's no cause for alarm. If anyone looks for me, you may tell them where I am."

She went quietly through the ship, slipping out the opening Light Traveler made for her in the hull of the ship. No tone sounded. No alert called her exit to the attention of the two on the bridge. The Light Traveler was merely facilitating the accomplishment of Ry Sing's goals.

✳ ✳ ✳

Bel'lar was taken to a local guard station where he was searched, his audio transmitter confiscated, and he was placed in a cell. Nothing like this had ever happened. No precedent existed for discovering someone who looked like Bel'lar. The request for orders continued up the chain of command. Several hours passed. Finally it reached the attention of the President of the Brotherhood of Syn.

He didn't hesitate. "Bring him to me," the President said, smiling as he speculated on the identity of this person.

All this time, Bel'lar had been silent, hoping to draw as little attention as possible. *Maybe they will believe my story and just let me go,* he thought. He knew from the bits of conversation he was overhearing that it was causing them a lot of trouble. Hours passed as he listened to the high level of activity outside his cell.

Then he heard voices coming nearer. The same two guards who had detained him opened his cell. They told him he was being taken to the President of the Brotherhood of Syn. He would decide what to do with Bel'lar.

They grabbed Bel'lar's arms and escorted him out to a transport. Bel'lar didn't resist. Every guard in the station was lined up, ready to stop him if he tried anything.

The trip to the President's office was only a few minutes away to a very tall building that gleamed golden in the daylight. The transport pulled up outside, and the two guards got out with Bel'lar. Four guards met them and joined Bel'lar's security detail. This building, unlike those he had been seeing in the city, was in good condition and well-maintained. No refuse cluttered the entry or the street around this building. He could see into the lobby, where many Brotherhood of Syn Security guards were visible. He recognized his insignia, ISOS, mounted in large gold letters over the main entry. *Was his order In Search of Shangri-La in charge? That would be a relief.* He turned to the guard on his left. "That insignia, ISOS. What does it mean?"

"You don't know what that means? That's our religious icon. Everyone knows this." The guard rolled his eyes and looked away. To Bel'lar's eye the guard's face had an uneven expression without eyebrows to shape his face.

Bel'lar persisted. "I know it's the icon, but what does it mean?"

The guard whispered, "In Search of Salvation. Now, quiet."

They took him in a side door and up in a vertical lift to the President's office on the top floor. It was a tight fit with six guards and Bel'lar. At the floor, only the two guards brought Bel'lar into the President's suite. The other four remained in the lift.

Bel'lar stood, his head down, his hood obscuring his head and the upper half of his face, while they handed a data card to the security guard on station there. The guard held it in front of a scanner and read the message. Then he nodded. The two guards took Bel'lar in through the open door to the President's private office.

The President walked around his desk and peered at Bel'lar's face. Then he dismissed the guards, leaving Bel'lar alone with him. He motioned him to sit in one of the two chairs in front of the desk and returned to his seat behind his desk.

Bel'lar got only a momentary sense of the luxuriousness of this office before his attention was wholly taken by this man. The President was a synthetic, older than Bel'lar, although it was difficult to determine his age. Like all of the Syns, no hair grew anywhere on the President's head and face, but his considerable physical size was elegantly attired. He wore a crisp black suit with a white shirt with a stand-up collar. A red tie was knotted at the neck. The jacket had two tails that dipped down the back.

Bel'lar suffered keen disappointment. This was not what he was hoping for after the relief upon seeing the ISOS insignia.

The President sat quietly and watched him for a time; then he said, "You're an Organic, aren't you?"

Bel'lar answered carefully, determined to hold on to his disguise, "No, I have a disease. I was going to my surgery when your guards stopped me."

The President leaned back in his chair, shaking his head in disbelief. "I'm known as Quasar. What are you known by?"

"Louie."

The President continued to watch Bel'lar. Then sat up. "Very well, Louie." He emphasized the name implying he didn't believe it. He contacted the security guards waiting outside the door and gave instructions for them to leave. "You can leave this man to me," he told them.

Bel'lar listened to the President's conversation as he looked around the office. The President had a large desk made of some kind of dark wood; it appeared old, even ancient. On either side of two very large windows were bookcases made of the same ancient wood. The sky through the windows was a pale yellow, suffused with bright but not direct sunlight, owing to the pollution layer. Under the windows was a bar with cabinets, again made of the ancient wood. Another doorway led into a room off to the opposite of the windows. The doorway was open, and he could see more shelves with books inside.

Quasar went to a cabinet behind his desk, where a bottle and glasses sat on a shelf. He poured a dark-purple liquid into two glasses and offered one to Bel'lar. Concerned about what it was, Bel'lar didn't drink it.

Quasar observed his reluctance and explained, "This is wine made from grapes grown in the soil." He drank from his glass and remained standing by his desk.

Real wine. Bel'lar was interested. He inhaled its scent and then sipped the wine. It was a very fruity, red wine. "This is very good, Mr. Quasar."

"Don't call me Mister. Call me Sir, or just Quasar." He gave Bel'lar a friendly smile.

Bel'lar raised an eyebrow; the President didn't see this as the hood was still pulled down. "Quasar. I didn't think any organic plants grew on this planet anymore."

"That is so, but this wine is from my private reserve. It's been stored for hundreds of years. I'm nursing it. I feel it will last the rest of my life at least. Every once in a while I have a little drink, or for a celebration. Today is one of those celebrations."

Bel'lar, intrigued but wary, asked him, "Why is that?"

"I've finally met the man that everyone feared." He approached Bel'lar, jerking back his hood, exposing his face and hair. Bel'lar's hand shot up, knocking Quasar's arm away. The older man stepped back. They stared into each other's eyes. Quasar smiled. Bel'lar wasn't sure what he saw in this man's eyes: excitement, interest, perhaps, but, for the moment, not aggression.

Quasar walked to the shelving, where old books were in rows. He pulled out one entitled *The History of Our Planet, Part I*. He walked to Bel'lar, thumbing through the book. Settling on a page, he showed it to Bel'lar. "You look like this picture."

The page depicted a likeness of the captain of the Light Traveler. It was a picture of Bel'lar, his name spelled out underneath.

"Perhaps there's a resemblance, but it's not me. Might be my great, great grandfather."

"The story is that this man went on a trip. He traveled so fast that, by the time he would have returned, hundreds of years would have passed here. If he came back, wouldn't that be cause for celebration?" Quasar continued to smile knowingly at Bel'lar.

Bel'lar smiled back at Quasar. "That would be a miracle worthy of a celebration." He couldn't fathom Quasar's purpose with these questions but realized that Quasar suspected his identity. How it was possible that this man would recognize him 350 years later he didn't know.

Quasar set the book down on his desk and returned to his chair. "Let's suppose you're that person, just to humor me. You went to a planet, or were supposed to have gone to a planet, but once you lifted off from here, there were no further communications. Why?"

Bel'lar debated how to answer, whether to answer, and then decided to go along with this fantasy of Quasar's. "Well, just suppose my grandfather was this man. If he was leaving the planet in a hurry, and there was some concern that someone would try to find him and bring him home before his mission was complete, he would have cut off any contact."

Quasar considered this idea, holding his glass up to the light. "That's very plausible. I'll have to think on it."

They both sipped their wine, and continued to watch each other. A knock sounded on the door. Quasar motioned to Bel'lar to put his hood back on. Once Bel'lar had complied, he called out for them to enter.

Two security guards escorted in another prisoner. Wearing a similar jacket to Bel'lar, he recognized immediately that it was Ry Sing. She shook off the hood, and her hair spilled out. She looked at Quasar with interest and anticipation. He smiled broadly, glancing from Bel'lar to this new woman.

Bel'lar stood, while inside his heart sank. Ry Sing smiled at him and then turned her attention back to Quasar. She shrugged her arms free from the two guards. Still smiling, Quasar motioned them to leave. They hesitated, and he glared at them. The guards hurried out.

Quasar walked around the desk and escorted the young woman to the chair next to Bel'lar's. She sat, keeping her gaze on Quasar.

Quasar clapped his hands together. "This is wonderful. Two of you. What a day for celebration."

Bel'lar frowned at Ry Sing but said nothing. What was she doing here? And why couldn't she listen to him? Now they were both in danger.

"You must be part of Bel'lar's crew. Where are the others? Surely there are more of you."

Ry Sing continued to look at Quasar, her gaze intensifying. She wanted to see inside this man to who he had been. He might have been Ka'aya.

"Oh, forgive me. I am called Quasar. And you are—."

She smiled. "Quasar. Is that the only name you respond to? Does 'Ka'aya' mean anything to you?"

Quasar grinned. This was too much fun. Two Organs. "The only other name I respond to is President. That's my title here. Who might this 'Ka'aya' be?"

"Someone dear to me. I know he's on this planet, and I must find him."

"Perhaps I'll help you find him. But for now, what are you called?"

She glanced at Bel'lar, and he shrugged. She looked back at Quasar and said, "I am called Ry Sing."

Quasar gave her a little bow. "Greetings to you, Ry Sing, and to our other illustrious guest, Bel'lar. You know, of course, that I didn't believe that name you gave me. This is indeed a great day. Let me get you a glass of wine to celebrate with us." He poured one for Ry Sing and brought it to her. She accepted it and, lifting it to her nose, breathed in its fragrance. With a happy sigh, she sipped.

Quasar sat on the edge of the desk in front of her. She leaned forward and touched his knee. Gazing into his eyes, she maintained her touch. Pitching her voice to be a caress, she said,

"Thank you. That was lovely. I would like to get to know who you have been. Just relax and open your mind to me. I'm only going to take a quick peek. That's it. Yes . . ."

Quasar's eyelids drooped, and his eyes slid out of focus. He entered a dream state as she used her sensitive abilities to probe his energy, seeking something that would indicate whether or not he had been Ka'aya. Almost there . . .

A knock at the door broke the hypnotic trance. Quasar jerked up straight. He blinked and looked at her and Bel'lar. Confusion registered on his face for a second. She smiled and sipped her wine while Bel'lar watched him.

Quasar called out, "Enter."

One of Quasar's staff stepped in. They were getting ready to leave for the day and wanted to know if he needed any more assistance. Quasar told them to go ahead. He was taking both of these people to the surgery at his compound.

It had taken hours throughout the chain of command for Bel'lar to be brought before President Quasar. It had been much faster for Ry Sing. She had been brought immediately to the President after being captured. Of course, she had simply walked up to the first guards she found and surrendered.

As a result, it was now late in the day when Quasar motioned them to come along with him. Taking the lift down, they emerged in the lobby and walked out to the waiting private transport which hovered just above the ground. It appeared to operate similarly to the public rail that Bel'lar remembered but no tracks were required. They got in, and the President's driver took them to the compound. Everyone on the street knew this was the Presidential transport. They waved and peered in the windows to catch a glimpse.

The transport made its way carefully through the people and arrived at a guarded compound enclosed by high stone walls. The sign identified it as the Compound of the Congress. A walled city within the city, the guards waved them in and closed the gate behind them. They traveled through another gate to an inner walled area, where the transport stopped. They got out. The transport was pulled over to one side and parked.

Bel'lar and Ry Sing followed Quasar inside the main entry and down a short corridor into a small room with a bench along one wall. Quasar left them inside and went away.

Bel'lar tried the door. It was locked, as he expected. He turned back to Ry Sing. She embraced him.

"I'm glad you're not hurt," she whispered. They didn't know if anyone was listening outside the door.

"What are you doing here? We don't know what these people are capable of. And now we're both captured."

"Easy, Bel'lar. I came for you. And we're only captured as long as we want to be."

"But what were you doing with Quasar back there?"

She looked away and then back at him. "I haven't told you before now because I thought you would be uncomfortable knowing this, but Ka'aya's soul has been with us on the ship until just a little while ago."

"What?"

She put her finger to his lips. "He left the ship to reach the home planet so that he would have enough time to be born and grow up to be someone living in this time. I have to find him. I was assuming that, with all of his past lives and knowledge, he would be someone of importance or a great holy man. But, Ka'aya, whoever he is now, may not know who he was. I was trying to discover Quasar's past lives to see if he was Ka'aya."

"It can't be Quasar, Ry Sing. He's a self-centered, completely physical person. I can't imagine Ka'aya being that way."

"You're probably right. That doesn't sound like Ka'aya."

"Then what's your plan? Are you just going to put everyone you think might be him into a hypnotic trance?"

"Frankly, that is my plan." She sounded sheepish. Then she grinned.

He grinned back. "Pretty stupid."

The door opened, and two men entered. One was a large, fair-skinned man, with short, red hair and light-blue eyes. An imposing older man, he was looking at Bel'lar as if he knew him. The other was a good-looking man in his middle years with dark, piercing eyes. He had black, wavy hair, which he wore smoothed back, curling behind his ears. Both wore long, white robes.

"Organs," Ry Sing sang out as she ran up to them. "Do either of you have any fond memories of being a holy man?"

The red-haired man glanced at her dismissively and then turned his complete attention back to Bel'lar. He stuck out his hand to Bel'lar and shook his hand. Bel'lar was dumbfounded. Who were these men? And could they really be Organs?

"Who are you?" he asked.

The man grinned and said, "It's me, Quasar."

Bel'lar stared at him, trying to make sense of what he was seeing. This couldn't be the Syn who had brought him and Ry Sing here. What kind of trick was this? Then he looked closer and found some resemblance. He did look like Quasar, but his body was entirely different, and he had hair and eyebrows.

"What game is this? You do look similar, but what happened to your body?"

The dark-haired man shook Bel'lar's hand and answered, "I'm Lotep. As you both can see, we are indeed Organs like you. We wear Syn suits that were created in the Time of the Dim. We could see then that the synthetic foods and chemical compounds were diminishing the brain capacity of our people. A secret project was begun to keep a few important people as Organs. We created this compound and the Syn suits at that time."

"Enough about this," Quasar interrupted. "You must tell me about your journey, Bel'lar. We couldn't understand why you didn't return all those years ago. Then we figured you took the ship and ran away. Why have you come back now?"

Relief flooded through Bel'lar as he drew himself up, his military bearing evident. Here was the Organ leader who would hear his report and decide the next steps. "I have returned to report my findings and receive new orders." He looked to Quasar for a response.

"Yes, yes, your mission. We'll get to that. Where is your ship?" Quasar looked directly at him.

Bel'lar's instincts were on alert. He wasn't prepared to give up his ship and the rest of his crew. His relief faded. He met that look with a wary smile. Wanting to seem friendly, he said, "It's safe."

"We didn't sense it."

"Maybe your sensors are malfunctioning."

"Well, we can look into that tomorrow. You must bring the ship into the compound in the morning. We have a vacant spot. Do you wish to contact your crew?"

"There's no other crew than Ry Sing. No one else came back with us."

"Oh, that's sad. Did they remain on the new planet waiting for you?"

Bel'lar simply nodded.

"We'll talk later. Lotep will find you some quarters afterward. You can't walk freely among the people outside anymore. You saw what happened when you were out there. They were afraid. You're an alien to them. But now, follow me. This dinner is in your honor, Bel'lar."

Bel'lar shook his head. "I wish you wouldn't."

Quasar ignored him and walked away.

Ry Sing linked her arm with Bel'lar's. "Come on. It will be fun." They followed Quasar, with Lotep walking behind them.

*    *    *

The dinner was being held in a big hall with about 300 Organs attending. He learned later that this was nearly all of the Organs who lived inside this compound. Lotep took them over to the front table while Quasar greeted people and then made his way to his seat of honor.

The people in the hall looked at these strangers in awe. A hush came over everyone. It made Bel'lar a little self-conscious. Ry Sing didn't seem to care. She looked about her with interest. He heard some of the people whispering and was disturbed to discover what they were saying. "Is that the great holy man? It can't be. He lived more than 300 years ago. Maybe he's a god. Gods don't die. They don't age—they just live on forever."

Another said, "Why is he here now? Have we done something wrong? And who is that with him?"

"I heard he's here to bestow his blessings on us."

Bel'lar wondered what he had gotten himself into as he sat next to Quasar at the President's table. He looked around and saw that one table ran along the front of the room where he was sitting. Other tables were lined up perpendicular to this table. There was room for the servers to move around the tables. Everyone could see the main table where the President, his advisors, and guests sat. Ry Sing sat next to Lotep, who was between Bel'lar and her.

Quasar stood, raising his arms. The whispering stopped as everyone stood with him. "We now give thanks to all those who do not partake of this meal. For this meal was intended for us. We have prepared this meal, and no Syns were involved in the preparation. Amen." Quasar remained standing as the people sat, chairs scraping, implements tinkling. When all were seated, he spoke.

"Before we eat, I would like to introduce a long-lost religious leader, Bel'lar, who has come back from the heavens beyond."

Bel'lar blinked quickly and felt the color drain out of his face. He looked down to hide his reaction. What was Quasar up to?

Quasar looked over at Bel'lar and then continued. "He will be among us for many days and nights to explain to us why we are the chosen ones of God. He will have the opportunity to take time to anoint all of you. Allow him, and you, to understand why God has picked us over all of the others to contain, direct, and run this great society of ours. We are the Congress of this planet. The Quasarian Congress will never be defeated."

The Organs began to murmur in positive response as Quasar continued.

"The Quasarian Congress of the world contains the chosen ones. The ones who rule and direct. We shall endeavor to become greater than ever before. As you go out and run your businesses, as you direct your Syns to do your bidding, you create the wealth you need to maintain this Congress." He laughed. Everyone laughed with him, except Bel'lar and Ry Sing.

"Now, we have Bel'lar. Stand up, Bel'lar. Stand up."

Bel'lar stood begrudgingly. Quasar leaned over to him and said quietly, "Smile. Let them know you're excited to be here. This is your home. You should be excited."

Bel'lar raised his hand in greeting. He smiled, but, inside, "happy" wasn't what he was feeling. He wasn't a religious leader, long lost or otherwise. This deceit on Quasar's part increased his wariness. He wished Ry Sing were safe on the ship.

"Please, sit down, Bel'lar," said the President. Bel'lar sat quickly. "Enjoy the bounty of this land. Begin."

Dinner was served. The fresh food was quite sumptuous, however, not up to the quality of the blue-white planet. The Organs ate and talked. Music was being played in the background. A small orchestra projected light, as well as music, which was very soothing and relaxing. All the foods and vegetables served were natural. Almost nothing was cooked, except for a few dishes. All the food was completely organic and all completely meatless. Cheese, milk, and creams were offered, but no meat.

Quasar ate for a few minutes, and then he began to speak to Bel'lar. "Look around you. Here are the few Organs left on this planet. We can only be Organs inside this compound. We live a completely different life inside here. The people of this planet don't know who we are and what we do. But our purpose is to take care of the Syns by producing synthetic foods for those lost souls."

Quasar lifted his utensil, indicating the people. "When we were all Organs, the government had a great vision. To feed the growing population and eradicate all known diseases, they created synthetic foods. But what happened, and we didn't realize it at that time, was that every time we got rid of one disease, we created, through synthetics, a similar ailment. That led to the creation of new synthetics to counteract the new disease."

Quasar signaled one of the attendants to take his plate. "Consequently, once you start doing this, you can't stop. Now, after 350 years, we're no better off. And the people are incapable of governing themselves because their mental capacity is much reduced. They are just a group of human animals directed by a few organic individuals. Of course, much wealth was created for those in control."

Bel'lar felt ill. Was this really how it was? Or was Quasar trying to manipulate him for his own ends, whatever they might be? Somehow, he was going to have to leave this compound and see the truth outside. "How is it that you escaped becoming a Syn?" he asked.

"My ancestor was one of those with great vision."

Bel'lar looked around this room at these Organs, who seemed to accept him as a religious leader. No one had disagreed or asked any questions. Now, no one was looking his way. They were absorbed in their dinner, chatting with their companions. He wondered if any of them would want to go to the blue-white planet. And after seeing the terrible condition of their home planet, he wondered, as Ry Sing would say, if any of them deserved to go. Were these people in this room too caught up in this privileged, albeit cloistered, life to want to leave? And outside this compound, could the Syns stop using the synthetic compounds? Was it too late for them to be anything else but what they had become? Depression settled down over him. Was his journey for nothing? He felt old. Even his bones seemed to hurt.

Quasar turned to the man sitting on his other side and didn't talk to Bel'lar again. Bel'lar spent the remainder of this dinner in silence, lost in his thoughts.

Ry Sing had turned her attention to Lotep. This man exuded a calm and comfortable confidence, not like the mercurial personality of the Quasar. Perhaps he was Ka'aya. She leaned closer to him, putting her hand on his arm.

"Tell me about yourself, Lotep."

He looked at her and smiled. "What would you like to know?"

"Where do you come from?" she asked.

"My family has lived inside this compound for at least the last two hundred years. Before that, I'm not sure. It was never spoken of by my parents."

"So you have been trapped inside here for a long time. I don't think I could accept living this way."

"That's how my sister felt. Currently, she's off with a religious group, attempting to see if it's possible for the Syns to return to an organic lifestyle."

"Your sister is religious, then. What about you? Do you have any religious leanings?"

"I think my sister was more swayed by the hope of change for the people rather than religion, but as for me, religion holds no interest. I see it as a means to control the population."

"So you have no propensity toward being a holy man?" Lotep shook his head. She continued, "Tell me about your childhood. Anything of importance occur? Something strange or unexplainable?" She watched his face as he considered his answer.

"I had a normal childhood. I excelled in learning and was prepared to follow in my father's footsteps. My position as Speaker of the Congress was my father's before me."

"I see. Do you believe in past lives?"

"No, I don't think so. There seems no point in being continually reincarnated here. And I have witnessed no evidence of it in my life. Is that something you believe in?"

"Yes, I most definitely do. My childhood was one of reconnecting to my past lives. It enabled me to become a sensitive and holy person. Many times, I have found that one's natural proclivities or interests in early life are memories from past lives. If you embrace these memories and seek to understand, you grow in spirit and understanding."

She ate the last few bites of the dessert pudding and put her spoon down. She was satisfied that Lotep was not Ka'aya. Looking around the room, she was aware that here were supposedly all the Organs on this planet. He had to be here. She would keep searching. She noticed Bel'lar was quiet and wondered what he was thinking. Unable to overhear his conversation with Quasar, she hoped they would have some privacy and a chance to talk after this dinner.

When dinner was over, everyone waited until Quasar was ready. Quasar stood, and Lotep motioned for Bel'lar and Ry Sing to follow him. The other people at his table left the room in single file. Then everyone else was free to get up and move about. Quasar walked away once outside the door, leaving Bel'lar and Ry Sing with Lotep.

Bel'lar watched the people pass by, but no one made any attempt to talk to him. In fact, they seemed to have forgotten about him. He was relieved. Yet, he found it strange. Why weren't they more curious?

"Come, I'll show you to your quarters," Lotep said. They walked along. "In the morning, I'll give you a tour. I'll show you how wonderful this compound is and what we've created here."

Lotep took Bel'lar and Ry Sing to a room down at the other end of the main corridor. He touched the door, and it opened. He stepped aside for them to enter. Then he bowed his head to Bel'lar.

"Don't do that," Bel'lar said. "You make me self-conscious." These Organs were not like the ones he remembered. "Why do you bow to me?"

"You are the Bel'lar who has returned after 350 years. So I honor you." Lotep smiled at Bel'lar's confusion. He had a commanding presence about him that was different than the Quasar because he seemed sincere. Bel'lar wondered if he might be a man, like himself, who ascribed to a higher ideal with the will to adhere to it. Bel'lar hoped there would be time to find out, but Quasar's words tonight gave him an indication of the delicate situation he was in being among these Organs.

"I'll come to your room at the third gong tomorrow and show you around the Compound. Goodnight." Lotep closed the door behind him and left.

Bel'lar inspected the room to make sure they were truly alone. Despite Quasar's having called him a "long-lost religious leader," the accommodations didn't reflect that status. The room was small and austere and white. He wanted to notify the ship and was going to try to use the implanted transmitter. He touched his temple three times. Aboard ship, a signal was heard. The signal of three indicated he was all right but couldn't speak to them now. They were to stand by and not leave the ship. Bel'lar was glad that Ry Sing had implanted this transmitter before he'd left the ship.

Bel'lar lay down and closed his eyes. He had just finished telling Ry Sing about his conversation with Quasar. She was unsurprised and hadn't any encouragement to offer him. She said that these people had strayed from the Sacred Ecology religion and destroyed themselves and this planet. She didn't want to stay here any longer than it took to find Ka'aya. He couldn't agree with her. He had to see what it was really like outside this compound. He had a deep-seated desire to determine if it was too late for these people. But he couldn't accept that yet. He had just returned home. Perhaps an opportunity would arise tomorrow. He had expected to be awake a long time, but he was exhausted and fell asleep almost immediately.

Ry Sing listened to his breathing and realized that he was asleep. She slipped out of bed and entered the bathroom. She closed the door without a sound. *Where on this planet are you, Ka'aya?* she thought as she looked into the mirror. Ka'aya was gazing back at her. "There you are," she whispered. "When you came to this planet to gain experience and knowledge, you would have been an Organ. To be a Syn would merely perpetuate a life that is unproductive, without stimulation, and, I feel, a waste. And I know you wouldn't do that because you're seeking the third aspect of your soul. So you must be in this compound. Any hints as to who you are?"

Ka'aya smiled. "Follow your intuition, dear one. We're here, but, at this moment, we are in hiding, even to us."

"You couldn't be more specific?"

"You sound like Bel'lar. Just remember, we are with you, and, together, we will find us. Don't give up." He faded away, and she remained for a few minutes staring at the mirror, her mind looking over the Organs she had seen tonight, separating out the ones she would pursue tomorrow.

✳ ✳ ✳

The next day, Lotep took Bel'lar on the tour he had promised. Ry Sing stayed behind. She had her own agenda to pursue, intending to wander around by herself. She didn't want to waste any time in her search for Ka'aya.

Bel'lar saw how efficient everything functioned. Yet not one Syn was in the compound. Only Organs lived and worked here. Even the vegetables were grown by Organs. Organs also prepared the food. They had realized that their life here was to serve and live in the Compound of the Congress forever. Their commitment was for their lifetimes. They had no other choice. Lotep said that they got so tired of wearing their Syn suits when they left the compound, but they knew that, if they were discovered among the Synthetic population, they would be killed.

The Compound of the Congress had actually been a park in the center of this city a long time ago. When it was determined to save this place, the outer walls were built. Then the pyramid-shaped roof, with semi-opaque glass that let in light, was placed over the Compound. This would ensure that what was inside would stay as it was. Everywhere in the inner compound were trees and plants, with areas set aside for growing food. In the center was a lake with benches around it in various spots and flowers growing. The lake was kept stocked with fish. It was quite beautiful, a completely different world from the outside, where the Syns lived.

It was amazing to Bel'lar that the Organs could keep this a secret from the Syns. "What about the trees, Lotep? Can't the Syns see them from the outside, or from up in the buildings?"

"We're careful to keep the trees lower than the walls of the inner compound. Over the years, we have raised the height of the Compound's inner walls on three different occasions. That way, they can't be seen. But as for the buildings, no windows are needed, for there is nothing to see. Only President Quasar has windows in his private office. If a Syn actually thinks he sees green somewhere, he will report it. It's against the law for anything to be green."

"So how old is this compound?" Bel'lar couldn't accept the dichotomy between the beauty in here and the stark reality that the Syns lived in outside.

"It was built in the Time of the Dim," Lotep said.

"What is that?"

"You're in luck, because right now, we are celebrating the Time of the Dim. The Dim was a period when much life was lost due to the people's ignorance. The Last Rights of Ester signified the end of the Time of the Dim. This celebration will be held in three weeks. It's a religious holiday held each year on the 13th day after the start of the New Year."

✻ ✻ ✻

A few days passed. Quasar had left Bel'lar to his own devices each day. Each morning, Bel'lar and Ry Sing were up and about, exploring. They watched the Organs put their suits on. These suits were incredible technology and enabled the Organs to masquerade as Syns. They left each day, picked up by the transports. They were in charge of all the Syns. The Syns on this planet did all the work. They created all the wealth for the few Organs who were living in the Compound of the Congress. Bel'lar pondered this, aware that he could go out amongst the people if he was wearing a Syn suit. Then he could get back to his ship. If he understood how the Syn suit worked, he could take one or two more for his crew. Then they could walk around and really see the state of affairs on this planet.

He and Ry Sing found the behavior of the Organs in this compound unusual, strange. These people seemed too calm, almost disinterested. He had been introduced to them as the Bellarian holy man, returned after 350 years. Yet this story that should have stretched their credulity didn't seem to stimulate any curiosity about him. No one asked him about his mission, what he had found. At first, he had been relieved to be left alone, but, now he found it disquieting. Some seemed to have forgotten about him. Others simply nodded deferentially as they passed him. This just wasn't normal behavior. Were they being "managed with synthetics" like the Syns outside? He didn't find any proof of his suspicion though, despite his concentrated effort.

Every night at the same time, Bel'lar sent the message by the three taps on his temple and signaled his ship that he was all right but not to leave the ship. Ry Sing had assured him that the ship knew where she was and would have told Mauleen. He hoped his crew would not get impatient and try to find them.

Then Bel'lar's unspoken wish for his own Syn suit was granted. Quasar decided to have him fitted him for a suit. He wanted to take Bel'lar out of the Compound with him. It took several days to construct. The suit completely covered him from head to toe. No part of his body was exposed. Even the face molded itself to his face and moved with his expressions. Underneath was a body-hugging garment of lightweight white material that left his head, hands, and feet bare. To wear over the Syn suit, Bel'lar was given a suit similar to Quasar's, except this one was gray.

Though it made him look three times his normal size, the Syn suit was actually lightweight and flexible like his own skin. Bel'lar was surprised that the suit was not more uncomfortable. It had its own system of ventilation which kept him cool and fairly comfortable—as comfortable as one could be totally encased in a suit.

Quasar was passing by in the main corridor and called over to him one morning, "I wish to take you to my office. From there the vantage point is great."

Bel'lar wondered what Quasar meant by the vantage point is great.

Quasar urged him, "Come with me, and you'll see."

Bel'lar went with Quasar to the tallest building in the capital, where the President had his office. This was where Bel'lar had been brought the first day. This time, Quasar took him into the library and invited him to sit.

On the wall behind Quasar's chair was a series of pictures. Hung in a row, the last one nearest the door was of Quasar. Bel'lar assumed that they were past presidents. One of the pictures, the third in the series, was covered with a black cloth. He wondered why that one was covered.

"We've been trying to locate your ship without success. You must bring it to the Compound. That's why I had you fitted with the suit," Quasar explained. "But I'm not really concerned, because, more than the ship, I have you."

Bel'lar didn't answer. It almost seemed that Quasar didn't want an answer. He just watched him, waiting to see where Quasar was going with this conversation. Then, the President turned the discussion to the blue-white planet. "This planet you found. Tell me. What was it like? Why did it take you 350 years to return?"

"It has to do with the speed we traveled at and its effect on time. As we increase in speed, it slows down time. To us, it was about one year and, to you, more than 300 years."

"Interesting. So, if I took this ship and circled the planet at beyond the speed of light, and then slowed down and came back to this planet, it could be that three or four hundred years had gone by in a matter of a few months. Is that right?"

"Well, in principle, I think it would work, but why would you want to do that?" Bel'lar was still wondering what Quasar's point was. Of course, he knew Quasar wanted the ship. Bel'lar would do everything to keep it from him.

"I would want to do that only if I could come back and see what's happened and then go back. Is there a way to go back in time?"

Bel'lar gave that some thought. "Maybe there's a reverse on the ship; I don't know. I'm not one of your technos. I was, and still am, one of the warrior class."

"Yes, yes . . . ," Quasar said. "I was just thinking. So tell me about the blue-white planet."

Bel'lar was relieved and a little excited to finally be able to talk about his mission. He sat up straight and told Quasar about the blue-white planet, the beauty and abundance, the race of Asians who inhabited it, and the great potential to live the organic life there, to work, to experience the natural way to live.

Quasar listened without interruption until Bel'lar had finished speaking. Then he chuckled. "But who wants to live like that, when you have all that you want on our planet here?"

Bel'lar sat stone faced, but, inside, he was disappointed and angry by Quasar's view. He had taken Quasar's silence as a sign of his interest. But the truth was this man didn't care about the organic lifestyle. Did he really want things to stay as they were?

Bel'lar had one more thing to say. "Sometimes, Quasar, you have to go back to the beginning. When the experiences of society . . ." —*What did the book say?* he asked himself— ". . . the experiences of society diminish and continue to repeat the same experiences. When those beings on that planet do not, and never will expect, to live the experiences any other way, then it's time to move on. It's time to change the reality. It's time to reinvent the future. Sometimes, when you are running on a treadmill, not going anywhere, just expending energy, it's prudent to step off of the treadmill and go in a different direction."

Quasar laughed and smacked his knee. "I knew you were the holy man we needed. We have many people who seem to want to do that very thing. Of course, I don't. Why would I? So your job is to convince those people that what we have here was created by God. And it will continue here with you as the religious leader."

"I'm not your religious leader, Quasar. I don't believe in what you're telling me. I won't do it."

Quasar stood and advanced on him. "Oh, yes, you will. And once you have convinced the Organs again, then maybe we can move you into the Syn community. You can teach them that the treadmill is the way to go." He pointed at Bel'lar.

Bel'lar sat up straighter and stared into Quasar's eyes, the two men locked for a moment in a power struggle. Then Bel'lar, maintaining eye contact, relaxed and smiled, diffusing the tension. He thought Quasar was the one on the treadmill. But he waited, wanting to know what he was planning.

Quasar continued, "Once you're on this treadmill, you never fall off. You're always in the same place. You know where you're going and where you've been. Isn't that wonderful and comforting? I think your return is a godsend. It will work out very well for me."

Quasar surveyed this library, his books, and then he returned to his seat. "One more thing I'm sure you want to know. A group of Syns is trying to repent and become Organs again. They have taken your religion to heart. They are indeed true Bellarians. They have a small community on a little continent off to the south. Wait a moment." Quasar grinned. "I believe it's on the continent of your birth. That's why they've chosen that place, isn't it? I sometimes forget things. You know, being around the Syns so much, sometimes I think I become one." He chuckled.

Then sobering, Quasar said, "This community won't work, but I allowed it because whenever you have a few discontented Syns, you have the potential for mass hysteria. Then we would have to crank up the factories to produce more synthetic countermeasures to reduce the anxiety of running on the treadmill. The people need more than these tranquilizing compounds. They need a focus. Dressed in a Syn suit, you could be that great focus. We shall announce at a later date that you have come back from the heavens to proclaim that this is the great society we had hoped it would be. Every person has a place; every person has the food they need and the drugs to sustain a wonderful and happy life.

"I know I laugh a lot, and you're probably thinking we have invented a chemical compound that will make people laugh. And you're right. Maybe I do partake in it once in a while, but you must understand I have great stress. I have great power. My authority is unlimited and unchallenged."

Bel'lar gripped the arms on the chair, angered by this speech. His apparent part in the president's plan was to manipulate the people and keep them happy despite the terrible lives they led. He had no intention of doing that. But that community of Bellarians . . . He would like to see it. Maybe someone from there might want to leave this place. He relaxed. Once again, he had hope that someone here would be able to go to the blue-white planet and give meaning to his mission. Focused within, he glanced at Quasar and saw him looking at him, questions in his eyes. He struggled to find something to say. "Do you have elections?"

"Yes, we do. Our government has a committee, and the population votes for the committee members. There are two parties. Every four years, the committee changes, and they appoint a president. For the past fifteen or so years, they seem to like me a lot. I keep getting reappointed. I'm what you would call the head of the bureaucratic state. It believes in freedom for all and all a voice. They have the ability to vote their minds and hearts. They choose to put into power whomever they want. Of course, they want whomever it is we decide to run. It all comes back to me." Quasar leaned forward. "Would you like a soda?"

"What's that?"

"It's a concoction we've made for the Syns that contains sugar, salt, caffeine, and a downer and an upper. It drives you crazy, but you like it because it's addictive. Try one." Quasar smiled again, in that unsettling way he had.

Bel'lar hesitated. This didn't sound like something he wanted to try. He wondered whether it was even safe to drink. If Quasar was drinking it, that wasn't a guarantee of safety. This man was very far from the Organs he knew.

"You must try one. I drink one every day when I get up. Otherwise I wouldn't be as much fun. You can also try these pills." Quasar reached into his pocket and took out a packet of pills. He offered them to Bel'lar.

Bel'lar shook his head. This man wasn't a true Organ. Was this what was wrong with the Organs in the compound? Did they indulge in these artificial substances?

Surprisingly, the President accepted Bel'lar's response, and they continued their discussion for a short time.

Then Quasar stood abruptly. "I have business to attend to. I will join you this evening. Lotep will meet you on the first level of this building. My staff will show you." Quasar went into his private office and closed the door.

* * *

While Bel'lar was being questioned by Quasar, Ry Sing wandered around the lake in the center of the Compound of the Congress. It was peaceful and quiet at this time of the morning. Everyone was about their duties, and she was relatively alone. There were some people on the other side of the lake, but they were too far away to disturb her. She sat down cross-legged under a tree and focused on the water. Every so often, a tiny ripple disturbed the surface. She cast her thoughts inside and ceased to notice her surroundings. She wanted to be able to leave this compound without the inhabitants noticing. She didn't have one of those Syn suits, but she felt there must be another way. If she were simply invisible, that would be the answer, but she didn't know how to do that. She sifted back through this life, seeking any training or any glimmer of an idea that she could expand on, but nothing surfaced in this life. So be it. Then she must search deeper. She must go back into a past life.

Breathing deeply, slower and slower, her heart slowed, and she passed over the barrier between lives and looked around. A crystal chair of golden topaz stood before her. Light streamed in from a myriad of angles in this structure housing this chair, setting the topaz alight with life. She sat in the chair, placing her hands on the arm rests. As she leaned back, the past life unfolded before her eyes. She was on Taurus. People who looked like her went about their activities. She saw the pyramid on a causeway with ocean around it and the city in the distance rising up into the clouds, it was so tall.

Then she was infused with memory and knowledge. And she knew that she had the ability in that dimension to create a vortex of energy that would allow her to appear invisible. This energy vortex would shift the perceptible light rays to make her appear as if she were floating in water. Her body would be hazy, out of focus. If anyone noticed her, they would dismiss it as an illusion or simply a shadow.

Concentrating on this idea, her body, seated beside the lake, began to vortex. As she vibrated faster and faster, the life on Taurus faded away. She rose to her feet, and, fully infused with this higher vibrational energy, she was an iridescent whirlwind that stirred no blade of grass; she glimmered with stardust.

Passing safely and unnoticed from the Compound, she turned unerringly in the direction of the Light Traveler's location. She and the ship were in communication. She passed through groups of people, some of whom turned toward her, thinking they saw something out of the corner of their eyes. One tried to touch the whirlwind, but his hand slid through it. He shrugged and turned back to his friends. She continued on her way, the ship guiding her in her mind.

✳ ✳ ✳

A Brotherhood of Syn Security guard escorted Bel'lar to the vertical transport and down to the first level of the building. As he rode in the vertical lift, he reflected on Quasar's words. He was going to claim he was the god of the Bellarian religion. *Didn't that present a conflict for him, since Quasar was the leader of the Quasarian religion?* Bel'lar asked himself. *Did he want to create conflict by exposing me as the holy savior of the Bellarian religion? Or, maybe, he just wanted dueling gods, the Bellarian versus the Quasarian. Maybe he was just fooling with my mind, and trying to drive me insane. But it seemed probable that Quasar was the one impaired by the substances he indulged in regularly. What an experience!* The doors to the lift opened, and he stepped out on the first floor. There he was met by a Syn who whispered to him, "Hello, Bel'lar."

Bel'lar looked at this Syn but didn't recognize him.

"It's me, Lotep. I'm here to take you back to the Compound."

Bel'lar looked closer and then saw that it was indeed Lotep. In the Syn suit, he looked 100 pounds heavier and had no hair. The Syn suit took on the characteristics of the person after the first wearing. Now he could see that this was indeed Lotep, and he must likewise be recognizable in his own suit.

"Hi, Lotep. What about a tour of the city first?"

Lotep looked around and then said, "Well, I don't see what that would hurt. No one will recognize you. Let's do it."

Lotep took him outside to his transport, and they began to travel around the city. This transport was large enough to seat six. It had a round dome over the top. Now Bel'lar had a chance to see that it levitated above the city streets by means of magnetized cables in the streets. They could ride along these cables throughout the city. There were no accidents, since they had outlawed wheeled vehicles. Lotep explained that wheeled vehicles used to kill and destroy too many people, so they adopted this system of transport. There were also a limited number of authorizations for these vehicles in the city. To receive one, you had to apply for it, and that was only if you needed it for business. Of course, members of the government had whatever they needed. Personal transport was accomplished through the use of public rails. This completely eliminated any accidents, because the system was monitored. The locations of all the cars were computed and fed back to the central control, avoiding the possibility of two cars ever being in the same place.

They traveled through the city. Some of it looked similar to when Bel'lar lived there. He was surprised, expecting much more change after 350 years. "You know, Lotep, this isn't much different than when I was here."

"Yes, at that time, there was much construction, which satisfied the needs of the city for many years. Later the government purchased all the buildings in the downtown areas of the city. Since then, they have determined that the building of new facilities was a waste of time and effort. There has been very little building, except on the outskirts, to house the expanding population. Once the people live in a building, they never move. They have no need. This eliminates a lot of excess confusion for everyone. The government likes to know where everyone is, and the Syns get confused with change, so it works out for the best."

Lotep parked the transport. They got out in the center of the city and walked around for a bit. They came upon a person in an extreme state of intoxication, lying on the ground at the side of the road. People were touching their lips and then touching this person as they walked by. They repeated as they did this, "For they are in the rapture of their life, and this is all we ever want."

Bel'lar couldn't keep himself from staring. "Why are they touching their lips and repeating these words? I saw this once before, on the first day, when I was alone in the city."

Lotep explained as they watched the people. "They touch their lips because that is where the consumption begins."

Bel'lar was repulsed by this twisted practice. How could this society have become this distorted? "Shouldn't we help him?"

"No. The Brotherhood will come, and he will be delivered from the bondage of consumption. At least that's what the holy men say. But, I suspect . . ." Lotep stopped talking, looking around.

Bel'lar waited, but Lotep said nothing. "Lotep, go on."

Lotep looked at him, confused. "What?"

"You were speaking; you said you suspect something, and then you stopped."

"I did? Oh sorry." Lotep shook his head. "I was going to say I suspect Quasar actually takes the lives of these poor individuals who have consumed beyond their abilities to understand. The Quasarian religion honors this, saying to consume all is the act of the most heavenly being. It has been written that God, the Quasar, did indeed consume all that lived on the first planet, the Planet of Abundance. Then he took his twelve disciples up into the heavens and created the Quasar of stars that filled the sky. There is the bounty. When we consume all there is," Lotep turned to look at Bel'lar, "while being in a conscious mind, then we shall have all the bounty the Quasar created."

Bel'lar shook his head sadly. These people were being manipulated in every aspect of life. It seemed too late for them. But what did Lotep believe? Bel'lar thought the only way this story might be acceptable was if one's mind were addled by drugs and synthetic foods as these people's were.

Lotep answered him, equally sad. "That's their belief. Everything is contrived to continue making them believe this."

"Then you don't believe this story?" Bel'lar was surprised and relieved to see Lotep's sadness. This man wasn't happy about the situation outside these compound walls.

Two men lifted a hand to Lotep in greeting as they passed by, recognizing the Speaker of the Congress. Like Quasar, Lotep was dressed in a black suit with white shirt. Lotep nodded in response; then, taking Bel'lar's arm, he tugged him back, out of the walk path, away from the many people around them.

Lotep leaned toward Bel'lar and lowered his voice, not wanting the people to hear any of this conversation. "None of the Organs have this belief. It's only outward allegiance to Quasar that makes it appear that we go along."

"Isn't that dangerous, pretending to believe? Surely Quasar knows none of you believe this."

"No, it's not dangerous. Quasar doesn't believe it, either. It's merely part of our role as providers for the Syns. It's become easier for us to follow the Quasarian religion. But lately, Quasar has begun acting strangely. I suspect he's indulging too frequently in the substances we make for the Syns. It's changing him, and he's becoming unpredictable."

They crossed the street and began walking back toward the transport's location.

"I see. Could we go out to the old teleport station? I'd like to see what it's like now."

"You don't want to go there. It's just a fenced area. It has the old pyramid, which is very rustic. We fenced it because people kept defacing it and stealing the stones."

"I'd like to see it. I spent many years on my last assignment there."

"Then, we'll go there."

They returned to the transport. Lotep steered it to connect to the route that led out to the teleport station. They had to wait at several places for people to cross. The streets were congested, and people crossed everywhere on the street, walking around Lotep's government transport. Some peered into the transport, nodding to Lotep. Finally, they reached the connection and proceeded more smoothly.

On the way, Bel'lar asked Lotep about his life, wanting to find out more about him. "Lotep, I've been meaning to ask you:

What is the Speaker of the Congress? How did you come to have such a responsible position?"

The route to the teleport was a raised loop around the city. Bel'lar could see the area they had walked through, but soon they were outside the city proper, and barren, dusty, brown fields stretched out on one side, buildings on the other.

Lotep said, "I was groomed for it. My father was the Speaker of the Congress before me."

"You followed in your father's footsteps."

Lotep nodded. "He was a great man in his own right, but, at the end of his career, he became disenchanted. When it was time to pick a successor, he chose me. I have been doing it for about ten years."

"What exactly do you do?"

"Basically, I run the Compound of the Congress. I'm in charge of this forbidden city. I'm responsible for everything that goes on, from security to making sure that the food supply is sufficient. I have a capable staff. The first day of the workweek, at the third gong, we meet and plan what is to be done for that week, month, and year beyond."

Bel'lar asked, "Do you like what you do?"

The elevated loop descended and connected to a road that Bel'lar remembered from that first day when he made the hike into the city. His journey had taken him much longer than this trip.

"I like the organizational aspects of the position, but, to be honest, there is no more adventure or excitement. It's mostly routine. I dream of going on an adventure."

"Could you set up a government and run it?" Bel'lar said.

Lotep's eyes lit up. "Oh, yes. I have the skills and am willing to travel."

Bel'lar chuckled. "I'll keep that in mind when I start my next government. What about your family?"

"My parents are retired. My sister, who was studying to be a holy man, found this, as she puts it, great sage. They call him the Saint. Now she's off with him, trying to change the world."

Bel'lar's thoughts were interrupted by the appearance of the old teleport station. Lotep turned his focus to parking the transport in front of the sign. They got out, and walked over to the fence.

Aboard ship, the Light Traveler alerted Mauleen and Enis to Bel'lar's presence outside. They were on the bridge, where they'd spent the last few days, monitoring the planet's transmissions and entertainment channels as well as scanning for Bel'lar and Ry Sing. They scanned the immediate area, but they couldn't see him.

Bel'lar walked toward where he knew the ship existed in the other dimension. He turned away to keep Lotep from seeing what he was going to do. He put his hand up to his temple. He was about to use the implant to signal when a hatch opened before him. He reacted instantly, jumping inside the ship.

Lotep saw the hatch open and Bel'lar disappear into it. He leaped toward the opening, but it closed, leaving him outside. Bel'lar was gone without a trace. He shouldn't have brought him out here. He hoped he could get his attention, talk him into returning. He had to take him back to the Compound, or Quasar would be furious.

Meanwhile, Mauleen saw only that it was a Syn who had entered the ship. She grabbed her light pistol and yelled, "We've been breached by a Syn." She took off at a run for the hatch. "Enis, you're in charge." Enis jumped up, with a grin on his face. At last to be in charge. He sat in Bel'lar's chair.

"First Officer," the Light Traveler said. "There is no need for a weapon. It's Captain Bel'lar that I have allowed to board. Cease your actions."

"No. We can't take any chances." Mauleen doubled her speed, racing to meet the intruder.

Inside the ship, Bel'lar discovered that he was inside the decontamination corridor. It was once again necessary.

When Mauleen got to the hatch, it was a Syn she saw, not Bel'lar, coming out of the decontamination corridor. This Syn handed his gray suit to her. Then she noticed an opening in the front of the Syn just under his chin. Mauleen jerked to a stop. As he pulled apart the neck and pushed the head up, it was Bel'lar inside it. What? It must be a suit. She stared, trying to comprehend.

"Help me get this off. It's so confining." As he struggled to get out of the suit, Mauleen continued to stare.

"Mauleen, some help here," he directed.

She started pulling on the suit at the back of the neck to help him out of it.

"Thanks, much better. Couldn't wait to get that off."

She stared at the white underwear that hugged his body. "Captain, finally you're here. Are we leaving?" Mauleen was breathing hard.

Bel'lar noticed the light pistol and grinned. "No, not yet. There are still some things I want to do. I'll talk to you in a moment, but first, we have someone outside our ship."

Mauleen followed him to the bridge, where Enis was in charge, still sitting in Bel'lar's chair. Bel'lar raised his eyebrow at this but said nothing.

"I have him in sight. Should we zap him senseless?" Enis was excited at this prospect.

"No, Enis. I want to talk with him. Turn on the outside communication, so he can hear me."

Mauleen stepped over and turned on the speakers, not waiting for Enis to do it.

Outside the ship, Lotep had figured out that Bel'lar's ship must be here somewhere. He tried to feel for it, but he couldn't find anything. He walked back to where Bel'lar had disappeared. He called out, "Bel'lar. I know you're there. Talk to me."

"Yes-s-s-s," Bel'lar answered Lotep.

"This is going to get me in a lot of trouble. You must come back with me. It's important for you to see what we're all about. Don't give up on us. We're not all like Quasar, even though it seems to be this way."

Bel'lar motioned to Mauleen to turn off the speaker. Then he turned to his crew. "What do you think?"

Mauleen answered immediately. "Don't let him in."

Enis said, "Let's vaporize him—make him dust, powder, smoke!"

*I've got to get Enis out of my chair,* Bel'lar thought. *He's undergoing some kind of transformation.* Then he focused on Lotep's presence.

"I'm considering letting him in," he said.

"Then we can vaporize him." Enis grinned.

Bel'lar stared at Enis and Enis squirmed, uncomfortable under that gaze. He vacated the captain's chair and backed up. Bel'lar opened the channel again. "Lotep, when you see the area in front of you turn black, step into it, and you will be aboard my ship." He motioned to Mauleen to meet Lotep. She hurried out, Enis behind her.

Light Traveler opened the hatch, and Lotep stepped in. Mauleen was already waiting for him at the end of the decontamination corridor, with Enis standing by her. Bel'lar hurried down after them. Lotep stood there, his hands in the air, Mauleen's pistol pointed at him.

"Mauleen, put your weapon down. He's one of us." Bel'lar pushed her pistol down as he stepped in front of her toward Lotep.

"He is? Is that a suit like the one you had on?" She looked curiously at Lotep, waiting for the suit to open up.

"It is. Let's help him out of it. Put your hands down, Lotep," Bel'lar directed.

Lotep lowered his hands and then pulled apart his suit. Bel'lar helped him out of it. Lotep, feeling at a disadvantage, put on his jacket, leaving the rest of his outer clothing with the suit.

Enis was surprised when he saw the real Lotep emerge. "You're an Organ." He stepped closer to look him over.

"Yes, the Organs run this planet now." Lotep looked around at these members of Bel'lar's crew, the curly-haired redhead in the military uniform and the tall, thin man with shaggy brown hair.

"They do? I can't believe that. All your transmissions show nothing but Syns." Enis frowned at Lotep.

"That's true. They feel they're in charge. But the government is really in charge. If you look at the government, they all look like Syns, but behind them all, behind the suits, they are Organs. Organs run this planet."

"Come, Lotep. Let me show you the ship." Bel'lar walked off, with the others following.

"That would be wonderful. I have dreamed of traveling on one of these crafts some day to distant stars, where I may explore freely who I am and share my knowledge."

Bel'lar grinned at Mauleen, shrugging his shoulders at Lotep's formal speech.

"Let me introduce my crew." The others stopped as Bel'lar spoke. "This is Mauleen, First Officer of the ship." Mauleen and Lotep nodded to each other. Lotep turned to Enis. "And Enis, this is Lotep. Lotep, this is Enis."

"Greetings, Lotep. I'm the ship's cook."

"No, he's more than that," Bel'lar said. "He's actually our Botanist."

"I am glad to meet you both. We've waited so long to be saved," Lotep said.

"What's this about being saved?" Mauleen looked from Bel'lar to Lotep for answers.

Bel'lar gave her a sheepish grin. "I'm kind of the savior, according to Quasar. Yet it doesn't seem that important to anyone here. There's a group that's still organic, just like Lotep. They are housed in the Compound of the Congress. There are about 300 of them. They live in a self-sufficient inner city that is forbidden to all Syns. They must never know what goes on in that inner city."

"That's the reason for the suits," Lotep explained. "It was very difficult until the suits were manufactured. Now, we can wear them at least eight or nine hours a day and be comfortable in them. We instruct the Syns and provide for them. The Syns expect their leaders to look like this. If we came out as Organs, they would stone us."

"It's a very good hoax, all right. But what started as good intentions always goes off course, never ending up as good as the intentions were," Bel'lar commented.

Mauleen looked at him curiously. "Are you feeling all right?" Was this her Captain with his philosophical comments?

Bel'lar laughed, and everyone laughed with him.

"Come into the lounge," Enis said, "and have refreshments. You must be thirsty." He walked on ahead.

Bel'lar led the way down the corridor, with Lotep and Mauleen behind him.

"I will take Mauleen's hand, if she will permit me. We'll follow you to the lounge." Mauleen, caught off guard by the formality of his request, allowed Lotep to take her hand and escort her. Lotep enjoyed the blush that spread over her face.

They arrived at the lounge and sat around a small table. Enis brought out fruit juice made from fruit he had gathered on the blue-white planet. They talked for a while. Lotep was impressed with the fruit juice. They couldn't get anything that good here, he said, because so much of the natural climate had been corrupted.

"I would love to be able to travel to the blue-white planet on this ship," Lotep said.

No one commented; they just smiled at him. He smiled back, hoping he would get the chance.

The four were becoming comfortable and relaxed, when everything changed.

A vortex of energy passed through the ship's hull and into the ship, continuing on until it entered the lounge. One minute it wasn't there. The next it appeared to Bel'lar and the others in the lounge. This vortex of energy swirled and glimmered, and bits of blue seemed to dart about inside it. It didn't advance any further into the lounge. Bel'lar jumped to his feet and, in a split-second decision, assumed it was some kind of energy weapon sent by Quasar. He grabbed Lotep, shoved him against the bulkhead. The whirlwind continued to spin.

"You had us followed," Bel'lar yelled. Lotep struggled, but Enis rushed over and grabbed Lotep's arm to prevent him from getting away.

"Wait. Wait. I don't know what this is," Lotep gasped out.

Mauleen pulled her pistol but was unsure if this would do anything when the vortex began to slow. With every revolution, more blue was visible until first a hand, an arm, and a bit of long dark hair could be glimpsed. Then it slowed even further, and now a person was visible. It was Ry Sing, wearing a blue dress that appeared translucent and shifting. Then they realized it was Ry Sing that was translucent, that they could see through her body. She seemed to be a mass of moving energy, and that slowed as well. As they watched, her transparency faded, and she seemed to solidify, if that were possible. She stood before them dressed in a blue, diaphanous gown, the trappings of Taurus, still a reflection of that past life.

Lotep ceased to struggle when Ry Sing became recognizable. Bel'lar and Enis forgot about him in the shock of her extraordinary appearance and released him.

"I'm so excited," Ry Sing said. "We have to go to Taurus. It's still as I left it."

Bel'lar's mouth dropped open.

"It's just as I left it," she repeated. She walked away from this group staring at her, toward the table.

Lotep looked at Bel'lar and said, "You don't understand. I'm not who you think I am. I'm like you. I'm searching, too. Searching for how I fit. It doesn't seem to be on this planet."

Ry Sing returned with a glass of juice. "I'm thirsty." The blue garment was fading now, being replaced by Ry Sing's lavender tunic and pants. Within moments, no trace of the blue Tauran gown remained.

Lotep looked at Ry Sing, a look of awe on his face. She smiled back.

Bel'lar didn't respond to Lotep. Instead, he turned his attention to Ry Sing. She was looking at him for the first time since her entrance. "What do you have on?" she stepped closer, looking at the white underwear. "I like it."

Bel'lar laughed. "How did you do that? Did you just pass through the ship's hull?"

Enis touched her on the shoulder and then pushed. She grinned at him. He grinned back.

Lotep watched all of this, still in awe. Who were these beings? Especially this Asian woman. Yes, he definitely wanted to travel with them.

"I did," she said. "Wasn't it wonderful? I wanted to leave the Compound, and you can't do that without a suit. Then I retrieved this ability to vortex from my past life on Taurus. I just entered that frequency and simply walked out of the Compound. No one noticed. There's a pyramid there, too. I mean on Taurus. When can we leave here?"

"Not just yet. I have something to resolve first," Bel'lar answered her.

"As do I. I almost forgot in all my excitement." She sat at the table, and the others followed suit. In a short time, the conversation continued.

Mauleen and Enis wanted to know what had been going on and where Ry Sing had been. Bel'lar filled them in on the last few days, with Lotep adding information to clarify. Bel'lar told them about the Syns and the distorted, synthetic world they lived in. And about the Organs—how they were trapped inside the Compound, never able to leave without wearing a disguise.

They gave Lotep a quick tour, showing him the bridge and telling him a bit about the ship, which he found fascinating. Then Lotep realized how long they had been gone and said, "I must take Captain Bel'lar and Ry Sing back to the Compound of the Congress, or there will be a search. You will certainly be discovered. We do have some technologies to discover frequencies, and eventually they'll figure out that you're hiding in this frequency. What are your plans, Bel'lar?"

"Yes," Ry Sing said, "what are your plans?"

"Your plans should be to let this man go and leave this place," Mauleen interrupted. "They want to take our ship and probably throw us in prison."

Lotep smiled at her, thinking she was quite attractive, this little redhead. "If you're not in agreement with Quasar, then you might wind up in prison. The people here are controllable by changing some of the ingredients in the foods. If you're Quasar, and you wish them to be angry, to rebel against something, you merely adjust the proportions of certain chemicals in the synthetic foods, capsules, or water."

"Like those sodas. I was tempted to try one. They sound wonderful, to hear Quasar explain it," Bel'lar said.

"They are quite wonderful but very addictive. You have to realize that, once you're addicted, it takes a lot of personal effort to stop using it," Lotep explained. Then he stood. "But we need to return."

"We do," Bel'lar said. "Mauleen, I can't give up on the planet yet. We've been here only a few days. I must try to see if there is anybody," he laughed ruefully, "to save. I have been announced as the savior. Let's have a little bit of fun here and see where it leads us."

"Fun, Bel'lar? This doesn't sound like fun. But if you're going to do it, I want to be with you." Ry Sing looked at Lotep. "I want one of those Syn suits. I can't repeat my earlier journey again today. I'm too tired. Why don't you bring one back for me? Then I'll consider returning to the Compound."

Enis spoke up. "I want one. I want to go out, too."

Lotep considered this. "It might be possible. I'll see what I can do." He turned to Mauleen. "What about you, Mauleen? Do you want one? I would be more than happy to bring one for you." He reached out and took her hand.

Mauleen smiled at him, not pulling away. He was quite attractive, she noticed. "No, I don't believe it's necessary for me to find out how bad things have gotten. I can view them on the crystal display. I can see all I need to from here. Thank you, but, no thank you, for the invitation." She let go of his hand.

"We really must be on our way. We have a curfew at the Compound of the Congress. If we're late, we'll be locked out. It's been a pleasure to meet you, especially you, Mauleen. I look forward to the next time." Mauleen flushed at this remark, embarrassed by his marked attention. He smiled at her reaction.

As the others walked to the hatch, Enis remained on the bridge. Bel'lar and Lotep put on their Syn suits. When they were ready, Bel'lar turned to Mauleen. "I'm expendable. Light Traveler is not. Take whatever action is necessary to protect yourself and the ship."

She straightened and tucked one loose strand of hair behind her ear. "Yes, Captain Bel'lar. I will."

Bel'lar turned to Ry Sing. They hugged and kissed. She put her hand on his cheek and whispered, "Take care, my beloved." He hugged her again.

"Open the hatch, Light Traveler," Bel'lar said.

"Indeed, Captain," the ship responded.

The hatch opened, and two Syns walked out into the early evening air and got into the transport. They traveled away to the Compound. On the way, Bel'lar told Lotep, "They will move the ship and change its frequency, so, if you had any thoughts of betraying me, it won't matter."

"If I wanted to betray you, I would have done it by now. Quasar told me you would probably want to go to your ship and that I should allow this. Once inside, I was to press the distress signal. Each suit comes with one. You merely touch your thumb and little finger together on both hands. Within minutes, the Brotherhood of Syn Security Special Forces come to your rescue. They would have been here in moments and seized the ship and your crew."

"I told Quasar that Ry Sing and I were the only ones."

Lotep smiled. "Do you think he believed that? You will just have to trust me." They lapsed into silence as they traveled.

Lotep was right. Bel'lar would just have to trust him. He rather liked him. And, truly, he didn't think that they could find the ship, let alone board her. They had no idea what Light Traveler was capable of.

There were a few clouds in the sky, and not much color was displayed in the sunset. Bel'lar noticed this and couldn't help but compare it to the blue-white planet. "What happened to the sunsets?"

Lotep regarded Bel'lar curiously. "Sunset? What's that?"

"You know—when the sun's rays cut through the atmosphere at a certain angle. It changes the sky to vibrant colors, like yellows, oranges, and burnt reds. The sunsets on the blue-white planet were spectacular. I miss them."

Lotep considered. "No sunsets in my lifetime. It sounds wonderful. But we've had problems once the vegetation was gone. The atmosphere is becoming lighter. That's why we supplement synthetic oxygen in the food supply."

"Of course, you do," Bel'lar commented. This planet seemed nearly unlivable without technological assistance. No food, no clean air. He had to assume no clean water, either. How did they survive? "Lotep, how do you maintain a clean environment in the Compound? Do the people take drugs?"

"It's becoming more difficult each year. We keep it to a minimum, but we have to purify the water and the air. There doesn't seem to be much reaction to those agents thus far."

"I see," Bel'lar responded. Lotep didn't notice, but Bel'lar did. That explained the strange behavior of the Organs. If they were ingesting all of these agents, they were altered in ways they no longer noticed.

They arrived at the Compound and proceeded into the inner wall. Quasar was waiting for them when they walked into the first room to take off their suits. He looked unhappy. "Why have you been gone so long? We thought you were just going to see the city."

"I wanted to see where I used to live and where I used to work. It's a lovely city. We stopped and talked to some of the people and had some refreshments." Nonchalantly, Bel'lar smiled at him, attempting to disarm him as he took off his suit and hung it up.

Quasar motioned Lotep to step away with him, leaving Bel'lar to finish changing. They walked a short distance, and Quasar turned to Lotep. "Simple orders are too difficult for you to follow, apparently. Perhaps you don't want to be administrator of this great city anymore." Quasar glared at Lotep. Lotep met his eyes but said nothing.

Quasar started to walk away but then turned and said more loudly, "Bel'lar, there is a meeting at my office in the morning. You will attend. I plan to reveal you to the holy men of the Syns." He walked away, chuckling.

When Quasar was out of earshot, Bel'lar asked, "Lotep, what are the holy men of the Syns?"

"The Quasarian Brothers. The Quasar may be doing something that I thought he wouldn't do."

"What, Lotep?"

"If you view them with your suit on, then it will be just introducing one of their own to them. But if he has you remove your suit, then I would have concerns." Lotep hesitated.

"What do you mean?"

"I don't really know. I need time to think about what's going to happen. Why don't you go to your quarters? We'll meet after dinner."

*I don't like this*, Bel'lar thought, as he walked away. What was going to happen now? And could he trust Lotep? Did Quasar order him to contact the BOS once he was inside the ship? Or did he just say that to trick Bel'lar into thinking he was on his side?

Bel'lar sat at Quasar's side again at dinner. Lotep didn't attend. No one asked after Ry Sing and Bel'lar didn't offer anything. The people noticed him when he took his seat, but then they seemed to forget he was there.

After dinner, as he passed people in the hallways and the gardens, some bowed their heads in honor toward this Bellarian. Bel'lar was being accepted as the savior who had returned. This disturbed him to his very core. He wasn't a savior but simply a military man on assignment.

Bel'lar was supposed to meet Lotep on a bench, near the lake on the north shore. As he walked, he saw that the hibiscus was in bloom. It was quite lovely here in this park, but he couldn't see the stars because of the opaque glass. Spotlights with star cutouts over the lenses projected the illusion of stars in the night sky up on the inside of the great canopy of glass. Outside in the city, when they looked up at night, they didn't see any stars. A dark haze covered the city.

Bel'lar found his way to the bench on the side of the lake. A small light illuminated it by the water's edge. As he approached, he saw a shadow that resolved itself to be Lotep sitting there.

He clasped his hands together and bowed to him. "Greetings, Lotep."

Lotep stood and greeted him in kind. "Greetings, to you, Bellarian. You are the one who sits at the right hand of God."

Bel'lar waved his hand dismissively. "That's what they tell me, anyway. Let's sit down." They both sat. "What's that you have there?"

Lotep produced a bottle of what turned out to be vintage wine. He held it out to Bel'lar. "Here, you take the first drink."

Bel'lar accepted the bottle and took a swallow. "It's good. Thanks." He handed it back and gazed out over the lake. Ripples, caused by something coming to the surface in the water, spread out in a circle.

Lotep took a long drink and glanced over at his silent friend. "You're starting to understand your religion."

"No. What I understand is when the people who pass me clasp their hands and bow in reverence, they want something from me. I have begun to offer that back to them. They smile serenely, and move on. It's as if I've recognized them and given them a free pass to heaven. It'd be laughable if they weren't so serious."

Lotep chuckled. "Then, after we talk tonight, I hope you will give me a special pass to sit at your right hand when I die and go to that place in the heavens where the Quasars are."

"I don't understand these two religions, Quasarian and Bellarian. How did this all begin? Can you tell me?"

"I'll try to explain," Lotep said. "I'm not a religious person, but I'll tell you what I know."

Lotep stood and walked a few steps away. He looked up into the artificial night sky. Bel'lar waited, but Lotep said nothing.

"Lotep?" This was the second time Lotep had lost his train of thought. Bel'lar wondered how seriously he was affected and if it was permanent.

"Yes."

"You were about to explain about the religions."

"Oh, was I? Sorry. Since the last time we changed the chemicals in the water, I've noticed I've had more of these spells." He looked at Bel'lar. Then he drew himself up tall. "Let us begin." He held his hand up as if pontificating to a large crowd. "I'm starting to sound like some of the religious leaders." He grinned. The wine was having an effect on him.

Bel'lar teased him, "With that white robe, you look very like one yourself, in this light." He was enjoying the wine's relaxing effect, too.

They both laughed as they looked out over the lake. They passed the bottle back and forth. They could see reflections of the simulated stars shining in the water.

Bel'lar pointed. "Look. It's almost as if I were back on the blue-white planet. The skies are clear there, and you can see the star of this planet."

"It sounds wonderful," Lotep said. "I'm going to do something for you, and then you will have to take me with you."

Bel'lar turned and peered up into Lotep's face with a grin. "It will have to be something wonderful." They both laughed again. "Please continue with the story."

Lotep sat down, took a drink of the wine, and passed it back to Bel'lar.

"Well, let's see . . . Everyone believed in the Sacred Ecology religion until you left this planet with your band of holy men, promising us salvation, promising us a place in heaven where we all could live out our lives in wealth and splendor. That's how the Bellarian religion began. It was an offshoot of the Sacred Ecology.

"The belief was that someday you would come back and save them, by taking them with you. This belief existed for about one hundred years after you left. But then, in the Time of the Dim, the Quasarian religion was born. You hadn't returned. Some of the Organs began to sense unrest and unhappiness in the Syns, so we created the Quasarian religion in response."

Bel'lar interrupted, "You created the Quasarian religion?"

"Let me explain. The Quasarian religion teaches that, through technology, we will be one. By consuming all there is to consume, you will ascend into the Quasars, which is the heavens' most heaven. Therefore, we had to discredit the Bellarian religion."

Bel'lar drank again, wondering why being the Bellarian was an advantage here, as the Quasar seemed to think. Maybe the better question was, advantage for whom? He drank again, finishing the wine. He held out the bottle to Lotep. "Sorry. It's all gone."

"Oh wait, I forgot." Lotep leaned down and pulled another bottle from under the bench. He opened it, took a drink, and gave it to Bel'lar.

"I must apologize again for the lapse in my memory. I must tell you the truth." He pitched his voice low. "Even though we believe we're truly organic, the true organic no longer exists on this planet. Everything must be purified and treated in some way to maintain the delicate balance in the Compound . . . over time, the chemicals have dimmed my mind . . . my thoughts . . . to the point where it's hard to grasp and remember certain concepts and other thoughts. Part of the time, I don't care that I forget."

"It's all right. Go on with your story," Bel'lar encouraged him.

Lotep patted him on the knee. "Thank you, friend." Then his forehead wrinkled as he struggled to remember where he was in the story. He smiled and continued, "In the Time of the Dim, the people were unhappy because some of the synthetic production was causing the population to become hostile. They vented their frustrations at the leaders of the government, the religion and the corporations. We created the Quasarian religion to find fault with the Bellarians, because we were afraid of the unrest.

"We needed to discredit the belief that Bel'lar would come back, anoint everyone, and take them up into the heavens, into the Quasars. The Quasarian religion said this was a lie. Bel'lar was not the savior but a thief who had stolen our technologies and left the planet. We gave them a focal point until we could create a synthetic to counterbalance the other synthetics that they were using at that time. We merely let them focus on the difference between the way they looked and the way Bel'lar looked. Bel'lar was an Organ. He was different looking. That meant he must be untrustworthy and evil.

"The President of the Brotherhood of Syn at that time took the title of the Quasar of the Quasarian religion. He's the one who took charge in the dim days. All the Organs who didn't live in the Compound were sought out and eliminated on his order."

"He killed Organs? But, he was an Organ." Bel'lar was beginning to see the futility of his mission. This government he came home to report to lived a lie that, if discovered, would be torn down around them.

"The Organs were trying to live with the Syns in harmony. They realized and accepted that the Syns wanted to live their lives as synthetics. It worked for a time. But the Quasar at the time had to prove to the Syns that he was truly a part of the Brotherhood of Syn. He didn't care about the Organs who lived outside the Compound because they were against what we were doing. So he sacrificed them. They didn't serve any purpose to him. It was a great loss. We carry that shame with us today."

Bel'lar gave the wine to Lotep and then walked down to the lake's edge. Lotep drank deeply, watching the captain.

Bel'lar bent down and collected a few stones. He felt their shape and edges, seeking the perfect flat shape; then, one by one, he skipped them out on the lake. He smiled at one that actually skipped three times, and then he turned back to Lotep.

"That's a horrible but interesting story. But why am I going to meet the holy men tomorrow? You still haven't answered that question."

"I don't know. It's just one of his ploys. I don't think it's anything to worry about."

"Well, that's encouraging," Bel'lar said and took a deep breath. "Any more wine in that bottle?"

Lotep grinned and shook the bottle. "Just a bit. Here."

Bel'lar drank the rest, and they began the walk back.

"Will you do me a great favor tomorrow when I go to see Quasar? This might be my last chance to speak with you."

"Anything, my friend."

"Would you would take some suits to my ship and allow my crew to visit their home planet? Then they can walk outside among their brothers. Let them feel and see firsthand as best they can with those suits on. Let them be exposed to what the planet is really like. That would be wonderful if you could do that for me, and them."

"Well, it will be difficult to get some suits, but I think I can borrow a few from people about that size. It won't conform to them, but it will possibly suffice."

"That would work very well, Lotep. Thank you. Thank you, for all you've done."

They walked in silence for a time.

Lotep inhaled deeply. "I always enjoy the evening hours, because it's quiet and peaceful," he said. "In the Compound, you can smell the plants, the water, the flowers and the fruits. Sometimes, I wish we could allow the Syns to be exposed to this, but they would just consume it, and it would be gone. But let's go in. You have a busy day in front of you tomorrow." Lotep left Bel'lar at the door of his room.

Bel'lar went inside, but, despite the wine, he was still agitated and unable to sleep. He paced for a time, but that didn't help. Ka'aya and Ry Sing had tried to teach him many times to relax in a meditative state. They would laugh if they found out that he'd finally decided to give it a try. He lay back on his bed, closed his eyes, and crossed his hands over his chest while he began breathing deeply. He thought of Ry Sing and was relieved that she was safe on the ship. Now if she would just stay there. Then he felt Ka'aya and Ry Sing's presences. He drifted off as he became more and more calm. They seemed to be there in spirit with him, stroking his forehead, helping him to be more relaxed. Then he heard the words of Ka'aya, "Allow what has begun to finish . . . through adversity much is learned . . . and the lives you live shall be as many and as different as the stripes on the back of the bumblebee."

He dozed off and awakened with the sounding of the first gong. The gong sounded every morning at the first three hours of the day. Each gong had a different tone, which Bel'lar had learned since his arrival. If you were still asleep at the third sounding, you would be late and disgraced according to the Quasarian religion. The people who lived in the Compound of the Congress tried to observe some of the Quasarian religious rituals. This enabled them to comment and talk like a Syn when they were out among them.

He heard the second gong and realized that he must get up and get ready for the day. He didn't eat because he was not settled enough. This could be his last day on this planet for all he knew. He was aware that Quasar was manipulating him into doing as he wished. It was not dying that he feared but not knowing what would happen.

A few minutes past the sounding of the third gong, there was a knock on his door. Bel'lar opened it to Quasar's driver, who had already donned his Syn suit.

"Are you ready, sir?"

"I am ready for anything." He followed the driver to the room where Bel'lar's suit was stored. Bel'lar put on his own suit while the driver waited, and then they went out to the transport. He was surprised that Quasar was not there. The driver explained that Quasar had left at the first gong and was already at his office.

✳ ✳ ✳

Lotep was up and out early, also. He was able to find suits for the two women, but there wasn't one available for Enis. It was after the third hour of the morning when he arrived at the location where the ship was the other day. As he got out of his transport, he was hoping they hadn't moved it. He walked over to where he thought the hatch was and stood there. He was holding two large bags. They almost looked like they could carry a body in each, but, in fact, they held the two suits. He looked around to make sure he was alone and then yelled out, "Mauleen. It's Lotep. Let me in. I have something for you."

He felt exposed, just standing there, waiting, without any good reason why he was way out here with these two suits. He looked furtively around again. Still he saw no one. Bel'lar had picked a spot to hide the ship where very few people went. It was an old part of town and was deserted at this time of day. No one lived in this area anymore.

Aboard the ship, Enis was standing watch. He had just relieved Mauleen, who had taken the early hours' watch. Enis heard Lotep calling out because they had been keeping the outside sensors active at all times. He notified the first officer by intercom. "Mauleen. It's that friend of Bel'lar's. He's come back."

Mauleen returned to the bridge quickly with Ry Sing, who had also heard Enis's intercom announcement. All three talked for a moment.

"Maybe he's a decoy," Mauleen suggested. "Are there any other Syns around? What about the BOS? Any out there?"

Enis confirmed that there were none, but Mauleen scanned the area within a hundred meters and was satisfied that no life signatures other than the man waiting outside were near. "Let's do this. Let him in, and we'll have our pistols drawn so that he won't be able to overpower us."

"I don't think that's necessary," Ry Sing said. "He's brought us something. I want to see what it is."

"You two go to the hatch," Enis said, "I'll stay here and keep monitoring the area around us. I'll let him in and be ready to direct Light Traveler to blast us out of here if it's a trap."

Mauleen agreed. "Let's pick up the pistols on the way. Come on, Ry Sing."

Ry Sing refused a pistol but didn't try to talk Mauleen out of hers. When they were in place at the hatch, Mauleen contacted Enis on the intercom and directed him to open it. The two stood ready as the hatch slid up.

"Hurry up, Lotep. Get inside," Mauleen said.

He picked up the bulky suits and dragged them inside; the hatch closed behind him. He carried them through the decontamination chamber and then put them down, took a deep breath, and looked at the two women. "I didn't know if you trusted me enough to let me in or not. But I really wanted to come back. Bel'lar said he wished more than anything for you to have the chance to walk on your home planet, to see what's been done here. I borrowed these suits for you. They won't fit quite right because new suits conform to your body type and facial features, but they should be comfortable enough."

Ry Sing eyed the bags excitedly as she said, "Get them out. I want to go shopping." They all laughed.

Enis walked in. "What are you doing down here? What's in the bags?"

"Bodies," Lotep answered.

"Live bodies or dead bodies?" Enis was interested now.

"Neither. They are synthetic bodies that we developed to cloak our identities. Without these suits, we would have been eliminated long ago, and this society would have ceased to exist.

The Syns don't know we exist because they think they killed us all in the Time of the Dim."

"What's that, the Time of the Dim? I heard people mentioning it when I was inside the Compound." Ry Sing helped Lotep out of his suit and hung it on a hook inside the walk-in locker, adjacent to the hatch.

"That was when the Syns captured all the Organs living outside the Compound and killed them."

"Why did they do that?" Enis asked.

As Lotep unzipped one of the bags, he explained the Time of the Dim and how the government at that time killed all the Organs not living inside the Compound. He went on to explain how currently they were experiencing the annual celebration of the Time of the Dim.

Ry Sing helped him unpack a suit. "This situation sounds serious. How is Bel'lar?" Her forehead wrinkled in concern as she straightened up.

"What have they done with him?" Enis said. "Do we need to break him out?"

"When I left him last evening, he was quite well. He and I talked in the park by the lake."

"When is he coming back to us?" Ry Sing said.

"I don't know. Today he had a very important meeting with Quasar and the religious leaders of the Quasarian religion."

"Is he safe?" she asked. "Tell me."

"Sometimes I fear that the Quasar has ulterior motives, but then he does something unexpected, and I find myself saying that he's the right leader of the people. But, then again, sometimes I'm afraid. To answer your question, I believe the Quasar wants something from Bel'lar. It's probably this ship and all of you. Right now, I believe he's safe."

"I see, but I'm still concerned for him. He continues to send the signal each night, and I will wait and see if he sends it tonight. But Lotep, understand this." She stepped closer to him, touching his shoulder. He looked up. "If, one night, he does not send the signal, we'll take this ship and destroy your Compound. We'll find and bring back my beloved at all costs," Ry Sing said.

Lotep had been pulling the other suit out of the bag. He looked up at her, considering her words. "I believe you would. I sense you're the one who hides in plain sight."

Now the suits were out of the bags. Enis realized there were only two suits, both female. "Where's my suit? I want to go, too."

"I couldn't get a suit for you today," Lotep said apologetically.

Enis smiled, "Then give me yours."

"No," Mauleen said, "Someone has to guard the ship. Someone has to be in charge."

"Oh. That would be me," Enis said. He stood taller and held up his head. "But I still want a chance to explore sometime."

"I'll try to find one for you next time. But I can't let you use my suit. If Quasar learned that I'd helped you, I would be punished, maybe even with death." Lotep was very earnest about this.

"You can trust me," Enis said. "I'm in charge." He started back to the bridge. "Let me know when you're ready. I'll release the hatch for you. Then, I'll remain on guard until you return, in total control of this vessel."

Mauleen watched him walk away, his head held high. She knew he would sit in Bel'lar's chair. She smiled and turned back to Lotep and Ry Sing.

Ry Sing and Mauleen found the suits very interesting. They were cool to the touch and made from a fabric which looked exactly like skin. In some areas, the fabric was fairly thick, and, in other areas, it was thinner to conform to natural body contours.

Ry Sing was the first to put on the suit. Lotep and Mauleen helped her. Once she was completely encased in it, she couldn't believe how big her breasts and buttocks were. Wearing the suit over her underclothes, she didn't make the connection that the suit made her look naked. She paraded around and tried it out, unaware of the picture she made.

Mauleen gasped out between laughs, "I don't think you can go out like that." She rolled her eyes and looked at Lotep, who was embarrassed but smiling at Ry Sing.

Ry Sing ignored them. "I have to see what I look like. I'll be right back." She ran off through the ship to her quarters. Enis caught a glimpse of something on the display that looked like a naked woman running through the ship. A very large naked woman. He did a double take as he exclaimed aloud, "Who was that?"

Ry Sing rushed into her quarters straight to the wardrobe to see her reflection. She turned around, looking at this body. She found it very impressive. *I can almost see why the Syns find this attractive. There's so much of me to share. Of course this isn't my face,* she thought. Lotep had chosen the suit of a woman in her midlife but one without any of Ry Sing's Asian features.

"Now what can I wear that will cover this suit." She looked through her clothes and found a casual, flowing garment with a lot of fabric in a bright-green color. It could be pulled over her head, and it covered the body. It hung to just below her knees because of the size of this body; on her own body it reached her ankles. She found a scarf to match and tied it around her head. "There. It can't get any better than this. That looks good," she said to herself. She tried shoes but couldn't get them on over her large feet. When she returned to the walk-in locker, Mauleen had her suit on and was wearing white clothes with shoes. A white scarf was wrapped around her head. She looked dignified in these clothes.

The two women wearing other women's faces grinned at each other. "You look great," Mauleen said. She looked down at her clothes. "These are so boring."

"No, no, Ry Sing," Lotep said. "If you go outside in that, you'll be arrested. Bright colors are not acceptable. And green is against the law."

"Against the law to look great? I find myself quite wonderful looking! I can see how the Syns think that what they are doing is right." She turned from side to side, posing for the other two.

Mauleen laughed again. "You've already turned into a Syn, and you've only had the suit on a couple of minutes. Ry Sing, you have such great compassion for human beings that you don't know."

"Of course. Isn't that life? Live it unafraid to the fullest, going all out at everything you do. That is me."

Lotep brought some clothes to her. "Yes, that may be, Ry Sing, but I'm not going anywhere with you looking like that. You must put on these clothes I brought for you."

Mauleen kept laughing as she helped her change.

Lotep put his suit back on. They called Enis. He released the hatch after scanning the vicinity for life signatures.

The three walked out onto the planet. It was the middle of the morning. Ry Sing was the first to comment on the smell. "That's horrible. I thought the suits must mask it somehow. How do you stand it, Lotep?" She put her hand over her nose and mouth. She had barely gotten through it when she left the ship that first day.

Mauleen began to cough. "You live with this smell every day?"

"I guess we just get used to it," Lotep said. "You will, too, in a little while. Come. We can go in my transport. It has conditioned air and government identification. No one will bother us. We'll be quite safe."

They climbed in, and, after a few minutes, they could breathe easier inside it.

Ry Sing wanted to go by the old apartment where she and Bel'lar had stayed before. Lotep was happy to comply and took them into that area of the city. They passed the public rail station. It was filled with many people, just as it had been that day a year ago—no 350 years ago—when she and Bel'lar had jumped on the back of the transport. The station had been new then, and the city had been very proud of it. Now it was falling into ruin yet still in use. The porte-cochere remained, but pieces of its ceiling had fallen and been simply pushed aside so as not to block the entry. The columns were darkened with age, and the edges looked as if something had been chewing on them, giving them a ruffled appearance.

The closer they got to the center of the city, the more people they saw. The two women noticed that everyone was dressed in shades of white. The difference between the clothes provided by Lotep and those worn by the people around them was that many of the clothes were stained, even tattered in some cases, and looked unclean. Ry Sing hadn't noticed this in the compound of Organs. But, in the city, it was the rule and not the exception.

Lotep explained that, as the Syns aged and the synthetics exerted a stronger influence on them, they lost the desire to care for themselves. Their mental and physical states degraded. They lived a basic existence controlled by the substances they ingested.

Lotep turned off the main road and directed the transport down a side street. Ahead was the apartment building. Long ago a deep salmon color with green trim, now it was painted a light gray. Lotep found a place to park the transport. They got out and walked through the grounds of the complex. In Ry Sing's time, these grounds had been planted with grass, trees and bushes accented by flower beds. All of this was gone, replaced by unrelenting gravel. This lack of color was everywhere in the city. Everything was bland and dilapidated, falling into ruin.

Ry Sing and Mauleen were still having trouble breathing the polluted atmosphere. Mauleen began to cough; her face flushed red, and tears streamed down her face.

Lotep pulled some packets of oxygenated wafers from his pocket. "Here, try these. They will help."

"No, thanks, Lotep. I don't want to take any synthetics," Mauleen said.

"Don't worry about these. A day or two won't hurt you. We have to take them when we're out in the city each day. It doesn't seem to have affected us too much after all this time." He twisted his face into a grimace. It scared Mauleen, and she gasped. Then Lotep laughed. Mauleen smacked him on the shoulder. Both women took a wafer and found that they did help—not with the smell, unfortunately, but with their breathing.

Ry Sing remembered there used to be a restaurant close by, so she encouraged the other two to find it. They found it on the next block. The building had undergone many repaints, but, as they were coming to expect, it was a neutral color, this time tan. The sign was readable and in good shape, although of a completely different design than the one from Ry Sing's time. Surprisingly, it did have the same name she remembered even after all this time: *The Star Fire Eatery.*

Ry Sing walked quickly to the entrance. "Let's go in and eat. The food used to be really good because they cooked everything on a grill." Her mouth was watering. Then she turned and whispered to Lotep, "Can we eat in these suits?"

He whispered back, "Yes, you can do everything in them, although some things might be more trouble than they're worth."

She reached for the door, and Lotep grabbed her arm. "That's probably not a good idea. I don't know what you would eat in there."

"Oh, let's try it, Lotep. It's fun to be here."

"All right, but be careful what you order. Things may sound the same, but they will be synthetic."

Ry Sing brushed his warning aside. She was not to be dissuaded. They went inside.

It was before midday, and the restaurant wasn't busy. An older couple sat by the door, and two men sat alone at separate tables. Mauleen was on guard, watching everything, but Ry Sing was really enjoying herself. She was talking to the people and looking around at the restaurant. They found seats, with Lotep sitting next to Mauleen and Ry Sing across from them.

Ry Sing looked over the menu and discovered that it seemed the same. She was excited now and ready to order. She leaned over to the other two and said, "Do you know how long it's been since we ate out?"

Lotep chuckled. "I don't eat out much anymore. We usually eat in the Compound." He wondered what they were going to think of the food when they got it.

Ry Sing ordered a sandwich of grilled vegetables. Mauleen was reluctant to order anything but settled on greens made from peat moss, which had been dried and shaped. Lotep contented himself with a colored water, it was blue. Mauleen and Ry Sing found this weird, but he explained that it was how water was always served. The color disguised the natural color and allowed them to add vitamins and other nutrients.

The order was made and delivered to them in five minutes. The service was unbelievably fast. Lotep explained that everything was already made and sealed in individual servings. The staff just heated it up or did some minimal preparations and served it.

The food was a serious disappointment despite its exotic colors. At first Ry Sing liked the bright colors, but, upon closer examination, the colors bore no resemblance to the organic version. Her initial feelings gave way to queasiness. The sandwich roll was yellow, and the vegetables were red and purple with black lines to simulate grill marks. The texture of the sandwich was rubbery, not even close to organic food. She picked at it, poked it, watched it jiggle. She pushed it away, not wanting to taste it.

Mauleen's salad was interesting but musty tasting. Like Ry Sing's food, it was strangely colored, a chopped mixture of blue, yellow, and pink leaves with tiny orange balls sprinkled over it—very far from the fresh greens and vegetables she was eating on the blue-white planet. She pushed the food around her plate.

Ry Sing struck up a conversation with the couple at the next table. This elderly couple was pleased to be eating next to Lotep, Speaker of the Congress and senior staff to the President. They were friendly and interested to talk. Ry Sing chatted on, telling them that they were from another city and were enjoying their visit here.

While they were chatting with the elderly couple, a man came in and ordered some food to take out. He was agitated, looking around constantly, his fingers tapping on the counter. He got angry and complained that the service was too slow when the food was brought out. He slammed the door on his way out, jarring everyone in the place. Ry Sing and Mauleen were surprised at his behavior.

"It seems it can never be too fast," Mauleen commented. "Some things never change."

Lotep leaned close to her, his voice pitched low. "That man has something wrong with his synthetic dosage. That's why he was angry. Brain chemistry is a delicate thing to keep in balance."

After their interesting meal, they decided to see where Mauleen grew up on 108th Street. When they were safely inside the transport, Ry Sing felt free to comment now that no one could hear her. "That was truly awful. No wonder the people are sick." Mauleen made a face in agreement.

Lotep just laughed. "I warned you," he said. Then he looked at the two women. "What's next? What would you like to do?"

Mauleen and Ry Sing exchanged a look. "Don't you remember, Lotep? You were going to take us to where I grew up," Mauleen said.

"That's right. Did we talk about this already?" He looked at them, noting their nods. "I'm sorry. Where do I need to go?"

Mauleen explained, and Lotep directed the transport to the connecting road.

Lotep took them out to 108th Street. Mauleen guided him to make the proper turns and reached her section of the neighborhood. He parked, and she was the first one out of the transport. Walking quickly, she stopped across the street from an ancient house. Parts of the roof had blown away, leaving holes that were covered with some kind of shiny material. A fence around the exterior had fallen down on one side. It was a sad, tarnished version of what she remembered as her childhood home. She just stood and looked. "This is where I lived most of my life," she whispered.

Of course, Mauleen didn't know anyone living there now. Both her parents had been alive when she embarked on this mission. She had left, not knowing if she would ever see them again. When they had arrived here and Bel'lar had given them time to adjust, she had blocked all thoughts of her family and thrown herself into work. She had pushed all that from her mind until this moment when the grief came crashing down. She realized that her parents were dead. Everyone she had known and loved except her fellow travelers were dead and had been for a long time. She was alone. A tear escaped, streaking down her cheek.

Lotep stood beside her. Sensing her grief, he took her hand. She stood stiffly in silence, trying not to cry.

A little girl, sitting outside on a porch step at this house, watched them. Mauleen saw the glint of red in the fuzz that was really a halo of hair on this little girl's head. It was red like Mauleen's hair.

Ry Sing crossed the street and greeted the little girl, asking her name.

"My name is Nina," the little girl said. She was home today because she was not feeling well. She was ten years old last week. She began the supplements that all Syns took for the rest of their lives. She was having trouble adjusting to them, but her parents said not to worry, she would adjust.

Ry Sing sat down on the step next to the little girl. She waved Mauleen over to come sit with them.

Mauleen crossed the street to join Ry Sing, Lotep at her side. She relaxed as Ry Sing talked to the little girl. She felt encouraged. Nina had the red hair like many in her own family. She might be one of Mauleen's descendants. But her spirits sank when Lotep told them as they walked away that the supplements would destroy the hair growth within a few weeks. The child would eventually be hairless like her family. Some children didn't adjust to the supplements and became very sick; some died. She was quiet on the walk back to the transport.

"Why do they take them?" Mauleen asked Lotep.

"The synthetics help their bodies mutate so that they can handle the food substances they eat. Everyone must look the same. If that little girl grew up looking like an Organ, she wouldn't be accepted in this society."

Mauleen and Ry Sing stared at him.

"Are you saying this little girl could be an Organ without the synthetics?" Ry Sing asked. Mauleen looked back at the little girl.

"Perhaps. I wouldn't go that far," he said. "But the synthetics also suppress the population growth, which is critical now." He opened the door to the transport and stood back to allow them to get inside.

Ry Sing realized that every aspect of these people's lives was directed without any of them knowing. She didn't see how it could be called life, this existence the Syns were living.

They climbed into the transport in silence.

"Well, ladies. What would you like to do next? We still have a little bit of time." Lotep looked at the two and saw Mauleen lost in thought, staring out the window. He and Ry Sing exchanged a look, and then Ry Sing said, "I would like to see the temple of the Sacred Ecology religion. I studied there when I was young."

They had trouble finding the location. They drove around the area twice. Then she realized that the temple had been eradicated, and a factory, shut up and falling down, had been built in its place, filling the extensive grounds that had once been a peaceful place to walk and meditate. She got out and walked along the front of the property, stopping to gaze inside. She sighed. This was not her home anymore. Once they left this planet, she would never return.

Ry Sing hurried on, Lotep and Mauleen following. They walked around the corner and found an old house that used to sit diagonally across from the school. Now it simply sat in a row with three other houses that were still inhabited. The remaining houses on this street were either demolished or had fallen down. Either way, the piles of remains were still in evidence. The demise of the factory had probably dictated the end of this neighborhood.

Ry Sing stopped and waited for the other two to catch up. "I used to know the people who lived here. When I studied at the temple, I would visit them often."

An old man, a Syn, lived in the house now. He was sitting on his porch, watching the three strangers on his street. He waved at them imperiously, calling them on to his porch for a chat. They all sat and talked to him for a little while. Ry Sing felt very at ease with him; he seemed familiar to her, but she couldn't determine why. He didn't look like anyone she had known. But his energy, his spirit, connected with hers.

"What do you do with your time?" Ry Sing asked him.

He leaned forward and looked at her closely. Then he sat back. "I have learned that you can't change the world, so I have tried to make the best of every day. I have seen much sadness in my life. Do you remember the flies? They used to buzz around me when I was a young man. They irritated me so much I tried to kill them all. I must have succeeded, for there are no more flies now." He gazed down the street, lost in thought. Then he focused back on Ry Sing. "It's the strangest thing, my dear. Every day, I long to be irritated by those flies again, because life without those flies doesn't seem fulfilling. If I ever see another fly, I would cherish it. I have finally realized that flies were a part of my life that is gone now."

She held his hand, giving it a squeeze, and smiled. He smiled back at her.

They said their goodbyes and left. The old man told them they were welcome anytime.

Mauleen had relaxed while they spent time with this old man and was in a lighter mood when they returned to the transport.

Lotep hoped to get her to smile and offered, "Would you like to do some shopping. Is that next? You can use my credits if you see something you want."

"Not me," Mauleen said.

"Thank you, Lotep," Ry Sing said. "But I've changed my mind. I don't want to shop; everything is white."

"What do you mean? They have off white, bright white, yellow white, and all these different styles, with pleats, without pleats, etc. Are you sure?" Lotep smiled at them and was rewarded with their smiles.

They returned to the ship in the afternoon. Lotep parked the transport at the side of the fence, where it was out of sight from the road. Enis let them back inside and then met them at the hatch. They were talking about how much fun and how interesting it had been to explore the city. They took off the suits, leaving them in the decontamination area. Once again, Lotep wore his jacket over his white garment, leaving the rest of his outer clothes with the Syn suit. They were about to leave the hatch area to have refreshments before Lotep had to leave.

"Wait," Enis said. "It's my turn."

"I'm sorry, Enis." He patted Enis on the shoulder. "Maybe next time. You can't go out without me to guide you. It wouldn't be safe. I have to be back in the Compound soon."

"This may be my only chance."

"I must get back. They keep a count of all of us when we're out of the Compound. There are no exceptions to the curfew."

Enis frowned, obviously disappointed.

Ry Sing tried to ease his feelings. "You'll get your chance. Don't worry. It just can't be now. Come and hear what we did today."

"No. I'll go back to the bridge. It's still my watch. Go have your refreshments. I'll see you when you're finished."

"If you're sure," Ry Sing said. She touched Enis's arm and smiled at him. He nodded and walked away.

The three had refreshments and talked about the day and the trip into the city. Inside the lounge, they were unaware that the sun had begun its journey to the horizon, the shadows lengthening outside the ship.

Lotep explained that the suits he had brought today were from two people who rarely left the Compound. Their suits had been serviced but hadn't been picked up yet. He used his position to borrow them, but they would have to be returned. He would leave them here for a while, but if they were needed, he would come and get them.

Enis returned to the bridge and his survey of the surroundings. He couldn't keep his mind focused on monitoring the crystal displays. He kept thinking about the suits, Lotep's in particular. Then he decided, just out of curiosity, to find out if Lotep's suit would fit him.

Back in the walk-in locker, he saw the two female suits were already packed away into the bags. He found Lotep's suit ready for Lotep to put on. He thought maybe he would just step outside the ship, and see what it was like, just for a few minutes. What would it hurt? Just a quick walk around the ship. Just to get the feel.

Quickly, he pulled off his outer clothes and tossed them on the floor. He took the suit off the hook and stepped into it. He hopped a bit as he got his other foot inside. Then, slipping his arms in, he secured it as best as he could. He stood upright. It felt good. Lotep was similar in height to him but thicker in the body. He checked for any holes. Good there, too. He grinned. Quickly he donned Lotep's black pants, white shirt, and shoes. Wasting no more time, he used the small emergency hatch, unaware that it sounded an alarm as he exited outside. The hatch closed behind him. The alarm sounded throughout the ship.

"Emergency hatch has been opened" was announced over the intercom system. Enis, fully immersed in his adventure and unaware of the excitement that he was causing on the ship, wandered around outside. He walked disjointed, getting used to the suit. He moved his arms around, watching them. They looked like real arms. He stared down at his hands, turning them this way and that. He flexed his fingers. Now he was excited.

The three heard the alarm and hurried up to the bridge. Enis was nowhere in sight. The crystal display was still trained on the area right outside the hatch. A Syn was out there wandering aimlessly around. Then he turned in the direction of the ship, and his identity was clear.

Mauleen laughed. "Lotep, it's your twin. We didn't know you had a twin, did we, Ry Sing?"

Ry Sing giggled. "If that's not your twin, then Enis is wearing your suit." Both women let out peals of laughter, but Lotep was angry.

Using the intercom, Lotep yelled, "Enis, get in here immediately, or you'll be in severe trouble." The ladies were still laughing. This just made him all the more upset. These three had no idea how dangerous it was for him to even be here with them on this ship, let alone someone wearing his suit.

Enis acted as if he couldn't hear them, holding his hands up to his ears and shaking his head. Then he turned and walked away.

"We have to go after him," Lotep said.

"I'm sure he's coming right back," Ry Sing said.

"You don't understand." Lotep was more upset now than angry. "Enis has to come back inside."

"It's too late." Mauleen pointed to the display, and they watched two Brotherhood of Syn Security guards run up to Enis. There was some conversation between them, but they couldn't hear it. They were waving their arms and pointing off in the distance. They started off, and Enis went with them without a backward glance.

Lotep sighed as he dropped into a chair. "Well, there goes my life. It's over. Enis will definitely get me in trouble."

"There's nothing we can do now," Mauleen said. "We'll have to wait for him to come back." She turned to look at Lotep. "You'll just have to stay here with us." She smiled.

For a second, in the midst of all of his fear, he smiled back. Then he shook his head. "No, no, you don't understand. I'm an important official in the Syn government. I'm the Speaker of the Congress."

Mauleen looked perplexed. "We know that. Why is that bad?"

"As Speaker of the Congress I control my party. When I speak I speak as them. Now, when Enis speaks, he speaks for the party." Lotep put his head down on the control panel. "I just hope he doesn't do anything foolish. I have to get back in a few hours, or I'll be missed."

"Well, there's not much you can do now. Light Traveler will notify us when he returns within a hundred meters," Ry Sing said.

"Thank you," he said. "Who is Light Traveler?"

"Greetings, Lotep. I am Light Traveler." The voice seemed to issue from the air around them.

He stood and turned around, looking for the source of the voice. "Greetings. Where are you?"

"I am the entity that you are now housed in," the ship explained.

"I'm inside you? How do I know this?"

The ship jiggled the deck on which they were standing.

Lotep fell back against the console. "I believe you. You can stop now." He looked at the two women. "This ship is alive."

Ry Sing grinned at his response to the ship. "Don't you know all things are alive? Just some things are more easily discerned as living."

"I kind of understand your thinking there," he said.

"There's nothing we can do now," Ry Sing said. "Even if we put the other two suits on and go after him, three people would be lost instead of one. Look on the bright side. He's a person in the suit of a powerful person."

"And if he doesn't say too much, he ought to get by," said Mauleen.

"I hope he doesn't say anything," Lotep mumbled.

Back in the lounge, Mauleen activated the display as they waited for Enis. Lotep brought up his concern that Ry Sing's absence would be noticed in the compound. He wanted her to return with him today.

"I've completed my search in the Compound. I have no reason to return."

"What were you searching for?" he asked.

"I was searching for Ka'aya."

"Is this the holy man from your voyage? I've heard the words of Ka'aya before. I hold him dear to me."

"That's wonderful, Lotep. I, too, hold him dear. I was his student. He traveled with us to the blue-white planet. Then, on the way home, he passed from physical, and his spirit reincarnated on this planet. He told me to find him and that we would be reunited. But I'm worried that he might not remember that he had been Ka'aya in his previous life. Somehow, I was to discover him and help him remember, if needed. I spent my time in the Compound meeting Organs and conducting small tests without any success. Ka'aya is not in the Compound." Ry Sing looked at Lotep. "I don't understand this because that's where all the

Organs live. He would surely be an Organ. I can't imagine that he would be a Syn."

"Perhaps he died. The only other Organs not here are Saint Significance and my sister. They are both on the Continent of Rebirth," Lotep said.

"Where is that?"

"It's the continent to the south. In your time, it was called the Island of Mauree."

"Isn't that where Bel'lar was born?" Mauleen asked.

"It is, yes," Ry Sing said.

"What are they doing there, Lotep, this holy man and your sister?" Mauleen sat forward.

"They have started a community of Syns attempting to return to the organic lifestyle."

Ry Sing put her elbows on the table and leaned her chin on her hands, deep in thought. "You mentioned that before, didn't you?" Ry Sing said. She sat back. "Bel'lar needs to complete his task here. Then I can continue my search there. I don't believe he is dead. Ka'aya must be this holy man."

It got later and later. For a while, the three chatted in a relaxed manner. But Lotep became increasingly nervous, glancing at the display every few minutes.

Finally four hours had passed. Lotep had given up glancing at the display and was staring at it while he paced back and forth in a high state of agitation.

Mauleen and Light Traveler were searching for Enis, so far, without success.

Ry Sing offered to attempt to communicate with Enis telepathically. "If I succeed in raising his awareness, that may get him to return."

Lotep was open to anything at this point. Ry Sing settled back and relaxed into meditation. After a short time, she sat up. She was confident that she had gotten Enis's attention for a moment but didn't know if he would respond. He had seemed erratic, and his thoughts were chaotic. Nothing to do but wait.

Two more hours had passed, when the ship alerted them that her sensors had picked up a life sign in the vicinity of the ship. Mauleen crossed the room to the display and could just make out a white shape come into view, walking very slowly, dragging something. The three ran up to the bridge to use the sensors to determine if it was Enis. It was dark outside now, and very close to the curfew time for Lotep. When this Syn got close to the ship, the sensors activated some exterior lighting. They saw that he was all dirty and had cuts on his forehead and his right arm. His forearm was dark—was that blood? He was dragging a large bag. He had a rope tied around the bag and pulled up over his shoulder. He was leaning forward, the rope stretched tight, dragging the bag very slowly.

"He's ruined my clothes and my suit," Lotep exclaimed.

"I'm sorry about your suit. But what does he have in the bag?" Ry Sing was smiling.

"I don't care about the bag," Lotep retorted.

"At least he didn't get arrested," she answered.

Mauleen sighed. "Oh, my God. He could destroy all of our plans." She scanned the area but found no one other than this Syn in the vicinity.

They waited as he approached, but he seemed disoriented. He stopped, looking around, pointing with one hand. Then he shook his head and turned away, pulling the bag a few feet. Then he stopped again. It was obvious to the three on board that he couldn't remember the location of the hatch.

Mauleen hailed him on the intercom. "Enis, turn around. You're facing the wrong way."

They watched as he turned around completely twice and stopped. Still facing away from the ship, he wavered like a tiny tree in a breeze.

"Turn around," Ry Sing directed him. They watched him turn again and then fall down. "Oh, my. Is he dead?"

"I hope my suit isn't dead," Lotep said exasperated. "What are we going to do?"

"Go out and get him. We turn off the lights inside the hatch, open it, and drag him inside. I'll stay here at the controls. You and Ry Sing do it. When the hatch opens, run out and get him. I'll monitor the area. No one can see him lying out there with this big bag of something."

Lotep and Ry Sing raced down to the hatch and waited for Mauleen to open it. The lights went out, and the hatch opened. They ran out to Enis.

Ry Sing whispered, "Are you alive, Enis?"

He struggled to sit up. "You won't believe . . ." he whispered. His eyes rolled up inside his head, and he collapsed. They each grabbed him under an arm and pulled. They dragged him in with difficulty because he was like a dead weight. As they lay him down in the decontamination corridor, he woke again and saw his bag outside. "Don't forget my bag. It wouldn't be worth it except for the bag. You must get it." He raised his arm, pointed, and tried to get up but he collapsed again.

Ry Sing shook her head at Lotep and then whispered, "I'll get it." She darted out the door, and, with great effort, she managed to get it inside. It was very heavy and clanked when she dragged it.

Meanwhile, Mauleen, viewing all this from the bridge, closed the hatch as soon as Ry Sing was inside. Then, she hurried down to join them. She didn't want that bag any farther inside than it was already. She wanted it fully decontaminated.

Lotep and Ry Sing dragged Enis into the walk-in locker, leaving the bag by the hatch. When Mauleen got there, she was relieved. "Good. Don't bring the bag any closer until we find out what's in it."

Lotep knelt by Enis and began unfastening the clothes and then the Syn suit. "We must hurry. I can't be back after curfew."

"I'm worried about Enis," Ry Sing said. "What's happened to him?" She leaned over Enis's face, patting his cheeks, looking at his eyes. He was unresponsive.

Mauleen said, "How's the suit?"

"It needs repair, but I think I can still wear it back." They opened up the suit, and there was Enis, exhausted but smiling. They pulled his arms out and then his legs, rolling him off the suit. Lotep grabbed up the suit while the two women rolled Enis on his back.

Enis lifted his head, "You should have seen them. They were all amazed at what I could do." He slipped back into unconsciousness.

"I've got to get out of here," Lotep said. He put on the suit quickly; it was cut, bleeding, and dirty. What could Enis have been doing to get it this way?

Ry Sing touched the blood. "These suits bleed? How is that possible?"

Mauleen brought over a cloth and proceeded to wipe the dirt and blood off the suit. Lotep smiled at her attention.

"They do everything," he said. "Some of these suits are more than one hundred years old. We keep those in the museum. We must smuggle you into the Compound to see them. Next time. It won't be long." He gently touched Mauleen's cheek. She put her hand over his. They smiled at each other. Ry Sing, watching this, smiled too, missing Bel'lar.

He finished fastening his clothes and walked to the hatch.

"I'll release the hatch from the bridge," Ry Sing said. "You stay here, Mauleen, and say your goodbyes. So long, Lotep." She ran off.

Mauleen looked at Lotep in his Syn suit and said, "I could even grow to like you as you are now. It would take some adjustments, but I feel you're a kindred spirit to me." She stopped abruptly and covered her mouth. "I'm sorry. I've never said that to anyone before." A blush spread over her face.

*What a lovely shade of pink she is,* he thought. "I understand. Don't be sorry. It was lovely. But now, I must go." The hatch opened, and he dashed out to his transport. Mauleen watched him go, her face flushed with embarrassment.

He arrived at the Compound just a few minutes after curfew, but he knew the guard. Since he was the Speaker of the Congress, they let him in. The guard was surprised at Lotep's appearance. "What happened to your suit? Were you in a fight?"

"It's a long story. Goodnight." He rushed into the inner compound and stripped his suit off quickly. Timing was on his side. He was alone as he dropped the suit at maintenance to be serviced. But he wasn't worried. He had a second suit, like all the senior staff. Tomorrow, he would be able to continue his work. He thought of his friends on the Light Traveler as he went to his room to wash up. He actually hoped Enis was fine in spite of his behavior. He kept remembering Mauleen's parting words. He felt happy. His boring life had suddenly become much more interesting.

Back on the Light Traveler, Mauleen and Ry Sing half dragged, half carried Enis to his quarters. They had to set him down frequently since he was heavy. Once, they thumped his head on the floor. They both giggled. He didn't seem to notice. His eyes fluttered open and then rolled around in his head as he tried to focus on the lights, the walls, and his friends. He smiled up at them: "Make a wish, for I shall grant . . . ," and he passed out again. They got him on his bed by pulling and pushing. But this didn't affect him, either. As he wavered in and out of consciousness, they left him to sleep off whatever it was he had taken.

✳   ✳   ✳

Earlier that same day, Bel'lar was en route to the President's office, being driven there by Quasar's driver. They arrived, and Bel'lar glanced up at the ISOS logo on the building again. He wished it held the same meaning—In Search of Shangri-La—as it had in his time here. But everything was turned around, distorted, remade in a bizarre manner. Deceit had eaten into the fabric of this society and rotted it from within. Even this congenial-appearing relationship he had with Quasar. He was really no more than a prisoner. Yet, for some reason, it amused Quasar to treat him in this way. Or was it that this society was docile from all the drugs and that Quasar didn't fully realize how much violence Bel'lar was capable of unleashing.

This time, he was escorted into the lobby. A BOS guard took him up in the lift to the President's floor. The guard was expecting Bel'lar. He notified Quasar's receptionist, and she came out and directed Bel'lar into the office.

Quasar said, "I'm glad you could meet with me today. I appreciate you taking the time."

"I didn't realize I had a choice." Bel'lar stood stiffly, irritated by this pretense.

Quasar smiled and said, "You're quite right, of course. You didn't. But it pleases me for you to come under your own power. Not restrained with chains."

"You'd do that? Isn't that kind of archaic?" Bel'lar asked.

"Sometimes we have to be assertive, let's say. But not with you. You're a reasonable man. Now come through here, and let's sit in the library again."

Bel'lar followed Quasar into the library. He could smell the old paper, its musty scent. It reminded him of his father's study, which had been filled with books, even stacked up on tables, leaving barely enough room for his father to conduct business. He wondered if some of these books had belonged to his father.

Quasar waved a hand, indicating the books. "I find it invigorating to be around all these old books. You know, they don't produce books anymore for the simple reason that we don't have any trees. The trees produced all the paper. That's why there are no trees. It's not from using wood to burn; it's not to build with. The building industry became quite adept at using and reusing all the parts of the trees. But the trees are gone because of paper. It was paper that destroyed the forests. Because of paper, the sky is yellow. The trees filtered the air. Sometimes I wish that we didn't have to run out of paper before we realized that we didn't need it.

"Technology created new ways to use paper more quickly. We could print in enormous quantities and run copies almost instantly. Before we knew it, thousands of trees were spewed out of our machines. It was very sad." He paused and looked at Bel'lar. Then he laughed. "Do you believe this?"

"I can't prove or disprove it."

"The story is true, but I was the one who encouraged the production of the machines to print faster. That's how I made all of my credits. That's how I got here. If it weren't for the trees, I wouldn't be in this office."

"So you owe your success to the trees. What do you owe to the civilization that has no trees?" Bel'lar said.

"I owe them nothing. Without me, there wouldn't be any society. And the trees would be gone anyway. Come and have something to drink."

Bel'lar sat in the same chair as last time, the one with his back to the door. "It's pretty early for something alcoholic."

"Then how about tea?" Bel'lar nodded. Quasar poured tea for both of them and brought it over.

Once the president was seated, Bel'lar looked at him impatiently. "Why am I here? Where are the holy men you wanted me to meet?"

"Yes, why are you here? You have never really answered this question. Tell me, Bel'lar, honestly, why you came back. Then I will tell you my thoughts." Quasar sat back with his tea and watched Bel'lar consider his question.

*I have nothing to lose,* Bel'lar thought, *and if nothing comes of this, I will escape the Compound and return to the ship.* He gathered his thoughts and began to speak. "I have been a soldier, in service to my planet all of my life. When I was given the commission to search out a new home for our people, I did it with a certain amount of pride because I loved my homeland and this planet where I was born. You understand, I would do whatever it took to achieve this, and I have done it. We found the blue-white planet. I came back to tell the people that there is a chance for a new beginning. I came back prepared to transport them to their new home. But what I found is a world gone mad, where the people believe that by consuming, they will benefit in heaven through your Quasarian religion. And now I'm in a quandary of what to do."

Quasar leaned forward. "I'll tell you what to do. You will do as I wish, for now you're in my domain."

"I concede that, but I'm not like the Syns. I'm not under your chemical-induced control. My mind is still my own."

Quasar laughed. "That's what I like—someone my equal in intelligence. That's why I'm going to give you a problem to solve. If you solve it then, maybe, I'll let you choose what you will do, who you will be, and where you will live."

Bel'lar watched Quasar, who continued to grin at him. This sounded like a challenge. "What's the problem?"

"My problem is with the religious elders. They are the holy men who sit on the right and left sides of me when I sit on the throne of gold, wearing the hat of the Quasarian, the leader of the Quasarian religion," Quasar said pompously.

Bel'lar coughed.

A flash of irritation moved across Quasar's face at Bel'lar breaking his thought flow. "My problem is very simple. The religious elders are questioning my authority. They know that I live in the Compound of the Congress. They see Syns go in and out every day, the presidents of large corporations, the senior staff of the government and others. But yet, the twelve elders have never had access to the forbidden compound. They have informed me that if they aren't allowed in to see all and to know all, they will dispute my absolute authority. That is the ultimatum sent to me by the senior member of the holy men.

"My first thought was for him to get a disease and die. But then I thought that I should use this to my advantage. While I was pondering my dilemma, you appeared. It was like a gift from heaven. Something to be used. I considered handing you over as an Organ. Let them use you to unite the Syns again. The holiest of all religious days, the Last Rites of Ester, will be here in three weeks. They could sacrifice you then and unite the Syns. Then the religious elders would swear allegiance to me again, for I have discovered the alleged savior, Bel'lar himself, the leader of the Bellarian faction of the Sacred Ecology religion."

"I'll tell them the truth," Bel'lar said. "That you're not a Syn. I'll tell them you're like me. That Organs are hiding in the compound."

Quasar laughed. "I thought you might say that, but I know you won't. If I felt you would actually do that, I would have you taken to the surgery, and, in a matter of a few hours you would truly be transformed into a Syn. We would inject fats from dead Syns and mass quantities of synthetic substances. This would damage your brain, putting you in the dim days of your life. You would wander and babble and be trapped in your body. Many in our society get this babble sickness. They babble on and on, never saying a coherent thing again. Eventually, over-consumption turns all the people into babbles. They babble until they die."

Bel'lar took a deep breath and shuddered. The idea of being mentally damaged, trapped in his body, was too horrible to contemplate. Worse than death. Quasar, it seemed, had some teeth after all. Bel'lar had no choice. Maybe, Quasar would grant him a chance to do something before he carried out this threat. "I'll help you under one condition. I want to journey to my birthplace to see how you're treating those who are trying to return to the organic lifestyle."

"Excellent," Quasar said, "You have one week to do this. The week before the celebration of the Last Rites of Ester, I will expect you to produce the solution I need." Quasar paused and stared at Bel'lar. "Or you will be the solution." He smiled again.

"Very well," Bel'lar said, as he thought, *I won't take orders from this man. What I'm really agreeing to is to leave this planet as soon as I'm satisfied that there's nothing more I can do, no way to rescue anyone from this place.* But, to be satisfied, he wanted to meet those who had returned to the organic lifestyle and see if any of them wanted to relocate to the blue-white planet.

Quasar led Bel'lar back into his office. Then he turned to face him. "Lotep will make all the arrangements and travel with you. Two of my security guards will also be present at all times."

Quasar smiled and patted Bel'lar on the back, again giving the appearance to his receptionist and guards that he and this man were friends.

Bel'lar was escorted back to the Compound of the Congress. He ate the midday meal and kept an eye out for Lotep, but he had learned that Lotep had taken the day off and was out somewhere. He hoped he was with his crew. He still hadn't returned by the evening meal, so Bel'lar went in alone. Everyone ate together in the Compound at this time of night. They treated this meal as a unification ceremony of the Organs every evening after the sun had set.

Afterward, Bel'lar joined the other inhabitants of this compound as they strolled past fruit trees and through gardens on a path that looped back to the main entrance to the building where Bel'lar was housed. No one accosted him, allowing the savior to walk in meditative silence. He was glad for this reprieve. He didn't want to interact with any of them. His mind was full of the events of the afternoon and what he was going to do. He certainly had no intention of staying to become a religious sacrifice.

On the fifth time around, he saw Lotep coming in and walked over to meet him. They walked away from the community stroll and out to the lake to talk. Lotep told him that he'd spent the day with Mauleen and Ry Sing. He could see that Bel'lar was restless and not really listening. He changed the subject and asked him about the meeting with Quasar.

It took Bel'lar a moment to respond, his mind focused on his conversation with Quasar. He pulled his attention back. "I'm sorry, Lotep. I wasn't listening. Quasar has given me authorization to go to the Continent of Rebirth. You're to go with me. I have to return in one week, because Quasar will be waiting for my solution to his problem of the holy men. If I don't come up with a solution that benefits him, he plans to give me to the Quasarian Brothers to sacrifice at the Last Rites of Ester."

"What?" Lotep blurted out.

Bel'lar stopped him. "I have some ideas about this, but I don't want to discuss them yet."

Lotep was silent, thinking rapidly. He didn't understand why Quasar would allow Bel'lar to make this journey. How would this benefit the President? Then he said, "All right, but I would like to help you if I can, Bel'lar. I consider you and your crew friends. Why don't we take Mauleen and Ry Sing with us to the Continent of Rebirth?"

"I would like to do that, but how, without endangering them?"

"I'll tell the security guards they're friends of mine. They'll accept that because they don't know everyone in the Compound. The two suits I borrowed are from women who rarely leave the Compound and spend all their time with their families. The guards won't know them, either."

"Good, but how do we get them here?" Bel'lar said.

"I'll bring them here in my personal transport when we're ready to go."

Bel'lar smiled at Lotep's creativeness. "You have it all worked out." Then he realized. "You've been thinking about it."

Lotep smiled and nodded. "I've been working on a plan to bring them into the Compound, but this will be easier."

They began to quietly discuss the next steps. Lotep pointed out that they would need to wear their Syn suits at all times on this trip. Only in private would they be able to take them off for a few minutes.

Small hovercrafts were available to the government for travel around the planet, so he would have the guards arrange for one. The trip to the Continent of Rebirth would take about three hours. Since only the government and military officials were allowed to travel, there wouldn't be any impediments.

They decided to go two days from now, early in the morning. Lotep would go at the first sounding of the gong to pick up the two ladies, giving them a few minutes to get ready. He would bring them back to the Compound and meet Bel'lar at the third gong in the area where the transports were parked. Ry Sing and Mauleen would not enter the Compound, to avoid having to take off their suits and risk exposure. They said their goodnights. Bel'lar hurried into his room to send the signal to his crew so they would know he was all right.

* * *

Two days later, the first gong was sounding as Lotep left the Compound to pick up Mauleen and Ry Sing. When he arrived at the site, it was deserted. He climbed out of the transport near the ancient pyramid and waited in full view. He knew someone was on watch inside the ship and would see him.

It was Mauleen's watch. She noticed him immediately and let him in. Ry Sing and Enis met her at the hatch to see Lotep. He quickly explained his reason for coming. He was there to take the two of them with him and Bel'lar to the Continent of Rebirth. They had a few minutes to get ready.

The two women hurried off. Lotep and Enis stared at each other. Both were uncomfortable.

"I'm s-s-orry about your suit," Enis stammered.

Lotep nodded, still too angry to say anything.

As Ry Sing made her way back to the hatch, she realized that she would get her chance to meet the Saint and find out if he was Ka'aya. Things just seemed to work out. She smiled as she met up with Mauleen.

Both men helped them into their borrowed suits.

Enis would remain in charge of the ship. Bel'lar's orders were if Enis had any concerns during this time, he was to leave the planet immediately and wait at a safe distance from the planet for further instructions. Enis was amenable to being in charge while they were gone. His desire to explore had been satisfied by his foray two days earlier.

Ry Sing patted Enis's cheek in farewell. The three left the ship.

They made the trip with Lotep to the Compound of the Congress. He took them through the first gate and then into the second gate. He parked the transport and asked them to wait. At the third gong, the prearranged time, Bel'lar came out. Lotep hurried him along. He didn't want anyone to question what they were doing. They got back into the personal transport and made the short trip to the new facility in the center of town, where the hovercrafts were kept.

Bel'lar grinned at the two ladies and said, "May I make your acquaintance, ladies? I'm Bel'lar and you are . . . ?"

Ry Sing giggled. Bel'lar said, "Well, that must be Ry Sing inside there, so you must be Mauleen." Mauleen laughed. Both had forgotten that Bel'lar wouldn't know who was who in these suits with someone else's face.

Bel'lar squeezed Ry Sing's arm. "There's so much of you. What have you been eating while I've been busy?"

She giggled again. Lotep laughed with this lighthearted group. He hadn't been this relaxed in a long time and was looking forward to this trip with these three.

A few minutes later, they arrived at the hovercraft port. Lotep parked his transport in a special place reserved for the government. Inside, they met the two security guards who would pilot the ship and accompany them. Lotep introduced the two ladies and Bel'lar to the guards. They boarded the ship.

Bel'lar and Mauleen were interested in learning about this vessel. Lotep explained that the ship was a C-class hovercraft that seated twelve. Two security guards sat up front to pilot it. It had an elongated, rounded body with a delta wing and a tail, with another delta wing on top of the tail. It was very comfortable inside, with many windows, affording an excellent view. Six large seats on each side swiveled toward the center and back to the windows. This craft was based on technology that used magnetics.

The four made themselves comfortable. Ry Sing sat next to Bel'lar on one side with Mauleen and Lotep opposite them. This way, they each had windows to look out of and could turn and talk to each other easily on the journey. As one of Quasar's fleet, it was possible to shut off the pilots from hearing any discussion in the passenger cabin. Lotep pressed the switch as soon as they got comfortable so they could talk freely. Within moments, they were airborne.

Bel'lar was quite amused by this little craft. "Do you think they'll let me fly it, Lotep?"

"Perhaps on the way back, but right now, I want to show you some sites and fly over some areas of importance."

Everyone settled into their seats as the craft gained in altitude. Lotep was the first to break the silence as they looked back over the city. "Isn't that a beautiful sight?"

Bel'lar and the two women looked at each other. What was Lotep thinking? The haze of yellowed pollution hung over the city.

"I've been meaning to ask," Mauleen turned to Lotep with this question. "Why are there no vibrant colors? There are no bright reds, blues, greens, or yellows. Except for the food, it's all colorless."

"I believe it has to do with the deterioration of the cornea in the Syns' eyes. Many are losing the abilities to see color now. This seems to increase as they age. That's why there are mostly shades of white and gray. To them these are vibrant colors, but, to us, they are subdued and lacking in color."

Ry Sing arranged her tunic as she commented, "That explains why everyone wears these similar fabrics."

Lotep nodded.

Ry Sing sighed. "That's too bad. Part of living is experiencing the great vastness of the spectrum."

"Speaking of experiencing life, your crewmember, Enis, must have made a spectacle of himself the other evening. He almost ruined my Syn suit. It's being repaired, but it's going to cost a lot of credits." Lotep sounded irritated.

Ry Sing smiled at him. "Wait until you hear the whole story. The repairs on your suit will be the least of it."

Bel'lar interrupted. "What are we talking about here?" Mauleen was also smiling. Bel'lar saw this and said, "When my first officer is smiling, something's going on. Tell me about Enis."

Ry Sing began to tell the story. "When Lotep came, he didn't have a suit for Enis. We left him on the ship while we toured the city."

Mauleen added, "And he didn't like it. We had to leave him in charge to get him to agree."

"The three of us visited some old places, like your old apartment, Bel'lar."

"It's still there, Ry Sing?"

"It is," she said. "We didn't go in. Someone lives there now. But guess what? The restaurant, your favorite restaurant, was still there."

Bel'lar thought for a moment. "The Star Fire Eatery?"

Ry Sing smiled and nodded.

"And did they have the griddle cakes with the maple syrup and currants?" Bel'lar's mouth watered just thinking about it.

"I'd forgotten. That was your favorite. Every weekend he would order that." Ry Sing watched Bel'lar, lost in his memory, and smiled again.

Mauleen said dryly, "That was still on the menu, but it probably wasn't what it used to be."

Ry Sing said, "The menu seemed similar but the food, if you could call it that, was not alive. Anyway, let's get to the good part."

"You mean the part about him destroying my suit?" Lotep snapped.

"Yes, that part. Anyway, Bel'lar, when we got back to the ship, we took off the Syn suits and went to the lounge. Meanwhile, Enis decided to try on Lotep's suit, and apparently discovering that it fit, couldn't resist exploring in the city. When he finally returned after many hours he was completely incoherent, and the suit was cut and bleeding."

"And filthy," Mauleen added.

Lotep was getting angry at the memory. "When I get the suit back, I'm going to present him with a bill."

Ry Sing, ignoring Lotep's anger, continued with the story. "He could barely walk. He was dragging this big bag. It looked like he was bringing one of the Syns back with him. We got him into the ship, and he could barely stand. We took him out of the suit and put him to bed to sleep it off. Now comes the good part. The next day, during the morning, we were in the lounge, eating, when Enis comes in dragging the bag with one hand. In the other hand, he has a bottle of what he called Happy Jack's soda."

Lotep rolled his eyes. "You have to watch out for Happy Jack's."

Ry Sing agreed. "Anyway, he drags this bag in. Mauleen and I had completely forgotten about it. Enis was grinning as if he knew a great secret. I asked him why he was happy. He told me he was exhausted from the night before. I asked him if the Happy Jack's sodas caused this. He said not completely. It was the CC that they dropped into the sodas." She paused for effect.

"He tried CC?" Lotep blurted out.

Bel'lar looked confused. Ry Sing was amazed that, as large as Bel'lar was in his suit, he could register this on his artificial face.

"What is this CC?" Bel'lar asked.

"They call it Crystal Cubes," Lotep explained. "They contain a chemical substance dispensed in a sugar cube. There have been cases known where people laugh themselves to death."

Ry Sing giggled.

Lotep looked sternly at her. "I'm very serious. The sugar cubes contain a substance that creates a chemical reaction in the brain. This creates a euphoric state that can cause brain hemorrhages. You can literally laugh yourself to death."

Bel'lar said, "That's the way I want to go."

Ry Sing raised her eyebrows, no mean feat in someone else's face that didn't have eyebrows, and looked at him. "I don't think Enis was trying to do that."

"What else was in the bag?" Lotep asked.

"I was getting to that part," she said. "Enis was excited that he'd found these treasures. We sat down on the floor next to the bag. He started pulling things out. He said he found a great antique store that had kitchen utensils. The storeowner didn't even know what they were used for. But Enis did. He pulled a cylindrical piece of wood with a handle at each end from the bag. He said it was for rolling out pastry. Then he pulled out what he said was a machine for grinding grains. It was very heavy. He had some other pieces, but I can't remember what they were now. Then, he pulled out his best treasure of all. Two cases of Happy Jack's soda and one small box full of sugar cubes."

Lotep was concerned now. "You have to take those away."

"I did," Mauleen said. "I hid them before we left the ship."

Lotep looked at her in surprise and then laughed. She was smart and attractive—although he couldn't see how attractive with the suit covering her up.

"And this is the best part," Ry Sing said and started to laugh, "I asked Enis how he could afford all of these lovely things."

Lotep stopped laughing. "Don't tell me. The shop owner recognized me and allowed Enis to buy on credit."

By then, Mauleen and Ry Sing were laughing. Bel'lar tried to contain his laughter; after all, this had been a potentially dangerous stunt that Enis had pulled and could have ended badly. But he wanted, they all wanted and needed, the release from the tense events of the past few days. He gave in and laughed with them.

Lotep huffed something about taking it out of Enis's hide. Mauleen moved closer, put her arm around him. "Maybe you can do odd jobs to pay back the credits you owe."

Lotep just sat there looking at his hands. Then he looked at her. "Maybe you'll just have to take me to the blue-white planet." He grinned at them, and then turned to look out the window. They were nearing a great gouge in the ground. It was an open pit mine.

Ry Sing noticed it, too. She leaned closer to the window, looking down. "What are all of these mines for?" she asked Lotep. Several more massive pits opened up as they flew over.

"That is where our food substances are mined. We use this material to make the foods the Syns eat. Do you want to see more?"

Mauleen and Lotep moved over to look out the windows by Ry Sing.

"I would, Lotep. Can we fly in closer?" Bel'lar asked.

Lotep activated the intercom and instructed the pilots to fly low and hover over one of the large open pits. They flew down over the nearest one. As they were looking down, Lotep explained what they were seeing. "They are mining the rock and stone minerals. We take these basic minerals and crush them. Then we synthesize them into a food substance. Plus, we use some clay, sand and grind and mill it, for texture."

"You mean what your people are eating is inert matter?" Ry Sing frowned. That explained the horrible food at the diner. And no doubt contributed to the mutation of their bodies and minds. What she didn't understand was how they were able to exist on this meager food supply.

"We have nothing else to make food from now, and, even then, it's not enough. Where did you think we get the food to feed billions of people?"

"We were kind of hoping that you had some secret ingredients, maybe from the seabed, or something that was still alive," Bel'lar ventured.

Lotep nodded as he continued, "We did use seaweed. It made a great salad. It was also good in cheese. But, when the atmosphere couldn't hold condensation anymore to create clouds and rain, the planet heated up. It systematically caused water vapors to rise up into the outer atmosphere and create water crystals. But, they were too far out of the gravitational pull, and they never came down. As the atmosphere diminished, the water crystals moved farther away. They have never fallen again on the planet as rain. Now we call that the Icelandic belt around this planet."

Mauleen said, "We passed through that ring of ice crystals when we returned here. We were wondering where it came from."

"What a waste of water," Ry Sing exclaimed. "Why haven't you unfrozen the water to let it fall?"

"How? We desperately need that water, but we don't have the technology. The oceans are very saline now, and the levels are extremely low. Maybe seventy-five years ago the last fish . . . ," Lotep grabbed his throat, "jumped out of the water and died." He coughed and then laughed.

"That's sick," Mauleen said.

The others smiled at this, but it was very serious. Lotep's attempts to amuse them were falling on deaf ears. He didn't realize how important this was to them. What he saw as great achievements they saw as monumental failures.

Bel'lar redirected the conversation. "What are they mining down below us?" He pointed at an open pit that spread out on the ground on his side of the craft.

"Calcium. This is how we make milk, cheese and byproducts. We pulverize calcium and add water distilled from the oceans. This also diminishes the oceans, because it never returns to them. We've broken the cycle of nature on this planet by diminishing the atmosphere and creating the pollution layer that hovers over the cities. The pollution creates hot zones over the cities. In these hot zones, this pollution layer hangs on. At this rate of evaporation of the oceans and with our mining abilities, we are projecting a balanced population growth. You notice there aren't many children. The Syns have lost interest in reproducing for they . . . ," he paused, searching for how to formulate a polite response.

Ry Sing said it for him. "They don't want to have sex anymore. It's too much of an effort. And I can see why." She looked down at her borrowed body. But to be fair, she thought, this was a suit, not her real body. She could take it off, but the Syns were trapped in their bodies, forced to endure their own mutated physiology.

"Indeed, Ry Sing. They would rather consume more and save energy. They don't have the sexual appetite to produce the children. And, as I was saying, at the current rate of population growth, we have estimated that fifteen years of food supplies remain. Then we don't know what we'll do. We thought about creating some sort of spacecraft to go to nearby planets to find food substances. But the religious zealots of the Quasarian religion believe that we won't achieve the sanctity of this planet by introducing outside substances. They wish to vanquish the planet completely, and, at the end, they will cease to exist here. This will ensure their place in the Quasars."

He sounded sad and hopeless for the first time that Bel'lar had noticed.

"But these beliefs, they're perverted," Ry Sing said. "It's hard to believe they would be willing to die for them."

Lotep shook his head. "This is their experience on this planet. You can't say they are perverted until you live with them and experience what it's like to be a Syn. My parents . . . ," He stopped, overcome by his emotions. "They were once Organs like me. They lived across the lake in the Compound of the Congress. But they despaired of their life. They came to believe that to live as an Organ was a crime against humanity. For the life of me, I can't understand why. But in their elder years, three years ago, they decided to undergo the surgery." Tears sparkled in his eyes. Mauleen put her hand on his arm in comfort.

"You mean the surgery to become a Syn?" Bel'lar blurted out.

Ry Sing interrupted, "There's a surgery to become a Syn? Why? It's one thing to play a Syn for a day as we are, but to change your whole body structure and metabolism and brain capacity. Why?" She focused intently on Lotep.

"And if that wasn't enough," he said softly, "once you're turned into a Syn, your remaining life expectancy drops to five to ten years. The average is only six or seven years." Lotep sat quiet, sadly thinking of his parents.

"Why do people do it?" Mauleen asked.

Inundated by grief, Lotep made no effort to answer. His mind was filled with how his parents looked that last time he saw them.

Bel'lar rubbed his synthetic face while he thought. Then he said, "Sometimes people need to belong to something. Something they feel is greater than them. The Quasar and the Quasarian followers have a goal, a mission. They're enjoying their lives. Let them finish it out. It's not for everyone. It wouldn't be for me. I would fight to the death before I would become a Syn."

"And look at you saying those words," Ry Sing said. "You're sitting here in that Syn suit. Even your face looks like you. At least this isn't my face."

"This conversation is depressing," Mauleen said.

Lotep sat up, recovered. "Thank you, Bel'lar, for your kind words." He instructed the pilots to go forward at maximum speed to the Continent of Rebirth and land at the village by the ocean.

The ship increased in speed, and they gazed out the windows. They passed over more open pit mines. Then they began to see abandoned pits. They saw a couple of cities. They all looked the same, but none as big as the capital city. Then they flew over the ocean, but the ocean wasn't blue. It was a dark green, almost black, as if it had died. It appeared flat because the waves had subsided substantially due to the reduction in winds. A closer look at the blackish-green water revealed that some kind of algae was growing in it. It could be seen clearly because of the much lower volume of water. The water level had been steadily decreasing over the years, exposing more land.

Ry Sing pointed to a large area of algae. "Lotep, what about the algae down there? Can't you harvest that?"

He looked down at the algae. "We've performed lots of experiments on it. We're still working with it as a food substance, but it's actually a poison. It's a seaweed derivative that thrives on the oxygen in the ocean. It eats the oxygen in the water. Along with the evaporation and the increased salt content, this algae helped killed all of the fish, creating this sludge. In some areas it's so thick you can almost walk on top of it. It's called Aristotle fungus, named after the scientist who discovered it. To date, the only thing it does is make a strong dye. Ironically, it's a green color, and green is illegal. Green was banned by the Quasar many hundreds of years ago."

Bel'lar thought it was more than ironic. It was twisted that green was the color of hope to him but illegal here. Green was what he was desperately hoping to see on the Continent of Rebirth. Anything to show that these people had a chance at living as Organs. Yet he knew he couldn't take them all, and he didn't know how he could choose who would stay.

They cruised along in silence for awhile. Then Bel'lar said, "Maybe, on the Continent of Rebirth, there may still be some green." He tried to look hopeful, but this trip to their home planet had been one disappointment after another.

Ry Sing squeezed his hand. "And some hope for this planet. I'm looking forward to seeing where you grew up. I haven't been to this part of the world before."

Mauleen had been watching for any signs of the approaching continent. "Don't get your hopes up."

"This will be my first time here as well," Lotep said. "I've wanted to come before, but was always too busy. Look over there. You can just see the edge of the continent."

"Where? I can't see anything." Bel'lar pressed his face to the window.

Ry Sing pointed. "At the edge of the water. It's that dark spot."

Bel'lar stood up to see what she saw and then sat back down in disappointment. "There's no green."

Ry Sing put her arm around him. "I'm sorry you had your hopes up. Remember what Ka'aya said. Allow what has begun to finish. Merely be the observer."

"I don't know if I can. My whole life has been devoted to helping my planet, and now it's too late." Bel'lar was becoming disheartened.

"Try to understand that they are living what they want," Ry Sing explained to him.

Bel'lar inhaled sharply. Despite what he'd said earlier about letting his people be happy, it hurt to think they were living their choices. Who would choose this willingly? He looked out the window again. "We're getting close. You can see the tip of it now."

Mauleen had changed sides, sitting in the seat by Bel'lar in order to see the approaching continent. "The brown you saw was the buildings. Maybe these Syns are starting to get their color sight back. Look. All the buildings in the village are dark brown."

*Some hope*, he thought, but he smiled as he said, "Maybe, Mauleen." He would take any bit of hope, no matter how small.

Down below, the ocean was less contaminated on the coast of the Continent of Rebirth. The algae hadn't completely taken over, and they saw spots of blue but still no fish.

Looking out over the continent, Bel'lar couldn't see any more signs of habitation. No cities, no smaller towns. Only this one village up ahead. "Where are all the cities that used to be on this continent?" Bel'lar asked.

"This is the only village left," Lotep answered. "The rest of the continent was extensively mined over the last two hundred years in the desperate search for food. But once the mines played out, they were abandoned. No other inhabitable areas exist now."

"Do any animals live here?" Ry Sing asked.

"There are no animals remaining on this planet. The last ones died out many years ago. Only some fish live in the Compound."

Ry Sing was sad and relieved. This planet wasn't hospitable to life any longer. It wasn't a fit place for animals, or people, for that matter. Perhaps Zander had removed them. She hoped so.

Bel'lar shuddered, unable to speak. His home was gone. Nothing was left of where he had grown up on the other side of the continent. He felt his past being ripped away. And his hope with it. He looked down, unable to continuing looking out the window.

"Forgive me," Lotep said. "I didn't realize how this would affect you."

Bel'lar lifted a hand and waved Lotep's apology away.

Ry Sing held his hand, giving comfort, knowing that it wasn't enough. If it wasn't for her search for Ka'aya, she almost would have wished they hadn't returned. The reality of this planet's spiral into death was causing too much pain for Bel'lar.

As they got closer, Mauleen had been scanning the land, looking for anything to ease Bel'lar's sadness, and she found something. "Look Bel'lar. There's something growing."

Indeed, on the outskirts of the village some spots of green were discernible. A few plants were growing here in this forgotten place.

Lotep said, "This is the only place that green is allowed on the whole planet. This was an experiment that was started many years ago by the Bellarian religion. They built a monastery and lived in peace and harmony with their own abilities to create their own food substances. No food substance is brought here. They have only what they can cultivate or make. Most of the minerals were depleted many years previous to them renaming it Rebirth.

"The fact that it is called Rebirth is both ironic and sad. About one hundred years ago, a new mineral was found on this continent, a fiber. This was the only place on the planet that this mineral was found. They felt it would revolutionize the food industry. It made food substances thicker, more luxurious and palatable. We thought it was going to be the rebirth of the society, but it was short lived when the substance ran out. By that time, however, this continent had been thoroughly explored and excavated, with all the cities destroyed in the process."

Bel'lar and Ry Sing exchanged a look, but neither commented.

As they flew in closer, they saw the landing site. It was on a plateau that jutted out into the ocean, with cliffs on three sides dropping into the ocean, the village on the other. The village was a small group of brown huts made from mud and grass. Very rustic but natural. Some larger buildings existed, probably old ones from an earlier time. It didn't look anything like Bel'lar remembered. This village had at one time been a busy port, built right down to the ocean's shore. And the cliffs weren't here before. It indicated how low the ocean had dropped.

Their pilots brought them in over the village, and set the hovercraft down on a clear spot meant for this purpose just outside the gate. The pilots busied themselves securing the craft. The others got out of the hovercraft and stretched. Ahead of them was a gate, and further on were the first huts, the start of the village. As they proceeded toward the gate, they saw people beginning to gather at the edge of the village. They must have been coming in response to the sound of the hovercraft landing.

The gate provided no security but served merely as a formal arched entry with a sign identifying the village's name. It sat alone on the plateau constructed of bricks with a mud coating, the same dark brown as the village buildings. The words set into the arch read, "Welcome to Shangri-La."

Bel'lar's sight blackened around the edges and he stopped abruptly, still some distance from this gate. Of all the names, they had chosen this one, he thought, feeling sadness tear into his chest. This name represented the guiding ideal that had sent him out to find the blue-white planet. He shook his head and brushed away a tear.

Ry Sing ran over to him. He looked at her. "Is this what I'm searching for?" he asked.

"No. What you have always been searching for is in your heart. Even though now your heart is breaking, and I feel it too." She put her arm through his. Mauleen came up on the other side of him and stood quietly. Ry Sing knew that Bel'lar was seeing the end of his purpose in this life, and he feared it was for nothing.

Lotep didn't want to intrude on Bel'lar's sadness. He walked on, intending to introduce himself to the people gathering at the edge of the village. He had noticed that a woman ran off, presumably to bring back someone in charge, from the snatches of conversation that he heard. By the time he reached them, the crowd parted, and two men walked to meet him.

Lotep introduced himself and explained that they had been sent by Quasar to see how the experiment in organics was progressing. The two men introduced themselves as the mayor and a holy man of the Bellarian religion.

Lotep kept his eye on Bel'lar, and, when he saw him look his way, he motioned him over.

Bel'lar had pushed back the sadness to a bearable level and regained control of himself. He walked up confidently with Ry Sing and Mauleen, turning his attention to the two people waiting to meet them.

Lotep performed the introductions. Bel'lar clasped his hands together and bowed to each one, while Mauleen and Ry

Sing just smiled. The older gentleman appeared to be a Syn, but, surprisingly, he had a few hairs growing on his head in various spots, about thirty very long gray hairs, which didn't look as if he had ever cut them. He was quite large, attired in a white robe. He was the leader of the Bellarian religion here on this continent. This was Saint Significance.

Ry Sing smiled, pleased that the Saint was here. She would get the chance to find out if he was Ka'aya's reincarnation.

The younger man with him was Vasquez, the mayor of this community. Vasquez also had a small growth of hair, a clump on the left side near the crown of his head. The hairs formed a tiny tail, extending to his shoulder. This surprised Bel'lar. He hadn't expected any hair at all. He hadn't noticed any in the capital city on any of the people there. Did this mean that this experiment was proving successful? He hoped it did.

A woman stepped out of the crowd and called out, "Lotep." Lotep recognized her immediately. It was his sister Mary. It had been three years since he had seen her, when she came here to work with the Bellarians. He missed her. Now that their parents had joined the Syns, she was all he had left. They embraced and stood hand-in-hand while Lotep introduced her to his friends.

Lotep hadn't mentioned that he had a sister to Bel'lar. She looked like a Syn, but he assumed that she was an Organ wearing a Syn suit like her brother. She was similar in height to Ry Sing, and if her Syn suit reflected her true appearance, she was pretty. He wondered if she had dark hair like her brother. He realized he probably wouldn't find out because she would be wearing her Syn suit the entire time they were here.

Saint Significance was staring at Bel'lar. He tilted his head to the side, looking him over. "You look vaguely familiar, and you carry the name Bel'lar, the savior of our race. Is it truly you?" He dropped down on one knee. "You're a Syn. I always assumed that Bel'lar was an Organ—that he would one day stand where you stand, coming back to take the Syns away. It's been my life's work to understand man's ability to get himself into situations that make no sense and hold no value. Are you this man from the past? This man who went on a journey hundreds of years ago in search of Shangri-La? Are you this man, who has come full circle, and discovered that Shangri-La is here?"

Mary and Vasquez hastily knelt, surprised by Saint Significance's behavior. Everyone was looking at Bel'lar. The crowd gathered behind them began to murmur, moving closer, unsure what to do.

Unable to stop his eyes from tearing up, Bel'lar spoke, "Yes, my name is Bel'lar. But I'm merely a military man doing my duty. Stepping upon this continent and seeing your village that you have named Shangri-La lifts my spirits. You were right to name this place what every man is searching for. Please get up. Show me your village."

The community drew aside, letting them enter the village. Some of them touched Bel'lar on the arm and on the shoulder. He smiled and nodded to them. He heard them saying his name and welcoming him. They were polite, but he could feel their excitement. It gratified him that finally here he was welcomed as the returning military man and honored for his search for Shangri-La. They wanted to hear what he had to say. He wanted to tell them the truth, all of it, let them understand what he had done and why he came back. But he didn't know if he should or what Quasar might do if he did.

The people followed behind as they walked slowly down the main street. It was a very small village. All the huts and buildings were painted brown. The yellow cloud that lay over the other cities they had flown over was absent here, and the air smelled cleaner.

"Your village, with its dark brown buildings, is a welcome relief from the capital city," Bel'lar said.

Vasquez stepped closer and answered, "Thank you. We wanted to establish a return to an original color. But you said brown. It's a dark gray."

"Indeed, you're correct," Bel'lar responded, realizing that Vasquez couldn't distinguish the difference in the color and didn't wish to offend him.

Bel'lar walked alongside Saint Significance at the forefront of the group. "How many of you are there, and how long have you been here?"

The holy man cleared his throat. "We've been here five years. When we came, there were almost 200 of us. Two-hundred anxious people, with positive attitudes, ready to tackle anything and everything."

"But it doesn't look like 200 now," Mauleen observed. She looked around at the villagers walking with them. Their faces were beaming with happiness.

"You're right. Only forty-five are left. After the first year, when many of our experiments in growing failed, and many more were not as successful as I had hoped, many left."

As they continued walking, Bel'lar saw, nestled against the buildings, glimpses of green. The inhabitants appeared to be growing small plants around everything, but on closer inspection, the plants were very tiny, and some were deformed.

Bel'lar directed the holy man's attention to the plants. "Why are the plants so tiny?"

The Saint sighed and Bel'lar stopped. "Ah, you see, that's our problem. Without pure water, the plants grow slowly and are deformed. Many do not bear fruit, and, if they do, the fruit doesn't grow to maturity. We have discovered that this planet can no longer support the growing of organic food."

The Saint shrugged. "We do what we can. Only a few can exist in this way."

The old man began to walk again, and the others followed. Ry Sing, watching Bel'lar's face, saw the reality of this situation sink in, and she felt his despair. It hurt her to see him this way.

The Mayor, Vasquez, was a friendly person who seemed very pleased to have Bel'lar here in their midst. He pointed out different places of interest as they walked: the library, a small café where most of the followers met each day for at least one meal, and the shrine of the Bellarian. The shrine interested Ry Sing, but Bel'lar found it to be too much. He didn't want to view a shrine to himself. He wasn't a god, but as he glanced at the people following, he realized that they had a different idea. He mumbled something about how lovely it was and that he didn't want to hold up the holy man, who had walked on.

Vasquez acquiesced gracefully, and said, "You're right. Let's go into the consul's quarters, and enjoy some refreshments."

The villagers continued to walk with them. A few other villagers crossed their path, nodding politely to the visitors. Bel'lar could sense their curiosity about him and his fellow travelers. These villagers joined the procession with the others. Whispering indicated they were being filled in on who Bel'lar was and what was happening.

Mauleen had been walking with Lotep and his sister Mary behind Bel'lar and Ry Sing. Mary had been telling Lotep that she was saddened, because, after three years, no progress had been made. They could see for themselves that progress was impossible. They were too far on their chosen path on this planet to turn back now. The end was inevitable. Mauleen, listening to this with one ear and, with the other, to the holy man's answer about the plants, understood Bel'lar's despair. There didn't seem to be anything they could do. They were 350 years too late. This was the only Shangri-La these people would ever know—unless some of these people would be allowed to return to the blue-white planet with them.

They followed the holy man and the mayor into a round building at the end of the main street. It had large windows that looked out over the ocean. The mayor stopped the villagers at the door, telling them something Bel'lar couldn't hear. Most of the villagers dispersed, but a few came inside to help the mayor with the refreshments.

"Come, let's sit over by the windows," Vasquez said. The room was large and, each evening, accommodated the entire village for their meal, just as in the Compound of the Congress. They followed Vasquez over to the windows and sat down.

Bel'lar said, "Thank you for this welcome. It's my honor to be here. I'm looking forward to speaking to all of you, but, right now, I'm tired. Could we postpone our discussion until tomorrow? We're planning to be here for a few days."

"Certainly. Join us for our evening meal tomorrow," Vasquez said. "We will formally welcome you then."

"We'll have the whole village here," Mary added.

Saint Significance nodded. "That would be the time and place to show the people who you are," he said.

After the refreshments, Mary offered to take them to where she was staying. Her hut was a bit larger as the sister of the Speaker and would accommodate them.

Outside, the two security guards were waiting for Lotep. One of the guards addressed him. "Where do you want the cargo? And your bags?"

"We will be staying at Mary's, so follow us. Then you can bring our bags and the cargo there."

"You brought something. What is it?" Mary said.

"A present for you," Lotep said. Mary looked excited.

This hut of Mary's was close to the gate. Mauleen and Ry Sing were given a room to share, Lotep and Bel'lar, the other guestroom.

"Please feel at home here," Mary invited them. She was happy that her brother was here and, unbelievably surprising, he had brought Bel'lar, the long-awaited holy man. What an honor. She didn't quite know what to do or how to act. Overwhelmed, she just stood in the common room, smiling.

Everyone was getting settled when there was a knock on the door. The sound broke through Mary's stasis, and she hurried to open it. One of the security guards/pilots who had arrived with her visitors entered and placed some bags on the floor.

"Where do you want the cargo?" the guard asked Lotep.

Lotep looked at Mary. "How much cargo is it?" she asked.

"A lot. As much as we could fit in the hovercraft," Lotep said.

"I have a shed out back where we could store it," Mary said, "but what is it?"

"It's food."

"Food! Bring it right in here, and set it down in front of me." Mary rubbed her hands together in excitement.

The guards brought in a small tug that levitated a stack of boxes. It took ten trips to bring in all the food. When they were finished, it was stacked all over her main room and entry. Mary was very excited when she saw how much food her brother had brought her. She opened a few boxes and then caught her brother in an embrace and danced around with him. Everyone was caught up in Mary's exuberance.

"Can I help you?" Ry Sing offered.

"Help me eat this stuff?" Mary laughed in delight, as she looked at all the boxes. There was enough food here to feed everyone in the village for months. "Thank you, Lotep." She gave him another hug. Then she turned to the others. "Thank you all for sharing my home with me. It's nice to have such honored guests, especially my brother. It's lonely out here."

One of the security guards spoke up, "Excuse me, Speaker. We've secured quarters down the street. We will be available at your request."

Lotep walked them to the door. "Very well. If I need you, I'll find you there. We'll be leaving two days from today."

"Yes, Quasar has given us the orders."

After the door closed behind the guards, Mary said, "I have to help prepare the evening meal now, but I'll be back in several hours. I'll make dinner for you, don't worry. And don't touch the boxes." She smiled at Lotep. "I'm glad you're here." Then she looked at her guests. "In the meantime, you're free to wander around. Everyone's friendly here, so enjoy."

She left them alone in the main room of her hut, which was stacked almost to the ceiling with boxes of food. They heard her singing happily as she walked away.

Lotep, who had walked his sister to the door, came back into the main room. "What would you like to do now? We have some free time. It might be wise to use it. Tomorrow, Saint Significance may have things he wishes to discuss with you, Bel'lar." He looked at each one of them in turn, coming to rest finally on Mauleen, who had taken a seat over by the window.

She smiled at him and said, "How about a walk, Lotep? We can let Ry Sing and Bel'lar have some time together. I would love to see this tiny village with you." She crossed the room, navigating around the boxes, to his side. She sent Ry Sing a quick look as she joined Lotep.

Ry Sing and Bel'lar were quick to react. "See you two later," Ry Sing said as they disappeared out the front door. Once outside, they turned toward the gate.

Mauleen and Lotep followed them out. The village was busy with people walking this way and that, congregating to talk about the visitors. They walked a short way. Then Mauleen leaned over to Lotep. "I forgot something," she whispered. "Can we go somewhere quiet and with no people?"

"Why, yes. Over here behind this building. It's deserted right now." They walked behind the building. Lotep stopped close to her with anticipation.

Mauleen noted his heightened interest with amusement. "Step back, Lotep. I'll only be a moment."

She lifted up her tunic, and Lotep thought, *This is getting interesting.*

She turned away and reached inside the suit to pull out her hidden transmitter. She turned back to Lotep, the transmitter in her hand. "Why are you frowning? I need to contact the ship. It won't take long, and then we can continue our walk."

Lotep's hopes evaporated.

Mauleen smiled as she keyed in a code and held the voice transmitter up to her mouth. In a moment, the ship responded. "Hi. This is Enis. I'm unavailable to answer at present. If you will leave a message I will . . . Hello, hello," Enis answered. He was out of breath as he said again, "hello."

"Enis," Mauleen said. "You're in charge of the ship. That means you must monitor all incoming communications."

"I am monitoring all the communications," Enis said, breathing hard.

"Where were you?"

"I'm very busy. Being in charge is a daunting task. Do you remember the box of sugar cubes?"

"Yes."

"I can't locate them. I was sitting here and thought that I might try an experiment to see what effects the sugar cubes and Happy Jack's sodas would have on my body without the Syn suit on."

Lotep, overhearing the conversation, frowned. "Can he be trusted to protect the ship?"

Mauleen stepped away from Lotep. "Enis," she said, in a commanding voice. "The sugar cubes are in a safe place."

Enis said, "That's great. Where?"

"You're the only one there, Enis. You can't be experimenting with those substances, leaving the ship unattended. You must protect the ship first."

"I hear you," he said, his voice dropping. "But we both know the ship doesn't need me to protect her." He sounded disappointed. There was a pause, and then he said, "But I will require the sugar cubes on your return."

"Yes, Enis," she said. "Now tell me. How is everything aboard?"

"Light Traveler reports to me every day, and the last report was that everything is in normal operational status."

"Excellent. Now, I'll contact you every day at this time for your report. The Captain will be expecting it."

"Very well, First Officer," Enis said. "You can count on me. I'll do as you request." The transmission terminated.

"Put that thing away," Lotep said. "Let's get out of here. He's exasperating. He's one of those people who one minute seems to do and say everything exactly right, but in the next . . . who knows?"

Mauleen said, "You're just saying that because he took your suit, but yes, he's liable to do something unexpected if left to his own devices. That's why he's in charge of the ship. He needs to be kept occupied."

✳ ✳ ✳

Ry Sing found it difficult to hold Bel'lar's hand because both their hands were unnaturally large in these suits. But she didn't let go because she wanted to be close to him as they walked. His face was sad, now that no one was watching him. It was amazing that his artificial face reflected his feelings. She wanted to get him alone so that they could talk and decide what they were going to do.

He didn't look up at the sign as they walked under it, but he did inhale deeply of the air as if passing through the gate released him from a part of the weight he carried. Then he said, "It's nice to be free of that stench in the capital city for a while. It's impossible to ignore."

They continued on, passing the transport parked on the plateau.

"I agree. That was horrible. Let's walk up near the edge of the cliff. I want to look out over the ocean. There are some rocks we can sit on." Ry Sing pulled Bel'lar along. They were slightly out of breath when they finally reached the rocks. The cliff area was deserted this late in the afternoon, leaving no risk of being interrupted. He simply sat on the first rock he came to and gazed out to sea in silence.

Brushing off the rock she had chosen, Ry Sing sat, putting her specimen bag on the ground by her feet. She watched him, realizing that he wasn't going to say anything. Well, that was fine with her. She began by telling him about her trip into the city with Mauleen and Lotep. She told him about eating in the restaurant and how the food was terrible. Now that Lotep had explained what they made the food out of, she understood.

He didn't look at her as she continued.

"We went out to where Mauleen grew up and found her parents' old house. We talked to a little girl who could have been Mauleen's descendant; she had the same red hair. Mauleen was melancholy and subdued after that. This little girl had just started taking supplements that apparently all Syns take from age ten up, but she wasn't adjusting well and was home sick. Lotep explained that some children didn't adjust and died. She was such a sweet little girl, Bel'lar."

He listened, allowing her voice, her words, to lull him into a relaxed state. He enjoyed her impressions and thoughts and didn't interrupt, although he smiled from time to time.

Marking those smiles, Ry Sing continued speaking, pleased that he was relaxing. "Then, Lotep took us to where the temple and my school used to be. It was all gone. They built a factory. It was such a beautiful place when I lived there." She stopped speaking and looked out over the ocean. In her mind, she saw the temple again and the grounds where she had spent many days. Sadly, nothing was as it had been. *Yet how could we expect it to be the same?* she thought. Then she gave herself a little shake and went on with her story. "We walked around the corner and found the house of the couple I used to visit when I was in school." Reminiscing, she said, "They were so nice to me and welcomed me at any time. They were like parents to me, since mine died when I was little. They had been dead many years before we left, a year ago.

"An old man lives in the house now. He invited us to sit on his porch and talk. He's at the end of his life and was reflecting on things he missed. He seemed familiar, but I couldn't place him. We spent an enjoyable hour with him; then we returned to the ship."

She had reached the end of her story. She stopped speaking and glanced at him.

He adjusted his position on the rock and said, "So, Ry Sing, you've seen the people and this world. They don't seem to care about anything but maintaining the system they have set up. What do you think?"

"They do care. You just don't like what they care about."

"I hear you, but I've devoted my life to serving the people. I come home, to take them to the blue-white planet, and they don't want to go. I thought that we'd be greeted as honored guests for our search for Shangri-La. And by now we would be planning our return trip and selecting those who were traveling back with us. Instead, since we arrived, I've been trading words with the Quasar, wasting time, involved in his political designs. The Quasar cares only about control and power. And there's only fifteen more years of food. It's too late. Look around here. No plants will grow. Everything has been destroyed. This planet's cycle is almost at an end. My reason for living is almost at an end." He dropped his head into his hands. His voice was muffled as he spoke. "Seeing that sign over the gate demoralized me. I don't know what to do. I was hoping we would see something here that would restore my faith and allow me to do my duty."

She put her arm around him and leaned on his shoulder.

After a few minutes, she said, "I agree with you. None of the Syns want to leave. They would die if we took them away from the food and supplements they're accustomed to and require for existence. This planet is dead now or soon will be. Nothing will shake it from its course. Is there anyone you want to take back with us to the blue-white planet? Have you met any Organs you feel would want this chance? Choose Bel'lar, for these chosen few will be all that will be left of our home planet."

As she fell silent, she heard a buzzing, and a little insect flew at her face. She laughed out loud when she recognized it as a fly. Bel'lar looked up quickly at her laugh.

"Oh, Bel'lar. Catch this fly. If it lives long enough, I want to give it to the old man I met in the city. He told me he had learned that you couldn't change the world, so he was trying to make the best of every day. He didn't like flies when he was younger and killed them. Now that he's approaching the end of his life, he realized that the flies were part of his life. He misses them; he even misses the irritation. Help me catch it, please."

Ry Sing pulled a small container with a perforated lid out of her bag and handed it to him. He smiled at her, this woman wearing a Syn suit with unfamiliar features. Yet, by her actions, he knew it was Ry Sing, always following her impulses. He watched the fly, waiting for it to land on something. Then a thought occurred to him. He simply held out the open container. The fly flew over it, then turned and landed inside it. He put the lid on. He turned to her in wonder at this little fly's seeming desire to help an old man. They both laughed.

Bel'lar was overcome by bittersweet happiness. "Maybe, I have just saved one life." Ry Sing hugged him. They both felt the jumbled happiness and sadness and sat quietly.

After a few minutes, Bel'lar said, "I wish Ka'aya was here to help me make the decision."

"You don't need Ka'aya. Relax and go within; you can discover the knowledge you need to make the right decision."

"It would be easier if Ka'aya were here."

"This isn't the time for easy. It's difficult, but I know that you'll make the right choice. I'm not going to influence you. This is your decision."

She looked out over the ocean and saw that the sun was making its way down the sky to the horizon in anticipation of night. "Look. The sun's setting. That's what your life feels like now. It's entering the darkness, the end times. But it will rise again on the other side of the world just as your life will rise again somewhere else. When you know this, going into the darkness is not that difficult. Make the decision without worrying about the darkness; make the decision by merely understanding that all life has cycles. Then allow what has begun. . ."

"I know," he interrupted her. "To finish. You sound like Ka'aya."

"Come back to Mary's house, and let's kick Lotep out of your room. I'm dying to get out of this suit. It's too confining. Then we can be together while we're here. I don't think they will argue. Mauleen likes him."

Bel'lar grinned. "You twisted my arm." They meandered back to Mary's house holding hands.

They entered the house and discovered the others sitting at the dinner table. Mary was the first to look up. "Oh good. I was getting ready to serve. My brother brought some bottles of wine. Would you like some?"

Ry Sing hurried over and sat down, bumping into Bel'lar as she passed him. He grinned at her excitement and squeezed her arm. He wasn't sure if she felt it because of her suit. Lotep began pouring wine, and Ry Sing held her glass out. They sat down with the others and enjoyed dinner.

With the first bite, Lotep realized this was organic food from the stores in the Compound. He stopped eating, filled with dread. When Mary found the wine, he had been surprised, but the food was a complete shock. He had asked Quasar for some supplies to bring for this religious community, assuming it would be the usual Syn food. Never in all the time he had been in charge in the Compound had the Syns been given organic food. This food was part of the secret the Organs kept. Why did Quasar do this? Was it a mistake? He didn't think so. He also didn't think it was a treat. Something was going on. He looked around at the others. His sister was totally absorbed in the pleasure of having this party, sharing this wonderful food without making the connection that it was organic. No one was looking at him. He hoped he hadn't given away his shock. He returned to eating, not wanting to say anything.

Mary didn't notice her brother's expression. Bel'lar did, however, and wondered what had caused it. But it passed quickly, and Bel'lar forgot about it.

At the end of the meal, they lingered afterwards, talking.

"Mary wants to live in the Compound of the Congress again," Lotep said. "She feels, well . . . ," he turned to her, "I'll let you tell them."

"I'm ready to leave. This has been a grand adventure," Mary began. "Now I want to go back to the Compound and never leave. I never want to interact in the society that the Organs have created again."

Bel'lar leaned back in his chair. "Why did you come to the land of Rebirth?"

"I learned about Saint Significance. He intrigued me with his simple philosophy. It was time to make anew, to merely and simply begin again, he said. That enticed me. Almost 200 people were here in the beginning. But we found, in the last three years that I have been here, that the planet can't sustain itself any longer. The remaining people in this community are simply existing."

"Is there no hope?" Ry Sing asked. She sipped, enjoying another glass of wine.

"Not in my heart," Mary said, "I'll go back and write a story. A story of hope and triumph."

"I thought you had no hope," Mauleen said.

"I don't. Maybe writing about it will help me understand what's happened to me, my family, and this civilization. But now, I must excuse myself. I'm accustomed to rising early in the morning." Mary stood.

Bel'lar got to his feet as well.

They all decided to go to sleep early. Lotep cautioned them about wearing their suits even when sleeping.

Bel'lar and Lotep were in their beds in the guestroom. The lights were out when the door opened. Ry Sing stood in the doorway without her Syn suit. She was wearing the same black dress that she found in the Asian pyramid. The light was shining behind her, creating an inviting silhouette. "Bel'lar."

Bel'lar sat up in bed and grinned. "That's the dress." Unable to bring himself to wear the Syn suit all night, he still had on the underwear garment in case he had to dress in a hurry.

"We have some unfinished business." She walked toward him.

Lotep turned over to see what was going on. He had been trying to sleep. His mouth dropped open. "Now that's an Organ," he whispered.

"Isn't there somewhere you need to be?" she said.

Lotep hastily grabbed a pillow and a blanket, mumbling something about guarding the food. He walked past her, the blanket dragging on the ground. She closed the door behind him.

"Come here, you Organ," Bel'lar said. He lifted the blanket in invitation.

"That's the nicest thing you've said to me in a long time." She slid into bed with him.

Out in the common room that was still full of cartons of food, Lotep thought he might sleep on the couch, but it was full of boxes, too. He considered sleeping in Ry Sing's bed, but that might be too forward, with Mauleen sleeping in the other bed. He walked around for another ten minutes. "This is silly." He knocked on Mauleen's door.

"Come in, Lotep," Mauleen called out.

He opened the door and stepped inside. "You knew it was me."

"Who else would it be? Besides, I've been waiting for you. It took you all this time to decide where to sleep. Don't you like me, Lotep?"

He was embarrassed. "It's because I like you that I couldn't decide."

Mauleen smiled in the darkness as she said, "How about for now, you take the other bed, and we'll talk?"

Relieved, Lotep lay down on Ry Sing's bed.

❋ ❋ ❋

Mauleen and Lotep were drinking tea and chatting at the table the next morning. Bel'lar and Ry Sing joined them when there was a knock on the door. Ry Sing answered it, and, seeing who it was, bowed her head. "Greetings, Saint Significance." She stepped back to invite him inside.

He bowed, and said, "Thank you, holy one."

They stood, looking at each other. She tilted her head to the side. A glow emanated from this old man's body, extending out to arm's length on all sides. With this large of an energy field, he had the ability to create his own reality, she noted. She narrowed her eyes. She knew from her discussion with Lotep that the Saint was an Organ, but the suit with the hair growth was amazing. She couldn't detect any artificiality. Then she said, "You remind me of my old friend and teacher Ka'aya. All I carry of him are my emotions and feelings. I carry them in my heart. It's comforting knowing that one day we shall touch each other again."

"I'm sure that is a great comfort, and I know you will see him again. But now, I'm here to see Bel'lar." He smiled. She smiled back.

Bel'lar heard his name spoken and came to the door. "Greetings, Saint Significance."

"Greetings, Bel'lar. I'm on my daily walk. Will you join me?"

Bel'lar looked at Ry Sing, and she smiled. Bel'lar glanced back at Saint Significance and said, "Why not? Let's go." Then he grabbed Ry Sing's hand and pulled her along with them.

The Saint walked ahead in silence, the other two following. They took the same path as yesterday when they left the village. Through the gate, past the transport. Again, Bel'lar didn't look up at the words on the sign.

"Can I call you Saint?" Bel'lar said.

"Yes. I added the Significance as part of my name, but I have always been the Saint."

A path ahead wound around and up to the edge of the cliff. The old man walked quickly, without any restrictions to his gait. Bel'lar lengthened his stride to keep up. Ry Sing followed behind him.

The old man turned onto the path. It was just wide enough for the two of them to walk side by side, but Bel'lar saw that it would narrow soon as it neared the top of the cliff. He glanced back at Ry Sing. She smiled and waved him on. He turned his attention back to the Saint.

"Ry Sing," the Saint addressed her, "what do you think of our endeavor to recreate an organic life?"

"Uh, uh, well, it's nicer here than in the capital city, but . . ." Ry Sing stuttered, not wanting to offend this old man.

Bel'lar interrupted, "It's sad. You won't survive here."

The holy man turned and looked at Bel'lar. The early morning light haloed his body, expanding his natural gleam, and spilled onto the rocks around him. They had reached the top of the cliff. "Yes, we're at the end. That's why it's so fortuitous that you're here now. Here is a quick lesson in life to carry you through the end days here. Watch closely as I walk on the edge of the cliff."

The Saint walked along the edge for a few steps; then he stepped out into nothingness, one foot on the solid ground of the path and one walking on air. Bel'lar instinctively reached for him, but he wasn't close enough. He caught himself from falling as the Saint smiled and waved him back; he continued with one foot off, one foot on the cliff.

"Once you have learned your fears and conquered them, then you will be able to live out the last days on this planet," the Saint said.

Watching the Saint perform this balancing act excited Ry Sing. "I want to try. Let me do it." She pushed her way between Bel'lar and the Saint. Then, without hesitation, she stepped out into the vastness and stood there without any visible means of support. Her body glowed brightly, and she beamed her happiness.

The holy man grinned. "You're good at this."

Ry Sing smiled. "I seem to have conquered all my fears but one."

Bel'lar stared at her, his stomach clenched, wanting to pull her back to the safety of the cliff path. "You don't look afraid," he said nervously. He hated it when she did things like this, terrifying him down to his very core.

"The fear that many cannot conquer is the loss or suffering of someone they love," the Saint offered.

Ry Sing's face filled with sorrow. She didn't speak, stepping back to the path, the glow about her diminishing. Her eyes were heavy, and she looked away.

"Fear not, my Ry Sing, for this, too, you will conquer." He glanced back at Bel'lar, who was looking apprehensively over the edge. "Come along, Bel'lar." Then he grabbed Ry Sing's hand and said, "We will walk. I have much to tell you two."

The three walked along the cliff for a long time and finally returned to the village gate. They stood looking at each other.

"Quasar has promised me a part in the celebration," Bel'lar said. "What happens at this celebration?"

"The Last Rites of Ester begins at evening on the Thirteenth and culminates in a ceremony at midday on the third day. The people eat a last supper that first evening. Then they fast until after the ceremony. No supplements or food or drink are taken during this time by law."

"How can they do that? It must be torture for them." Bel'lar didn't think the Syns could endure this without suffering.

"It's very difficult. It can lead to hysteria, and some fall into babbling. The ceremony is followed by an orgy of consumption. Everyone tries to consume more than they have ever consumed before. The hearts of many may give out. They will cease to exist. It is a great honor to cease to exist on this day. Many live for this event."

Bel'lar shuddered, wondering how these people could believe in a god that would demand this type of celebration. "Is someone sacrificed?"

The Saint glanced at Bel'lar. "Sometimes Quasar has a special guest."

"Will it be Bel'lar?" Ry Sing asked.

"Yes," the old man answered without hesitation.

Ry Sing's stomach tightened with fear. She grabbed Bel'lar's arm and said, "We've got to get off this planet."

"It's all right. I'm smarter than Quasar." He grinned at her.

The Saint watched these two. What he saw made him smile. Then he said, "Now, my son, it's time for me to go." He raised his arms to embrace Bel'lar. Bel'lar responded and then shivered at the jolt of energy he received and stepped back quickly.

Bel'lar felt a strong connection to this old man, a connection he couldn't explain. He felt compelled to speak of it. "You remind me of my father, but in a good way. My father and I never got along, and I always wished we did. But for some reason, and I really don't understand this, I can picture you as being the ideal father to me. The feeling is very strong. I will always hold you dear to me."

"I'm glad you feel this way. As my connection to you is very strong." The Saint paused, looking on Bel'lar with affection. Then he looked at Ry Sing and said, "I have a connection to someone else here, and I'm concerned about him."

She regarded him, waiting for him to continue.

"You're here to find him," he further explained.

"You mean Ka'aya," she said and stepped closer.

"Yes. He's on this planet but cut off from his higher self. He did this to have a visceral experience but became lost in the physical being that consumes him."

"I've been looking, but I just can't find him. Tell me who he is."

"He's the one in plain sight," the holy man said.

"You can't be more specific?" Bel'lar said.

"I cannot tell you. I have many talents, but one I do not possess is that of living your lives." He looked at both of them once more. He smiled.

"It's been my pleasure to have encountered both of you. I shall hold you deeply in my thoughts." He turned and walked away, waving at them.

Ry Sing called after him, "Tell me who Ka'aya is! Where is he?"

Bel'lar waved the Saint off. "Let him go. All holy men are alike. They tease you with tidbits but never give you anything substantial." Then he looked at her. "Do you really think Ka'aya's alive?"

"Absolutely," she said.

"Come on," Bel'lar said. "And they wanted me to be a holy man. What a joke."

Ry Sing smiled and linked her arm with his, and they walked back into the village.

✳ ✳ ✳

That evening, Vasquez stepped through the open door of Mary's hut and called for the Captain. Mary went to greet him, Bel'lar behind her. Vasquez was attired in a white robe tonight, honoring the special guests. "It's time. Bel'lar—you're speaking at the feast tonight, aren't you?"

"Yes, I am."

"Wonderful! The Savior Bel'lar coming here is a miracle." He bowed his head reverentially to Bel'lar. "Everyone will be there."

"Remember Vasquez, I'm just a military man," Bel'lar said.

"Yes, I remember," Vasquez said. "We're just honored that you're here." He looked at Lotep. "We've prepared some of the food you brought us. We thank you for that, Speaker. Come down as soon as you're ready. We'll be waiting for you."

"We'll be right there," Mary said.

Bel'lar and Mary watched Vasquez walk steadily through the village.

"I don't know what we would have done without Vasquez," she said. "He's been a solid influence here, maintaining a firm, benevolent hand on this community. Everyone looks to him for help and guidance." She looked at Bel'lar. "Did you talk to Saint Significance?"

"Yes, I did. He's a very—how can I put this?—interesting, but strange, and enlightening, but cryptic, individual."

"Doesn't he get under your skin?" she said with a smile.

"That's one way of putting it," he answered. "He reminded me of Ka'aya."

Ry Sing came up behind him. "Exactly like Ka'aya," she said. "I hope I get the chance to talk to him again."

"I don't think we're done with him," Bel'lar told her.

Lotep and Mauleen joined the others as they made their way to the round building at the end of the street. When they walked in, the people got to their feet and said in unison, "Greetings to the Bellarian." Oddly formal, it almost sounded like a prayer.

This embarrassed Bel'lar. He wasn't a holy man. Yet he responded with, "Greetings." He wanted to help these people somehow. Looking around this room full of smiling faces, he felt closer to this group than he had to those in the Compound of the Congress.

He and his friends were shown to a table, where Saint Significance was already seated. On his way through the room, people touched him, on the arm, his back. He clasped hands extended to him. He heard them call him "savior" and he was disturbed.

Vasquez joined them, and the dinner began. Already exhilarated by the presence of the Savior Bel'lar, the villagers kept staring at him, whispering among themselves. The whispering ceased when the food was served. Today they were truly blessed by his visit, and this meal was an unheard-of treat for these people attempting to return to the organic lifestyle. They had been existing on minimal nutrition and were considerably thinner than the Syns in the capital city. The food brought by Lotep was from the stores within the Compound. No Syn had eaten this before or known of its existence. The freshness and flavors were overwhelming to these people, and, for a time, everyone was caught up in the joy of eating real, natural food.

Vasquez couldn't get enough of the fruit. First he had an apple. The juice ran down his chin as he crunched into it, but he kept eating, not caring that it dripped on to his clothes. Then some cherries. After that he ate two bunches of grapes. He was almost beside himself with the sweetness and texture of this food. With each bite, he allowed the grape to explode in his mouth, spilling out its juices. His eyes almost rolled up inside his head, and Bel'lar smiled. Never before had Vasquez or the others known anything like this.

In contrast, the Saint ate sparingly of the food and had one glass of wine.

Bel'lar, sitting next to him, asked, "Don't you like the food?"

The Saint shook his head. "The food is very good. I do not subscribe to the Quasarian philosophy of consumption, preferring to eat minimally. I do not allow the physical to impair my spirit. I see that you and Ry Sing agree with me."

And indeed, Bel'lar and Ry Sing's dishes contained small amounts of food similar to the Saint's.

Bel'lar thought the gift was a great gesture on Lotep's part as he watched the community enjoy this meal. But then he remembered Lotep's shock at dinner last night, and a dark thought squeezed in. He wondered why they were given this particular gift. These people were unaware that this kind of food even existed. And, it seemed to Bel'lar, now it was very possible that the secret life of the Organs within the Compound might be exposed. Why would anyone risk that? Was this purely Lotep's idea, or was the Quasar behind it? This made him uneasy and spoiled his enjoyment of the meal.

Ry Sing noticed his disquiet and squeezed his hand. He looked at her and saw the question in her eyes. He shook his head slightly and squeezed her hand back.

The wine that Lotep had brought was passed around freely, and laughter was heard from all corners of the gathering, as the people relaxed under its effect.

Ry Sing leaned over to Bel'lar and whispered, "I thought they'd look more organic. More like us."

"So did I," he answered.

Finally, everyone was finished. Vasquez wiped the juice from his chin with a grin. He thanked Lotep for bringing the food and for bringing Bel'lar. Then he introduced the Saint.

The Saint got to his feet, and looked out over these people he had been ministering to these past five years. A few were still eating, but the majority focused on him.

"To have here in our midst the Savior Bel'lar is truly a miracle. And with him is the holy one, Ry Sing, with the rare attainment of Sower. We are honored by their visit and look forward with eagerness to Bel'lar's words tonight."

Then a man's voice carried from somewhere in the room, "I knew I was right. I believed no matter what. Thank God. It's the Savior."

Saint Significance turned to Bel'lar and motioned for him to stand. "Bel'lar, it's time for you to share who you are. Please talk to us a little bit."

Bel'lar stood reluctantly, his eyes cast down as he pondered what to say. He looked around the room. All eyes were on him, expectant. Two ladies in the middle of the room had their hands over their hearts, waiting for him to speak. An older man smiled encouragingly at him from a nearby table.

Bel'lar smiled back and began, "I know you think I'm someone special. That I'm the holy man of the Bellarian religion. But I'm merely a simple military man who had a mission to discover a new world. During that mission, I've learned that the only thing you can do is be true to yourself. Live your lives as you believe they should be lived. Don't regret what should have been, what could have been, but understand that your lives are opportunities to experience life itself. And, in the future, I'm going to try to live up to that. That's all I can tell you. Thank you." He sat again. Ry Sing squeezed his hand. A few people applauded.

Vasquez stood; bowing his head deferentially, he said, "Forgive me, Bel'lar, that's a really nice speech, but it's not what we want to know. We've read many things about you and your mission. We want to know what really happened. Please tell us." He sat and the villagers were nodding and murmuring.

"Yes, please tell us what happened," one of ladies with her hand over her heart asked.

The older man nearby said, "Did you really go in search of Shangri-La?"

Bel'lar glanced at Ry Sing. She nodded. "Go on," she said softly. "Tell them."

The villagers leaned forward, intent on him.

Bel'lar cleared his throat and stood. "You have a right to know." He cleared his throat again. "My original orders were to find a new habitable planet for our people to relocate to. Information was discovered regarding a planet known as the blue-white planet, and we were sent to prove its existence. And we did. We found it. And it's truly wonderful. It is perfect for you. A new home for this civilization."

"Why did it take you so long to return home?" Vasquez asked.

"It's because of the speed and distance that we traveled. We were only gone a year, but to you it's been 350 years."

A man stood up in the back. "We're ready to go. Just say the word. How long do we have to get ready?"

"I wish I could answer that, but it's not my decision. I'm waiting for Quasar to make those decisions."

"When will he decide?" Vasquez asked.

"I don't know," Bel'lar answered. "It's out of my hands."

"But you're the Savior. You should decide," someone called out.

"Yes, aren't you the true god? Can't you just smite him or something?" someone asked.

Bel'lar shook his head in apology. "I'm just a military man, as I told you."

The man in the back, who said they were ready to go, spoke up again. "Well, if you're not the Savior, tonight you are because of this food. We've never eaten like this before." Those sitting near him agreed.

"Where did this food come from? Did you bring it from the blue-white planet?"

Bel'lar glanced at Lotep, who looked nervous. He wondered what Lotep was thinking. Then, not wanting to upset these people, he said, "We brought it from the blue-white planet." He smiled. "The blue-white planet has the potential to provide for all of us for many years to come." He glanced at Lotep again and saw his surprise.

Ry Sing touched Bel'lar's arm, getting his attention. He nodded to her; she stood and said, "Please . . . , I want to warn you about this new planet. Its abundance may seduce you. A very long time ago, there was a planet called the Planet of Abundance; some of you may know of it." Many of the villagers were nodding. "It was like this new blue-white planet. Its bounty seemed unlimited and led the inhabitants into over-consumption. The only solution to that situation was to annihilate that planet completely. It sits dormant now, unable to sustain life. And here you're in the same quandary on this planet, having over-consumed. Don't repeat these mistakes and destroy the blue-white planet."

Vasquez turned to the Saint. "Is this true about that planet? Was it annihilated?"

The Saint inclined his head to the mayor. "Indeed, it was. The holy one, Ry Sing, is correct in making you aware of your past. Heed her warnings."

The villagers listened to this warning, but they quickly returned to the prospect of relocating, wanting to know all about the blue-white planet. Bel'lar answered all their questions, describing the planet and its many continents and environments. He told them about the Asian race and its intermingling with the indigenous peoples. They refused to accept that he wasn't the Savior, and he gave up trying to explain. They bowed to him as they left, paying homage to the Savior. Many hugged him. They wanted to show him the shrine, but he shook his head, saying that was for them and not for him. He thanked them for their kindness and stifled his impatience at all of this attention. Soon he would leave, and these Bellarians would have something to remember.

He heard many of the villagers talking about packing. They were planning to return to the capital city to be ready to leave when Bel'lar made his next trip to the blue-white planet. He hoped that their wishes came true, but he didn't think the Quasar cared about them and would allow any of them to leave.

✳ ✳ ✳

Mary's hut was quiet. Time had passed, and everyone was asleep inside. Indeed, the entire village was asleep. Then Ry Sing was awakened by a spiritual nudge. Bel'lar was sound asleep next to her. Not fully awake, she allowed the nudge to guide her. She gathered a robe about her body, not bothering with the Syn suit, and left the room. She walked softly through the house to the door. Feeling the desire to go outside, she stepped into the cool darkness. She opened her eyes, surprised she was there. She collected her thoughts, not completely understanding but also not disturbed by this, and closed her eyes. Seeking direction, she was drawn to the cliff where they had walked with the Saint earlier.

She reached the cliff path and made her way to the top. A breeze blew through her hair, her robe. She separated from her physical body; her eyes closed again, and she heard a faint sound.

"You need not open your eyes to see me, for my energy now is greater than the physical. But come, walk with me, for it is the time of understanding. It is the time of revealing. For I am the one, the soul you've been seeking. But, in this time, we have fragmented the soul of Ka'aya into many parts."

She recognized the voice of the Saint. "Will I be able to do this?"

The voice changed, and now it was her beloved Ka'aya's. "Of course, my dear. All shall be revealed to you. You must only allow."

"Is that my Ka'aya?" she asked, her voice filled with joy.

"I am the essence of Ka'aya. The fragmented soul still lives a tormented existence in a physical body on this planet. But this will remain a mystery to you for a short time longer. We must not interrupt this life. And it will be revealed."

She looked upon the Saint as he stepped out into the air beyond the cliff. He smiled and waved. Then his body plummeted down the cliff toward the ocean. Her eyes followed him, but, before he hit the bottom, his body vaporized into a mist, and the mist dissipated into nothingness. She understood that he was so light that his body almost didn't exist.

She inhaled a deep breath, attempting to compose her thoughts as she turned from the edge and made her way in silence back to Mary's hut.

*　*　*

Early the next morning, Bel'lar and his group, joined by Mary, carried their things to the ship. No one saw them off, because they had already said their goodbyes to the village last night at the dinner. Now the village was silent.

The security guards hustled them aboard, and Bel'lar felt like they were sneaking out, leaving these people to their fate. As they took off, he couldn't shake this feeling. But he had decided last night that he would come back for Vasquez and his wife and any others here who would want to make the voyage to the blue-white planet. This group of people knew what it meant to embrace an organic lifestyle. They deserved a second chance.

The ship lifted off; then it turned and came back around over the village, where it hovered. While everyone on board was trying to figure out what the pilot was doing, a loud explosion rocked the vessel. Looking out the windows, Bel'lar spotted the site of the explosion. Down in the village, the library and the area around it had been destroyed.

Villagers ran from their homes only to be confronted by smoke and fire. Some were caught in the rubble, hurt and crying.

Mary jumped to her feet, shocked. "What's happening? We have to help them! Turn back, turn back!"

Lotep spoke urgently to the pilots, but they refused to take his orders. Instead they shut off the intercom and maintained the stationary hovering position over the village, leaving the passengers helpless to intercede as the destruction continued.

Then another explosion buffeted the airborne vessel, and the houses near the café were gone. Down below, Vasquez and his wife helped their neighbors get to safety. Fire spread quickly through the village. Flames shot across their path and Vasquez pulled his wife out of the way. He looked up to the ship hovering above and yelled out, "I knew you weren't the true god. I just knew it."

Inside the craft, Bel'lar was furious. He jumped across the cabin and punched Lotep in the mouth. Slamming him down into his seat, Bel'lar towered over him, yelling in his face. "What have you done?"

Lotep put up his hands, his synthetic mouth bleeding, all the while trying to explain. "It wasn't me. I didn't know anything about it." He didn't try to fight back.

Another explosion rocked the ship, and the village below was consumed in flames. Black smoke rose into the air. The pilots turned the ship from the village and sent it speeding away from the Continent of Rebirth.

Bel'lar straightened up from Lotep and looked out over the burning village. It had been incinerated, he realized with horror. Vasquez and his community no longer existed. Bel'lar dropped into his seat. He clenched his hand into a fist and slammed it into the wall of the ship, drawing a glare from the security guards. He looked at Ry Sing. "That was the last opportunity for life on this planet."

She nodded. "We need to get out of here."

Lotep moved to a seat away from Bel'lar. Mauleen opened the ship's healer's kit and proceeded to treat the cut on Lotep's mouth. The cut on the suit didn't hurt, it was the bruise that was developing on his own face underneath that stung. He gave her a small smile and then turned away. She didn't know what to say, divided as her loyalties were between her Captain and this man she was growing to care for. Instead, she sat silently between them.

Mary had collapsed, grief-stricken. The remainder of the trip she passed in silence, dozing on and off. Lotep stared out the window, clenching and unclenching his hands. He seemed as devastated as Mary.

Bel'lar watched him closely. He actually liked him, but he didn't know if this man could be trusted, as he had hoped. Lotep had repeatedly denied knowing anything about Quasar's plans, but he was, as all the Organs on this planet were, expert at pretending to be something else.

Bel'lar moved to sit by Lotep. The Speaker drew back, afraid he was going to be hit again. Bel'lar touched his arm, shaking his head. He leaned close and whispered, "I'm calm now. I won't hit you again. Did you really not know anything about this?"

Lotep glanced at the pilots up front and checked the inter-com. It was still shut off, but he whispered back, "I didn't know anything. But the food bothered me. When Mary opened the first crates, I realized it was organic food. I was shocked. I expected it to be Syn food. I still don't understand. The Quasar must have ordered it, but, why, I don't know. We've never given organic food to the Syns before."

"Maybe it's my fault. I shouldn't have told them about the blue-white planet. Quasar has kept all this secret since we arrived. I just felt they deserved to know. And now they're all dead."

Ry Sing leaned toward them, her voice soft, "It's not your fault, Bel'lar. You're not responsible for the evil that lies in Quasar's heart. You have to get away. Don't go back to Quasar."

Bel'lar looked at Lotep. "Can you help me?"

Lotep nodded. "I can take you to the ship once we're in my private transport. But I want to go with you. I'll do this if you'll take me and my sister with you."

Ry Sing was nodding. Bel'lar stuck out his hand to Lotep. They clasped hands in agreement. Then they sat back, lost in their own thoughts.

As they approached the capital city, they were confronted again with the yellow fog of pollution that hung over everything. They landed at the hovercraft port. Lotep's personal transport was still parked over at the side. No security guards waited on the landing pad. *We're in luck*, Bel'lar thought. The second the craft stopped, Bel'lar and the others jumped out and ran to Lotep's transport. The women climbed inside the vehicle.

Then two guards charged out of the port's station and came at Bel'lar. He punched one, but the other grabbed him around the neck. He struggled, kicking out. The arm around his neck tightened. He dug his fingers into the arm choking him while the other guard tried to grab his arm.

Ry Sing jumped from the transport, yelling, "Let him go, let him go!" She reached Bel'lar and hit the one choking Bel'lar on the back of the neck and jerked on his ears. He cried out, and the other guard grabbed her off him and pushed her away. She stumbled to her knees and then just came back, scratching him on the face and kicking him in the leg. Mauleen and Lotep rushed up and grabbed her, pulling her back.

The two guards wrestled Bel'lar to the ground. One shoved his knee into Bel'lar's back, twisting his arm, forcing his face into the ground. He stopped fighting.

"They won't kill him, not until the last rites," Lotep hissed in her ear. He had Ry Sing around the waist and lifted her off the ground. She kicked her feet, trying to get free.

"Stop fighting, Ry Sing. Before we're all in danger," Mauleen said.

Lotep carried her to the transport and forced her inside. They watched as Bel'lar was hoisted to his feet by the guards and propelled inside the station.

Lotep sped away in his transport, taking the women to safety.

Quasar waited inside the station, his arms crossed. He was scowling. Two more guards were standing on either side of him.

*It begins*, Bel'lar thought, as he walked to meet Quasar. He stared at this man who he knew now was an unconscionable monster. He wanted to kill him. He tried to get free, but the guards held him tighter, twisting his arm painfully up behind his back.

Quasar smiled and turned to the security guards beside him and then pointed at Bel'lar. They bound Bel'lar at his wrists, snapping the restraints on tight, almost cutting off the circulation in his arms. These wrist restraints had a short bar between them so he couldn't hold his hands together.

Bel'lar held up his restrained hands. "Don't you trust me?"

The Quasar looked him over with a sneer. "I'm very disappointed in you. You didn't do what I wanted, but now you will." He laughed and walked away.

Only one week remained until the Last Rites of Ester celebration.

* * *

Ry Sing was still furious and terrified about Bel'lar being captured but had stopped fighting once inside the transport. She wiped away tears as she watched them drag Bel'lar inside the station. She had to get him free. The Light Traveler would know how. But where were they taking him?

Mary had seemed numb since the massacre of her village and her outburst on the transport and completely unaware of what had happened to Bel'lar. Now she suddenly spoke. "Lotep, I want to see our parents."

"No," Ry Sing said. "We have to get back to the ship so we can save Bel'lar."

"Don't worry," Lotep said. "He'll be safe until the Last Rites."

"I don't care about that. We have to get him back now!" Ry Sing yelled.

"Please," Mary said. "It will take only a few minutes to see my parents. It's my last chance."

Lotep glanced back at Ry Sing. "It's on the way."

Ry Sing exchanged a look with Mauleen. They realized that they couldn't overpower him. There was nothing to do but to go along.

* * *

The guards roughly hauled Bel'lar outside the hovercraft station and loaded him into a transport. Again he was taken to the presidential building. This time, however, they took him into the lower levels and shoved him into a small room. They removed his restraints and were about to leave when he stopped them, asking, "What am I doing here?"

One of the guards said, "Quasar wishes it."

"What does that mean?" He rubbed his wrists, getting blood back into them.

This guard smiled meanly. He slammed and locked the door. Both guards laughed as they walked away.

* * *

Lotep stopped the transport in front of the tenement where their parents lived. The color of the building had faded and flaked off, leaving much exposed block. Refuse was piled in the gutters. This was typical of the living conditions of the city's inhabitants. The city was crumbling around them, all the structures in varying degrees of disrepair. The Syns lacked the desire and the inclination to clean and repair their city.

A transport like the one Lotep was driving was an unusual sight. One old man ran his hands along the front of it in awe. Lotep cautioned him to be careful. Then he followed his sister and the other two women inside the building.

Trash was scattered on the floor in the hallway, and a broken-down cart was pushed up against one wall. They stepped around this and toward the stairs.

Mary looked around distastefully. "This is worse than I remember."

"It's not that bad," Lotep said. But he didn't like it here, either. It bothered him that the Compound of the Congress didn't care about the state of the city. The Organs had taken on the task of caring for the Syns, but they did nothing to change or improve their living conditions. Consequently, the buildings were maintained just enough to be functional.

Mauleen and Ry Sing followed quietly behind the brother and sister, looking around. The building was dark and dingy inside, and neither wanted to touch anything. They went up several flights of stairs to the third floor. By the time they reached the third floor, the exercise, combined with the poor air quality, had them all out of breath. Mary knocked on the door and stepped back. An eye appeared in the hole in the door, looking at them.

*       *       *

Bel'lar looked around at his new accommodations. Not too bad. Not too good. The only light came from the small window in the door. One bunk against the wall. At least it seemed clean and unused.

He had been brought to the Retention Basin, which was what they called the prison in the Quasar's building. He was the only one down here as far as he could determine. No one answered when he called out.

*       *       *

"Who is it?" a woman's voice called out.

"It's me, Mom," Mary said. "Open the door." She stood on tiptoe so her mom would be able to see her.

"Whose Mom are you?"

"Mom, it's Mary, your daughter."

"Daughter? I have no daughter." The woman sounded confused.

"Open the door, please," Lotep said in his official voice.

There was some fumbling with the lock, and then the woman opened the door. Mary had opened her mouth to greet her mother when the words were knocked from her mind. She stood on the threshold staring. She didn't recognize this woman. Dressed in a dingy white shift, this woman was very old. Unlike most Syns, her body hadn't thickened. Her skin sagged from her arms, her neck. Her face was creased, wrinkled. All of the hair on her head had fallen out. Only sparse eyebrows arched over her dull eyes. Mary sucked in a sob that escaped as a tiny cry. Lotep reached for her, but she walked quickly past the woman into the room. The others followed.

Ry Sing looked this woman over. The woman stood, her head down, her hands shaking. She was polite, but she was lacking in cognitive abilities. She didn't recognize her children. She led them into a living room, where an older man sat in a tawdry chair, staring into a display mounted on the wall. Circles widened and then diminished around a dot on this display. The old man was in a hypnotic state, unaware anyone was here.

The old man appeared ancient, wrinkled, and weak. His physical state was similar to his wife's.

Ry Sing noticed the ancient wallpaper. Shabby and torn, it was a mere echo of its once-pretty yellow rose pattern. The tiny place was in disarray. The only seating was an old couch stacked with blankets on one end and the chair the old man was sitting on. The furnishings looked like they were from Ry Sing's time on this planet, if that were even possible.

Lotep approached the old man. "You don't mind if I turn this off?" The old man didn't react. Lotep turned off the display. "Father." No response. Lotep's father continued to stare.

"Please excuse him," their mother said. "It will take him a few minutes to return to reality."

Mary, watching all of this, was beside herself at her parents' behavior. Her voice rose as she said, "What's going on here, Mom? Why is Father in this stupor?"

"What do you mean? That's his recreation. It stretches Melvin's mind capacity."

Mary paced back and forth, clasping and unclasping her hands, while Ry Sing and Mauleen just watched. Mary stopped in front of Lotep. "How could we let them do this?"

He answered, "This is to be expected. Sometimes the surgery takes very well. In this case, it did. Usually it takes longer to become the complete Syns that our parents have become." He had tears in his eyes as he stared at his dad.

The old woman looked up. "We're very proud to be Syns. Once we were different, and we didn't want to be. Now we're the same as all the rest. It's comforting to know that I'm . . ." She stopped and looked around confused.

"Mom. That you are what?" Mary asked.

"That I are what?"

"Never mind, Mom," Lotep said.

The woman, his mother, said, "Who is your mom?"

He shook his head sadly. "Mary, they are much farther gone than I anticipated."

"They're not our parents anymore," she said. "They are merely cogs caught up in the progress of society."

"Don't be disappointed," Ry Sing said, her voice filled with compassion. "What you're seeing, you're seeing through your eyes, not theirs. This is what they wished."

"But is this what they really wanted?" Mary said in disbelief. She sank down on the old couch. The blankets fell over on her. She pushed them away.

"It doesn't matter what they really wanted," Ry Sing said. "This is who they are now. You must learn to let them be. You must let them live their lives to the fullest. If this is their choosing, then so be it."

Mary hung her head. "I hate seeing them like this." She looked at Ry Sing. "Where is your family?"

"My parents died when I was six, and I was put in an orphanage. But I would trade your parents for mine. For even though they aren't what you wish, at least you have known them. Don't judge them. Allow them to be. That's all you can do."

Mauleen sat down beside Mary and hugged her.

They stood up together, and Mary said to Lotep, "I think it's time to leave."

"What about our father?" Lotep said. "You haven't spoken to him yet."

"I can't," Mary said, with tears in her eyes. "I will speak to them in my heart, remembering them as they once were, not as they are now." She kissed her father on his cheek. He was still tranquilized and didn't respond. She approached her mom to give her a kiss, but her mother stood back, uncertainty on her face. Mary's tears began to fall, and she turned away, crying. Then she hugged her anyway. "Goodbye, Mom." Lotep put his arm around his sister, and the four left. The woman stood at the door, watching them walk away, confusion on her face. After a few minutes, she closed the door.

"You have learned a great lesson," Ry Sing said. "You have seen people you love dearly, but they are not as you wish. And you have left them now as they wish." No one else spoke as they walked to the transport.

Once inside the transport, with the doors closed, Ry Sing said, "Is this the norm of society here? Is this what the people can expect to be?"

"This is all that can be expected today," Lotep answered. "The drugs and synthetic foods that they eat drive them to this state. So yes, this is normal. And our parents are only in their fifties. Life expectancy is rarely past sixty. And I don't think they will live that long."

Ry Sing looked at Lotep. "You understand that your society is dying, don't you? There is only a short time left." This tiny apartment, inhabited by two beings who were only shadows of their former selves, told her the end was near. The stench of death permeated this city. She wrinkled her nose.

He just stared at her without answering.

She couldn't wait to leave this planet. "Take us back to our ship. We have to save Bel'lar from that madman."

Ry Sing felt Mary's sadness and asked her, "Come with us, Mary. You will be safe on our ship."

"Go, Mary," Lotep said. "You'll like it there."

She looked from Ry Sing to Mauleen and then said, "All right. Thank you."

"Wait till you meet Enis. You'll like him, or should I say, he'll like you," Mauleen said.

Mary smiled a little and wiped her eyes. "It would be good to meet someone new. Thank you both."

Lotep was pleased with this arrangement because he wanted Mary out of harm's way, as well, over the next week. He still had hopes that he could help Bel'lar and be able to leave on that ship.

✳ ✳ ✳

Ry Sing hurried to the bridge. Enis was sitting in Bel'lar's chair.

"Anything? Did he check in?"

"Not yet, Ry Sing," Enis answered. "It's too soon. He won't send the signal for several hours."

"As soon as you know, tell me." Ry Sing was anxious, restless. She paced back and forth. Then she hurried off the bridge. In the lounge, she entered the preparation area. She had a drink of water and then paced some more.

Mauleen came in. "There you are."

Ry Sing didn't look over at her; she just kept pacing.

"Are you all right? What's wrong?" Mauleen asked.

"I'm fine. I'm just trying to figure out what's going on. I'm trying to find Bel'lar." She shook her cup, and drops splashed out. She didn't notice.

"He'll check in at the usual time. Don't worry. He's fine. Relax." Mauleen hadn't seen Ry Sing like this before.

"I'm too anxious," Ry Sing said. "I can't bear it if something happens to him." She left her cup on the counter, opened the cold storage, and poked through the containers. She discovered some celery. Taking a piece, she broke it in half and munched on it as she searched through more containers.

"The ship hasn't indicated anything wrong with Bel'lar. She has access to his transmitter," Mauleen said, trying to help her.

"But where is he?" Ry Sing said.

"He's in the Presidential building somewhere below ground," Mauleen answered.

"Light Traveler, locate Captain Bel'lar," Ry Sing said.

"His location has been determined," the ship answered.

"Then bring him aboard," Ry Sing demanded.

"I am unable at this time."

"Why not?" Ry Sing paced.

"There are events in his life which he must continue until completion. This is one of those times when I can't interfere. But he is safe at this time," Light Traveler explained.

Ry Sing threw up her hands in frustration.

"Thank you, Light Traveler," Mauleen said.

Enis entered the room. Noting Ry Sing's frantic behavior, he took a bottle of Happy Jack's soda from the cold storage. He opened it and offered it to her. "This is what you need."

She grabbed it and took a drink. Then she paused, holding the liquid in her mouth. She tilted her head to the side as if she were thinking. Then ran to the water service drain and spit it out. She gave the bottle back to Enis. "Are you crazy? That's poison." Under her breath she mumbled, "Bel'lar's all right, Bel'lar's all right, Bel'lar's all right. I've got to find Ka'aya, I've got to find Ka'aya . . ." She continued repeating to herself as she left the lounge.

Enis watched her leave and then looked at Mauleen. "My philosophy is if you're gonna go, go happy." He took a big drink of the soda. "Ahhh. So refreshing."

Mauleen finished wiping up the spill from Ry Sing's cup and threw the towel down on the counter. "You're becoming a Syn," she snapped and walked out.

He smiled and drank again.

✳ ✳ ✳

Later that evening, at the agreed-upon time, Bel'lar sent the message with the transmitter hidden in his temple. Along with this signal, his vital signs were sent, reassuring Ry Sing that he was safe. Now they could only wait, for the end was near. He had plenty of time to contemplate what he had done and what he would do.

✳ ✳ ✳

Ry Sing entered her quarters still in a highly agitated state. She paced around and then stopped. She raised her arms and then swept her hands through the air down past her face, continuing the motion down over her body, clearing the energy around her. She took a deep breath. "I am the Ry Sing Su Tong." She sank into a cross-legged position on the floor. Breathing calmly, she slid into a meditative state.

In her mind, she spoke, "Ka'aya, even though you're in physical somewhere on this planet, and you don't remember who you are, I shall find you and save you from yourself. That is my promise."

Sinking deeper now into a trancelike state, she envisioned the image of Ka'aya as she knew him before and spoke to him. "Find yourself in this life. Who are you now?" In her mind's eye, she watched Ka'aya's image begin to change form. First Lotep appeared. She felt nothing, and the image faded away. Lotep's father appeared. He faded away. Vasquez was next, but he faded too. One of the guards from the journey took form; *no*, she thought, and he faded away. Then the image coalesced into Saint Significance. Yes, there was something there. She knew this already. But he was no longer in physical form.

"Who are you now in this life?"

Her mind filled with the answer. "We are of importance in this society, but we have not completed this experience yet, so you will not know our true identity. When it's necessary, you will understand who we are." Then he faded away.

She let the trance state go, uncrossed her legs, and stretched out on the floor. She breathed deeply. She had accomplished something, but she wasn't sure what yet. But it didn't matter because she had decided to let what had begun finish. She fell into a deep sleep.

✳ ✳ ✳

Bel'lar had been confined in this otherwise-empty prison in the basement of the Presidential building for a couple of days. He was still wearing his Syn suit because he didn't dare remove it. He was positive that the guards in this prison were Syns, and removing his suit would expose him for the Organ that he was. He wasn't sure what would happen then.

Bel'lar had a good view of the guard on duty in the hall because the upper half of his cell door was open, with only bars preventing his escape. He called him over. "I want to see Quasar. I have his answer."

The guard smirked. "The answer's not important. It's the question that's needed." He walked away.

*What does that mean?* Bel'lar thought. He thought Quasar wanted to hear his answer, but he hadn't seen Quasar since he was captured at the hovercraft station. Didn't Quasar care about it anymore? What was going on? Angry and impotent, he paced back and forth, trying to figure it out. *I grew up on this planet that I've come back to save. And now I'm a prisoner, betrayed by the very ones that I serve.*

He yelled at the guard, "What's the question?"

The guard said, "It's not the question but the answer that's important."

Bel'lar's anger intensified. How dare they keep him locked up? "I'm sick of this," he said under his breath. He returned to his bed and sat, his arms crossed, leaning against the wall. The guard ignored Bel'lar and walked away. Several times during the day, the guard would walk the length of this hall and back and then sit in the chair by the vertical transport.

The guard came over again. "Hey, Bel'lar. Have you figured this out yet, the questions and answers?"

Bel'lar came up to the door of his cell. "There are three questions and three answers, but only I know which goes with which."

Bel'lar turned around and stared at the back wall of his cell. He was getting nowhere with these two. He reminded himself that they were only functioning within their parameters. The mental capacity of the Syns was limited to normal activities such as taking orders, caring for themselves, buying food. But they were incapable of creating music, art, architecture or science.

They didn't sing or dance. They had achieved the ultimate de-evolution from apelike hairy bodies to ones completely devoid of hair with completely diminished brain capacity.

The guard stared in at Bel'lar but didn't comment. He was becoming curious about this individual Quasar was having them guard.

Later that night, Bel'lar was awakened with a jolt. He looked around his darkened cell. It was very quiet and dark and airless. The Syn suit was sticky and hot after being worn continuously these past days. He could smell his body odor and wished for water to wash. Mostly he wanted to rip it off. He settled for opening the front of the suit and felt some relief.

He began to think about why he had come back. He could have had a great life with Ry Sing and his other friends on the blue-white planet. But no, not Bel'lar. Bel'lar had committed himself to a higher calling. What higher calling? Maybe it didn't matter if he was considered a god in the eyes of some and the skinny devil in others. But he was a prisoner, and he couldn't see how he was going to complete his mission. Quasar was entirely uninterested in the blue-white planet and Bel'lar's mission.

And Bel'lar didn't know what Quasar was going to do.

He didn't want to die here on this planet.

These thoughts threatened to overwhelm him. He tossed and turned, and couldn't relax his thoughts. These thoughts drove his restlessness. What would Ka'aya do? *Ah yes. Ka'aya would go within. I'm already within, and I don't like it.* Then he remembered a prayer his parents had taught him as a child. He knelt beside his bed. He knew that, if he knelt, the body would be distracted, because kneeling hurt, and this floor was hard. He clasped his hands together and leaned on the bed.

"Oh God in heaven, I know I'm only a small part of you. When I doubt this, give me courage and show me the . . . book?"

What about the book? He had forgotten that the book was inside a pocket under this suit. He got it out. *This is what I've been looking for all along. Thanks, Mom.* The prayer worked.

The book was luminous in the darkness of his cell, infused with its own light. Surprised, and not surprised—after all it was the property of many holy men—he hoped it was enough light to read by. He put the book on the bed in front of him while he continued to kneel. How was it that Kowangii had used it? He saw the old man in his mind leaning over the book. He would just open it to any page, not worrying what that page was. Holding it with both hands, Bel'lar let it fall open. It arbitrarily opened to a page near the back. He scanned down the page. There.

He began to read. "When there comes a time in your life that you feel utterly alone, and the fear begins to overwhelm you, realize this fear is part of the despair. This despair is what you are dealing with now. Allow yourself to become utterly and voraciously consumed by the guilt and worthlessness of your insignificant being."

Bel'lar blinked. Maybe this was the wrong part of the book to be reading. *Now I just want to kill myself. Oh, well. I'll just read on.* "Now that you have realized your death is a way out, pause for a moment. Close your eyes and picture what it would be like if this life were over. Would you be walking in a meadow on a warm, sunny day with the birds singing and wildflowers everywhere? You turn around and realize you are alone. All of your friends are still back in the physical realm. You accept that, and you walk on. A little farther on, you wonder what would have happened if you had stayed in that life. As you look off down the path, you might wonder if it was that tough to stay on it. Now you realize that the question has not been answered. You realize the meaningless life you are now living has meaning, because, when there is one question to be answered, there is a purpose. This somehow miraculously pulls you up from the depths of despair and plants you firmly in the present, with the understanding that the fear that brought you here was merely the fear of not answering the question."

He set the book down. *So what is God trying to tell me here? Never give up? Never give up what? Is what I have read before, about me destroying this planet, true? Is that really my duty? Ka'aya, help me. What would he say?* Then chills shivered throughout his body. *Oh, yes. I will allow what has begun to finish in the way it's supposed to.* That thought released much of his anxiety. He smiled and climbed back into bed, clutching the book to his chest. He turned over on his side, pulled up his knees, and fell fast asleep.

✳ ✳ ✳

A different guard brought Bel'lar his morning meal. "Eat. Today you see Quasar.

"It's about time."

This morning, the food was presented in a bowl. Heaped inside the bowl were synthetic crunchy grains with artificially shaped and colored purple berries, with a white liquid to soften it. Alongside was some kind of bread-like roll with a bright red spread in a blob on the top. He poked the berries with his finger. They were gooey. The intense purple and red colors were so unnatural they held no appeal for his appetite, but he overcame that and ate. In the military, one learned to eat when there was food. Bel'lar smiled at what Ry Sing's reaction would be to this food. He knew she wouldn't touch it.

The guard watched Bel'lar eat. Then he leaned on the cell door and said, "I can't remember the last time we had a prisoner down here for longer than a day."

"Were they released?"

"Well, hmm, I don't know," the guard answered.

Bel'lar considered him. "Are you familiar with the Bellarian religion?"

The man looked at Bel'lar. "A little bit, but I'm Quasarian. You can't work in government without being Quasarian." He studied Bel'lar. "You have the same name as that ancient holy man. He left the planet and was to return and save us." He laughed. "Are you going to tell me that's who you are?"

Bel'lar laughed, too. "I've been on a journey for three hundred years."

"You look pretty good for three hundred years old."

"Never mind that. I'm back now. I've found our new home, and I'm here to take you all there."

"What? Oh, sure." The guard walked back to his post, laughing. Bel'lar continued to eat.

One of his usual guards arrived. It was time to take this prisoner to Quasar.

"What is the question?" the guard asked, continuing the game he had been playing with Bel'lar since he had arrived.

Bel'lar answered, "If I'm not a god, how can I be more than 300 years old?" He watched the guard's reaction and was rewarded.

The guard blinked and swallowed. "You're not 300 years old." He stuck his chin out aggressively at Bel'lar.

Bel'lar noted the guard's nervousness and said, "Go to the old books of the Sacred Ecology. I'm in there. In those days, I had hair, but, of course, I was younger." He laughed. "Go look. See if it's not me."

The guard didn't know how to answer that. Instead he said, "It's time to see Quasar."

The guard made Bel'lar stick his hands through the hole in the cell to put on his wrist restraints. This time they were not as tight as before. *Progress,* Bel'lar thought. *I've become more than a prisoner to them.*

"Thank you," he said. "I will remember this kindness."

The guard looked away at this and opened the cell. They escorted Bel'lar to the Quasar's office, where he was taken right in.

Quasar, seated behind his desk, motioned Bel'lar to sit. The guard pushed him into the chair and stepped away. "Wait outside," the President said. The door closed behind the guard, and Quasar turned his full attention to Bel'lar.

Bel'lar opened his mouth to speak. Quasar jumped up and put his finger to his lips for Bel'lar to be silent. He walked around his desk and then around Bel'lar, and stopped in front of him. "I have come full circle." He laughed.

Quasar walked away.

"You want a Happy Jack's? I'm going to have one."

"It's difficult to drink with these restraints on." Bel'lar held out his wrists.

Quasar ignored that as he got two Happy Jack's sodas from the refreshment bar under the window. He put one in front of Bel'lar but on the desk, out of reach. He took his and sat in his chair behind the desk. He took a drink. "Have you solved my problem, Bel'lar? Or should I say 'The Bellarian'? What should I call you? I'm losing my patience with you."

Bel'lar tried to speak again, but Quasar interrupted, "I'm getting impatient. We're very close to the Last Rites of Ester. This is very important to me and to my whole philosophy of life. I will give the Syns what they want. So, unless you give me a good reason, you're going to be attending the ceremony." Quasar laughed cruelly. "Why don't you speak? What's the matter with you?"

Bel'lar stared at Quasar. He wanted to shove that bottle right down his throat.

"Why did you kill all those people on the Continent of Rebirth?" Bel'lar spit the words out.

Quasar's response was cool, almost bored. "I didn't kill anyone. It was their time to be consumed. And what a prize to get Saint Significance, too. Besides, you needed to learn a lesson. You needed to see how powerful I am. My way is the only way. Those going off on their own can't survive. You understand now, don't you?"

Bel'lar's eyes bored into Quasar. Hatred filled him.

He leaped from his chair and charged the desk to get at Quasar. Using his hands he vaulted over the side of the desk.

Quasar jumped up, overturning his chair, throwing his soda aside, and running to the door.

The guards rushed in. One tackled Bel'lar, bearing him to the ground. He fought, but the second guard jumped in. Together, they pulled him to his feet.

Quasar pointed to the chair.

Bel'lar was forced into the chair, but, this time, his restraints were shackled to one of the chair arms. A guard stood on either side of him. Quasar walked around his desk and righted his chair. Then he pointed to the door. Both guards filed out.

Quasar meandered over to get another soda. He began to mumble to himself. "Did he spill his? Does he want another one?" He shook his head. Then he smiled and drank.

Watching this man, Bel'lar couldn't detect any shred of compassion in Quasar. And what about the mumbling? Was he crazy?

Then he realized that, if he wanted the chance to save these people, he had to convince Quasar to allow it. He sucked down his anger and lowered his eyes. He thought about who might want to go with him. Lotep and his sister. And there must be others in the Compound who would want this chance. He gritted his teeth, thinking about Vasquez and the others on the Continent of Rebirth. Then he pushed the anger down.

He looked up, his anger under control. "I have done my duty. I discovered the beautiful blue-white planet, where everyone can live in harmony with nature, as God intended. I am the prophet. I've returned and offered you this paradise. And you reject this. For what?"

"Why would I want to start over when I have everything I want here?"

"But the people are suffering," Bel'lar said.

Quasar looked out the window, drinking his soda. "How does that affect me?"

"You would deny this opportunity for others?"

Quasar turned to face Bel'lar. "My people have everything that they could want here on this planet. No want has been denied. I have made sure of it. They have no reason to leave."

Quasar gazed out the window into the distance again. He took another drink of soda.

Bel'lar made a monumental effort not to give in to the raging desire to toss Quasar, chair and all, right out the window. He sucked it down into his gut. He appeared calm as he stared at Quasar. "What about your Compound of the Congress?"

Quasar turned. Bel'lar's calmness irritated him. "What do you mean?"

Bel'lar spoke clearly. "In the Compound of the Congress lies a threat to you from other Organs who have the mental capacity to overthrow you." He watched the President's face.

That threat hit home. Quasar returned to his desk and put his bottle down. Then, slamming his hands on the desk, his body stiff, he leaned toward Bel'lar, the antagonism plain in his eyes. "Is this supposed to frighten me? Don't you think I've thought of that?" He straightened and drank more soda. His face relaxed, and he laughed heartily. He had flipped from furious to relaxed in the space of a heartbeat. "I have a failsafe plan." He sat in his chair and leaned back, once more drinking his soda as he watched Bel'lar.

"When your ship was discovered, I bet you didn't know that documents were found hidden in the pyramid. These documents were taken away before you were made Captain and kept a secret. But nothing is secret from me." Quasar drank again and appeared to be looking out the window, but he was actually watching his adversary out of the corner of his eye. "I found them and discovered information about a device originally built by the Sacred Ecology holy men. Of course, I had it built with its network of nuclear devices. I couldn't resist."

Bel'lar's mind raced to digest what he was hearing. Did Quasar really have a device like that of the Great One? He had to be lying, didn't he?

Now Quasar's face was sly, calculating and gave nothing away other than his enjoyment at baiting Bel'lar. "I discovered other things, too. I found historical logs from an ancient voyage. They tell all about how the holy men used this Device to consume the Planet of Abundance."

Bel'lar shook his head and fidgeted. It wasn't possible that this man knew anything about the Great One. "I don't know what you're talking about."

Quasar laughed.

Bel'lar searched Quasar's face, tried to read his mind, somehow get at the truth here. "You would destroy all that you have created here? Everyone?"

Quasar stood. "Who better to decide than the one who giveth and the one who shall taketh away?" He walked over to a large mirror mounted on the back wall and began to admire his reflection.

Bel'lar could detect the madness in Quasar, fed by the absolute power he held and, he was horrified to discover, driven by boredom. This man could not be allowed to continue to lead this society. And Bel'lar was afraid. It was very possible that he wouldn't see Ry Sing again.

Quasar looked at Bel'lar in the mirror. "You know, Bel'lar. I heard the words that came from my mouth. They sounded so eloquent that I had to look in the mirror to see the most magnificent god that I am. Don't you agree?"

He walked back to Bel'lar. "Of course, you do. I must thank you for solving my problem. I needed a gift for my people, and what better gift than the life of a holy man? And, since you have nothing more to say, I shall see you at the Last Rites of Ester." He touched the panel on the corner of his desk, which signaled the guard.

The guards entered and removed Bel'lar.

Quasar yelled after him, "You didn't drink any of your soda. Didn't you like it?"

✳ ✳ ✳

Ry Sing paced back and forth in her quarters. She couldn't bear to sit still and wait. Bel'lar had been checking in each evening, and his vital signs indicated that he was unhurt. Despite this, she was afraid for his life. She and Mauleen had discussed this over and over. But they hadn't been able to discover how to free him. She had to see him. Maybe she could enter the vortex and bring him back with her. *That's it,* she thought. *I can do it.*

She stopped pacing and closed her eyes. She focused inside, crossed the barrier between lives and stepped into the most recent past life. She saw the topaz chair glowing softly. Drawing its energy, she began to vibrate, faster and faster. This energy swirled about her, was her. She stepped out of her quarters and into a room.

A man looked up and beheld an iridescent whirlwind, glimmering with stardust. Something was inside it, but it was too vague to identify. Stunned but unafraid, he simply watched.

This whirlwind floated closer and slowed just enough that he could see Ry Sing inside it. Her clothing phased in and out between the blue, flowing garment from Taurus and the lavender tunic and pants she had been wearing, as he watched, still too fascinated to speak.

She inhaled a deep, steadying breath, and the phasing stopped. In control of the translocation, she was wearing the blue dress from Taurus and remained fully infused with that past life. She faced a doorway. She turned around and saw Quasar looking at her. Shocked, she plummeted out of the vortex and fell to her knees.

Quasar stood, looking over his desk at her. Overcome by the beauty of this being, he didn't recognize Ry Sing.

Struggling to salvage her control, she pulled herself up straight while still on her knees and said, "I'm here for Bel'lar. Let me take him, and we'll leave. It will be like we've never been here." She got to her feet.

Quasar shook his head. "You don't understand. This is fun. This is perfect. What is better than to consume a false god at the ceremony?"

She stepped closer. "I won't let you hurt him. You don't know what I'm capable of."

He laughed. "You can't stop me, little girl. Bel'lar is mine to do with as I wish."

He raised his arms and turned to the window. His body began to glow with a golden light. "Then all may witness that I, the Quasar, am the true god. The light shall expound from me and only me." He spoke as if in a trance, wrapped up in his vision.

She watched him in fascination. The light around him intensified as he spoke. Where did he get all this energy to create this spectacle?

Who was he? *No,* she thought. *That's not possible.*

She had to get out of here. Inhaling a deep breath, she closed her eyes and strove for calmness. She saw the topaz chair on Taurus, she felt the energy, pulling it into her . . . she lost it.

Looking, she saw that he was still facing the window.

She stilled her shaking hands. Again she strove for calmness as she breathed in, seeking an inner focus. She felt her focus slipping, slipping . . . gone. She shook it off.

Was he looking? No.

Again. Breathing in calming energy, it filled her as she brought her focus in, narrowing it, almost . . . then, struggling to save it, she took a deep breath, another. Yes. Success. Changing her awareness, she was consumed in the vortex of energy, and stepped from the room and into her quarters on the ship.

When Quasar turned, she was gone. He hurried around his desk and then to the door, looking for her. He yelled at the guards. "Lock down this building! There's an intruder! Find her!"

Back inside her quarters, Ry Sing shook herself free of the energy and returned to pacing. Why had she ended up in Quasar's office? She had been clear in her intention to see Bel'lar. She paced faster, filled with fear for him.

✳ ✳ ✳

"What great words of wisdom do you have for me today?" the guard asked Bel'lar. It was now the Thirteenth, the first day of the Celebration of Ester.

Bel'lar came up to the cell door to receive the tray of food and said, "Remember. Your President Quasar is the reflection of your society. When you disagree with him, or you're unhappy with what he's doing, look to yourself for the reason." Bel'lar took his tray and sat on his bed.

The guard appeared to be considering Bel'lar's words. Then he shook his head. "You're an idiot." He stalked away.

Bel'lar glanced up. "Indeed, I may be." He turned his attention to his food.

*　*　*

The fly buzzed around inside the terrarium in Ry Sing's quarters. Enis had planted this for her, filling it with tiny plants from the blue-white planet. He called it a microcosm of the blue-white planet. This was the fly that she and Bel'lar had captured on the Continent of Rebirth. It reminded her of the old man she'd met when she and Mauleen had visited the city with Lotep. Somehow he was familiar to her, and her mind kept mulling it over, seeking the reason. She must have known him in a past life. Did he really mean what he'd said about cherishing a fly if he found one? Why not find out? Besides, she needed to improve her ability to vortex.

She opened the terrarium and put her hand inside. The fly buzzed about and then settled on her index finger. She lifted her hand out carefully and held it next to a small specimen dish. The fly hopped inside the dish, and she covered it. Tucking the dish inside her pocket, she contacted the bridge with her request.

Mauleen looked up as Ry Sing entered the bridge. "The display is focused on the old man's house," she said.

Ry Sing thanked her and walked to stand in front of the display. Enis watched with interest.

On the planet, the old man was sitting in a rocking chair on his porch, his eyes staring off into the distance. His eyelids drooped, his chin dropped to his chest. He seemed to have fallen asleep.

Ry Sing closed her eyes and clasped her hands in front of her. Breathing in deeply, she went within, seeking out that past life, accessing the well of energy that would allow her to translocate from here to where the old man was sleeping.

As Enis watched, her body broke into millions of tiny bits of light that seemed to stretch toward the display, gather themselves, and she was gone. He quickly searched the display and identified a hazy, out-of-focus blur that he knew was Ry Sing. This shimmering haze appeared to drop away from her as she stepped out on the ground in front of the house. She wasn't wearing a Syn suit.

She stopped at the porch. "Hello," she called out.

The old man jerked, and his eyes flew open. He stared at this Asian woman looking back at him. "I know you."

"Yes," she said. "I've been here before."

He shook his head.

Belatedly, she realized that she had been wearing someone else's Syn suit that time. He couldn't recognize her from then. So what did he mean?

"I want to feel your energy." He closed his eyes and held out his hands to her. Without hesitation, she moved closer and put her hands in his.

He smiled. "I know that I was a holy man of the black race on a distant planet. I instinctively feel that you were there. I asked to feel your energy because, from life to life, your signature energy never changes. That's why, when you came toward me, you recognized me, and I, you."

She looked deep into his eyes for the truth and recognized him. This old man was Kowangii, the holy man from the Light Wanderer. Even his features held a similarity to Kowangii's that she could now discern. They hugged each other.

"Now that I've found you, I don't want to let you go. Come with me. You can leave this planet and begin a new life." She held onto his hand.

"I'm not ready to leave here. This is my home and this experience is not yet ended." He smiled at her.

"But I can't . . ." she began.

And he finished, ". . . let me go? Yes, you can."

She regarded him with sadness.

"When I touched you, I sensed another," he said. "Is she happy with her choice?"

Ry Sing realized immediately that he meant Char. He truly was Kowangii. She stepped aside in her mind to allow Char to come forward. As Kowangii watched, her visage changed, at first a blend of Ry Sing and Char; then a ripple traveled throughout her body from her head to her feet, and, at its completion, Char was standing before him, the beautiful young woman of the black race. She hugged him, weeping tears of joy at this reunion. "I have not regretted my choice. It was the right thing to integrate with Ry Sing. I have been learning so much. And we have become more than I ever could alone."

Then a buzzing filled her ears. The fly was impatient to be set free. Char said, "We have something for you."

"Is it a ticket to get into the heavens?"

"Something much better." She handed him the clear dish. As she withdrew her hand, a wave of energy traveled through her being again, and Ry Sing was standing before him.

The old man looked down and smiled. "It's a fly." He took it and held it with reverence.

Ry Sing said, "It's more than a fly. This tiny being was created by God, and you have learned that, when you destroy all of God's creatures . . ."

The old man finished the sentence, "You are left alone to ponder what you have done."

The old man quickly opened the dish. The fly, immobile for a moment, seemed to stare up at him. Then it tried its wings, recognizing freedom. It was airborne.

Ry Sing smiled. "As God intended."

The old man was smiling from ear to ear now, tears running down his cheeks. "My whole life has come down to this moment of understanding. That I should allow what God has created. It will live in my heart forever."

Ry Sing touched the old man who knew he was Kowangii gently on the top of his head. "I, too, will remember this moment, for these are the moments of my life also." She turned and walked away. She could hear the fly buzzing around the old man.

Ry Sing easily entered the state of mind that accessed the well of energy and dissolved, reappearing on the bridge.

There, the old man's face filled the display. As everyone watched, the fly landed on his nose. A look of ecstasy came over the old man's face as his eyes crossed to see the fly. Tears fell freely from Ry Sing's eyes as she laughed. Enis and Mauleen cried with her.

✳ ✳ ✳

Bel'lar had been attempting to sleep for the better part of the afternoon. He rolled back and forth, unable to contain the restlessness he felt. The holiday had begun the day before, but there was nothing he could do about it. He hadn't talked to Quasar again. Ry Sing's beautiful face filled his mind. He wished he had the chance to see her once more, to hold her in his arms. He wondered if she would take some of the people to the blue-white planet once he was dead. He shook himself.

He wouldn't think like that. There was still time for something to happen. He wouldn't give up hope. He sat up. The guards had brought water a short time ago. He drank from the container. *I will allow what has begun to finish,* he thought. *And be alert to opportunities.*

Staring out the door, he drifted into a contemplative state. Time passed. Then, from the periphery of his vision, he noticed a brightening of the corridor. It grew brighter. He heard no footsteps, no sound of any kind. Yet something was coming. He watched the door, unwilling to look away. The light intensified until it reached his door and floated through the bars, blinding him. He covered his eyes, and, simultaneously, the light dimmed until he could look at it directly.

As he stared, stupefied, the light came closer. Something began to take shape. A face, not recognizable yet, a torso, the body of a man, although it couldn't be taken for a physical being. Then the vision cleared, and Bel'lar saw Saint Significance floating before him.

Bel'lar jumped to his feet and looked, beguiled by this magnificent being before him. "Are you real?"

"I'm in a form you might not be familiar with."

"Why are you here?" Bel'lar asked; then he halted, trying to order his thoughts. "Are you here for me?"

The vision raised one arm in Bel'lar's direction and said, "I have come to hear your last confession."

Bel'lar was confused. "My confession. What do I have to confess?"

"Tomorrow is a very important day for you and this world."

"I know that. I have to get out of here. Will you help me?"

The Saint floated closer. This glowing apparition was disconcerting to Bel'lar. "No," the Saint said. "You have been running your whole life from your greatest fear. It's time to face it."

Bel'lar shook his head, struggling to understand. "What do you mean? Of being killed? Of course, I'm afraid of that."

"You have a greater fear."

Bel'lar watched the Saint. He didn't know what to think. Then his birthmark on his chest began to burn. He rubbed it in reflex.

"You have been running your whole life. As a child, you refused to embrace the wisdom of your calling."

"You mean being a holy man? You sound like my father. That's all he ever wanted me to be."

"This life you lead now has a purpose. You can't escape that purpose." The Saint lifted his hands to the sky. "You must embrace the truth. Tomorrow will present you with a tremendous opportunity that you have been hiding and running from all your life. Tomorrow, you must free the souls."

The Saint's words triggered a memory of the Great One's face as he delivered his message to Bel'lar on the ship. He rubbed the birthmark harder.

The Saint said, "My son, I shall be with you on that day."

The magnificence that was the Saint began to wane, to dim.

Bel'lar called out, "Wait, don't go. Don't go."

All that remained of the Saint was one tiny sparkle of light, suspended in the air in front of Bel'lar. He held out his hand, and it dropped gently into it. Then, cradling it with both hands, he held it up to his face, looking it over from different angles. Then, knowing, he brought it closer and blew on it. The tiny light winked out.

He rubbed the birthmark again, attempting to will it into submission, but he couldn't shake the memory of that day. And the voice of the Great One filled his head. "The one who carries the mark shall continue me. Do not deny this sacred trust. Do as you are intended upon. These are the souls that can be saved."

He shook his head, attempting to clear it. He paced as he spoke out loud. "Was that really the Saint? Or was I just hallucinating? Was he here to try to force me to do something he couldn't or wouldn't do?

"What did he mean 'free the souls'? And what am 'I intended upon'?" he asked the air around him. Why did this have to be so obscure? Couldn't someone, just once, tell him straight out? But what was the real truth? Was it that he was here to destroy them? No, he couldn't accept that. He was here to take them to the blue-white planet. Yes, that was it. If there was any way possible, he would do that. He would hold onto that thought and let it sustain him.

✳ ✳ ✳

Ry Sing stood in front of the large display on the bridge, her hands tightly clasped. Mauleen scurried about, making adjustments to the instruments. Enis sat in Bel'lar's chair, but he wasn't relaxed. He sat forward as if ready to leap out. They were viewing the platform on the planet below, where the celebration of the Last Rites of Ester was about to begin.

Without turning, Ry Sing said, "Can't we get a better view?"

Mauleen spoke softly to the small display at her station. The view of the platform slid to fill half of the display, and two more views ranged on the side. The first view was a closer view of the door at the back of the platform, the other, a view of the crowd gathered in the immense square that faced the platform.

Ry Sing turned around, and all three exchanged a look. They were ready. She hoped that they would have a chance to use that readiness.

✳ ✳ ✳

The immense square was packed to bursting. People jostled against each other as the sun shone down on the yellow haze, creating a stifling, dense environment, heating them into impatience. Many had been waiting since the sun came up. They were hungry. This was the third day without food.

The platform, four meters high, with steps leading down and off in three directions out into the crowd was permanently installed against the Presidential building. After years of exposure, the platform's original yellow color had weathered to a grayish-white. At the back of this platform, stairs led up to another, smaller level, where the chalice of the eternal flame sat, a symbol of eternal consumption, looming over the ceremony. Horn blowers were positioned behind the chalice. At the back of the lower platform was a door through which Quasar and others would enter.

Around the base of this platform, Brotherhood of Syn guards stood shoulder to shoulder, holding shields displaying the BOS insignia and standards with Brotherhood of Syn flags attached. These standards had pointed ends, doubling as weapons. The guards tightened their holds on their standards. The crowd was growing agitated.

The horns sounded, and Quasar appeared at the back of the platform. A shout went up as the people cheered him. He walked out into full view, his arms up, his hands held wide, the people cheering him on. His robe, buttoned down the front, embroidered with trees and animals, was green and gold. On his head was a golden crown, shaped like a cone, glowing in the muted sunlight. He lowered his hands and the people quieted down.

The horns sounded again.

Quasar called out, "Welcome my brothers," and out of the door filed the twelve Quasarian Brothers, all wearing green robes and gold masks, each carrying a shepherd's crook. Each gold mask was an animal face, each one representing an animal that had been consumed completely. It was an honor to consume something living, absorbing its essence. It was believed that when they consumed something to extinction, they were closer to god.

The twelve brothers split into two groups. Six brothers stood on each side of Quasar, forming an inverted "v" with Quasar as the vertex. They fanned out to either side of the platform. The crowd cheered and applauded.

Quasar waited, enjoying his people's homage. The people relaxed and quieted, yet maintained an air of expectancy.

He raised his hands to the multitudes and began to speak, his voice and image broadcast throughout the city and across the planet. "I am the Lord thy God, and you shall bow down to me."

The crowd bowed, and Quasar was pleased.

"Over the past year much has been accomplished. We have consumed much. But our work in this place is not yet finished. We have much more to consume before God the Father will take us into his realm. Together, on this gorgeous day, we shall move one step closer to eternal salvation in the Quasars."

"Amen," the crowd responded.

Again Quasar waited as the crowd settled down.

He stepped forward and said, "And now. The twelve who have been consumed, the Brothers of the Quasar, shall walk in procession amongst you."

The brothers paraded forward, down into the crowd; six walked into the crowd on the right side and six walked into the crowd on the left. The green and gold of their robes was in great contrast to the soiled white of the people's garments.

Quasar breathed in the magnificence of this ceremony, his presence expanding with the energy. "As we walk amongst the multitudes, and touch and gather those who believe, it makes my heart proud to be your god. I'm humbled by your loyalty and obedience to me. For without me, the Quasars above would not be attainable. Without me, your lives would not be bountiful. Without my guidance, this great society would not exist." His arms spread wide to embrace his people.

The people spontaneously made way for the brothers as they waded into the crowd. They pushed and shoved, endeavoring to touch the robes of the brothers as they passed. The brothers were bumped and nudged but they continued walking, turning toward the center of the crowd where they met, crossed over, and returned to the platform, climbing up again to stand behind Quasar.

From all over the square, people began yelling, "We love you, Quasar! We love you, Quasar!"

These people had been there early, seeking good vantage points to view the celebration. They had endured three days without food, drink and the supplements that controlled their moods and were in a severely weakened state. The heat trapped under the haze of pollution intensified. Throughout the seething mass of people, some had already succumbed to delirium, falling down in a fit, babbling incoherently. The mass of humanity surged toward the guards. The guards around the platform were provoked into shoving back.

Quasar held up his hands for silence. It took a few moments, but, finally, everyone seemed focused on him. "Today we celebrate the Last Rites of Ester." He turned again toward the door.

A small child walked out, carrying a pillow of gold-colored fabric with an object draped in scarlet silken cloth resting on it. This child's head had been shaved to maintain the Syn persona, as he was too young to have begun the process of becoming a Syn. Dressed in a white tunic and short pants, his attire mirrored those of the multitudes spread out below, except his garments were clean. He walked proudly to stand beside Quasar.

Quasar looked back at the audience and continued, "Many years ago, it came to the knowledge of the Quasar that the skinny ones, the ones who could not consume, were not worthy of sharing this place and living their lives among us. They corrupted us. But we knew better."

He lifted the scarlet cloth from the pillow, uncovering a ceremonial dagger. The handle of this blade was gold and ornate. Holding it over his head to show the congregation, he pulled it out of the jeweled scabbard.

The congregation erupted in shoving, yelling, "Me, me, take me! I want to go to the Quasars!"

Shrieking and babbling, they worked themselves into a religious fervor. They surged as one entity toward the guards surrounding the platform. The guards shoved back, their ranks unbroken but stretching; the crush of people had them pinned against the platform. They were rattled. They knew how easily they could be swallowed up in this crowd.

Quasar put the scabbard down on the pillow and with both hands grasping its hilt, held the dagger up, its blade pointing down. He raised it above his head. Sunrays cut through the pollution barrier to spark light on the blade. The light reflected off the haze, sparkling on the desperate crowd, anointing them with its light.

Again some tried to push their way through the guards.

"Choose me! Choose me!"

A fight broke out at the side of the platform. A guard was knocked down. A man climbed over him and gained the platform. He ran to Quasar, two guards hard on his heels. Quasar turned to meet him, the dagger in his hand. The guards grabbed this desperate Syn, his hands outstretched to Quasar, crying,

"I lived my whole life honoring you. You owe me this honor. Consume me!"

Quasar motioned to the guards to remove this man.

The Syn kept crying, "Consume me, consume me!" as he was dragged from the platform and pushed down into the heaving mass of people, where he disappeared from view.

Quasar called out, "Silence!" But the frenzied crowd couldn't hear him. He smiled with anticipation as he slid the dagger back into the scabbard and tucked it inside his belt. He whispered something to the child and the child hurried off the platform.

* * *

Aboard the Light Traveler, Mauleen called out to Ry Sing, "I think Captain Bel'lar's coming out."

Ry Sing walked a few steps closer to the large display.

Enis, still seated in Bel'lar's chair, scanned the people on the platform. "I don't see him yet."

"Mauleen, now you know what to do," Ry Sing said.

"Don't worry. I have it under control," Mauleen answered grimly.

* * *

Quasar seemed to expand as he threw out his arm toward the door. "Behold, I give you a gift from the gods."

A man emerged from the door at the back of the platform. Two guards prodded him along. He wore a long sleeveless robe of yellow, trimmed in gold, open at the chest and belted with a golden rope. His face was hidden by a golden mask depicting a man with a long beard wrapped with leather. A gold and yellow scarf covered the top of his head and hung down to his shoulders. The motion of walking ruffled the scarf, and the crowd glimpsed the long hair beneath it.

Many gasped at his hair, and they began to murmur, "Organ. He is truly an Organ." The word ran through the crowd until all were focused on this prisoner.

The man's hands were held in front of his body with gold restraints. A gold bar separated his hands. Precious stones of rubies and emeralds decorated the bar. The two guards brought him up to Quasar and then stepped back.

Quasar swaggered over and, taking his time, began to walk around this prisoner, looking him over.

The twelve brothers moved closer to see this Organ. No one had seen an Organ before other than in books.

Quasar expounded to the audience, "Who is this man that I have brought before you, on this glorious day?"

A man's voice shouted back, "He looks like a skinny devil Organ!"

"Here is the traitor Bellarian!" Quasar yelled triumphantly. "My gift to you on this holiest of all days." He threw his hands into the air.

The prisoner stood there watching the Quasar without any reaction. He appeared drugged.

"You may ask," and Quasar gestured to the audience, "why he came back now." Quasar walked a few steps forward. He was near the edge of the platform now, and people tried to push through the guards to touch him. The line of security held. "I brought him here to prove that the Bellarian religion is false. The one true religion is . . ." He paused, lifting his arms, waiting for the congregation to respond. And he wasn't disappointed.

"Quasarian! Quasarian! Quasarian!" thundered through the crowd as every voice answered.

Then the people cheered. Quasar grinned. And waited, working the crowd, absorbing the excitement. He raised an arm, inciting them to continue cheering.

A woman called out, "Show us. Let's see what evil looks like."

Quasar approached the prisoner and slowly lifted the man's mask.

Bel'lar stood before them, completely exposed as the Organ that he was. He glanced at Quasar. He felt sick when he saw how suffused with power Quasar was, obviously thriving on the excitement of the crowd.

The crowd shrieked; they couldn't believe what they were seeing. Then, in an instant, they became incensed, shouting, "Look at how evil, how distorted it looks!"

Others shouted out, "Consume him! Consume him now. I can't bear to look into his eyes."

And another shouted, "It's the skinny devil himself."

Bel'lar drew back, involuntarily, at the intensity of fear and hatred in the crowd. He turned his head around to see what was behind him. He noticed the twelve brothers. He looked for a familiar face. But, they all had masks on. He was on his own out here.

Steadying his breathing, he scanned the crowd. Never before had he felt the overwhelming emotion of hate that radiated from this mass of people. And that odor that burned his nose and throat, it was more than the pollution. It was the odor of hatred. He thought, *If I get out of this, I will never again allow anyone to think of me as more than a man.*

*       *       *

"Light Traveler," Ry Sing called out, "can you bring Bel'lar aboard?"

"It's not time yet. He still needs to complete his task. You know that allowing what has begun to finish is written in my stellar physiology. So allow him to finish what he has started."

"Please don't wait. Save him now."

                    *We Are The Destroyers*

"I cannot," the ship answered.

Ry Sing turned to Mauleen.

The first officer answered, "I've tried. Light Traveler won't allow this to happen. There's nothing I can do."

Ry Sing paced, frustrated, furious, trying to put all that aside and focus. She knew now that she had to do something to save him. She couldn't let Bel'lar die down there.

*       *       *

Quasar was almost beside himself with glee. He walked back and forth. This was the most perfect day. He put up his hands for attention. "Patience. Patience. I shall do as you wish. Today is a great day. For, today, we consume the last remnants of the Bellarian religion."

He pointed at Bel'lar. "But first, I will allow him to speak. Our tradition is to allow the chosen one this honor."

They shouted from the audience, "He doesn't deserve it. Don't waste our time—just do it!" The crowd pushed at the line of guards around the platform. The guards tightened their stance, raised their shields, and pushed back to maintain their position.

Quasar watched all of this and said, "Wait. We are beings of the god Quasar. We shall show our compassion."

He grabbed Bel'lar by the arm and pulled him close to the front of the platform.

Bel'lar pulled back and stumbled. Then he saw it. On the other side of Quasar. The Device in the shape of a pyramid, made from stone, with a metallic rod with a cross bar. Bel'lar staggered, as if all the blood had been drained from his body. It was just like the Device used by the ancient holy man. This must be Quasar's failsafe plan.

Recovering his balance, he saw the dagger at Quasar's waist. He looked into Quasar's eyes and saw unholy excitement and anticipation. He asked, "What do you want of me?"

Quasar laughed. "I want you to tell them of my greatness. Tell them what an honor it is to be consumed by me, their god."

Bel'lar turned back to the angry mob. These were the people he had discovered the blue-white planet for and had come home to save. Despair weighted his limbs; he almost sagged to the floor.

"Make it quick!" one yelled.

Another Syn yelled, "I haven't eaten in three days! You're starting to look good to me!"

Bel'lar turned pale and took a deep breath. Then he walked a few steps forward unsteadily to address the audience. His voice was low as he said, "It's my honor to be here."

* * *

Ry Sing, watching from the ship, cried to see him this way. "What's wrong with him? Is he hurt? I have to help him."

She watched as Quasar touched the dagger, smiling. Without warning, he jerked his head up, and his face filled the Light Traveler's display, staring at something he couldn't possibly see, Ry Sing looking back at him. It seemed that Quasar was looking directly into her eyes, that he knew she was there. His eyes were wild, and she knew he was engorged with the emotions coming from the Syns, feeding on the crowd. Now she was terrified for Bel'lar.

* * *

Bel'lar shook his head, attempting to clear the grief from his mind. He couldn't think of anything to say. What difference would it make to these people, anyway? They wanted, craved a spectacle.

Another of the people Bel'lar had come back to save yelled, "Louder, I want to hear the words!"

He looked out over the crowd, no longer seeing individuals, but a seething mass of mouths clamoring to be fed. This was what his people had become at the hands of the Compound of the Congress. Anger began to burn inside him, replacing his despair at failing his mission.

Bel'lar began again, louder, "It's an honor and a privilege for me, to have this opportunity to speak to you." He raised his head, he straightened, shoulders back. Marshalling his anger, he allowed it to strengthen him. Proudly, his military bearing evident in his body, he stepped forward.

His voice, strong and unwavering, carried out over the multitude as he spoke. "You have a burning rage inside to consume. But the reason God hasn't come to take you up to the Quasars is that the planet is not yet pure. The skinny devils still live among you, and until you seek them out and cleanse the planet of this evil, you will not be saved."

Quasar put his hand on the dagger. This prisoner couldn't be allowed to destroy his moment. He didn't want to hear any more and would end it right now. As he moved toward Bel'lar, the two guards who had brought Bel'lar out stepped in front of him and crossed their standards, blocking Quasar's advance.

Quasar glared at the guards, "How dare you?"

The one guard glared back. "It's our custom to allow the chosen one to speak. Allow this."

Quasar huffed angrily and backed up, but he kept his hand on the dagger.

Bel'lar, unconcerned, continued. "Look to your Congress for the answer. Within them lies the deceit that your great society is founded upon." Bel'lar looked out over the congregation and pointed with both hands in the direction of the Compound of the Congress. The gems in his restraints sparkled. "I am the true god, Bel'lar, who ascended 350 years ago. I'm here to see if you're worthy of my blessing. To prove this, I will call back the lightning bolts that I took with me when I left."

The crowd fidgeted. They didn't understand what he was talking about. He heard nervous laughter. Some tried to back away from their proximity to the platform, but those behind them were packed too tight. They didn't know what lightning bolts were or what would happen.

Bel'lar, mentally praying that Mauleen was listening and had understood, raised his hands above his head, straining as high as he could, and yelled out, "Oh God of my God, bring back the lightning bolts to show these infidels the true God."

Dead silence cut through the square as if everyone had sucked in their breath and held it at the same instant. Then a booming crack of thunder was heard, and a searing white bolt of lightning streaked down from nowhere, cutting through the gold bar separating the wrist restraints on Bel'lar's hands. The lightning bolt shot through the bar and struck the platform in front of Quasar, throwing him and the two guards down.

Unnoticed in the excitement, the Device began to shimmer.

The guards surrounding the platform ducked and hid under their shields.

The crowd was terrified, and, almost to a person, they dropped to their knees and bowed down, covering their heads with their arms, in mortal fear as ozone filled the air and smoke floated over the platform.

The holy men were driven back by the lightning strike. They cowered at the back, by the door, but continued watching.

Bel'lar inhaled a deep breath. He brought his hands down and saw the reddened skin from the lightning bolt. It had worked, although he had only narrowly escaped a fiery death thanks to Mauleen's excellent shooting.

Relief mixed with adrenaline and fury filled him with purpose as he spoke to the crowd. "Am I not the god I said I was? You should be afraid, because the next lightning bolt I send will destroy you."

He clenched his hands in fists that, in his rage, felt like iron. "Now listen to me. If consumption is what you want, I shall provide it."

He turned and walked back to where Quasar and the guards were now getting to their feet. "Back off," he ordered the guards. "I am the god on a mission to consume this false god before you."

The guards backed up in fear. Quasar sent a furious glance at them before focusing on Bel'lar.

Bel'lar grabbed the dagger from Quasar's belt and raised it over his head.

Quasar was stunned. He just stood there. Then he smiled as he said, "It would be my greatest honor to be consumed for my god."

Bel'lar stared, the dagger in his hand, and time seemed to freeze. Then a voice entered Bel'lar's mind. Saint Significance said, "You can't kill evil, for it lies in the hearts of men. Just expose it, and it will die."

Bel'lar's arm shot out, the dagger slashed into Quasar. Bel'lar jerked the blade free, but blood didn't pour from this wound. Instead Bel'lar had cut Quasar's Syn suit, slicing it open down the front, exposing Quasar for what he really was—a skinny devil. An Organ.

Quasar saw this great slash that had opened up his suit and looked up at Bel'lar in confusion. "Why have you done this?" He acted surprised.

Bel'lar said, "I am the god, and I shall allow what has begun to finish."

One of the guards recovered from his shock at seeing Quasar's real body. He grabbed Quasar and held him tight, pushing him toward Bel'lar. "Let's really show who you are."

Bel'lar cut again, slicing up one arm and more of the body, he pulled open the suit revealing Quasar's thin Organ body and his bare arm. His head was still intact, but his Syn suit hung in pieces about his body.

The other guard peered at Quasar's body and then lifted his arm to cover his eyes. "I don't want to know this. Quasar, make it go away. Make it like it was before. I can't live knowing this." Filled with overwhelming despair, he turned and ran, escaping through the door at the back of the platform.

Now Quasar's body was clearly visible to the crowd. They shrieked in shock and anger and grew ugly. They wanted blood.

"You have deceived us!" someone shouted.

Another yelled, "Is everyone who lives in the Compound skinny devils, too?"

A woman, hoisted on the shoulders of others, looked out over the mob. "We shall burn down the Compound and consume it. For then the righteous shall be left to inherit the planet."

A section of the mass of people surged out of the square, the Compound their destination. More followed. Others attacked the Brotherhood of Syn guards stationed all around the platform.

Quasar, taking everything in at a glance, realized he had no alternative. He had been exposed, and, now, there was nothing left but to die. *But I won't die alone*, he thought. Casting about he saw the Device; he jerked free of the guard and scrambled toward it. He didn't even know if it would work.

The guard, quickly assessing the desperate situation with the crazed mob, abandoned Bel'lar and ran.

Bel'lar followed Quasar's look and realized his intention in an instant. "I won't let you."

He launched himself at Quasar, slamming into him and bearing the man to the floor. They rolled, fighting. Quasar was a big man, and, despite being hampered by the torn Syn suit and his robe, he was strong. Bel'lar tore at the robe, ripping it. Quasar twisted away, but Bel'lar didn't let go. Instead he transferred his grip to Quasar's neck, pulling him back into his chest as he tightened his hold.

Suddenly, he was being pulled from behind and someone was yelling his name. Ry Sing had appeared on the platform in a vortex of energy. "Let him go. Come on, Bel'lar."

He tightened his grip on Quasar's neck, cutting off his oxygen. He ignored Ry Sing. He just needed to finish this. Then, in a superhuman effort, Quasar twisted again, this time loosening Bel'lar's grip, but Bel'lar didn't let go. They rolled across the platform toward the Great One's Device. Quasar struggled to his knees and crawled toward it, dragging Bel'lar hanging on his back.

Ry Sing pulled at Bel'lar's robe, trying to get him to stop, but she was as ineffectual as a child.

Bel'lar fought Quasar with everything he had, but his hands lost their grip, and he slid back. Quasar moved inexorably on and reached the Device. He stretched out his arm, and his fingers touched the rod. Bel'lar dug his fingers into Quasar's Syn suit, reaching to get a better hold. He hooked one hand into Quasar's robe and one around his leg and jerked him back. He leaped to his feet as Quasar scrambled to his and rushed back to the Device. Bel'lar threw himself at Quasar, intent on knocking him away from it. But Quasar turned and grappled with Bel'lar. Ry Sing was screaming something—he couldn't understand her. Quasar knocked Bel'lar back. Unable to catch himself, Bel'lar fell, and something jammed into his side. Then he dropped further as his body drove this thing he had fallen on down. He had done the unthinkable. He had driven the rod down into the Device. He lay over the Device, his mind unable to understand what had happened.

Then he rolled off of it, slowly got to his feet, and stood, staring at the Device glowing brightly. "No. I didn't mean to . . ."

Off in the distance, light flashes cut through the haze. Then an explosion and a wave of energy roared toward the square. But he ignored it, or perhaps he just didn't notice. Nothing else mattered to either him or Quasar, who had walked up beside him.

Without a second to lose, Ry Sing surged forward, expanding her energy field, encompassing Bel'lar. Quasar reached for Bel'lar and the three disappeared from sight as explosions ripped the air in this square, sending up plumes of smoke and debris. People, screaming and crying, ran to escape.

But there was nowhere to escape to, because this was the end. Their wishes were granted on this holiest of all days. Today they would be consumed and join their god in the Quasars.

❊ ❊ ❊

Mauleen and Enis sat silent, unmoving, as the display filled with the destruction unfolding in the square below. All they could do was watch, unable to look away, as more explosions tore apart the platform and the Presidential building behind it.

Then glittering lights flashed in the periphery of their vision, breaking their trance, and they turned to see an iridescent whirlwind of energy pass through the wall of the bridge on the Light Traveler and three people tumble out of it.

Enis jumped to his feet and rushed forward, ready to intercede. He helped Ry Sing to her feet, and Bel'lar stood. His yellow and gold finery was tattered and dirty.

"Oh, no," Ry Sing exclaimed. "Light Traveler, what have you done now?"

"I'm finishing what has begun," Light Traveler answered her.

They all turned to the focus of her surprise. Quasar was getting to his feet, trying to adjust his clothing. His suit gaped open.

"Light Traveler, get us out of here. That planet is exploding," Bel'lar ordered.

"Yes, Captain," the ship responded at the same time as she rose up and shot away from the planet.

Mauleen looked at Enis and pointed at Quasar. Together, they restrained him. He didn't react. All the fight had gone out of him. Completely demoralized, he sagged between them, looking down.

Bel'lar turned his attention to the display. The square filled the view, showing them the broken ruin of exploded buildings and bodies that it was now.

Enis stared at the destruction. "Captain Bel'lar, what have you done?"

Bel'lar flinched as the enormity of what he had done—even if unintentionally—hit him. He sat in his chair, his shoulders slumped, unable to look away from the carnage.

Ry Sing stood by Bel'lar, her hand on his shoulder. "Enis, he's only fulfilled his destiny."

Bel'lar looked at her with sadness in his heart.

Lotep entered the bridge and, glancing about, saw what was happening and made his way immediately to Mauleen's side. She released Quasar into his care and hurried to her station.

"Oh, my God!" Ry Sing cried out. "Mauleen, find the old man with the fly. Hurry. We have to save him."

Mauleen displayed the old man's house, then zoomed in. There he sat on his front porch, listening to the explosions going off around him. A fly was buzzing around his face, and he seemed completely unafraid. Actually, he looked happy. The fly landed on his nose. His eyes crossed as he gazed upon it.

Ry Sing rushed up to the display and put her hand up to touch him. "Kowangii. We need to save him." She looked at Bel'lar, but he shook his head.

Light Traveler interrupted, "We will reach maximum velocity in three seconds."

Ry Sing broke into tears. She knew it was too late. "I've lost Ka'aya. And now I've lost you, Kowangii." She collapsed to the deck, weeping.

A bright flash of light appeared from the right of the old man. The fly sensed this and looked in that direction. But it remained on the old man's nose, honoring the bond between them. The old man who knew he was Kowangii turned; his eyes grew large, as if he was seeing the future. A tear escaped from his eye and began to dry on his face as the wind blew, stronger and stronger. The fly was buffeted about but wouldn't leave. The light intensified. Then, in an instant, the rumbling increased to a deafening sound, the light blinding. The force of the wind blew at the old man's body, at the fly. As they watched, his body began to shred before their eyes until he was no more. His chair, his porch, his house were no more.

"Mauleen, the whole planet. Put it up!" Bel'lar yelled.

Helplessly, they watched as the chain reaction of nuclear explosions that had begun in the capital city spread out in four directions as if the planet were being drawn and quartered. For a moment the planet expanded further in four directions in a perfect cross. Four solid pieces of the planet exploded out. Then it began to withdraw into itself until it emerged as a white, red, and yellow ball of fire.

"Light Traveler, move it!" Bel'lar yelled.

Then Mauleen called out, "Bel'lar, a strange energy is issuing from the planet. It's coalescing into a long, cylindrical tail. It's coming right at us."

"It's got to be some kind of weapon," Bel'lar said. "We need more speed."

As the energy gained on them, their speed seemed negligible against the impossible speed of this tail of light. It was going to hit them. They braced for impact.

The ship lurched. Then a small thud was felt, and the ship absorbed the light, passing it through and into the bridge. Not a weapon but the souls from the home planet, millions of little singularities of life, in all their sparkling glory, poured into the bridge.

Many sped on, intent on their path, but one singularity expanded into almost a figure and called out to the woman weeping her heart out. "Ry Sing, Ry Sing, weep not. For I, the Kowangii, have not died."

She sat up and looked, wiping the tears from her face.

Kowangii was now fully figured before her, dressed in his familiar leopard-cloth robe. His face was gentle as he smiled down at her.

"I was the man and even the fly. I've merely transpositioned my life energy," he said.

All around this figure, tiny singularities continued their journey through the ship in a seemingly never-ending sparkling torrent.

Then another singularity slowed and began to form next to Kowangii's apparition. Ry Sing got to her feet and looked at this being.

Bel'lar was so distraught he said nothing, barely able to comprehend what was happening.

The others simply stared, speechless from the wonder they were witnessing.

This second singularity coalesced into a figure. As it formed, it spoke, "I am the significance of sainthood. I am all that needs to be and the essence of Ka'aya." They recognized the Saint.

The energies of the two singularities blended, and, instantly, they recognized each other. Sparks shot out from them; the sparkling lights intensified as they moved their singularities into a common field of familiarity and then joined as one.

The Saint spoke, "Ahh. That's what I have been waiting for. I am now the disembodiment of Kowangii and the higher self of Ka'aya. We are now one." This singularity grew, scanned the occupants of this bridge, and floated to a stop in front of Quasar. Then he looked back at Ry Sing. "Ry Sing, how thoughtful—you've saved my body."

"What do you mean?" she asked.

"This is my body," the singularity explained, indicating Quasar.

Shocked, she gasped out, "Oh, no."

"It can't be," Bel'lar blurted out. "It just can't be." He had just grasped what was happening. The Quasar was Ka'aya.

The combined singularity floated to face Bel'lar and spoke in Ka'aya's voice. "But it is."

Bel'lar covered his face with his hand. He couldn't bear to look.

The torrent of sparkling souls continued their path through the bridge as Ry Sing walked closer to Quasar, looking him in the eye. "I knew it was you. But how could you be so evil?" She tilted her head to the side, examining him.

The Quasar didn't respond; he was in shock as well, confronted by his higher self. If Lotep and Enis hadn't been holding him upright, he would have slid to the floor.

Ka'aya's voice explained, "When one cuts off from their higher self, one only embraces the evil that lives in the hearts of men. We shall prove to all this truth."

The singularity floated to Quasar. Then, in a revolution of light, this energy descended over him and took possession. He began to shake, vibrating so hard that Enis and Lotep hastily let him go and stepped away. What was left of his Syn suit dissolved, laying him bare, and before them stood a red-haired Organ, clad only in an undergarment. He fell to his knees, and, as they watched, underwent a further metamorphosis. This man's hair turned gray and lengthened to his shoulders, and a beard grew on his chin. When the metamorphosis was complete, he looked up. The man Quasar was no more. Ka'aya had returned.

"Ka'aya!" cried Ry Sing and ran to his side. She covered him with a blanket, keeping her arm around him.

He smiled at her and said, "We are the souls that can be saved."

The remaining sparkling singularities passed through the bridge and through the ship, leaving the Light Traveler behind as they sped off into space.

The End

The story will continue in *We Are The Souls That Can Be Saved.*